MIDNIGHT
RISING

LARA ADRIAN

ROBINSON

Constable & Robinson Ltd
3 The Lanchesters
162 Fulham Palace Road
London W6 9ER
www.constablerobinson.com

First published in the US in 2007 by Bantam Dell,
1745 Broadway, New York, NY 10019

This edition published by Robinson,
an imprint of Constable & Robinson Ltd, 2010

A copy of the British Library Cataloguing in Publication
Data is available from the British Library.

ISBN: 978-1-84901-110-5

Printed and bound in the EU.

With my humble gratitude and deepest respect
to all veterans of war

⊰ CHAPTER ONE ⊱

The woman looked completely out of place in her pristine white blouse and tailored ivory pants. Long, coffee-dark hair cascaded over her shoulders in thick waves, not a single strand disturbed by the moist haze that hung in the air of the forest. She was wearing tall elegant heels, which hadn't seemed to keep her from climbing up a wooded path that had the other hikers around her huffing in the humid July heat.

At the crest of the steep incline, she waited in the shade of a bulky, moss-covered rock formation, unblinking as half a dozen tourists passed her by, some of them snapping pictures of the overlook beyond. They didn't notice her. But then, most people couldn't see the dead.

Dylan Alexander didn't want to see her either.

She hadn't encountered a dead woman since she was twelve years old. That she would see one now, twenty years later and in the middle of the Czech Republic, was more than a little startling. She tried to ignore the apparition, but as Dylan and her three traveling companions made their way up the path, the woman's dark eyes found her and rooted on her.

You see me.

Dylan pretended not to hear the static-filled whisper that came from the ghost's unmoving lips. She didn't want to acknowledge the connection. She'd gone so long without one of these weird encounters that she'd all but forgotten what it was like.

Dylan had never understood her strange ability to see the dead. She'd never been able to trust it or control it. She could stand in the middle of a cemetery and see nothing, then suddenly find herself up close and personal with one of the departed, as she was here in the mountains about an hour outside Prague.

The ghosts were always female. Generally youthful-looking and vibrant, like the one who stared at her now with an unmistakable desperation in her exotic, deep brown gaze.

You must hear me.

The statement was tinged with a rich, Hispanic accent, the tone pleading.

'Hey, Dylan. Come here and let me get a picture of you next to this rock.'

The sound of a true, earthly voice jolted Dylan's attention away from the beautiful dead woman standing in the nearby arch of weathered sandstone. Janet, a friend of Dylan's mother, Sharon, dug into her backpack and pulled out a camera. The summer tour to Europe was Sharon's idea; it would have been her last great adventure, but the cancer came back in March and the final round of chemotherapy several weeks ago had left her too weak to travel. More recently, Sharon had been in and out of the hospital with pneumonia, and at her insistence Dylan had taken the trip in her place.

'Gotcha,' Janet said, clicking off a shot of Dylan and the towering pillars of rock in the wooded valley below. 'Your mom sure would love this place, honey. Isn't it breathtaking?'

Dylan nodded. 'We'll e-mail her the pictures tonight when we get back to the hotel.'

She led her group away from the rock, eager to leave the whispering, otherworldly presence behind. They walked down a sloping ridge, into a stand of thin-trunked pines growing in tight formation. Russet leaves and conifer needles from seasons past crushed on the damp path underfoot. It had rained that morning, topped off with a sweltering heat that kept many of the area's tourists away.

The forest was quiet, peaceful . . . except for the awareness of ghostly eyes following Dylan's every step deeper into the woods.

'I'm so glad your boss let you have the time off to come with us,' added one of the women from behind her on the path. 'I know how hard you work at the paper, making up all those stories—'

'She doesn't make them up, Marie,' Janet chided gently. 'There's got to be some truth in Dylan's articles or they couldn't print them. Isn't that right, honey?'

Dylan scoffed. 'Well, considering that our front page usually runs at least one alien abduction or demonic possession account, we don't tend to let facts get in the way of a good story. We publish entertainment pieces, not hard-hitting journalism.'

'Your mom says you're going to be a famous reporter one day,' Marie said. 'A budding Woodward or Bernstein, that's what she says.'

'That's right,' Janet put in. 'You know, she showed me an article you wrote during your first newspaper job fresh out of college – you were covering some nasty murder case upstate. You remember, don't you, honey?'

'Yeah,' Dylan said, navigating them toward another massive cluster of soaring sandstone towers that rose out of the trees. 'I remember. But that was a long time ago.'

'Well, no matter what you do, I know that your mom is very proud of you,' Marie said. 'You've brought a lot of joy into her life.'

Dylan nodded, struggling to find her voice. 'Thanks.'

Both Janet and Marie worked with her mother at the runaway center in Brooklyn. Nancy, the other member of their travel group, had been Sharon's best friend since high school. All three of the women had become like extended family to Dylan in the past few months. Three extra pairs of comforting arms, which she was really going to need if she ever lost her mom.

In her heart, Dylan knew it was more a matter of when than if.

For so long, it had been just the two of them. Her father had been absent since Dylan was a kid, not that he'd been much of a father when he was present. Her two older brothers were gone too, one of them dead in a car accident, the other having cut all family ties when he joined the service years ago. Dylan and her mom had been left to pick up the pieces, and so they had, each there to lift the other one up when she was down, or to celebrate even the smallest triumphs.

Dylan couldn't bear to think of how empty her life would be without her mom.

Nancy came up and gave Dylan a warm, if sad, smile. 'It means the world to Sharon that you would experience the trip for her. You're living it for her, you know?'

'I know. I wouldn't have missed it for anything.'

Dylan hadn't told her travel companions – or her mother – that taking off for two weeks on such short notice was probably going to cost her her job. Part of her didn't really care. She hated working for the cut-rate tabloid anyway. She'd attempted to sell her boss on the idea that she was sure to return from Europe with some decent material – maybe a Bohemian Bigfoot story, or a Dracula sighting out of Romania.

But selling bullshit to a guy who peddled it for a living was no easy task. Her boss had been pretty clear about his expectations: if Dylan left on this trip, she'd better come back with something big, or she didn't need to come back at all.

'Whooee, it's hot up here,' Janet said, sweeping her baseball cap off her short silver curls and running her palm over her brow. 'Am I the only wimp in this crowd, or would anyone else like to rest for a little bit?'

'I could use a break,' Nancy agreed.

She shrugged off her backpack and set it down on the ground beneath a tall pine tree. Marie joined them, moving off the path and taking a long pull from her water bottle.

Dylan wasn't the least bit tired. She wanted to keep moving. The most impressive climbs and rock formations were still ahead of them. They had only scheduled one day for this part of the trip, and Dylan wanted to cover as much ground as she could.

And then there was the matter of the beautiful dead woman who now stood ahead of them on the path. She stared at Dylan, her energy fading in and out of visible form.

See me.

Dylan glanced away. Janet, Marie, and Nancy were seated on the ground, nibbling on protein bars and trail mix.

'Want some?' Janet asked, holding out a plastic zipper bag of dried fruit, nuts, and seeds.

Dylan shook her head. 'I'm too antsy to rest or eat right now. If you don't mind, I think I'm going to take a quick look around on my own while you all hang out here. I'll come right back.'

'Sure, honey. Your legs are younger than ours after all. Just be careful.'

'I will. Be back soon.'

Dylan avoided the spot where the dead woman's image flickered up ahead. Instead, she cut off the established trail and onto the densely wooded hillside. She walked for a few minutes, simply enjoying the tranquillity of the place. There was an ancient, wildly mysterious quality to the jutting peaks of sandstone and basalt. Dylan paused to take pictures, hoping she could capture some of the beauty for her mother to enjoy.

Hear me.

At first Dylan didn't see the woman, only heard the broken-static sound of her spectral voice. But then, a flash of white caught her eye. She was farther up the incline, standing on a ridge of stone halfway up one of the steep crags.

Follow me.

'Bad idea,' Dylan murmured, eyeing the tricky slope. The grade was fierce, the path uncertain at best. And even though the view from up there was probably spectacular, she really had no desire to join her ghostly new friend on the Other Side.

Please . . . help him.

Help him?

'Help who?' she asked, knowing the spirit couldn't hear her.

They never could. Communication with her kind was always a one-way street. They simply appeared when they wished, and said what they wished – if they spoke at all. Then, when it became too hard for them to hold their visible form, they just faded away.

Help him.

The woman in white started going transparent up on the mountainside. Dylan shielded her eyes from the hazy light pouring down through the trees, trying to keep her in sight. With a bit of apprehension, she began the trudge upward, using the tight growth of pines and beech to help her over the roughest of the terrain.

By the time she clambered up onto the ridge where the apparition had been standing, the woman was gone. Dylan carefully walked the ledge of rock, and found that it was wider than it appeared from below. The sandstone was weathered dark from the elements, dark enough that a deep vertical slit in the rock had been invisible to her until now.

It was from within that narrow wedge of lightless space that Dylan heard the detached, ghostly whisper once again.

Save him.

She looked around her and saw only wilderness and rock. There was no one up here. Now, not even a trace of the ethereal figure who lured her this far up the mountain alone.

Dylan turned her head to look into the gloom of the rock's crevice. She put her hand into the space and felt cool, damp air skate over her skin.

Inside that deep black cleft, it was still and quiet.

As quiet as a tomb.

If Dylan was the type to believe in creepy folklore monsters, she might have imagined one could live in a hidden spot like this. But she didn't believe in monsters, never had. Aside from seeing the occasional dead person, who'd never caused her any harm, Dylan was about as practical – even cynical – as could be.

It was the reporter in her that made her curious to know what she might truly find inside the rock. Assuming you could trust the word of a dead woman, who did she think needed help? Was someone injured in there? Could someone have gotten lost way up here on this steep crag?

Dylan grabbed a small flashlight from an outer pocket of her backpack. She shined it into the opening, noticing just then that there were vague chisel marks around and within the crevice, as if someone had worked to widen it. Although not any time recently, based on the weathered edges of the tool's marks.

'Hello?' she called into the darkness. 'Is anyone in here?'

Nothing but silence answered.

Dylan pulled off her backpack and carried it in one hand, her other hand wrapped around the slim barrel of her flashlight. Walking forward she could barely fit through the crevice; anyone larger than her would have been forced to go in sideways.

The tight squeeze only lasted a short distance before the space angled around and began to open up. Suddenly she was inside the thick rock of the mountain, her light beam bouncing off smooth, rounded walls. It was a cave – an empty one, except for some bats rustling out of a disturbed sleep overhead.

And from the look of it, the space was mostly man-made. The ceiling rose at least twenty feet over Dylan's head. Interesting symbols were painted on each wall of the small cavern. They looked like some odd sort of hieroglyphics: a cross between bold tribal markings and interlocking, gracefully geometric patterns.

Dylan walked closer to one of the walls, mesmerized by the beauty of the strange artwork. She panned the small beam of her flashlight to the right, breathless to find the elaborate decoration continuing all around her. She took a step toward the center of the cave. The toe of her hiking boot knocked into something on the earthen floor. Whatever it was clattered hollowly as it rolled away. Dylan swept her light over the ground and gasped.

Oh, shit.

It was a skull. White bone glowed against the darkness, the human head staring up at her with sightless, vacant sockets.

If this was the *him* the dead woman wanted Dylan to help out, it looked like she got there about a hundred years too late.

Dylan moved the light farther into the gloom, unsure what she was searching for, but too fascinated to leave just yet. The beam skidded over another set of bones – Jesus, more aged human remains scattered on the floor of the cave.

Goose bumps prickled on Dylan's arms from a draft that seemed to rise out of nowhere.

And that's when she saw it.

A large rectangular block of stone sat on the other side of the darkness. More markings like the ones covering the walls were painted onto the carved bulk of the object.

Dylan didn't have to move closer to realize that she was looking at a crypt. A thick slab had been placed over the top of the tomb. It was moved aside, skewed slightly off the stone crypt as if pushed away by incredibly strong hands.

Was someone – or something – laid to rest in there?

Dylan had to know.

She crept forward, flashlight gripped in suddenly perspiring fingers. A few paces away now, Dylan angled the beam into the opening of the tomb.

It was empty.

And for reasons she couldn't explain, that thought chilled her even more than if she'd found some hideous corpse turning to dust inside.

Over her head, the cave's nocturnal residents were getting restless. The bats stirred, then bolted past her in a hurried rush of motion. Dylan ducked to let them pass, figuring she'd better get the hell out of there too.

As she pivoted to find the crevice exit, she heard another rustle of movement. This one was bigger than bats, a low snarl of sound followed by a disturbance of loose rock somewhere in the cave.

Oh, God. Maybe she wasn't alone in here after all.

The hairs at the back of her neck tingled and before she could remind herself that she didn't believe in monsters, her heart started beating in overdrive.

She fumbled around for the way out of the cave, her pulse jackhammering in her ears. By the time she found daylight, she was gasping for air. Her legs felt rubbery as she scrambled back down the ridge, then raced to rejoin her friends in the safety of the bright midday sun below.

He'd been dreaming of Eva again.

It wasn't enough that the female had betrayed him in life – now, in her death, she invaded his mind while he slept. Still beautiful, still treacherous, she spoke to him of regret and how she wanted to make things right.

All lies.

Eva's visiting ghost was only a part of Rio's long slide into madness.

His dead mate wept in his dreams, begging him to forgive her for the deception she'd orchestrated a year ago. She was sorry. She still loved him, and always would.

She wasn't real. Just a taunting reminder of a past he would be glad to leave behind.

Trusting the female had cost him much. His face had been ruined in the warehouse explosion. His body was broken in places, still recovering from injuries that would have killed a mortal man.

And his mind . . . ?

Rio's sanity had been fracturing apart, bit by bit, worsening in the time he'd been holed up alone on this Bohemian mountainside.

He could bring it all to a halt. As one of the Breed – a hybrid race of humans bearing vampiric, alien genes – he could drag himself into the sunlight and let the UV rays devour him. He'd considered doing just that, but there remained the task of closing the cave and destroying the damning evidence it contained.

He didn't know how long he'd been there. The days and nights, weeks and months, had at some point merged into an endless suspension of time. He wasn't sure how it had happened. He'd arrived there with his brethren of the Order. The warriors had been on a mission to locate and destroy an old evil secreted away in the rocks centuries ago.

But they were too late.

The crypt was empty; the evil had already been freed.

It was Rio who volunteered to stay behind and seal the cave while the others returned home to Boston. He couldn't go back with them. He didn't know where he belonged. He'd intended to find his own way – maybe go back to Spain, his homeland.

That's what he'd told the warriors who'd long been like brothers to him. But he hadn't carried out any of his plans. He had delayed, tormented by indecision and the weight of the sin he'd been contemplating.

In his heart, he'd known he had no intention of leaving this tomb. But he had put off the inevitable with weak excuses, waiting for the right time, the right conditions, for him to do what he had to do. But those excuses were just that. They only served to make the hours stretch into days, the days into weeks.

Now, easily months later, he lurked in the darkness of the cave like the bats that inhabited the dank space with him. He no longer hunted, no longer had the desire to feed. He merely existed, conscious of his steady descent into a hell of his own making.

For Rio, that descent had finally proven too much.

Beside him on a hollowed-out ledge of rock ten feet up from the floor of the cave rested a detonator and a small cache of C-4. It was enough boom to seal up the hidden crypt forever. Rio intended to set it off that night . . . from the inside.

Tonight, he would finish it.

When his lethargic senses had roused him from a heavy sleep to warn him of an intruder, he'd thought it to be just another tormenting phantom. He caught the scent of a human – a young female, judging by the musky warmth that clung to her skin. His eyes peeled open in the dark, nostrils flaring to pull more of her fragrance into his lungs.

She was no trick of his madness.

She was flesh and blood, the first human to venture anywhere near the obscure mouth of the cave in all the time he'd been there. The woman shined a bright light around the cave, temporarily blinding him, even from his concealed position above her head. He heard her footsteps scuffing on the sandstone floor of the cavern. Heard her sudden gasp as she knocked into some of the skeletal litter left behind by the original occupant of the place.

Rio shifted himself on the ledge, testing his limbs in preparation of a leap to the floor below. The stirring of the air disturbed the bats clinging to the ceiling. They flew out, but the woman remained. Her light traveled more of the cave, then came to rest on the tomb that lay open.

Rio felt her curiosity chill toward fear as she neared the crypt. Even her human instincts picked up on the evil that had once slept in that block of stone.

But she shouldn't be there.

Rio couldn't let her see any more than she already had. He heard himself snarl as he moved on the rocky jut overhead. The woman heard it too. She tensed with alarm. The beam of her flashlight ricocheted crazily off the walls as she made a panicked search for the cave's exit.

Before Rio could command his limbs to move, she was already slipping away.

She was gone.

She'd seen too much, but soon it wouldn't matter.

Once night fell, there would be no further trace of the crypt, the cave, or of Rio himself.

✦ CHAPTER TWO ✦

*H*idden Crypt Unlocks Secrets of an Ancient Civilization! Dylan scowled and held down the backspace key on her notebook computer. She needed a different title for the piece she was working on – something sexier, less *National Geographic*. She pecked out a second attempt, trying for something that would shout just as loudly from the newsstands as the latest Hollywood starlet in rehab story plastered on the front pages any given week.

Ancient Human Sacrifices Discovered in Dracula's Backyard!

Yeah, that was better. The Dracula bit was a stretch since the Czech Republic was several hundred miles away from bloodthirsty Vlad Tepes's place in Romania, but it was a start. Dylan stretched her legs out on her hotel room bed, balanced her computer in her lap, and began typing the first draft of her story.

Two paragraphs into it, she stalled out. Pressed the backspace key until the page was blank again.

The words simply weren't coming. She couldn't focus. The ghostly visitation she'd had on the mountain had put her on edge, but it was the phone call to her mother that really had Dylan distracted. Sharon had tried to sound cheerful and strong, telling her all about a river cruise fund-raiser the shelter was putting on in a few nights and how she looked forward to attending.

After losing another girl to the street life recently – a young runaway named Toni, whom Sharon had really thought was going to make it – she had ideas for a new program she wanted to pitch to the runaway shelter's founder, Mr Fasso. Sharon was hoping for a private audience with him, a man she had admitted on more than one occasion that she was a little infatuated with, to no one's surprise, especially not her daughter's.

Where her mother was always ready – even eager – to fall in love, Dylan's romantic life was a complete contrast. She'd had a handful of relationships, but nothing meaningful, and nothing she'd ever allowed to last. A cynical part of her doubted the entire concept of forever, despite her mother's attempts to convince her that she would find it, someday, when she least expected it.

Sharon was a free spirit with a big, open heart that had been stomped on far too often by unworthy men, and, now, by the unfairness of fate. Still, she kept smiling, kept soldiering on. She had been giggling as she confided in Dylan that she bought a new dress for the shelter's cruise, which she chose for its flattering cut and the color that was so similar to Mr Fasso's eyes. But even while Dylan joked with her mom not to flirt too outrageously with the reportedly handsome and evidently unmarried philanthropist, her heart was breaking.

Sharon was trying to act her normal upbeat self, but Dylan knew her too well. There was an out-of-breath quality to her voice that couldn't be explained away by the long distance phone service in the little Bohemian town of Jičín, where Dylan and her travel companions were spending the night. She'd only spoken with her mother for about twenty minutes, but when they hung up, Sharon had sounded thoroughly exhausted.

Dylan exhaled a shaky sigh as she closed her computer and set it beside her on the narrow bed. Maybe she should have gone for beer and brats in the pub with Janet, Marie, and

Nancy, instead of staying behind to work. She hadn't felt much like socializing – still didn't, in fact – but the longer she sat by herself in the tiny bunk room, the more aware she became of just how alone she truly was. The quiet made it hard to think about anything but the final, dreaded silence that was going to fill her life once her mother . . .

Oh, God.

Dylan wasn't even prepared to let the word form in her mind.

She swung her legs down off the bed and stood up. The first-floor window looking out over the street was open to let in some air, but Dylan felt stifled, suffocating. She lifted the glass wide and took a deep breath, watching as tourists and locals strolled past.

And damn if the ethereal woman in white wasn't out there too.

She stood in the middle of the road, unfazed by the rush of cars and pedestrians all around her. Her image was translucent in the dark, her form far less delineated than it had been earlier that day, and dimming by the second. But her eyes were fixed on Dylan. The ghost didn't speak this time, just stared with a bleak resignation that made Dylan's chest ache.

'Go away,' she told the apparition under her breath. 'I don't know what you want from me, and I really can't deal with you right now.'

Some part of her scoffed at that, because with her job on the line like it was, maybe she shouldn't be so eager to turn away visitors from the Other Side. Nothing would please her boss, Coleman Hogg, more than having a reporter on staff who could honest-to-God see dead people. Hell, the opportunistic bastard probably would insist on bankrolling a brand-new side business with her as the main attraction.

Yeah, right. So not happening.

She'd let one man exploit her for the peculiar, if unreliable, gift she'd been born with – and look how that had turned out. Dylan hadn't seen her father since she was twelve years old. Bobby Alexander's last words to his daughter as he drove out of town and out of her life for good had been a nasty string of profanity and open disgust.

It had been one of the most painful days of Dylan's life, but it had taught her a good hard lesson: there were precious few people you could trust, so if you wanted to survive, you'd better always look out for Number One.

It was a philosophy that had served her well enough, the only exception being when it came to her mom. Sharon Alexander was Dylan's rock, her sole confidante, and the only person she could ever truly count on. She knew all of Dylan's secrets, all of her hopes and dreams. She knew all of her troubles and fears too . . . except one. Dylan was still trying to be brave for Sharon, too scared to let on to her about how petrified she was that the cancer had come back. She didn't want to admit that fear just yet, or give it strength by speaking it out loud.

'Shit,' Dylan whispered irritably as her eyes began to sting with a warning of oncoming tears.

She willed them into submission with the same steely control she'd been practicing most of her life. Dylan Alexander did not cry. She hadn't since she was that brokenhearted, betrayed little girl watching her father speed off into the night.

No, getting sloppy with self-pity and hurt never did her a lick of good. Anger was a much more useful coping method. And where anger failed, there were few things that couldn't be fixed with a healthy dose of denial.

Dylan turned away from the window and shoved her bare feet into her well-worn pair of trail shoes. Not trusting to leave her computer unattended in the room, she slipped the slim silver laptop into her messenger bag, grabbed her pocketbook, and headed out to find Janet and the others. Maybe a little company and chitchat wouldn't be so bad after all.

By dusk, most of the humans traipsing through the woods and along the mountain paths had gone. Now that it was fully dark outside the cave, there wasn't a soul around to hear the explosion Rio was rigging to go off from within the lightless space of rock.

He had just enough C-4 on hand to permanently seal the cave's entrance, but not so much that he would bring the whole damn mountain down. Nikolai had thought to make sure of that before the Order had left Rio there to secure the site. Thank God for that, because Rio sure as hell didn't trust his cracked brain to remember the particulars.

He cursed sharply as he fumbled one of the tiny wires on the detonator. His vision was already starting to swim, irritating him even more. Sweat broke out on his brow, dampening the overlong hanks of hair that hung down into his eyes. With a snarl, he swept his hand over his face and up his scalp, staring fiercely at the lumps of pale explosive material in front of him.

Did he stuff the blasting caps into the cakes yet?
He couldn't remember . . .

'Focus, idiot,' he berated himself, impatient over the idea of something that should come so easily to him – and had, before he'd gotten his bell rung in that warehouse back in Boston – should now take him literally hours to even get started.

Add to that his body's sluggishness from deprivation of vital blood and he was a real piece of work. A goddamn waste of space, that's what he was.

With a surge of self-hatred fueling him, Rio stuck his finger into one of the small puttylike blocks of C-4 and tore it open.
Good. The charge was in there, just like it should be.

It didn't matter he couldn't remember placing it there, or that based on the mangled appearance of another of the cakes, he'd probably gone through this very exercise at least once before. He gathered up the supply of C-4 and carried them into the narrow mouth of the cave. He packed them into carved niches in the sandstone, just like Niko had told him to do. Then he went back into the cavern to retrieve the detonator.

Damn it!

The wires on the thing were all fucked up.

He had fucked them up. How? And when?

'Son of a bitch!' he roared, glaring down at the device, blind with a swift, sudden rage.

He felt dizzy with anger, his head spinning so badly it buckled his knees. He went down on the hard ground like his body was made of lead. He heard the detonator skid into the dust somewhere, but he didn't reach for it. His arms were too heavy and his head was weightless, his consciousness floating, detached from reality, like his mind wanted to separate from the wreck of the body that caged it and fly away to escape.

A thick nausea pressed him down, and he knew if he didn't work fast to get a hold of himself he was going to pass out.

It had been foolish to stop hunting all those weeks ago. He was Breed. He needed human blood for strength, for life. Blood would help him to stave off the pain and madness. But he could no longer trust himself to hunt without killing. He'd come too close, too many times, since he'd arrived here on this towering forest crag.

Too often on those few times he ventured out in hunger he'd nearly been seen by the humans living in the surrounding towns and villages. And since the explosion he'd survived in Boston a year ago, his was a face not soon forgotten.

Maldecido.

The word hissed at him from somewhere distant. Not the

night outside, but from deep out of his past, in the language of his mother's country.

Manos del diablo.

Comedor de la sangre.

Monstruo.

Even through the fog of his tormented mind, he recognized the epithets. Names he heard from his earliest childhood. Words that haunted him, even now.

The cursed one.

Devil's hands.

Blood-eater.

Monster.

And so he was, more now than ever. Ironic that his life would begin in hiding, skulking like an animal among the night-dark woodlands and hills . . . only to end much the same way.

'*Madre de Dios,*' he whispered as he made a feeble, but failed grab for the detonator. 'Please . . . let me end it.'

Dylan had barely set down her empty pilsner glass before another full one came to rest in front of her. It was the third round for the table since she'd arrived in the tavern and met up with her travel companions – this latest serving delivered with an extra-wide grin from the young man tending the bar.

'With my compliments, ladies,' he announced in thickly accented English, one of the few locals in the rural village who spoke anything more than Czech or German.

'Oh, my goodness! Thank you, Goran,' Janet exclaimed, giggling as she surrendered her empty for a fresh glass of frothy amber beer. 'What a dear you are, telling us all about your lovely town and now bringing us free drinks. You really don't have to do this.'

'My pleasure,' he murmured.

His friendly brown eyes lingered the longest on Dylan, which she might have taken as a bigger compliment if her companions weren't all qualified for AARP membership. Dylan herself probably had five to ten years on the boyishly handsome barkeep, but that didn't stop her from working his obvious attraction to her best advantage.

Not that she was interested in drinks or dating. It was Goran's talk of the surrounding mountains and their various lore that held Dylan captivated. The young Czech had grown up in the area, and had spent a good amount of time exploring the very range where Dylan had been climbing that morning.

'It's so beautiful here,' Nancy told him. 'The tourist brochure didn't lie; this truly is a paradise.'

'And such a vast, unusual terrain,' Marie added. 'I think we'd need a whole month to see everything out there. Too bad we have to return to Prague tomorrow.'

'Yes, that is too bad,' Goran said, directing the comment at Dylan.

'What about caves?' She'd been trying to gather details for her story without being too conspicuous, knowing that the locals probably wouldn't appreciate the fact that she'd ventured off the established trails to climb the mountains on her own. 'I saw a few caves marked on our map, but I imagine there's a lot more out there. Even some that haven't been uncovered yet, stuff that's not open to the public?'

The young man nodded. 'Oh, yes. There are maybe hundreds of caves and several abysses too. Most of them are still being documented.'

'Dylan saw an old stone coffin in one of the caves today,' Janet blurted innocently as she sipped her beer.

Goran chuckled, his expression dubious. 'You saw a what?'

'I'm not sure what I saw.' Dylan gave a nonchalant shrug, not wanting to tip her hand if she had truly discovered something significant. 'It was pitch-black inside, and I think the heat was playing tricks on my mind.'

'What cave were you in?' the young man asked. 'I know it, maybe.'

'Oh, I don't remember where I was exactly. It doesn't really matter.'

'She said she felt a presence,' Janet piped in again. 'Isn't that how you described it, honey? Like a . . . a dark presence coming awake while you were in the cave. I believe that's what you said.'

'It was nothing, I'm sure.' Dylan shot a pained scowl across the table at the well-meaning, but aggravatingly chatty older woman. For all the good it did. Janet gave her a sweet little matchmaker's wink as Goran leaned down next to Dylan at the table.

'You know, there used to be talk of evil in those mountains,' he said, his voice lowered to a confidential, if amused, tone. 'Many old legends warn of demons living in the woods.'

'Is that right?' she asked drolly.

'Oh, yes. Terrible beasts that looked like humans, but were not human at all. The villagers were convinced they were living among monsters.'

Dylan scoffed lightly as she lifted her glass. 'I don't believe in monsters.'

'Neither do I, of course,' Goran said. 'But my grandfather does. So did his grandfather before him and all the rest of my family who farmed in this area, going back hundreds of years. My grandfather owned the property at the edge of the woods. He said he saw one of these creatures just a couple of months ago. It attacked one of his field workers.'

'Is that so.' Dylan glanced at the barkeep, waiting for a punch line that didn't come.

'According to my grandfather, it was just after dusk. He and Matej were bringing some equipment into the barn for the night when Grandfather heard an odd sound coming from the field. He went to look, and saw Matej on the ground.

Another man was bent over him, holding Matej's neck to his mouth – bleeding him from the throat.'

'Good Lord!' Janet gasped. 'Did the poor man survive?'

'Yes, he did. Grandfather said by the time he ran back inside the barn to get something to use as a weapon against the creature, Matej was lying there alone. There were no marks on him except a bit of blood on his shirt, and he had no memory of the attack at all. The man who attacked Matej – or the demon, if my grandfather's account can be believed – has never been seen again.'

Janet clucked her tongue. 'And good riddance! Why, it's like something straight out of a horror movie, isn't it?'

Nancy and Marie looked equally aghast, all three women evidently buying Goran's tall tale – hook, line, and sinker. Dylan remained skeptical to say the least. But in the back of her mind she wondered if her story about an empty mountain crypt littered with old human remains might be even juicier with a firsthand account of some kind of demon vampire attack. Never mind the fact that the alleged victim couldn't corroborate with either memory or physical evidence; her boss at the paper wouldn't hesitate to go to print on the word of a superstitious, likely vision-impaired, backwoods old man alone. Hell, they'd gone to print on far less than that before.

'Do you think I could talk to your grandfather about what he saw?'

'Dylan is a journalist,' the ever-helpful Janet, to no one's surprise, felt compelled to explain. 'She lives in New York City. Have you ever been to New York City, Goran?'

'I have never been there, but I should like very much to see it one day,' he replied, glancing at Dylan again. 'You are a journalist, really?'

'No, not really. Maybe someday. Right now, the stuff I write is . . . I guess you could call them human interest stories.' She smiled up at the bartender. 'So, do you think your grandpa would be willing to speak with me?'

'He is dead, I'm sorry to say. He had a stroke in his sleep last month and never woke up.'

'Oh.' Dylan's heart clenched with true remorse, her hunger for a story taking an immediate backseat. 'I'm very sorry for your loss, Goran.'

He gave a tight nod. 'He was a lucky man. If only we all live to be ninety-two, like my grandfather, eh?'

'Yeah,' Dylan said, feeling the gazes of her mom's friends fixed on her in sympathy. 'If only.'

'I have new customers,' he announced as a small group of people came into the tavern. 'I must go now. When I come back, Dylan, maybe you will tell me about New York City.'

As he left, and before Janet could enthuse over what a great idea it would be for Dylan to invite the adorable young Goran to the States, marry him, and have his babies, Dylan faked a brilliant, big yawn.

'Wow, guess I had too much fresh air today – I'm really beat. I think I'm going to turn in early. I have a bit of work to do yet tonight, and some e-mails I need to take a look at before I hit the hay.'

'You sure, honey?'

Dylan gave Janet a weak bob of her head. 'Yeah. Long day.' She got up and grabbed her messenger bag from the back of her wooden pub chair. Pulling out enough Czech *koruny* to cover her portion of the bar tab and a nice tip for their host, Dylan set the money down on the table. 'I'll see you back at the room.'

As she made the short walk from the tavern to the hotel down the street, Dylan's fingers were itching to hit her keyboard. She closed herself inside the room, fired up her computer, and tried to keep up as the story spilled out of her. Dylan smiled as the piece took shape. It was no longer simply a report of an old cavern tomb and some dusty skeletons, but a blood-curdling account of a living, breathing evil that may well be still at large in the wilderness terrain above an otherwise tranquil European town.

She had the words.

All she needed now were some pictures of the demon's mountain lair.

❧ CHAPTER THREE ❧

It was early morning in the mountain region, too early for most of the tourist groups and day hikers to be out and about. Still, Dylan avoided the main entrance and ventured into the woods on her own. A light rain began soon after she entered the forest, the soft summer shower falling from gunmetal gray clouds overhead. Dylan's trail shoes padded wetly on the damp pine needles beneath her feet as she picked up the pace and located the mountain path she'd been on the day before with her companions.

There was no sign of the dark-haired lady in white today, but Dylan didn't need the apparition's help in finding her way to the cave. Guided there by memory and a rising thrum in her veins, she climbed the steep, tricky incline to the ledge of sandstone outside the hidden cave.

In the overcast haze, the narrow crevice opening seemed even darker today, the sandstone giving off an earthy, ancient scent. Dylan swung her backpack down off her arm and grabbed her small flashlight from one of the pack's zippered pockets. She twisted the thin metal barrel and sent a beam of light ahead of her into the dark passageway of the cave.

Go in, get a few pictures of the crypt and the funky wall art, then get the hell out.

Not that she was afraid. Why should she be? This was just an old burial site of some sort — and a long-abandoned one at that. Absolutely nothing to fear.

And wasn't that just what those clueless horror movie actresses would say right before they ate it in gory detail on-screen?

Dylan mentally scoffed at herself. This was real life after all. The odds of a chainsaw-wielding lunatic or a flesh-eating zombie lurking in the dark of this cave were about the same as her coming face-to-face with the blood-sucking monster Goran's grandfather claimed to have seen. In other words, less than nil.

With the rain pattering gently behind her, Dylan stepped between the narrow walls of rock and carefully navigated her way into the cave, the beam of her flashlight leading the way. Several feet in, the passageway opened up onto more darkness. Dylan swung the light around the perimeter of the cave, as awestruck as she had been yesterday, by the elaborate wall markings and the rectangular slab of stone at the center of the space.

She didn't see the man lying in a careless sprawl on the ground until she was nearly on top of him.

'Jesus!'

She sucked in a startled breath and leaped back, the beam of her flashlight ricocheting crazily in the second it took for her to get over the shock. She angled the light back down to where he lay . . . and found nothing.

But he'd been right there. In her mind she could still see his head of shaggy dark brown hair, and his dusty, tattered black clothing. A vagrant, no doubt. It probably wasn't that unusual for some of the region's homeless poor to squat in this area.

'Hello?' she said, swinging the beam across the entire floor of the cave. A couple of ancient skulls and scattered bones lay about in morbid disarray, but that was it. No sign of anything living – not within the past hundred years or so, by Dylan's guess.

Where had he gone? She slid a glance at the large, open crypt a few feet away.

'Look, I know you're in here. It's okay. I didn't mean to frighten you,' she added, even though it seemed absurd that she should be reassuring him. The guy had to be more than six feet tall, and even from the brief glimpse she'd gotten of him, she noted that his long arms and legs were thick with muscle. But his broken crumple on the floor of the cave had emanated pain and despair. 'Are you hurt? Do you need some help? What's your name?'

No reply. Not a sound of any kind.

'*Dobrý den?*' she called, trying to reach out to him with her pitifully limited knowledge of Czech. '*Mluvíte ánglicky?*'

No such luck.

'*Sprechen zie Deutsch?*'

Nothing.

'Sorry, but that's about all I've got unless you want me to break out some of my rusty junior high Spanish and really embarrass myself.' She pivoted with her flashlight, angling it upward as she scanned the high walls of the cavern. 'Somehow I don't think *¿Como esta usted?* is going to get us any further here. Do you?'

As she slowly turned, the light glanced off a jutting ledge high above her head. Some ten feet up was a sheer, arcing rise of sandstone. No way anyone could get up there.

Or was there . . . ?

No sooner had she thought it than the thin stream of light shooting up to the ledge began to flicker. It dimmed steadily, then went utterly dark.

'Shit,' Dylan whispered low under her breath. She banged the barrel on her palm a couple of times before somewhat frantically attempting to turn the damn thing on again. Despite fresh batteries installed before she left the States, the light was dead. 'Shit, shit, shit.'

Engulfed in total blackness, Dylan felt the first twinge of unease.

When she heard the scrape of rock overhead, every nerve in her body went tense. There was a long beat of silence, followed by the sudden crunch of booted feet hitting solid earth as whoever – or whatever – had been hiding in the shadows above now dropped to the floor of the cave beside her.

She smelled like juniper and honey and warm summer rain. But beneath all that was a sudden, citrusy spike of adrenaline now that he was near her. Rio circled the woman in the dark of the cave, seeing her perfectly while she stumbled in the abrupt lack of light. Her feet carried her backward . . . only to connect with a wall of stone at her spine.

'Damn it.'

She swallowed audibly, pivoting to try another tack, then swore again as her useless flashlight slipped out of her fingers and clinked on the hard floor of the cave. Rio had burned precious energy in mentally extinguishing the device. Manipulating objects by thought was a simple Breed talent, but in his current weakened state, Rio didn't know how long he could hold it.

'Um, you're probably not in the mood for company,' the woman said, her eyes wide in the darkness as they darted left and right, trying to locate him. 'So, I'm just going to leave now, okay? Just gonna . . . walk right out of here.' A nervous moan caught in her throat. 'God, please, where is the frigging way out of this place?'

She took a step to the right, edging along the cavern wall. Away from the exit, although Rio saw no point in telling her that just yet. He kept moving, trailing her deeper into the cave, trying to decide what to do with his repeat intruder. When he'd first awakened, startled to find he was still alive and not alone, he'd reacted on instinct – a vulnerable beast fleeing to the safety of the shadows.

But then she'd started talking to him.

Coaxing him out, even though she could not have known how dangerous a proposition that really was. He was furious and half-mad in the head, a deadly enough combination on its own, but being near the female now reminded him that even though he was broken, he was still very much male.

To his marrow, he was still Breed.

Rio breathed in more of the female's scent, finding it hard to resist touching her pale, rain-dampened skin. Hunger flooded him – hunger he hadn't known for some long time. His fangs surged from his gums, the sharp points jabbing the soft flesh of his tongue. He was careful to keep his eyelids low over his eyes, knowing the topaz-colored irises would soon be awash in the glow of fiery amber, his pupils thinning to vertical slits as the thirst for blood rose in him.

That she was young and beautiful only deepened his desire to taste her. He wanted to touch her . . .

He flexed his hands, then fisted them at his sides.

Manos del diablo.

He could hurt her with those hands. The strength given him by his vampire genes was immense, but it was Rio's other skill – the terrible talent he'd been born with – that could do the most damage here. With a centered thought and a simple touch, he could draw away human life in an instant. Once he'd come to understand his power, Rio had managed it with judicious, rigid control. Now anger ruled his deadly gift, and the blackouts he suffered since the warehouse explosion had made it impossible for him to trust himself not to do harm.

It was part of the reason he'd left the Order, and part of his eventual decision to stop hunting for blood. The Breed seldom, if ever, killed their human Hosts while feeding; that was all that separated them from the worst of vampire kind, the Rogues. It was the blood-addicted Rogues who knew no better, who had so little control.

As Rio stared with feral, thirsting eyes at the woman who'd wandered into his hellish domain, fear of losing control with her was the thing that kept him at heel.

That, and the simple fact that she'd been kind to him.

Unafraid, if only because she couldn't see the beast he really was.

She gave up on following the wall and moved toward the center of the small cave. Rio stood right behind her now, so close the curling ends of her flame-red hair brushed his ragged shirt. That springy strand of silk tempted him sorely, but Rio kept his hands at his sides. He closed his eyes, wishing he had stayed on the ledge above. Then she might still be talking to him, not stiff and panting with rising anxiety.

'You shouldn't be here,' he said finally, his voice a rough growl in the darkness.

She sucked in a quick breath, spinning around as soon as her ear had triangulated his location. She backed away, retreating from him again. Rio should have been glad for that.

'You do speak English,' she said after a long moment. 'But your accent . . . you're not American?'

He saw no reason to say otherwise. 'You are, evidently.'

'What is this place? What are you doing up here?'

'You need to leave now,' he told her. The words sounded thick to him, hard to push out of his mouth for the obstruction of his extruded fangs. 'You're not safe here.'

Silence hung between them as she weighed the warning. 'Let me see you.'

Rio scowled at the pretty, peach-freckled face that searched the gloom for him. She reached out as if to find him with her hands now. He recoiled from her sweeping arm, but only barely.

'Do you know what they say in town?' she asked, a note of challenge in her voice now. 'They say there's a demon living up here in the mountains.'

'Maybe there is.'

'I don't believe in demons.'

'Maybe you should.' Rio stared at her through the overgrown thicket of his hair, hoping the long hanks would conceal the glow of his eyes. 'You have to go. Now.'

She slowly lifted the backpack she was carrying and held it in front of her like armor. 'Do you know anything about this crypt? That's what it is, right – some kind of old crypt and sacrificial chamber? What about the symbols on the walls in here . . . what are they, some kind of ancient language?'

Rio went very still, very silent. If he thought he could let her simply walk away, she'd just proved him wrong. Bad enough she saw the cave once, now she was back and making assumptions about it that were far too close to the truth. He could not permit her to leave – not with her memory of the place, or of him, intact.

'Give me your hand,' he said as gently as he could. 'I'll show you the way out of here.'

She didn't budge, not that he expected her to obey. 'How long have you been living on this mountain? Why do you hide up here? Why won't you let me see you?'

She asked questions one after the other, with an inquisitiveness that bordered on interrogation.

He heard a zipper rasp on her pack.

Ah, hell. If she pulled out another flashlight, he wouldn't have the mental strength to douse it – not when he'd need all his concentration just to scrub her memory.

'Come,' he said, a bit more impatiently now. 'I'm not going to hurt you.'

He would try his damnedest not to, but already the task of staying upright was draining him. He needed to conserve all he could in order to blow the cave and not black out again before he could finish it. Right now, he had to deal with the more immediate problem in front of him.

Rio started toward her when she remained unmoving. He reached out for her, meaning to grab her backpack and haul her out, but before his fingers could close around it she withdrew something from one of the bag's pockets and brought it up in front of her.

'Okay, I'll go. I just . . . there's something I need to do first.'

Rio scowled in the darkness. 'What are you—'

There was a faint click, then a stunning blast of light.

Rio roared, wheeling back on instinct. More explosions of light fired off in rapid succession.

Logic told him it was a digital camera flash blinding him, but in a startling instant, he was hurtled back in time . . . back inside that Boston warehouse, standing beneath an airborne bomb as it detonated.

He heard the sudden boom of the explosion, felt it vibrate into his bones and knock the breath from his lungs. He felt the shower of heat in his face, the suffocating thickness of clouding ash as it engulfed him like a wave.

He felt the bite of hot shrapnel as it ripped through his body.

It was agony, and he was right there, living it – feeling it – all over again.

'Nooo!' he bellowed, his voice no longer human but transformed to something else, as he was, by the fury that ran through him like acid.

His legs gave way beneath him and he sank to the floor, his vision blinded by reverberating light and ruthless memories.

He heard footsteps scuffing past him in a rush, and through the phantom stench of smoke and metal and ruined flesh, he smelled the faint, fleeting traces of juniper, honey, and rain.

⇥ CHAPTER FOUR ⇤

Dylan's heart was still racing later that morning, after she and her companions had boarded the train that would take them from Jičín to Prague. It seemed ridiculous to let herself get so rattled by the vagrant she'd run into in the cave, even if he probably was a little bit psycho to be living up there like some kind of wild man. He hadn't harmed her after all.

Based on his bizarre meltdown when she tried to get some pictures of the cave before he could physically toss her out of there, she had probably scared him even more than he had her.

Dylan sat back in her compartment seat on the train, her computer open on her lap. Thumbnail images from her digital camera queued up on-screen as they downloaded to her computer from the thin black cable that connected the two devices. Most were from the past couple of days' travel, but it was the final handful Dylan was most interested in now.

She double-clicked on one of the dark images from the cave, the first of the sequence. The photo expanded, filling the small screen of her laptop. Dylan considered the face that was all but concealed by a growth of overlong, unkempt hair. The dull, espresso-brown waves hung limply over razor-sharp cheekbones and fierce eyes that reflected back at the lens in the strangest shade of amber she'd ever seen. The jaw looked as rigid as iron, the full lips peeled back in a vicious snarl that wasn't quite hidden behind the large hand that had come up to block the shot.

Jesus, it wouldn't take much Photoshopping back at the office in New York to make the guy look positively demonic. He was more than halfway there already.

'How did your pictures come out, honey?' Janet's curly silver head leaned over from beside Dylan on the cushioned bench seat. 'Good Lord! What is *that*?'

Dylan shrugged, unable to take her eyes off the photo. 'Just some whack-job squatter I ran into up at the cave this morning. He doesn't know it yet, but he's going to be the star of my next story for the paper. What do you think? Just look at that face and tell me if you don't see a blood-drinking savage who lurks in the mountains, waiting for his next hapless victim.'

Janet shuddered and went back to her crossword puzzle. 'You're gonna give yourself nightmares dreaming up stories like that.'

Dylan laughed as she clicked over to the next image on the screen. 'Not me. Never had a nightmare. In fact, I don't dream at all. Blank slate, each and every night.'

'Well, consider yourself lucky,' the older woman said. 'I've always had the most vivid dreams. When I was a young girl, I used to dream recurrently about a white poodle with painted toenails who liked to sing and dance at the end of my bed. I would beg him to stop and let me sleep, but he just always kept singing. Can you imagine? He sang old show tunes mostly, those were his favorite. I've always enjoyed show tunes, myself as well . . .'

Dylan heard Janet's voice beside her, but as she scrolled through the rest of the cave photographs on her computer, she was only half-listening at best. In her frantic pan of the place, she'd gotten one decent shot of the stone crypt and a couple of the elaborate wall art. The designs were even more impressive now that she had a chance to really study them.

Interlocking arcs and graceful, swirling lines ran the entire length of the cavern wall, rendered in a dark russet-brown ink. It looked semi-tribal yet oddly futuristic – unlike anything she'd ever seen before. Still more symbols and intertwining lines decorated the side of the crypt . . . one in particular that made the fine hairs at the back of Dylan's neck tingle.

She zoomed in on the strange design.

What the hell?

The teardrop-and-crescent-moon symbol was unmistakable, nestled within a series of curving lines and geometric patterns. Dylan stared at it in astonishment, and not a little confusion. This one mark was not unfamiliar to her at all. She'd seen it before, countless times. Not in a photograph, but on her own body.

How on earth could that be?

Dylan brought her hand up to the nape of her neck, bewildered by what she was seeing. Her fingers ran over the smooth skin at the top of her spine, where she knew she bore a tiny crimson birthmark . . . exactly like the one she was looking at on the screen.

With a steady, cold gaze fixed on the mouth of the cave, Rio jabbed the button on the C-4 detonator. There was a quiet beep as the remote device engaged, barely a half-second pause before the plastic explosives packed into the rock went off. The blast was loud and deep, a tremor that rumbled like thunder in the surrounding night-dark forest. Thick yellow dust and pulverized sandstone shot out of the passageway, tapering off as the walls of the cave's entry closed in, sealing the chamber and its secrets tight within.

Rio watched from the ground below, knowing that he should have been inside – would have been, if not for his own weakness and the intrusion by the female earlier that day.

It had taken a great deal of his strength to climb down

from the mountain as dusk fell. Determination had carried him most of the way; self-directed rage had kept him focused and clearheaded as he took up his position below the cave and triggered the detonator.

As the smoke and debris dissipated on the breeze, Rio cocked his head. His acute hearing picked up movement in the woods. Not animal, but human – the brisk, two-legged stride of a hiker straggling alone past dark.

Rio's fangs stretched at the thought of easy prey. His vision sharpened on instinct, his pupils narrowing as he pivoted his head to pan the area.

There – coming down a ridge just south of him. A lean human male with a camper's pack slung onto his back tromped through the thicket, his short blond hair glowing like a beacon against the darkness. Rio watched the hiker casually skid and jog down a leafy incline to the trimmed path below. In another few minutes, he would be walking right past the very spot where Rio stood.

He was too depleted to hunt, but everything Breed in him was on full alert, ready and waiting for the chance to spring.

To feed, as he so desperately needed to do.

The human strode nearer, unaware of the predator watching him from the cover of the trees. He didn't see the strike coming, not until Rio launched himself out of hiding in one great leap. The human screamed then – a sound of sheer terror. He flailed and struggled, all for nothing.

Rio worked quickly, throwing the young man to the ground and pinning him prone under the bulk of his large backpack. He bit down on the bared column of the human's neck, and filled his mouth with the sudden, hot spill of fresh blood. The nourishment was immediate, sending renewed strength into muscle and bone and mind.

Rio drank what he needed from his Host and no more. A sweep of his tongue sealed the wound; a sweep of his hand over the human's sweat-soaked brow erased all memory of the attack.

'Go,' he told him.

The man got up, and soon the flaxen head and bulky pack disappeared into the night.

Rio glanced up at the crescent moon overhead, feeling the hard pound of his pulse as his body absorbed the gift of the human's blood.

He needed this strength, because his night's hunting had only just begun.

Rio tipped his head back and dragged the night air through his teeth and fangs, deep into his lungs. His Breed senses sharpened, searching for the scent of his true quarry. She had been on this path hours ago, tearing out of the woods in fear. As well she should fear him. The flame-haired beauty had no idea of the secret she'd stumbled upon in that cave. Nor of the beast she'd roused in the process.

Rio's mouth curved into a smile as he sifted through the olfactory stew of the woodland air, finally registering the scent he sought. He breathed in the trace, lingering fragrance of her. Her trail was hours-old and fading fast in the humid night wind, but Rio would know her anywhere.

He would find her.

No matter how far she'd run.

⇥ CHAPTER FIVE ⇤

As the topper to a day that had started out weird and gotten even weirder, Dylan probably shouldn't have been surprised to find an e-mail from Coleman Hogg waiting for her when she fired up her computer after dinner that night in Prague. She'd submitted her story and a few pictures from the mountain cave once she'd arrived at the hotel around noon, not expecting to hear anything from her boss until she got home in a couple more days.

But he was interested in what she'd found on the mountain outside Jičín – so interested, in fact, he had taken it upon himself to hire a freelance photographer in Prague to go back with Dylan and get a few more shots for the piece.

'You have got to be kidding me,' Dylan grumbled as she scanned the message from her boss.

'You'd better get packing, honey. We don't want to miss our train.' Janet dropped a collection of half-empty toiletry bottles into a plastic bag and zipped it closed. 'Would anyone like the hotel hand lotion from out of the bathroom, or can I have it? And there's also a bar of hand soap in there that hasn't been opened . . .'

Dylan ignored the chatter from her traveling companions as the trio of them continued rounding up their things in preparation of their departure from Prague that evening.

'Shit.'

'What's wrong?' Nancy asked as she zipped up her small

suitcase and propped it on one of the two queen beds in their shared room.

'My boss must not realize that when I said I was leaving Prague tonight, that meant I was leaving Prague tonight.'

Or rather he did understand, and didn't care. According to his e-mail, Dylan was supposed to meet the Czech photographer tomorrow for a return trip to Jičín.

Marie came over and glanced at the computer. 'Is this about your story?'

Dylan nodded. 'He thinks it could be interesting with a few more pictures. He wants me to meet someone about it in the morning. He's already set up the appointment for me.'

'But we're due at the train station in less than an hour,' Janet pointed out.

'I know,' Dylan said, as she started typing a reply message to that effect.

She explained that she and her companions were taking the evening train to Vienna – their last stop on the tour before they departed back home for the States. She wouldn't be able to meet with the photographer because as of ten o'clock tonight, she wasn't going to be around.

Dylan finished typing the reply, but as she moved her cursor over the *Send* button, she hesitated to let the message go. She already had a reserved seat on Coleman Hogg's shit list. If she turned down this appointment – for any reason – she knew without a doubt that she would be kissing her job good-bye.

And as tempting as the thought actually was, getting herself fired was something she really couldn't afford to do right now.

'Damn it,' she muttered, sliding her mouse over to click the *Delete* button instead. 'It's too late for me to cancel this meeting, and I probably shouldn't anyway. You all are going to have to continue on to Vienna without me. I have to stay behind and take care of this story.'

*   *   *

Rio disembarked in Prague from a train packed with humans. Thanks to the blood he'd consumed and the rage that was coursing through every nerve ending in his body, his Breed instincts were locked on full alert as he stepped onto the platform of the busy station. Apparently his quarry had fled here, to Prague, after their confrontation earlier today. He'd been able to track her scent from the mountain into Jičín. From there, with a bit of mental persuasion, the operator of the small hotel in town had been cooperative enough to direct him toward Prague, where the American female and her companions had mentioned they were heading for the last leg of their stay abroad.

The tranced human had also been persuaded to fit Rio with a lightweight trench coat from the hotel's lost-and-found. Although the taupe garment was out of season and several sizes too small, it did a decent job hiding the worst of the filthy, bloodstained rags he wore underneath. He didn't give a shit about style or his looks, or even his certain stench, but he didn't need to draw undue attention by walking into a public place like some kind of castaway freak show.

Rio tried to mask his muscular bulk and height, assuming a hunched yet purposeful shuffle as he ambled through the busy station. No one gave him anything more than a passing glance, the humans subconsciously dismissing him as one of the dozen-plus homeless unfortunates who loitered near the platforms or slept in corners of the station as the trains screeched and roared through the terminal.

With his head down to hide the scar-riddled left side of his face, eyes intense beneath the fall of his unkempt hair, Rio headed for the exit that would put him on a direct path into the heart of the city, where his hunt for the woman and her damning pictures would resume.

Anger kept him focused, even when his head began to spin in the noisy, harshly lit cavern of the station. He ignored the swamping feelings of dizziness and confusion, pushing them down deep so he could find his course and keep it.

Forcing his vision to clear, he moved through a tight knot of young men engaged in a sudden argument in the middle of the terminal. The verbal contest turned physical as Rio passed, one skinny kid from the group getting shoved into a well-dressed English tourist who was yammering on a cell phone as he hurried for the train. The unwitting mark scowled as he recovered from the very deliberate collision and continued on, unaware that he'd just lost his wallet to the gang of professional pickpockets. The thieves moved off with their score, dispersing into the crowd where they would probably pull the same stunt a few more times before the night was through.

In another time, another place, Rio might have gone after the juvenile deliquents, just to set them straight. To show them that the night had eyes . . . and teeth, if they were too cocky to take a helpful hint.

But he was through playing the dark angel to the humans who lived alongside his kind. Let them cheat and kill one another. He frankly didn't care. As of lately, there wasn't much of anything he cared about – save his oath of honor pledged to his brethren of the Order.

Damn fine job he'd done upholding that vow.

He'd let them down by not sealing the mountain crypt as they'd trusted him to do several months ago. Now that failure was compounded. Now there was a witness. With photographs.

Yeah, absolutely stellar job he'd done so far.

Now the situation was as fucked up as he was.

Rio strode hard for the station exit, inhaling the countless scents that filled the air around him and processing them with a ruthless, determined concentration.

His feet stopped moving at the first trace of juniper and honey.

He swung his head around, following the tickle in his nose

like a hound let loose on felled game. The scent of the one he sought was fresh – too fresh to be anything but immediately present.

Madre de Dios.

The woman he hunted was here, in the train station.

'You sure you're going to be okay by yourself, honey? I don't feel right about leaving you behind like this.'

'I'll be fine.'

Dylan gave Janet and the other two women quick hugs as the group of them stood inside Prague's central train station. It was busy even at this time of night, the art deco building crowded with travelers, panhandlers, and quite a number of sleeping homeless people.

'What if something should happen to you?' Janet asked. 'Your mom would never forgive us – and I would never forgive myself – if you get hurt or lost or mugged.'

'Thirty-two years in New York hasn't killed me. I'm pretty sure I can survive a day here on my own.'

Marie's brow furrowed. 'And what about your flight home?'

'Already taken care of. I changed everything online back at the hotel. I'll be flying out of Prague the day after tomorrow.'

'We could wait for you, Dylan.' Nancy hefted her backpack up over her shoulder. 'Maybe we should forget about Vienna and rebook our flights too, so we can all go home together.'

'Yes,' Marie agreed. 'Maybe we should.'

Dylan shook her head. 'Absolutely not. I'm not going to ask any of you to spend the last day of your trip babysitting me when it's really not necessary. I'm a big girl. Nothing's going to happen. Go on, I'll be perfectly fine.'

'You're sure, honey?' Janet asked.

'Positive. Enjoy yourselves in Vienna. I'll see you back home in the States in a couple of days.'

It took a further round of fretting and tongue-clucking before the three women finally made their way to the departure platform. Dylan walked along with them, waiting as they boarded. She watched the train roll out of the station, then turned to leave with the rest of the people who'd come to see loved ones off that night.

As she walked toward the station exits, she couldn't shake the feeling that she was being observed. Paranoia, no doubt, brought on by Janet's worrying on her behalf. But still . . .

Dylan glanced around her in a casual pan of the area, trying not to look anxious or lost – emotional beacons for the types of people who liked to prey on stupid tourists. She held her purse in front of her, one arm locked down over it to keep it close to her body. She knew public transportation areas were prime targets for thieves, just like in the States, and she didn't miss the fact that the group of local teens hanging at a bank of pay phones near the exit were casting measured looks at the crowds as they dispersed. Pickpockets, most likely. She'd heard they often ran in packs around these places. ·

Just to be safe, she cut a wide berth and avoided them, taking the farthest door from the group.

She was feeling pretty street-savvy when she noticed a uniformed security guard walk up to the guys and show them the door. They loped off, and Dylan reached for the push bar on the glass door in front of her.

In the reflection coming back at her from the glass, she saw a familiar face – one that made her heart seize up in her chest.

Behind her, almost close enough to touch her, was a very large man barreling at her from the direction of the train platforms. Fierce eyes seemed to burn like coals under the fall of his dark hair.

And his mouth . . .

Good God, she'd never seen a more terrifying sneer in her

life. A row of perfect white teeth were clamped tightly behind the lips that were peeled back in a feral snarl, pulling the muscles of his lean face into a stark, deadly mask.

It was him – the man she'd found in the mountain cave outside Jičín.

He'd followed her all this way? Evidently so. She'd thought he might be crazy when she saw him earlier that day, but now she was certain. The way he looked at her now, he had to be an utter psychopath.

And he was gunning for her like he meant to tear her apart with his bare hands.

Dylan shrieked; she couldn't hold back her sharp gasp of fear. She ducked away from the exit, pulling a hard left and running, hopefully out of his path. A quick glance backward only made her pulse slam harder.

'Oh, Jesus,' she murmured, fright arrowing through her.

It couldn't be him. He couldn't be here looking for her . . .

But it *was* him.

And from the knot of terror that was lodged in her throat, she wasn't about to stand around and ask him what he wanted from her.

She raced over to the station security guard and grabbed the man by the arm. 'Help, please! Someone's after me.' She flung a look over her shoulder, pointing behind her. 'He's back there – light trench coat and long dark hair. Please. You have to help me!'

The uniformed Czech frowned, but he must have understood her because he followed her panicked gesture, his narrowed eyes scanning the station. 'Where?' he asked, his English thickly accented. 'Show me this man. Who is bothering you?'

'I don't know who he is, but he was right behind me. You can't miss him – more than six feet tall, shoulders like a linebacker, dark, dingy hair hanging over his face . . .'

Feeling safer now, she turned around, ready to confront the lunatic and hopefully watch him be carted off to the local asylum.

Except he wasn't there. Dylan searched the crowds for the big man who would stand out like a rabid, snarling wolf in the center of a herd of milling sheep. There was no sign of him at all. People filed past in ordered calm, nothing out of sorts, no hint of disruption anywhere.

It was as if he'd simply vanished.

'He's got to be here somewhere,' she murmured, even though she couldn't find him – not among the throngs entering and leaving the terminal, nor among the station's population of homeless people. 'He was right here, I swear. He was coming after me.'

She felt like a fool as the security guard's gaze swung back to her and he gave her a polite smile. 'Not anymore. You are okay now?'

'Yeah, sure. Okay, I guess,' Dylan said, feeling anything but okay.

She cautiously headed for the front entrance of the station. Although it was a beautiful summer night, with clear skies and plenty of people walking through the surrounding park and on the streets leading deeper into the city, Dylan hailed a taxi to take her the few blocks back to her hotel.

She kept telling herself that she must have been imagining things – that she couldn't possibly have seen the man from the mountain cave stalking up behind her in the train station. Still, as she climbed out of the taxi and hurried into the posh lobby of her hotel, her nape continued to prickle with anxiety. The feeling persisted as she stood outside her room door, fumbling with her electronic key card.

As she finally got the door open, a noise behind her made her pause. She glanced around but saw nothing, despite the continued wash of paranoid apprehension that hung over her.

She rushed inside like her life depended on it, feeling a star-tling blast of ice-cold air envelop her in the dark of her room.

'Air conditioner, doofus,' she told herself as she reached for the light switch and flipped it on. She had to laugh at her own paranoia, even as she quickly turned all the locks behind her.

She didn't see him until she took a step farther into the dimly lit room.

The man from the mountain cave, the lunatic from the train station, was somehow – impossibly – standing not ten feet from her.

Dylan's mouth dropped open in shock.

And then she screamed.

⊰ CHAPTER SIX ⊱

Rio closed his hand around the female's open mouth just as the first high note of terror ripped through the room. He'd moved too quickly for her human eyes to track him, employing the same Breed ability he'd used to tail her taxi from the station and follow her up into her hotel room. She'd probably felt him move past her as he had entered ahead of her – registering him only as a sudden draft of chill air – but even now he could tell that her mind was struggling to make sense of what her eyes were seeing.

She twisted her head, attempting to break free of his unrelenting grasp. Another scream formed in the back of her throat and blasted hotly against his palm, but the effort was useless. The hard clamp of Rio's fingers snuffed out all but the barest tremor of her cries.

'Quiet.' He held fast, and pinned her with a look that demanded obedience. 'Not one more sound, do you understand? I'm not going to hurt you.'

Even though he meant it – at least for now – he could see that she was far from convinced. She was trembling hard, her entire body taut and rigid, fear pouring off her in vibrating waves. Over the edge of his palm, her gold-flecked green eyes were huge and wild. Her fine nostrils flared with every short, panicked breath she took.

'Do as I tell you, and you won't get hurt,' he said, holding that wide, wary gaze. Very slowly, he began to ease some of the pressure from her mouth. The moist heat of her lips and sawing breath seared his palm as she adjusted to the tiny bit of freedom he'd granted her. 'Now, I'm going to take my hand away. I need you to stay quiet. Agreed?'

She blinked slowly. Gave him a faint, tremulous nod.

'All right.' Rio began to lift his hand. 'All right, that's good.'

The female didn't scream.

She bit him.

No sooner had Rio relaxed his hold than he felt the sudden, blunt force of her teeth latching on to the web of flesh between his thumb and forefinger. He spat a vicious curse, more pissed off that he hadn't seen the attack coming than he was put off by the pain of her bite.

She drew back just as swiftly as she'd struck and managed to break away from him. She lunged for the locked door but didn't even make it one step. Rio tackled her from behind, his arms wrapped around her like iron bands.

'Oh, God – no!' she cried, and went down hard on her knees, too fast for him to cushion her fall.

She collapsed in a clumsy, face-first sprawl on the floor. Rio heard her breath whoosh out of her on the abrupt impact and knew her lungs had to be screaming. Not that it sapped her of her determination. Damn, she was tenacious.

She made a last-ditch, frantic scrabble on her belly, trying to drag herself over the carpeted floor to get away from him. But she stood no chance, certainly not against one of his kind.

Rio crawled up the length of her, trapping her under the weight of his body. She was panting as he flipped her over onto her back and sat himself astride her. She wriggled, still fighting him for all she was worth, but she wasn't going anywhere. Rio had her imprisoned beneath him, holding her arms tight against her sides with the strength of his muscled thighs.

She was completely at his mercy now, and from the look

in her eyes as she stared up at him, she didn't expect he had much to give.

Rio could guess what he looked like – Jesus, what he smelled like too. This close, he couldn't hope that his scars were hidden behind his overlong hair. He saw her terrified gaze flick to the left side of his face, where the flames and flying shrapnel had left their mark a year ago. The tight, reddish-silver tangle of ruined skin must look especially hideous underneath all his grime. He must look like some kind of half-crazed monster . . .

Yeah, he did, because that's just what he was.

And he was also suddenly, acutely aware of the soft, warm woman trapped beneath him. Where he was dressed to offend, in torn clothes that were too far gone months ago to even make decent rags, she was wearing a curve-hugging, cap-sleeved tee-shirt with a pleasantly deep V-neck and light tan cargo pants that rode just below her hips. She smelled clean and fresh, infinitely female.

And she was beautiful.

Holy mother, was she ever.

He'd never seen eyes of her precise color, a rich, verdant green flecked with pale gold. A thick fringe of dark brown lashes framed those intelligent, mesmerizing eyes, which stared up at him now in such wary uncertainty. Her cheekbones were delicate and high, accentuating the graceful line of her jaw. She had the kind of beauty that made her seem both innocent and wise, but it was the shadows in her incredible eyes that intrigued Rio the most.

This woman had known disappointment and hurt in her life. Maybe even betrayal. She'd been wounded before, and now here he was adding a new brand of terror to her life experience.

Even worse, she aroused him.

Not only the knowledge that he had her caught between

his thighs, but the sight of her pretty mouth, which was stained with a trace smear of his blood from when she'd bitten him. Everything male in Rio was alert with the feel of her beneath him. Everything Breed in him was tuned in to that scarlet smudge on her tempting lips . . . and to the thrumming tick of her pulse where it beat so quickly at the base of her creamy throat.

He wanted her.

After the months of exile in that godforsaken cave, after Eva's deception that had left him dead in so many ways, Rio looked at this woman and felt . . . alive.

He felt ravenous, and she likely picked up on that fact from the low growl he could do nothing to suppress. He felt his vision sharpen as his pupils began to narrow with his interest. His gums ached as his fangs began to elongate behind the tight line of his lips.

And his cock was suddenly, achingly erect. There was no hiding that fact, even as he shifted his hold on his captive.

'Please . . . don't do this,' she said, a tear sliding down her cheekbone and into her silky red hair. 'Whatever you're thinking, just . . . let me go. If it's money you need, take it. My purse is right over there—'

'I don't want you or your money,' Rio ground out tightly. He got off her, angered with himself for the twin physical reactions he was having a hard time holding at bay. 'Come on, stand up. All I want is your camera.'

She slowly pulled herself to her feet. 'My what?'

'The camera you had with you in the cave, and the pictures you took. I need all of it.'

'You want . . . the pictures? I don't understand—'

'You don't need to. Just give them to me.' When she didn't move to comply, Rio trained a piercing look on her. 'Get them. Now.'

'O-okay,' she stammered, and hurried over to a large backpack that stood in the corner of the room. She dug through it and pulled out the slim digital camera.

When she started to open it up to pop out the image disk, Rio said, 'I'll do that. Give it to me.'

She held the camera out to him with shaking fingers. 'You followed me all the way to Prague for this? What's so important about those pictures? And just how did you find me anyway?'

Rio ignored her questions. In a few minutes, none of this would matter. He'd have the images and then he'd scrub the female's memory of the entire chain of events.

'Is this all of them?' he asked her as he turned the camera on and scrolled through the contents of the disk. 'Have you downloaded them to any other devices?'

'That's it,' she replied quickly. 'That's everything, I swear.'

He reviewed the handful of shots from the cave, the ones of himself in partial transformation, and the ones that showed the Ancient's hibernation chamber and the *glyphs* painted in human blood on the walls. 'Have you shown these to anyone?'

She swallowed, then shook her head. 'I still don't understand what this is about.'

'And that's how we're going to keep it,' Rio said.

He walked toward her, only three steps between them. She backed away, but came up against the window on the far wall of the room. 'Oh, my God. You said you weren't going to hurt me . . .'

'Be calm,' he instructed her. 'It will be over soon.'

'Oh, shit.' A strangled moan curled audibly in the back of her throat. 'Oh, my God . . . you're really going to kill me . . .'

'No,' Rio said grimly. 'But I need your silence.'

He reached out for her. All it would take was a brief settling of his hand on her forehead to erase her knowledge of the mountain cave and him from her mind.

But as his hand descended toward her, she drew in her

breath, then let it out on a string of words that made him freeze in place where he stood.

'I'm not the only one who knows!' She panted with fear. Words tumbled out of her mouth in a rush. 'Other people know where I am. They know where I've been, what I've been doing. So, whatever you think those pictures mean, killing me won't protect you because I'm not the only one who's seen them.'

She lied to him. Rio's anger spiked at the deception. 'You said no one else knew.'

'And you said you weren't going to hurt me.'

'Jesus.' He saw little point in arguing with her, or in defending his intentions. 'You need to tell me who you've shown the pictures to. I need names and locations.'

She scoffed, too bold for her own good. 'Why? So you can go after them too?'

Rio's mind switched into immediate reconnaissance mode. He threw a glance at her belongings and saw a messenger bag slung over the hotel chair. The bag looked like it probably contained a computer. He stalked over to it and withdrew a thin silver laptop.

He opened it and hit the power button, which must have given the woman an idea that she could make another break for the door. She bolted, but Rio cut her off at the pass. He stood in front of her, his back against the heavily locked panel, before she even had a chance to imagine freedom.

'Holy shit,' she gasped, blinking at him in disbelief. 'How did you get – ? You were all the way across the room—'

'Yes, I was. And now I'm not.'

Rio stepped forward, away from the door, forcing her to retreat. She backed up as he kept advancing, obviously unsure what to make of him now.

'Sit down,' he ordered her. 'The sooner you cooperate, the sooner this will be over.'

She took a seat on the edge of the bed, watching as he went back to her computer and fired up her Internet connection. Her e-mail was a revelation. Aside from the usual personal garbage and a recent airline ticket change, Rio found several messages in her *Sent* folder going out to some kind of news organization – a few of them complete with photos. He clicked one open and quickly scanned the contents.

'Ah, Christ. You've got to be kidding me,' he muttered. He swung a glare at her over his shoulder. 'You're a goddamn reporter?'

She didn't answer, just sat there biting her lip like she wasn't sure if a yes might get her killed faster than a no.

Rio put down the laptop and started pacing tightly.

He thought the situation had been bad before? Well, now he was faced with a nuclear-grade disaster. A reporter. A reporter with a camera and a computer and an Internet connection. No amount of mind-scrubbing was going to take care of that.

He needed an assist here, and he needed one pronto.

Rio grabbed her computer and called up the instant messaging software. He typed in a masked ID that would route to the Order's tech lab at the compound in Boston. The address was monitored 24/7 by Gideon, the warriors' resident computer genius. Rio entered a cryptic message using code that identified him, his location, and his need to contact.

The response came back from Gideon almost immediately. Whatever Rio needed, the Order would provide. Gideon was standing by for details.

'You got a cell phone?' he asked the reporter sitting mutely near him. When she shook her head, Rio snatched the desk phone and typed in the hotel's landline. 'What room number is this? The number, damn it!'

'Uh, it's 310,' she replied. 'Why? Who are you calling? Are you going to tell me what's going on?'

'Damage control,' he said, about a second before the telephone started ringing.

He picked up the receiver, knowing it was Gideon even before he heard the slight English accent on the other end. 'I'm calling on a scrambled signal, Rio, so speak freely. What's up? More importantly, where the fuck have you been all this time? For crissake, it's been five months since you went off grid. You don't write, you don't call . . . don't you love me no more?'

God, it was good to hear a familiar voice. Rio might have smiled at the thought but things were too far south on his end. 'I've got a situation here – it's not good, my friend.'

Gideon's humor vanished and the warrior was all business. 'Talk to me.'

'I'm in Prague. There's a reporter here with me – a female. American. She's got pictures from the mountain, Gideon. Pictures of the hibernation chamber and the *glyphs* on the walls.'

'Jesus. How did she get in there to take pictures? And when? That cave's been sealed up since you guys were there in February.'

Ah, hell. No getting around it. He had to just spit the truth out. 'The cave wasn't sealed. There were some delays . . . I didn't secure the damn thing until today. After the pictures were taken.'

Gideon blew out a curse. 'All right. I'm assuming you've scrubbed her, but what about the photos? Do you have them?'

'Yeah, I have them, but here's where it gets worse, Gid. She's not the only one who's seen them. They've already gone out via e-mail to the paper she works for and several other individuals. If I could've contained this by scrubbing her, I would have. Unfortunately, it's bigger than that, my friend.'

Gideon was quiet for a long moment, no doubt calculating the endless ramifications of Rio's fuckup, even though he was too much of a diplomat to list them off. 'First thing we need to do is get you out of there and somewhere secure. The woman too. Think you can hold her until I can arrange a pickup?'

'Anything you say. This is my mess, I'm sure as hell going to do whatever I need to in order to clean it up.'

Rio heard the vague clatter of a keyboard in the background. 'I'm contacting Andreas Reichen in Berlin.' There was a few seconds' pause, then Gideon started talking on another phone line back in Boston. He came back to Rio in no time. 'I've got pickup for you and transport to Reichen's Darkhaven, but it might take up to an hour for his contact to reach you.'

'That's no problem.'

'Confirming now,' Gideon replied, deftly handling the logistics like hauling Rio's ass out of trouble was nothing but cake. 'Okay, you're all set. I'll call again when the transport is in place.'

'I'll be ready. Hey, Gideon . . . thank you.'

'No problem at all. Good to have you back, Rio. We need you, man. Things don't feel right around here without you.'

'I'll report in from Berlin,' he said, thinking that now probably wasn't the time to tell Gideon that he wasn't coming back into the fold.

His date with death had been postponed, but as soon as he had this current situation under control, he was checking out for good.

⇥ CHAPTER SEVEN ⇤

Dylan sat quietly on the bed and watched as the dark stranger confiscated her computer and camera, then rifled through the rest of her belongings. She had little choice but to stay out of his way. Her slightest movement drew his attention every time, and after the mind-boggling, warp-speed maneuver he'd pulled when he blocked her from reaching the hotel room door, she hadn't found the nerve to attempt another escape.

She had no idea what to think of him.

He was dangerous, no question. Probably deadly when he wanted to be, although she didn't think murder was foremost on his mind at the moment. If he wanted to harm her, he'd had plenty of opportunity already. Like when she'd been trapped underneath him on the floor, very attuned to the fact that she'd had more than two hundred pounds of hard, muscular male on top of her and little to no hope of throwing him off. He could have wrapped those big hands around her throat and strangled her, right there on her hotel room floor.

But he hadn't.

He hadn't acted on the other impulse that had so obviously occurred to him either. Dylan hadn't missed the way he'd looked at her, his eyes fixed intensely on her mouth. The very male response of his body as he'd straddled her had been swift, unmistakable, yet he hadn't laid a finger on her. In fact, he'd seemed about as alarmed by his arousal as she'd been.

So, he apparently wasn't a cold-blooded psychopath or a rapist, regardless of the fact he'd stalked her all the way from Jičín to Prague.

So, what did that make him?

He moved too fast, was far too precise and agile, to be some kind of crazed survivalist or a garden variety vagrant. No, he wasn't either of those things. He might be filthy and ragged, one side of his face scarred from some horrific event she could only speculate on, but underneath all the grime he was something . . . else.

This man, whoever he truly was, was huge and strong, and dangerously alert. His keen eyes and ears missed nothing. His senses seemed to be tuned to a higher frequency than was humanly possible. Even if he was half insane, he carried himself like he was well aware of his own power and knew just how to use it.

'Are you military or something?' she asked, guessing aloud. 'You talk like you could be. Act like it too. What are you, some kind of special forces? Ex-military, maybe. What were you doing on that mountain near Jičín?'

He shot her a glare as he stuffed her computer and camera back into her messenger bag, but he didn't answer.

'You know, you might as well fill me in on some of what's going on. I'm a journalist' – well, admittedly, that was a bit of a stretch—' but I am a reasonable person. If those pictures are sensitive or classified or a matter of national security, just say so. Why are you so concerned about people seeing what was in that cave?'

'You ask too many questions.'

She shrugged. 'Sorry. Hazard of the job, I guess.'

'That's not the only hazard of your job,' he said, slanting her a look of dark warning. 'The less you know about this, the better.'

'You mean, about the 'hibernation chamber'?' He stiffened

visibly, but Dylan kept going. 'That's what you called it, right? That's what you told your friend Gideon. Some kind of shit is about to hit the fan because I took pictures of this hibernation chamber thingy and the, uh, 'glyphs' as you called them.'

'Jesus Christ,' he hissed. 'You shouldn't have been listening to any of that.'

'It was kind of hard not to. When you're being held against your will and pretty damn certain you're going to be killed, you tend to pay attention.'

'You're not going to be killed.'

His cold, matter-of-fact tone wasn't exactly reassuring. 'Sounded to me like you thought about it, though. Unless 'scrubbing' someone means something different to you than it does to everyone else who's ever seen a mafia movie.'

He scoffed, giving a curt shake of his head.

'What was in that cave?'

'Forget it.'

Not likely. Not when he seemed so protective of the information. As in, do-or-die protective. 'What do all those weird symbols on the walls mean? Is it some kind of ancient language? Some kind of code? Just what are you so desperate to hide?'

He came at her so fast, she didn't even see him move. She blinked and suddenly he was bearing down on her, the broad bulk of his body towering over her, making her shrink back on the bed.

'Listen to me and hear me well, Dylan Alexander,' he said tightly. The sound of her name rolling off his lips was jarring in its intimacy. 'This is not a game. It's not a puzzle for you to piece together. And it sure as hell isn't a story that I'm going to permit you to tell. So do us both a favor and stop asking questions about something that doesn't concern you.'

His eyes were livid, the topaz color of them flashing with anger. It was that hot, penetrating gaze that scared her the most – even more than the threat of his coiled strength or the terrible scars that stretched across the left side of his face and made him look so frightening.

But he was wrong when he said that the cave and whatever secrets it might contain did not concern her. She was personally invested in the story, and not just because it was beginning to feel like the kind of story that would not only save her so-called career, but quite possibly make it.

Dylan's interest in the cave and its strange wall art had gotten very personal from the moment she noticed the teardrop-and-crescent-moon symbol that identically matched the birthmark she had on the back of her neck.

She considered that bizarre coincidence as the hotel phone began to ring. Her uninvited guest picked it up and carried on a short, confidential exchange. He hung up, slung her messenger bag over his shoulder then went over to grab the backpack containing the rest of her belongings. He took her pocketbook off the nightstand and tossed it to her.

'That's our ride,' he said as she caught the small handbag. 'Time to go.'

'What do you mean, *our* ride?'

'We're leaving, right now.'

A wave of dread roared up on her, but she tried to maintain a brave front. 'Forget it. You really are crazy if you think I'm going anywhere with you.'

'You don't have a choice.'

He came toward her, and Dylan knew that she stood little chance of overpowering him or outrunning him. Not when she had to navigate three floors of the hotel in order to get away from him. But she could sure as hell scream for help – and would, the very second he dragged her into the hotel lobby.

Except he didn't bring her into the very public lobby so she could make her escape.

He didn't even open the door that led out into the hallway outside her room.

With that same speed and strength she couldn't help but be amazed by, he grabbed her at the wrist and pulled her to the window that overlooked a side street several dizzying yards below. He threw open the glass and climbed out onto the fire escape, still holding fast to her arm as he started to haul her outside with him.

'What the hell are you doing?' Dylan dug in her heels, her eyes wide with fear. 'Are you insane? You're going to break both our necks if you—'

He didn't give her a chance to finish the thought, let alone speak it.

Before Dylan realized what was happening, she was lifted out the window and over the solid bulk of his shoulder. She heard his boots clanking on the rattling iron of the fire escape. Then she felt her whole world shift as he incredibly – *impossibly* – vaulted over the railing with her.

They hit the dark pavement three stories below.

It wasn't the bone-breaking crash she anticipated, but a soft, almost graceful connection between his feet and the ground. She was still trying to process how that could be when suddenly she was pushed into the back of an open delivery truck that idled near the place they'd touched down.

Dylan tumbled in with her abductor right behind her. Disoriented and thoroughly confused, she was too stunned to form a single word as he brought the heavy trailer door down with a hard thump and enclosed them in darkness.

The truck's engine roared to life, and with a sharp squeal of tires, the vehicle took off with its cargo.

Back in Boston, it was nearly five A.M. and the last of the Order's warriors were heading in from their night patrols. Lucan, Tegan, and Dante – the mated ones, like Gideon, with females awaiting their return to the compound – had been in for about an hour already. Sterling Chase, the ex–Darkhaven Enforcement Agent who'd joined up with the Order last year and had proven to be a formidable – enthusiastically lethal – addition to the group, was present and accounted for too.

Now, as the three remaining members of the Order filed in, Gideon wasn't surprised to find Nikolai bringing up the rear. Although he was the youngest of the warriors, Niko was also the most relentless fighter Gideon had ever seen. An adrenaline junkie and vicious combatant, the Russian-born vampire never called it a night until dawn was creeping over the horizon, forcing him off the streets.

And when it came to high-octane weaponry, Niko was an absolute demon.

Tonight, as the black-clad warrior with the golden-blond hair and glacial blue eyes sauntered in behind the two newest members of the cadre, Kade and Brock, Gideon noted that he was armed with some of his latest creations. A nasty-looking 9mm semiauto with a clip full of titanium hollowpoint rounds rode at Niko's hip, and a laser-sighted sniper rifle tricked out with the same custom ammo was slung from a strap over his shoulder.

Even from behind the glass enclosure of the compound's tech lab, Gideon could smell fresh death on the warrior. Not human, as the Breed in general tried to maintain as peaceful a cohabitation as possible with their *Homo sapiens* cousins. They fed from humans in order to survive, but it was rare that a vampire killed his Host. It was a matter of simple logic after all. No sense wiping out your sole food source, or, for that matter, exposing yourself as a mortal threat to that food source and encouraging them to wipe you out instead.

But there was a small, splintered percentage of the vampire nation that didn't give a damn for solid logic. Rogues – vampires who'd become addicted to blood and gone feral, living only to feed that addiction – were the ones who found themselves in the crosshairs of the Order's lethal brand of justice.

The Order had been combating the problematic minority within the Breed since the Middle Ages, a task that had given the warriors a reputation as merciless killers among the vampire nation at large. Not that Gideon or any of his brethren were looking for accolades or public adoration. They had a grim job to do, and they did it very well.

Gideon met the three returning warriors in the corridor outside the lab, wrinkling his nose at the Rogue stench that Nikolai carried in with him.

'I take it the hunting was decent tonight.'

Niko grinned. 'It ended on a good note at any rate. Tracked and smoked a suckhead out of the city after he attacked a woman walking her dog in Beacon Hill.'

'My man here tracked the Rogue thirty-five miles – on foot,' Brock added, giving a roll of his dark brown eyes. 'Had the Rover gassed up and waiting on the corner. We could have run the son of a bitch to the ground in three minutes flat, but Jackie Joyner decides to hoof it instead.'

Niko chuckled. 'Hey, might as well make it interesting. Besides, it was a slow night up until then.'

'Been a slow month,' Kade replied, his tone not complaining so much as stating fact.

Things around the city had become considerably quieter since last February, when the Order had finally killed the vampire responsible for a rash of violence in and around Boston. Marek was no more, and following his death the warriors had been hunting down and eliminating all those who'd served him. As far as that went, Marek's human Minions were no problem – the blood-depleted mind slaves could not survive without their Master; wherever they were, they simply stopped breathing at the same time he did, and dropped dead of what would appear to be abrupt, yet perfectly natural, causes.

Marek's personal retinue of Rogues, on the other hand, were not as accommodating as their human counterparts. The blood-addicted vampires who'd been recruited, and sometimes forced, under Marek's command as his bodyguards and lieutenants were now left to their own misrule. Without Marek around to keep them in line and provide the victims required to slake their Bloodlust, the Rogue vampires had dispersed into the surrounding human populations to hunt like the insatiable predators they were.

Since the winter, the Order had smoked ten of the suckheads between Boston and Marek's last known headquarters in the Berkshires region two hours to the west. Eleven Rogues, counting the one Niko took out tonight.

And although what Kade had said about the current state of quiet was true, Gideon had lived long enough to know that a calm like the one they knew now wasn't meant to last. It was often just the lull preceding a hellish storm.

Given what the Order had uncovered on that Bohemian mountain last February, there was little question that a storm of epic proportions was on the rise. An ancient evil had been sleeping in the crypt on that mountain – a vampire unlike any in existence today. Now that powerful, alien creature was loose somewhere, and the Order's newest, most critical mission was to find it and destroy it before its terror was unleashed on the world.

That job was going to prove a lot harder if the secret realm of the Breed – and the escalating trouble within it – were suddenly exposed to humankind by way of a curious reporter who'd somehow wandered into the middle of all this.

'Got an interesting call from Prague tonight,' Gideon said. 'Rio's back on grid.'

Nikolai's tawny brows crashed together. 'He's not in Spain? When did he get back to Prague?'

'Doesn't sound like he ever left. He ran into some trouble there, in the form of an American reporter. She knows about the cave. She's been inside the Ancient's hibernation chamber. Took a bunch of pictures too, evidently.'

'What the fuck? When did all this go down?'

'I don't have all the details yet. Rio's working on getting the situation secured. He and the woman are on their way to Reichen's place in Berlin as we speak. He's going to report in once he arrives so we can determine how to best contain this potential disaster.'

'Shit.' Brock exhaled, running a hand over his dark brow. 'Rio's actually still breathing, eh? Gotta say, I'm surprised. Since he's been AWOL for so long, I kind of expected he wasn't coming back, you know what I'm saying? Edgy guy like that, seemed to me like a prime candidate to off himself.'

'Maybe he should have,' Kade put in, chuckling. 'I mean, hell, we've got Chase and Niko to contend with already. Does the Order really need another raving lunatic in the ranks?'

Nikolai sprang on the other warrior like a viper. There was no warning, no hint that Niko was going to grab Kade's throat in his hand and slam the big male up against the wall of the corridor. He was seething with defensive anger as he held Kade in a near death grip.

'Jesus Christ!' Kade hissed, clearly as shocked as anyone else by the unexpected reaction. 'It was just a joke, man!'

Nikolai snarled. 'Do you see me laughing? Do I look like I'm fucking laughing?'

Kade's sharp silver eyes narrowed but he didn't say anything else to provoke him.

'I could give a damn what you say about me,' Niko growled, 'but if you know what's good for you, lay the hell off Rio.'

Gideon might have guessed this wasn't about Kade unintentionally insulting Nikolai. It was about Niko's friendship with Rio. The two warriors had been as close as true brothers in the time before the warehouse explosion that left Rio scarred and broken. Afterward, it was Niko who made sure Rio fed,

Niko who dragged Rio's ass out of the infirmary to train in the compound's weapons facility as soon as the wounded warrior was able to stand up.

It had been Nikolai who argued the most vehemently every time Rio announced that he was too far gone to be useful and he was pulling out of the Order. In the nearly five months that Rio had been currently off grid, not a week passed that Niko didn't ask if there had been any word from him.

'Niko, damn, buddy,' Brock said. 'Ease up.'

The huge black warrior moved in, looking like he was about to peel him off Kade, but Gideon held him back with a look. Although Nikolai relaxed his grip, his anger was still a palpable force filling the hallway.

'You don't know dick about Rio,' he told Kade. 'That warrior has more honor than the both of us combined. So this is the last time I want to hear you talking shit about him. Understand?'

Kade nodded tightly. 'Yeah. Like I said, it was just a damn joke. I didn't mean any offense.'

Nikolai stared at him for a long moment, then stalked away in silence.

⊰ CHAPTER EIGHT ⊱

Dawn was inching up over the horizon as the delivery truck from Prague wheeled into a gated, heavily secured lakefront estate on the outskirts of Berlin.

The Darkhaven was held by a Breed vampire named Andreas Reichen, a civilian, but also a trusted ally of the Order since he'd assisted with the discovery of the mountain cave a few months ago. Rio had only met him briefly that past February, but the German greeted him like an old friend as he came around to the back of the truck and opened the trailer door.

'Welcome,' he said, then sent an anxious glance up at the pinkening sky overhead. 'You made excellent time.'

The male was dressed in an impeccably tailored suit and a pristinely pressed white shirt that lay unbuttoned at the throat. With his thick chestnut hair loose around his shoulders, the perfect waves setting off his striking, angular features, Reichen looked like he'd just come off a photo shoot for a men's designer ad.

One dark brow lifted slightly as he took in Rio's negligent appearance, but he remained the consummate gentleman. With a nod, Reichen offered his hand in greeting as Rio climbed out of the truck. 'No trouble along the way, I hope?'

'None.' Rio gave a brief shake of the vampire's hand. 'We were stopped at the border into Germany, but they didn't search the truck.'

'For the right price, they don't,' Reichen said, smiling pleasantly. He glanced behind Rio into the darkened trailer, to where Dylan Alexander lay on the floor. She was curled up on her side and resting peacefully, her head cushioned by the lumpy edge of her backpack. 'Tranced, I take it?'

Rio nodded. He'd put her out about an hour into the trip, when her endless, probing questions and the swaying motion of the truck had been too much for him to deal with. Even though he'd fed earlier that night, his body was still in need of nourishment and not yet operating on all cylinders. To say nothing of his other problems.

He had spent most of the five-plus-hour drive fighting off nausea and blackout – a weakness he wasn't about to risk exposing to the woman he'd just forcibly abducted. Better that she spend the duration of the trip in a light, psychically induced doze than have her make some desperate bid to overpower him and attempt an escape while they were in transit.

'She's attractive,' Reichen said, a casual observation that didn't even begin to do the female justice. 'Why don't you take her inside. I have a room prepared for her upstairs. One for you as well. Third floor, end of the hall to the right.'

Reichen waved off Rio's murmured thanks. 'You are welcome to stay as long as you require, of course. Anything you need, just ask. I'll be along with her things as soon as I compensate my Czech friend for doing this favor on such short notice.'

As the German went around to the front of the truck to pay the driver, Rio climbed back inside to retrieve his sleeping captive. She stirred lightly as he lifted her into his arms and carried her outside. He walked briskly toward the mansion and up the short climb of steps that led into the opulent foyer.

None of the Darkhaven's residents were around, even though it wouldn't have been unusual to see some of the civilian vampires or their female mates who lived together as a community in the vast estate. Reichen had probably made sure the house would be quiet for Rio's arrival, devoid of curious eyes and ears. Not to mention, protecting those same civilians from being identified by someone like Dylan Alexander.

A goddamn reporter.

Rio's jaw clamped tight at the thought of the damage the woman in his arms could do. Just a stroke of her pen – or keyboard, as it were – and she could put this Darkhaven and the hundred or so others like it in Europe and the United States in terrible danger. Persecution, subjugation, and, ultimately, wholesale annihilation were certain outcomes if humankind were to have proof of vampires living among them. Aside from some assorted, mostly incorrect, vampire folklore widely dismissed as fiction by modern man, the Breed had kept itself hidden from discovery for thousands of years. It was the only way they'd survived this long.

But now, through his own carelessness – his weakness – Rio might have undone all of that in one reckless moment. He had to make it right, no matter what it might take to stanch the bleeding wound this woman's story could cause.

Rio carried her through the empty foyer and up the massive staircase at the center of the elegant mansion. At the third floor landing, he followed the walnut-paneled hallway to the end of the line and opened the guest room door on his right. It was dim inside; like any Darkhaven residence, the windows were outfitted with electronic, UV-blocking shades to shut out deadly sunlight. Rio brought Dylan into the room and placed her on the large four-poster bed.

She didn't look so dangerous like this, coming to rest there in the middle of the plush, silk-covered mattress. She looked innocent, almost angelic in her silence, her skin as clear as milk except for the spatter of tiny freckles that marched across her cheeks and the bridge of her small nose. Her long red hair fell around her head and shoulders like a halo of fire. Rio couldn't resist touching one of the molten strands that had fallen over her creamy cheek. The tendril rasped against his callused fingers, which looked so dark and unclean against the coppery silk.

He had no right to touch her – no good reason to sift the beautiful lock between his fingers, marveling at the resilient strength contained within so much mesmerizing softness.

There was no cause at all for him to bend his head down to where she lay, passive only because he made her so, and to breathe the appealing scent of her into his lungs. Saliva surged into his mouth as he held himself very still over her, his face mere inches from the side of her neck. His thirst rose swiftly, along with a hot, swelling need.

Madre de Dios.

Had he really thought her to look like no threat to him now?

Wrong again, he thought, recoiling from her bedside as her eyelids fluttered with waking consciousness. The lull of the trance was dissipating; it would fall away completely once Rio wasn't in the room to hold the effect in place.

She stirred a bit more and he turned away from her briskly. He'd better get out of there, before he revealed himself any further with the current, rather obvious presence of his fangs.

When he looked up, he found Andreas Reichen standing in the hall outside the open door. 'Do you find the room suitable, Rio?'

'Yes,' he replied, stalking over to take the backpack and pocketbook from the German's hands. 'I'll keep these with me for now.'

'Of course. As you wish.' Reichen stepped back as Rio came out to the hallway and closed the guest room door. The German handed him a key for the lock beneath the antique crystal knob. 'The window shades are centrally controlled, and the glass behind them is equipped with alarms. Outside, the estate grounds are secured by motion detectors and a perimeter fence. But these measures were designed to keep people off the property, not in. If you think the woman is a flight hazard, I can post a guard at the door—'

'No,' Rio said as he turned the key in the lock. 'It's bad enough she can ID me. The fewer individuals we bring into this, the better. She's my responsibility. I'll make sure she stays put.'

'Very well. I've had the adjoining suite prepared for you. You'll find the wardrobe fully stocked with brand-new men's attire. Help yourself to anything you like. There's a bath and sauna in the suite as well, if you'd, ah, like to freshen up.'

'Yeah.' Rio nodded. His head was still pounding from the long ride in the back of the truck. His body was taut and edgy, hot all over, and he couldn't blame any of that on the trip or his rocky state of mind. Behind his closed lips, he ran his tongue over his still-present fangs.

'A shower sounds great,' he told Reichen.

Preferably an ice-cold one.

If Dylan was confused before she and her abductor left Prague, their arrival in what she could only assume was somewhere in or around Berlin made things all the muddier to her. When she woke up in the middle of a large, silk-covered bed in a darkened room that looked like an upscale European bed-and-breakfast suite, she wondered if she'd dreamt the whole thing.

Where the hell was she? And how long had she been here?

Even though she felt fully awake and alert, there was a kind of cloudiness to her senses, like her head had been wrapped in thick cotton.

Maybe she was still dreaming.

Maybe she was still somehow in Prague and none of what she recalled had actually happened at all. Dylan turned on a nightstand lamp, then got off the bed and walked over to the tall windows on the other side of the luxurious room. Behind the beautiful drapes and curtain sheers, a tightly fitted panel shade covered the glass. She looked for a pull-cord or some other means to open it, but she couldn't find anything. The blind was completely immobile, as though it was locked in place over the glass.

'The shade is electronic. You won't be able to open it from in here.'

Startled, Dylan spun around at the sound of the deep, but now familiar male voice.

It was him, sitting in a delicate antique chair in the opposite corner of the room. She knew the unmistakable dark, accented voice, but the man staring at her from the shadows didn't look anything like the filthy, ragged lunatic she expected to see.

He was clean now, and wearing fresh clothes – a black button-down dress shirt with rolled-up sleeves, black trousers, and black loafers that were probably Italian and probably very expensive. His dark hair gleamed from a fresh washing, no longer the dingy hanks that hung limply into his face but swept back now in glossy espresso-brown waves that set off the unusual color of his intense, topaz eyes.

'Where am I?' she asked him, taking a few steps closer to where he sat. 'What is this place? How long have you been sitting there watching me? What the hell did you do to me that I can hardly remember coming here?'

He smiled, but it couldn't be called friendly. 'Barely awake and already starting in with the questions. You were a lot easier to take when you were sleeping.'

Dylan wasn't sure why she should feel insulted by that. 'Then why don't you let me go if I annoy you so much?'

The smile quirked a little, softening the grim line of his mouth. Good God, if not for the scars that ran from temple to jaw on the left side of his face, he would have been drop-dead gorgeous.

No doubt he had been, before whatever accident had happened to him.

'I would like nothing better than to let you go,' he said. 'Unfortunately, the decision of what to do with you is not mine to make alone.'

'Then whose is it? The man you were talking to in the hallway before?'

She'd only been half-conscious, but she'd been awake enough to hear the exchange of two male voices as she was placed in the room – one of them belonging to the man glaring at her now, the other clearly German based on the accent. She glanced around at the wealth of antique furniture and fine art, at the ten-foot ceilings and ornate crown moldings, all of which practically screamed multimillion-dollar estate. And then there were those light-blocking, Pentagon-grade window shades.

'What is this place – headquarters to some kind of government spy ring?' Dylan laughed, a bit nervously. 'You're not going to tell me you're part of a well-funded foreign terrorist cell, are you?'

He leaned forward, resting his elbows on his knees. 'No.'

'No, you won't tell me, or no, you aren't a terrorist?'

'The less you know, the better, Dylan Alexander.' The corner of his mouth lifted as he said it, then he shook his head. 'Dylan. What kind of name is that for a female?'

She crossed her arms over her chest and shrugged. 'Don't blame me, I had nothing to do with it. I happen to come from a long line of hippies, groupies, and tree-huggers.' He just looked at her, those dark brows lowering over his eyes. He didn't get it, apparently. The reference seemed to go right past him, like he had never bothered with pop culture and probably had better things to do with his time. 'My mom named me Dylan – you know, as in Bob Dylan? She was really into him around the time I was born. My brothers were named after musicians too: Morrison and Lennon.'

'Ridiculous,' her captor replied, scoffing under his breath.

'Well, it could be worse. We're talking the mid-seventies, after all. I had just as good a chance of being named Clapton or Garfunkel.'

He didn't laugh, just held her in his piercing topaz gaze. 'A name is no insignificant thing. It frames your world as a child, and it lasts forever. A name should mean something.'

Dylan shot him a sardonic look. 'This coming from a guy named Rio? Yeah, I heard your German friend call you that,' she added when he pinned her with a narrowed gaze. 'It doesn't seem that much better than Dylan, if you ask me.'

'I didn't ask you. And that's not my name. Only a small portion of it.'

'What's the rest of it?' she asked, genuinely curious, and not just because it seemed like a good idea to gather whatever information she could about this man who was holding her captive.

She looked at him – at his scarred, yet ruggedly attractive face, the powerful body contained within his expensive new clothes, and she wanted to know more. She wanted to know his name and all the rest of his secrets, which she was certain had to be plentiful. He was a mystery she wanted to solve, and she had to admit that interest had very little to do with the cave, her story, or even her own sense of self-preservation.

'I've gone through your computer files and e-mail,' he told her, ignoring her question like she fully expected him to do. 'I know you've sent the cave photos to several individuals, including your employer.' He calmly rattled off the full names of her boss, Janet, Marie, Nancy, and her mom. 'I'm sure we could find them with little effort, but this will go much faster if you give me their current addresses and places of employment.'

'Forget it.' Dylan bristled at the idea of her privacy being so casually invaded. Inappropriately intrigued by him or not, she was not about to unleash this man or his shady cohorts on anyone she knew. 'If you have a problem with me, fine. But don't think I'm going to drag anyone else into this.'

His face was grimly set, unflinching. 'You already have.'

Dylan's heart sank at the flat statement that seemed so calm, yet so ripe with threat. When she said nothing else, he got up out of the dainty chair. God, he was huge, every inch of him swathed in lean, powerful muscle.

'Now that you're awake,' he said, 'I'll see that you have something to eat.'

'And give you the opportunity to drug my food? No thanks, I'd rather fast.'

He exhaled a low chuckle. 'I'll bring you some food. Whether or not you choose to eat it will be up to you.'

Dylan hated that her stomach seemed to churn eagerly at the thought of eating. She didn't want to accept anything from this man or his associates, even if it meant starving to death in the process. But she was beyond hungry and she knew that even if he brought her a bowl of lumpy, ice-cold gruel she'd gratefully gobble it down.

'Don't get any ideas about leaving this room,' he added. 'The door will be locked from outside, and I'll know the instant you try anything. I think you know that you wouldn't get far before I caught you.'

She did know that, in a place inside her that was all raw, animal instinct. This man, whoever he was, now held her completely at his mercy. Dylan didn't like it, but she was smart enough to know that whatever she was dealing with here was deadly serious. Like the woman in her, the journalist couldn't deny a certain fascination too, a need to know more − not only about what was truly going on, but also about the man himself.

About Rio.

'What, um . . . what happened to you . . . to your face?'

He threw a scowl at her, one that said of all her many questions, this one angered him the most. She didn't miss the way he turned his head slightly to the left, an almost unconscious move that helped to hide the worst of the damage. But Dylan had already seen the burn scars and pebbled skin. From the look of them, she guessed that they had to be combat wounds. Very grave, frontline combat wounds.

'I'm sorry,' she said, although whether she meant she was sorry for asking or sorry for what he went through, she wasn't totally certain.

He reached up with his left hand and raked it through the thick hair at his temple, like he didn't care if she stared now. But it was too late for him to call back his initial self-conscious reflex, and no matter how darkly he glared at her, Dylan knew he was bothered by his condition.

And as he moved, she caught a glimpse of an intricate pattern of tattoos on his forearm. They peeked out on both arms from under the rolled sleeves of his shirt, quasi–tribal markings done in a unique, variegated color blend of pale scarlet and gold. On first glance, she thought maybe they were some kind of membership markings, like the kinds American gangs used to show their allegiance.

No, not like that, she decided the longer she stared at them. *Not like that at all.*

The markings on Rio's arms were very much like the symbols and strange writings that were on the walls and crypt inside that cave.

He brought his hand down and the flash of warning in his eye all but dared her to question him about them.

'Tell me what they mean,' she said, looking up to meet his hard gaze. 'The tattoos. Why do you have the same kind of symbols on your body that were in that mountain cave?'

He didn't answer. In silence, he stood there unmoving,

looking even more dangerous in his civilized, tailored clothing than he had in the tattered rags he'd been wearing before. She knew he was immense, tall and broad and covered in lean, hard muscle, but he looked even more so as she approached him, determined to have this answer.

'What do the markings mean, Rio?' She took hold of his arm. 'Tell me.'

He stared down at her fingers wrapped around him. 'It doesn't concern you.'

'Like hell it doesn't!' she replied, her voice rising. 'Why would you have the same kind of markings on your body that are in that cave – on that crypt?'

'You are mistaken. You don't know what you saw. Then or now.'

It wasn't an argument so much as a complete refusal to take the conversation any further. And that really pissed Dylan off.

'I'm mistaken, am I?' She grabbed her long, loose hair and lifted it around to one side of her neck. 'Look at this and tell me I don't know what I saw.'

She bent her head, putting the exposed base of her neck – the patch of skin that bore her unusual birthmark – in plain view to him.

The silence seemed endless.

Then, finally, a hissed curse.

'What does it mean?' she asked him, lifting her head and letting her hair fall back in place.

Rio didn't answer her. He backed up as if he didn't want to be near her for another second.

'Tell me, Rio. Please . . . what does all of this mean?'

He was quiet for a long moment, his dark brows low over his eyes as he stared at her.

'You will know soon enough,' he said softly as he went to the door and stepped outside.

He closed her in, then turned the lock, leaving her in there alone and confused, and very certain that the path her life had been taking had just irrevocably changed course.

◄═ CHAPTER NINE ═►

A Breedmate.
  Madre de Dios, but he hadn't been expecting that. The small crimson birthmark on the nape of Dylan Alexander's slender neck changed everything. The teardrop-and-crescent-moon skin marking she bore wasn't something that occurred very often in nature, and its meaning was indisputable.

Dylan Alexander was a Breedmate.

She was a human female, but with the specific, extremely unusual blood properties and DNA that made her cellular physiology compatible with that of the Breed. Females like her were rare, and once women like Dylan were known to Rio's kind, they were cherished and protected as closely as blood kin.

They had to be. Without Breedmates to carry the seed of future vampire generations, Rio's kind would cease to exist. It was the curse of the Breed that all offspring of its hybrid race were born male – a genetic anomaly that occurred when the cells of the vampiric otherworlders mixed with those of the special human females that bore their young.

Women like Dylan Alexander were to be revered, not stalked like common prey and abducted off the street in fear for their lives. They were to be treated with great respect, not locked up like prisoners and held against their will, no matter how elegant the cage.

'Cristo en cielo,' Rio muttered aloud as he stormed down the

Darkhaven estate's gleaming mahogany staircase to the foyer below. *'Un qué desastre.'*

Yes, this truly was a disaster. He himself was a disaster – one that worsened by the moment. His skin was tight with hunger, and he didn't have to check the *dermaglyphs* on his forearms to know that they were probably no longer their normal pale henna hue, but reddish-gold, reflecting his mounting need to feed. A nagging throb was kicking up in his temples, portent of the blackout he'd be dealing with if he didn't lie down soon or get some nourishment to stave it off.

But sleep was out of the question and so was hunting for a blood Host. He needed to check in with the Order and fill them in on the added complication to a situation that had been fucked-up royal to begin with, all thanks to him.

He took the stairs a couple at a time, wishing like hell he could just continue walking right out the front door of the Darkhaven and into broad, deadly daylight. But he'd made this mess, and he'd be damned if he was going to leave it for anyone else to clean up.

As he hit the marble of the foyer below, Andreas Reichen was just opening the double doors from within one of the many rooms situated on the first floor. He wasn't alone. An anxious-looking Darkhaven male with a mop of strawberry blond hair was with him, both of the vampires coming out of the dark-paneled study in the midst of a hushed conversation. Reichen looked up at once and met Rio's eyes. He murmured something reassuring to his civilian companion as he clapped him gently on the shoulder. The younger male nodded, then politely got the hell out of the area with only the most furtive glance at the scarred warrior standing nearby.

'My nephew, bringing me some unpleasant news from one of the region's other Darkhavens,' Reichen explained once they were alone in the foyer. 'It seems there was an incident a couple of nights ago. A rather high-profile individual was found missing his head. Unfortunately for him and his family, the killing occurred at a blood club.'

Rio grunted, thoroughly unmoved. Blood clubs had been outlawed as barbaric underground sport decades ago, and most of the vampire population agreed with the ruling. But there were some within the race who still got off on the secret, invitation-only gatherings where human victims could be chased down in a contained area, raped, fed upon, and murdered like wild game. Helpless wild game, since not even the strongest *Homo sapiens*, male or female, was any match for a pack of bloodthirsty vampires.

The blood club killing was obviously a Breed-on-Breed altercation.

'Did they get the vampire who did it?'

'No. They're still investigating the murder.' Reichen cleared his throat and went on. 'Since the deceased was an elder – Gen One, in fact – and a member of the Enforcement Agency, there is understandable concern that the whole thing is set to explode into scandal. It's a very sensitive situation.'

Rio gave a wry snort. 'No doubt.'

Well, at least he wasn't the only one among the Breed with piss-poor judgment lately. Even the fully sane, cultured members of the vampire nation had their bad days. Not that it made Rio regret his own fleet of mistakes any less.

'I need to touch base with Boston,' he told Reichen, running his palm over his brow to wipe away the sheen of cold sweat that was beginning to gather there. A wave of nausea tried to rise up on him but he held it back with sheer willpower. Damn. He had to hold his shit together at least until sundown, when he could run out for a while and feed.

If the coming blackout didn't drop him before he got the chance.

'Is anything wrong?' Reichen asked him, concern furrowing his brow.

'I'm fine,' Rio muttered.

The other vampire didn't look the least bit convinced, even if he was too well-bred to say so. His dark gaze flicked down to Rio's arms, where beneath the rolled-back sleeves of his shirt, his *glyphs* were infusing with deeper, more intense color. He could claim from here to Sunday that he was right as rain, but those skin markings would give him away every time. The damn things were emotional barometers that visually broadcasted a Breed vampire's state of mind – from hunger to satiation, rage to joy, lust, contentment, and everything in between.

At the moment, Rio's *dermaglyphs* had saturated in hues of deep red, purple, and black – plain evidence that he was hurting and hungry.

'I need a phone with a secure line,' he told Reichen. 'Now. If you could, please.'

'Of course. Come, you may use my office.'

Reichen gestured for Rio to follow him back into the room where he'd been meeting with his nephew. The study was large and richly appointed, full of Old World elegance like the rest of the Darkhaven estate. Reichen went around a claw-footed monstrosity of a desk and opened a small hidden panel built into the polished mahogany surface.

He pushed a button on an electronic keypad, which made two of the tall bookcases across the room begin to separate, revealing a large, flat panel screen mounted behind them.

'Video teleconferencing, available if you wish,' he said, as Rio came farther into the room. 'Dial an eight to reach our operator for a secure outside line. And take as long as you like in here. You'll have complete privacy.'

Rio nodded his thanks.

'Do you need anything else right now?' his generous host asked. 'Or anything for our, ah, guest upstairs?'

'Yeah,' Rio said. 'Actually, I told her I'd bring her something to eat.'

Reichen smiled. 'Then I'll go have something special prepared for her.'

'Thank you,' Rio said. Then, 'Hey, Reichen. There's something you probably should know. That female up there . . . she's a Breedmate. I didn't realize it until just a few minutes ago, but she's got the mark. It's on the back of her neck.'

'Ah.' The German vampire considered that for a moment. 'And does she know what that makes her? What that makes the rest of us?'

'No. Not yet.' Rio picked up the cordless phone on Reichen's desk and hit the number eight on the keypad. Then he started dialing the private line that would route him to the Order's compound. 'She doesn't know anything about any of that. But I have a feeling I'm going to be spelling it all out for her real soon.'

'Then perhaps I'd better have a cocktail prepared for the lady as well. A strong one.' Reichen strode to the open double doors of the study. 'I will let you know when her meal is ready. If there is anything you need, just ask and it is yours.'

'Thanks.'

When the heavy wood doors clicked shut, Rio turned his full attention to the ringing phone line on the other end of his call. The compound's computerized answering intercepted and he punched in the code for the tech lab.

Gideon picked up without hesitation. 'Talk to me, buddy.'

'I'm at Reichen's,' Rio said, unnecessary information since the compound's system had certainly already confirmed the incoming phone number. But Rio's head was pounding too hard for him to do a lot of extraneous processing. He needed to convey his relevant intel while he was still making sense. 'The trip was uneventful, and I'm here with the woman at Reichen's Darkhaven.'

'You got her contained somewhere?'

'Yeah,' Rio replied. 'She's cooling her heels in a guest room upstairs.'

'Good. Nice work, man.'

The unwarranted praise made him clamp his teeth together hard. And the combination of his churning hunger and the spin of his head made him suck in a ragged breath of air. He let it back out on a low curse.

'You all right, Rio?'

'Yeah.'

'Yeah, my ass,' Gideon said. Not only was the vampire a genius when it came to technology, but he also had the uncanny ability to smell a load of horseshit when it was being shoveled at him. Even when it was being shoveled at him from another continent away. 'What's going on with you? You don't sound good at all, amigo.'

Rio rubbed his drumming temple. 'Don't worry about me. We've got a bigger problem over here. Turns out the female reporter is a Breedmate, Gideon.'

'Ah, fuck. Are you serious?'

'I saw her birthmark with my own eyes,' Rio replied.

Gideon murmured something urgent yet indiscernible to someone else apparently in the lab with him. The answering deep growl of a cool Gen One voice could belong to none other than Lucan, the Order's founder and leader.

Great, Rio thought. Although it wasn't as if he was planning to keep the news from the highest-ranking warrior of the group, so he might as well clue him in on all the facts now.

'Lucan's here,' Gideon informed him, in case he missed that fact. 'You alone over there, Rio?'

'Yep. Sitting all by my lonesome in Reichen's study.'

'All right. Hang on. I'm gonna put you on video telecom.'

Rio's mouth twisted grimly. 'I thought you might.'

He glanced up as the large flat-panel blinked on across

from him. Like a window opened on a next-door room, the screen filled with a real-time image of Gideon and Lucan seated in the Boston compound's tech lab. Gideon's eyes were intense as he gazed over the rims of his pale blue shades, his cropped blond hair a spiky, mad-scientist mess, as usual.

Under Lucan's furrowed black brows, his gaze was also serious, his light gray eyes narrowed as he leaned back in one of the big leather chairs that circled the Order's conference table.

'The female is safe here at the Darkhaven, and she has not been harmed in any way,' Rio began without preamble. 'Her name is Dylan Alexander, and from what I've gathered off her computer files she lives and works in New York City. I'm guessing she is in her late twenties, but there's a chance she could be near thirty—'

'Rio.' Lucan leaned forward, peering intently at the video screen where Rio's image was being projected back home. 'We'll get to her in a minute. What's going on with you, man? You've been out of contact since February, and no offense, but you look like hell.'

Rio shook his head, raked a hand through his sweat-dampened hair. 'I'm good. Just want to take care of this problem and be done with it, you know?'

He wasn't sure if he was talking about Dylan Alexander and her photos, or the other, longer-term problems he'd been dealing with since the warehouse explosion that might have killed him. Should have killed him, damn it.

'Everything's cool with me, Lucan.'

The vampire's expression held steady, measuring on the other end of the video feed. 'I don't appreciate being lied to, my friend. I need to know if the Order can still count on you. Are you still with us?'

'The Order is all I have, Lucan. You know that.'

It was the truth, and it seemed to satisfy the shrewd Gen One. For now.

'So, the reporter you're holding over there is a Breedmate.' Lucan sighed, rubbing his palm over his strong square jaw. 'You're going to have to bring her in, Rio. To Boston. You need to explain a few things to her beforehand, about the Breed and about her link to us, and then you need to bring her in. Gideon will handle the transportation.'

The other warrior was already typing away furiously at his keyboard, making it happen. 'I can have our private jet waiting to pick you up at Tegel Airport tomorrow night.'

Rio acknowledged the plans with a firm nod, but there were still a few loose ends to consider. 'She was booked on a flight out of Prague to New York today. She has family and friends who'll be expecting her home.'

'You've got access to her e-mail,' Gideon put in. 'Send a group message using her account, explaining that she's been delayed for a few days and will be in contact as soon as possible.'

'What about the pictures she took of the cave?' Rio asked.

Lucan answered that one. 'Gideon tells me you have the camera and her computer. She needs to understand that everyone who has copies of those pictures is a risk to us – one we can't afford to let slide. So, she'll have to help us by killing her story and destroying every copy of every photograph she's let loose.'

'And if she won't cooperate?' Rio could already imagine how well this conversation was going to go with her. 'What do we do then?'

'We track down those individuals she's been in contact with, and we obtain the images by whatever means necessary.'

'Mind-scrub them all?' Rio asked.

The set of Lucan's mouth was grave. 'Whatever it takes.'

'And the woman?' Rio wanted to be clear. 'As a Breedmate,

we can't just scrub her arbitrarily. She would be given some choice in this, wouldn't she?'

'Yes,' Lucan said. 'She does have a choice. Once she knows about the existence of the Breed and the mark she bears that links her to us, she can decide whether she wants to be a part of our world, or return to her own and give up all knowledge of our kind. That's the way it has always been done. It's the only way.'

Rio nodded. 'I'll take care of it, Lucan.'

'I know you will,' he said, no challenge or doubt in the statement, just pure trust. 'And, Rio?'

'Yeah?'

'Don't think I haven't noticed those livid *glyphs* on you, my man.' Narrowed silver eyes fixed on him over the distance. 'Make sure you feed. Tonight.'

⧉ CHAPTER TEN ⧉

Dylan sat near the head of the four-poster bed, staring intently at the illuminated digital display on her cell phone.

Looking for service . . . Looking for service . . .

'Come on,' she whispered softly under her breath as the message repeated in agonizing slow motion. 'Come on, work, damn it!'

Looking for service . . .

No signal available.

'Shit.'

She'd lied to her abductor about having a cell phone. Her razor-thin mobile had been stashed in one of the side pockets of her cargo pants all this time, not that having it was doing her much good right now.

Her expensive international service was sketchy at best. Dylan had tried dialing out for help several times in the past hour, with the same frustrating result. All she was doing by refusing to give up was wasting precious battery time. She'd lost the cell phone charger and the power converter doohickey a few days into the trip; now she only had two bars of juice left, and this current ordeal seemed far from over.

As if to punctuate that fact, the lock on the door snicked free and someone twisted the crystal knob from outside.

Dylan hurriedly powered the device down and stuffed it

under the pillow behind her. She was just bringing her hand out as her posh prison door swung open.

Rio strode in carrying a wooden tray of food. The aromas of fresh sourdough bread, garlic, and roasted meat drifted in ahead of him. Dylan's mouth watered as she caught a glimpse of a thick, grilled sandwich heaping with sliced chicken, marinated red peppers and onion, cheese, and crisp green lettuce. *Oh, God, did it look wonderful.*

'Here's your lunch, as promised.'

She forced a careless shrug. 'I told you, I'm not going to eat anything you give me.'

'Suit yourself.'

He set the tray down on the bed next to her. Dylan tried not to look at the scrumptious sandwich or the cup of ripe strawberries and peaches that accompanied it. There was also a bottle of mineral water on the tray and a short cocktail glass with a generous two-and-a-half-finger pour of pale amber liquid that smelled sweet and smoky, like very pricey Scottish whisky. The kind her father used to pickle himself in nightly, despite that they couldn't afford his habit.

'Is the liquor to help me wash down the sedatives you put in the food, or did you put the mickey in the drink?'

'I have no intention of drugging you, Dylan.' He sounded so sincere, she almost believed him. 'The drink is there to relax you, if you need it. I'm not going to force anything on you.'

'Huh,' she said, noticing a subtle change in his demeanor from before. He was still immense and dangerous-looking, but when he stared at her now, there was a sober, almost pained resignation about him. Like he had some unpleasant business that he needed to get out of the way. 'If you're not here to force anything on me, then why do you look like you're delivering me my last meal?'

'I came to talk to you, that's all. There are some things I need to explain to you. Things you need to know.'

Well, it was about time she got some answers. 'Okay. You can start by telling me when you're going to let me out of here.'

'Soon,' he said. 'Tomorrow night we'll be leaving for the States.'

'You're taking me back to America?' She knew she sounded too hopeful, especially when he was still including himself in the scenario. 'Are you going to release me tomorrow? Are you letting me go home?'

He walked slowly around the foot of the bed, over to the wall with the shaded window. He leaned one shoulder against the wall, his tattooed, muscular arms crossed over his chest. For a long minute, he didn't say anything. Just stood there until Dylan wanted to scream.

'You know, I was supposed to meet someone in Prague this morning – someone who knows my boss and has probably already called him to ask about me. I'm booked on a flight back to New York this afternoon. There are people expecting me back home. You can't just pluck me off the street and think no one is going to notice I'm gone—'

'No one is expecting you now.'

Dylan's heart started to thud heavily in her chest, as if her body was aware something big was coming even before her brain was fully on board with it. 'What . . . what did you just say?'

'Your family, friends, and your place of work have all been informed that you are safe and sound, but expect to be out of contact for a while.' At her certain look of confusion, he said, 'They all received an e-mail from you a few minutes ago, letting them know that you were taking some extra time off to see more of Europe on your own.'

Anger flared in her now, even stronger than the wariness she knew just a second before. 'You contacted my boss? My mother?' The job was of little concern to her at the moment, but it was the thought of this man getting anywhere near her mom that really set Dylan off. She swung her legs off the bed and stood up, practically shaking with rage. 'You bastard! You manipulative son of a bitch!'

He drew back, out of her path as she charged at him. 'It was necessary, Dylan. As you said, there would have been questions. People would have been worrying about you.'

'You stay the fuck away from my family – do you hear me? I don't care what you do to me, but you leave my family out of this!'

He remained calm, considerate. Maddeningly so. 'Your family is safe, Dylan. And so are you. Tomorrow night, I will be taking you back to the States, to a secret location that belongs to those of my kind. I think once you're there, a lot of what you're going to hear now will be easier for you to understand.'

Dylan stared at him, her mind stumbling over his odd choice of words: *those of my kind.*

'What the hell is going on here? I'm serious . . . I need to know.' Ah, hell. Her voice was quaking like she was about to lose it in front of him – this stranger who had stolen her freedom and violated her privacy. She would be damned before she showed any weakness to him, no matter what she was about to hear. 'Please. Tell me. Give me the truth.'

'About yourself?' he asked, his deep, accented voice rolling through the syllables. 'Or about the world you were born to be a part of?'

Dylan couldn't find words to speak. Instinct made her hand move up to the back of her neck, where her nape seemed to tingle with heat.

Rio nodded soberly. 'It's a rare birthmark. Maybe one in half a million human females are born with it, probably less. Women bearing the mark – women like you, Dylan – are very special. It means that you are a Breedmate. Women like you have certain . . . gifts. Abilities that separate you from other people.'

'What kind of gifts and abilities?' she asked, not even sure she wanted to have this conversation.

'Extrasensory skills, primarily. Everyone is different, with different levels of capabilities. Some can see the future or the past. Some can hold an object and read its history. Others can summon storms or command the will of living things around them. Some heal with a simple touch. Some can kill with just a thought.'

'That's ridiculous,' she scoffed. 'Nobody has those kinds of abilities outside of tabloid magazines and science fiction.'

He grunted, his mouth lifting at the corner. He was studying her too closely, trying to peel her apart with that penetrating topaz gaze. 'I'm certain that you have a special skill too. What is yours, Dylan Alexander?'

'You can't be serious.' She shook her head and gave a dismissive roll of her eyes.

But all the while she was thinking about the one thing that had always made her different. Her unreliable, inexplicable link to the dead. It wasn't the same thing as what he was describing, though. It was something else completely.

Wasn't it . . . ?

'You don't have to confide in me,' he said. 'Just know that there is a reason you are not like other women. Maybe you feel that you don't fit in with the world at large. Many women like you are more sensitive than the rest of the human population. You see things differently, feel things differently. There is a reason for all of that, Dylan.'

How could he know? How could he understand so much about her? Dylan didn't want to believe anything he was saying. She didn't want to believe that she was part of anything he was describing, yet he seemed to understand her more intimately than anyone ever had.

'Breedmates are uniquely gifted,' Rio said when she could only look at him in incredulous silence. 'But the most extraordinary gift possessed by each is the ability to create life with those of my kind.'

Jesus. There it was again – the deliberate reference to his *kind*. And now he was talking about sex and breeding?

Dylan stared at him, reminded swiftly and vividly of just how easily he'd been able to pin her beneath his powerful, fully aroused body in that hotel in Prague. It didn't take much to recall the heat of all that muscle pressed against her, though why the thought should make her heart beat faster, breath come harder, she really didn't want to know.

Was he setting her up here for a repeat performance? Or did he actually think she was gullible enough to be seduced into believing any of this stuff about being different, about belonging to some mysterious other world she knew nothing about until now?

And why should she believe it? Because of that tiny birthmark on the back of her neck?

One that still felt kind of warm and electric against her palm. She brought her hand down and tucked her arms around herself.

Rio tracked her movements with his keen, too-sharp gaze. 'I think you've noticed that I'm not quite like other men either. There is a reason for that as well.'

A heavy silence filled the room as he seemed to take his time measuring his words.

'It's because I'm not just a man. I'm something more than that.'

Dylan had to admit he was more man than any other she'd known before. His size and power alone seemed to put him in a separate class. But he was all male, that she knew by the way he looked at her, his eyes hot as they traveled over her face and down her body.

He stared at her, unblinking, heatedly intense. 'I am one

of the Breed, Dylan. In your lexicon, for lack of a better term, I am a vampire.'

For one stunned second, she thought she had misunderstood him. Then, all the unease and tension that she had been feeling since Rio had walked into the room vanished in a great rush of relief.

'Oh, my God!' She couldn't hold back her laughter. It barked out of her almost hysterically, a flood of disbelief and amusement washing away all her anxiety in an instant. 'A vampire. Really? Because, you know, that makes *so* much more sense than everything I was guessing you might be. Not military, not a government spy, or a terrorist operative, but a vampire!'

He wasn't laughing.

No, he simply stood there, unmoving. Watching her. Waiting until she looked up and met his unsmiling eyes.

'Oh, come on,' she chided him. 'You can't possibly expect me to believe that.'

'I realize it must be difficult to grasp. But it's the truth. That's what you asked for, Dylan. What you've been asking for since the moment you and I first saw each other – the truth. Now you have it.'

Good Lord, he seemed so serious about all of this. 'What about the other people living here? And don't try to tell me that there's no one else in this huge estate because I've heard them walking the hallways, and I've heard muffled conversations. So, what about them? Are they vampires too?'

'Some,' he said quietly. 'The males are Breed. The females living here in this Darkhaven are human. Breedmates . . . like you.'

Dylan recoiled internally. 'Stop saying that. Stop trying to pretend that I'm a passenger on this crazy train with you. You don't know anything about me.'

'I know enough.' He cocked his head at her, a move that seemed almost animalistic. Unconsciously so. 'The mark on you is all I need to know about you, Dylan. You are a part of this now, an inextricable part. Whether or not either of us like that fact.'

'Well, I don't like it,' she blurted out, getting anxious again. 'I want you to let me out of this room. I want to go back to my home, back to my family and my job. I want to forget all about that fucking cave and you.'

He gave a slow shake of his dark head. 'It's too late for that. There's no going back, Dylan. I'm sorry.'

'You're sorry,' she hissed. 'I'll tell you what you are. You're insane! You're sick in your goddamn head—'

With a smooth flex of muscle, he came out of his lean near the wall and within one instant he was standing in front of her. Not even a bare inch separated them. He reached out as if he was going to touch her cheek, his fingers hovering so near, yet resisting.

Dylan's heart slammed in her chest but she didn't move away. She couldn't – not when he was holding her in that smoldering, almost hypnotic, topaz gaze.

Was she breathing? God help her, she wasn't sure. She waited to feel his touch light on her skin, astonished to realize just how badly she wanted it. But on a slow growl, he let his hand fall back down to his side.

He bent his head close to her ear. His deep voice was a whisper of heat across her throat. 'Eat your meal, Dylan. It would be a shame to waste good food when you know you need the nourishment.'

Well, that went down about as smoothly as a glass of razor blades.

Rio locked her door, then stormed into his adjacent guest room, hands clenched at his sides. There had been a time when he would have carried out a task like this with charm and diplomacy. Hard to imagine himself in that role now. He'd been blunt and ineffective, and he couldn't blame all of that on his lingering head trauma or the hunger that was gnawing at him like wolves on carrion.

He didn't know how to handle Dylan Alexander.

He didn't know what to make of her, or what to make of his own unwilling reaction to her.

Since Eva, there hadn't been another woman to pique his interest beyond the most basic physical need. Once he'd been strong enough to leave the compound – long weeks into his recovery – Rio had satisfied his carnal itch the same way he slaked his hunger for blood. With cold, impersonal efficiency. It seemed so strange to him, a male who had unrepentantly enjoyed life's many pleasures as a vital part of living itself.

But he hadn't always been that way. It had taken him many years to rise above the dark origins of his birth and do something meaningful, to make something good of his life. He thought he had. Hell, he'd really thought he'd had it all. It vanished in an instant – one blinding, white-hot instant a summer ago, when Eva sold the Order out to their enemy.

Rio had long thought his Breedmate's betrayal had ruined him for anyone else, and a part of him had been glad to be rid of emotional entanglements and the complications that came with them.

But now there was Dylan.

And she was in that next room thinking he was a lunatic. Not that far off the mark, he admitted grimly. What would she think once she realized that what he'd told her just now was the truth?

It didn't matter.

Before long, she would know everything. A decision would be placed before her, and she would have to choose her path: a life in the sheltering arms of the Darkhavens, or a return to her old life, back among humankind.

He didn't plan on sticking around to find out which door she picked. He had his own path to walk, and this was merely a frustrating detour.

A rap on the closed door of his guest suite snapped Rio out of his grim thoughts.

'Yeah,' he barked, still glaring with self-directed anger as the panel swung wide and Reichen entered.

'Everything go all right?' the Darkhaven male asked.

'Just fucking great,' Rio growled, as sharp as a blade. 'What's up?'

'I'm going into the city tonight and I thought you might like to join me.' He glanced meaningfully at Rio's *dermaglyphs*, which were flushed with deep color. 'The place is decadent, but very discreet. As are the women who work there. Give any of Helene's angels an hour of your time, and I guarantee you they'll make you forget all your troubles.'

Rio grunted. 'Where do I sign up?'

⇥ CHAPTER ELEVEN ⇤

The Berlin brothel that Reichen brought him to that evening was everything Rio had been told to expect – and then some. Prostitution had been legalized here a few years ago, and as far as beautiful, ready, willing, and able women went, the sex club Aphrodite was clearly home to the cream of the crop.

Three of the club's finest examples, wearing nothing but minuscule G-strings, danced together in a slow grind in front of the private table where Rio and his Darkhaven host were seated with the club's stunning female owner, Helene. With her long dark hair, flawless face, and sinuous curves, Helene herself would fit right in with the flock of gorgeous young females in her employ. But beneath her blatant sex appeal, it was obvious that the woman had a shrewd business mind and enjoyed being the one calling the shots.

Reichen certainly seemed content to let Helene have her head with him. Situated beside her on the crescent-shaped velvet seat across from the one Rio occupied by himself, Reichen lounged against the tufted squabs with one foot propped on the squat round cocktail table in front of him, his thighs spread wide in order to give Helene's roaming hands free access to whatever they might find intriguing.

At the moment, she seemed focused on teasing him, sliding her scarlet-polished nails up and down the inner seam of his tailored pants while she conducted a hushed, don't-bullshit-me conversation in German on her cell phone.

Reichen met Rio's gaze from across the short distance and nodded in the direction of the three females gyrating and stroking one another just an arm's length away.

'Help yourself, my friend – to one or all of them. Your choice. They're here for your personal amusement, compliments of Helene when I told her I'd be bringing you by tonight.'

Helene sent a catlike smile at Rio as she continued to conduct her club business like the tigress she no doubt was. As she spoke curt instructions into her cell, Reichen smoothed her dark hair off her shoulder and traced his fingertips tenderly along the side of her neck.

They were an odd pairing, even as frequent but casual lovers, which Reichen insisted them to be.

Breed males seldom took a prolonged interest in mortal human women, even in a mainly sexual way. The risk of exposing the Breed's existence to humankind was generally seen as too great for a vampire to dare any kind of relationship for the long term. And there was always the danger that a human might fall into Rogue hands, or worse, be turned Minion by one of the more powerful, but corrupt, members of the Breed.

Helene was not a Breedmate, but she was a trusted ally of Reichen's. She knew what he was – what Rio and the rest of the Breed were too – and she held that secret as closely as she would one of her own. She'd proven trustworthy and loyal to Reichen, something Rio hadn't even been able to claim about the Breedmate female he'd bonded to all those years ago.

He tore his gaze away from the couple and stared out at the club's surroundings. Walls of smoked glass enclosed the low-lighted private room they were in, affording a 360-degree view of the action taking place on Aphrodite's main floor just outside. Sex acts in every variation, and in every combination of partners, filled Rio's line of vision. Closer still, were the three lovely females evidently on tap for his personal service.

'Beautiful, aren't they? Touch them if it pleases you.'

Reichen curled his finger at them and the three prostitutes made a deliberately seductive approach to Rio's side of the table. Bare breasts bobbed with artificial firmness as the girls ran their hands over themselves and one another, a show they'd probably performed a thousand times before. One of them sauntered closer and placed herself between his knees, her tan hips moving in time with the drone of bass and smoky vocals coming through the sound system in the background. Her two friends flanked her, caressing her body as she performed her little private dancer routine, the scrap of satin covering her sex hovering mere inches from Rio's mouth.

He felt oddly detached from the whole event, willing to let it happen, yet uninterested in anything being offered to him at the moment. He'd be using them as much as they intended to use him.

Helene ended her phone call on the other side of the table. As she closed the slim device, Reichen stood up and offered her his hand. She slid off the velvet seat and under the sheltering curve of her vampire lover's arm.

'They will provide everything you wish,' Reichen said.

When Rio glanced up at him in question, the other Breed male read his look without hesitation or error. His gaze slid to Rio's livid *glyphs*, subtly acknowledging his rising state of blood hunger. 'The glass in this room is one-way, completely private. Whatever your appetite demands, no one will know anything that occurs in here. Stay as long as you like. My driver will take you back to the mansion whenever you're ready.' He smiled, flashing only the very tips of his emerging fangs. 'I'll be late.'

Rio watched the pair stroll over to the elevator situated in the center of the private space. They were already caught in a fiercely passionate kiss as the doors closed and the car began its ascent to Helene's apartment and offices on the top floor of the building.

A pair of hands began unbuttoning Rio's black shirt.

'Do you like my dance?' asked the female grinding between his legs.

He didn't answer. They weren't really interested in making conversation, but then, neither was he. Rio looked up into the trio of beautiful, painted faces. They smiled, and pouted, and arranged their glossy mouths in sensual poses meant to titillate . . . but not one pair of eyes would meet his for more than the most fleeting instant.

Of course, he thought, smirking at their polite avoidance. None of them wanted to look too closely at his scars.

They kept pawing at him, rubbing against him like they couldn't wait to get busy with him . . . just like they were trained so well to do. They stroked him, cooing over how well-built he was, how strong and sexy they found him.

Carefully averting their gazes from his so they could continue pretending that what they saw didn't repulse them.

He hadn't been happy when Dylan confronted him about his scars. He wasn't used to that kind of head-on honesty, or the true compassion he'd heard in her voice when she'd gently asked him how he'd been injured. Rio had been caught off guard, self-conscious under Dylan's sincere interest, and it had made him want to crawl into the floor to get away from it.

But at least she hadn't hit him with this kind of infuriating falsehood. These women, so professionally trained to charm and seduce, couldn't mask their aversion.

They writhed and undulated in front of him, and as the minutes passed, the room began to swirl along with them. The club's garish colors blended into a dizzying smear of red and gold and electric blue. The music swelled louder, crashing against Rio's skull like a hammer dropping on fragile glass. He choked on the cloying odors of perfume, liquor, and sex.

The floor beneath him was spinning now. His temples were being crushed, madness rising like a black wave that would pull him under if he didn't get a grip.

He closed his eyes to block out some of the sensory bombardment. The darkness lasted only a moment before an image began to form out of the ether of his cracked mind. . . .

Amid the storm of pain and fear suddenly churning around him, he saw a face.

Dylan's face.

Her creamy, peach-freckled skin seemed close enough for him to touch. Her golden-green eyes were half-closed, but fixed on him, beautiful and unafraid. As he gazed at her behind his dropped eyelids, she smiled and slowly bent her head to the side. Her fiery, silken hair slid loosely over her shoulder, as gently as a caress.

And then Rio saw the scarlet kiss of twin punctures below her ear.

Cristo, but the sight of her like this was so real. His gums ached, and the tips of his fangs pressed sharply against his tongue. Thirst rolled up on him hard. He could almost taste the juniper and honey sweetness of the blood that pearled from her wounds.

That was how he knew for certain this was merely illusion – because he would never know the taste of her.

Dylan Alexander was a Breedmate, and that meant drinking from her was out of the question. One sip of her blood would create a bond breakable only by death. Rio had been down that road before, and it had nearly killed him.

Never again.

Rio snarled as his lap dancer decided it was a good time to get cozier. When he snapped his eyes open, she murmured something dirty, then planted her hands on his thighs and spread them wide. Licking her lips, she sank down onto her knees before him. When she went for the zipper of his trousers, it wasn't lust that turned his veins molten, but a spike of hot fury instead.

His head pounded, mouth felt as dry as sand.

Shit. He was going to lose it if he stayed any longer.

He had to get the fuck out of there.

'Get up,' he growled. 'Get off me, all of you.'

They scrambled back like they'd just provoked a wild animal. One of them tried to be brave. 'You want something different, baby? It's okay. Tell us what you like.'

'Nothing you've got,' he said tightly, giving them a long, hard dose of the ruined left side of his face as he shot to his feet.

None too steady, he staggered out of the private room, out of the throbbing, musk-heavy club. He found the quiet back entrance where he and Reichen had come in, shoved past the bouncers who wisely moved out of his way when they saw him coming.

The street outside was dark. The summer night air was cool on his heated skin; he drank it in through his mouth, breathing deeply in an effort to calm his roiling head. Cursed when it didn't do anything to soothe him.

His vision was sharper out here in the darkness, but it was more than just his basic nocturnal acuity giving everything a crisp edge. His pupils were narrowed from his anger and need, the amber glow of his transformed irises throwing faint light on the concrete under his feet. His steps were uneven, the limp he'd almost overcome now creeping into his gait.

His fangs filled his mouth. One look at the *glyphs* on his forearms and he knew he was in bad shape.

Damn it. He should have taken the vein of one of the

females back there. He needed to feed hours ago, and now his shit was getting critical.

Head down, fists shoved deep into the pockets of his pants, Rio started walking at a fast, none-too-graceful clip. He thought about heading for one of the city's parks, where the homeless and itinerant made easy prey for creatures of the night like him. But as he cut up a side street off the main drag, he saw a young punky woman puffing on a cigarette at the head of the alleyway. She was leaning back against the side of a brick building, picking at her fingernails as she blew out a cloud of noxious smoke.

If her black platform stilettos and tight miniskirt didn't give her away, the gravity-defying tube top she wore over her large breasts certainly would. The low-rent version of what Rio had just left behind glanced up and caught him watching her.

'*Ich bin nicht arbeiten,*' she said, her voice a caustic snarl as she went back to massacring her nails. 'Not at work right now.'

He walked toward her undeterred, a wraith moving out of the shadows.

She snorted, getting annoyed. 'My work tonight is done, *ja*? No sex.'

'That's not what I need from you.'

'Huh,' she scoffed. 'Well, then, fuck off—'

Rio moved on her so fast, she didn't even have time to scream. He crossed the several yards' distance in a blink and flipped the woman around so that she was facing the bricks. Her dark hair was short, making easy access to her neck. Rio struck with viper speed, sinking his fangs deep into yielding flesh and drawing hard from her vein.

She struggled only at first, twitching through the initial shock. But then she loosened as his bite drew out and the pain gave way to pleasure. Rio drank quickly, gulping down what his body so desperately needed. He licked the wound he'd made, sealing the bite with his tongue. The mark would be all but gone in a few minutes, and as for her memory of what just transpired? Rio reached around her head and placed his palm over her eyes.

It took only a second to erase the last few minutes of her recollection, but it was time enough for a man to come around the corner of the building and see the two of them standing there.

'Hey! *Was zur Hölle ist das?*'

He was beefy and bald, and he didn't seem happy at all. Wiping his hands on a stained bar apron, he barked something at the whore in German – a stern command she jumped to follow. Evidently not fast enough for Big Man. As she scrambled away, he lashed out and cuffed the side of her head with his fist. When she yelped and ran off around the corner of the building, Big Man started approaching Rio in the alleyway.

'Do yourself a favor and leave,' Rio growled in a voice that no longer sounded human. 'This doesn't concern you.'

Big Man shook his jowly head. 'You want sex with Uta, you pay me.'

'Then come and try to collect your piece,' Rio said, low enough that anyone with half an ounce of sense would have taken it as the warning it truly was.

But not this guy. He reached behind him and withdrew a knife from somewhere at his back. It was a deadly mistake. Rio saw the threat, and he was still too far gone to let it slide. As the pimp came forward like he meant to cut some cash out of Rio's hide, Rio sprang at him.

He took the human down onto the pavement, his hands wrapped around the thick neck. A frantic pulse hammered against his palm, beat after beat of warm blood rushing beneath the rough skin.

Distantly, Rio registered the drum of the human's heart, but his mind was not fully his own. Not anymore. His blood hunger was temporarily appeased, but rage had him firmly in its grip. The squeeze on his mind, on his own will, was relentless, bringing on the darkness he feared the most.

Maldecido.

Monstruo.

He felt himself sliding into that oblivion . . .

The names he was called as a young boy rose up in his ears like a battering storm. He remembered the dark forest and the smell of spilled blood on rough earth. The cottage where his mother had been killed before his eyes . . .

As darkness descended over him, he was that wild foundling he'd been in Spain so long ago. A confused and frightened child with no home, no family, and no one like him to show him the way of what he truly was.

Comedor de la sangre.

With a roar, he bent over his quivering prey and bit into the fleshy throat. He was savage, not from hunger but from fury and an old anguish that made him feel like a monster. Like the accursed. A terrifying blood-eater.

Manos del diablo.

Those devil's hands were no longer his own. The blackout was rising fast now, swamping him. Rio could no longer see the street in front of him. Logic and control shorted out like wires popping in his brain. He could hardly think. But he knew the instant the human's heart went silent beneath his fingers.

He knew, as the darkness pulled him under, that he had killed tonight.

A loud thump in the adjacent room woke Dylan out of a fitful sleep. She sat up, completely awake now. More noises sounded next door, low groans and heavy-footed stumbling, like someone – or some*thing* – large was in a world of agony.

The connecting suite was Rio's. He'd told her so earlier that evening, when he'd come back with a light dinner and her backpack of clothes, and told her to make herself comfortable for the night. He'd warned that he would be right on the other side of the wall, never more than a few seconds out of reach. Which hadn't exactly added to her comfort level in any way.

In spite of his threat, Dylan had suspected he'd gone out at some point. The neighboring room had been quiet for several hours, until this four A.M. wake-up call.

So much for Rio's claim that he was a deadly creature of the night. From the sloppy arrival going on over there, it sounded as if he was just another drunk, coming back from a hell of a bender in town.

Dylan sat there, arms crossed over her chest as she listened to him groan, knock into a heavy piece of furniture, curse ripely as his legs gave out beneath him.

How many nights did her father come home in similar condition? Jesus, far too many to count. He'd stumble in from the bar, so polluted it took her mom, Dylan, and both of her older brothers to haul him to bed before he fell and cracked open his skull. She'd developed a rigid lack of sympathy for men who let their weaknesses own them like that, but she had to admit that the noises Rio was making now seemed something other than your basic drunk-and-disorderly.

She climbed off the bed and moved quietly over to the connecting door. With her ear pressed to the cool wood, she could hear his breath rasping shallowly. She could almost imagine him lying on the floor where he crumbled, unable to move for whatever it was that he was dealing with over there.

'Hello?' she asked softly. 'Um . . . Rio, is that you?'

Silence.

It dragged out, long and uneasy.

'Are you okay in there?'

She put her hand on the doorknob, but it didn't give at all. Locked, just like it had been all night.

'Should I call for someone to help y—'

'Go back to bed, Dylan.'

The voice was low and snarly – Rio's voice, yet somehow very different than she'd ever heard it before.

'Move away from the door,' came the strange growl of words again. 'I don't need help.'

Dylan frowned. 'I don't believe you. You don't sound good at all.'

She tried the knob again. It was old hardware; maybe she could jiggle it open.

'Dylan. Get away from the goddamn door.'

'Why?'

'Because if you stay there one more second, I'm going to open it.'

He exhaled sharply, and when he spoke again his voice was raw gravel. 'I can smell you, Dylan, and I want to . . . taste you. I want you, and I'm not sane enough to keep my hands off you if I were to see you right now.'

Dylan swallowed. She should be terrified of the man on the other side of that door. And yes, part of her was. Not because of his unbelievable claim that he was a vampire. Not because he had abducted her and seemed intent on keeping her prisoner, albeit in a gilded cage. She was terrified because of the honesty in what he'd just said – that he wanted her.

And as much as she wanted to deny it, deep down, that knowledge made her burn just a little to know Rio's touch.

She couldn't speak. Her feet started moving beneath her, pulling her back from the door. Back to reality, she hoped, because what she'd just been considering was not only unrealistic but downright stupid. She padded over to the bed and got in, sitting there with her knees drawn up to her chest, her arms locked tightly around her shins.

There would be no more sleep for her tonight.

❧ CHAPTER TWELVE ❧

She didn't expect to see him in her room first thing that morning.

Dylan came out of the guest suite's spacious shower and dried off with one of the half dozen luxurious towels folded neatly on a built-in shelf in the bathroom. She rubbed out most of the water from her hair, then threw on the last of her clean clothes from her bag. The layered double camisoles and drawstring capris were rumpled, but it wasn't like she had anyone to impress. Barefoot, her damp hair clinging to her bare arms, she opened the bathroom door and padded out to the main room.

And there he was.

Rio, seated in the chair near the door, waiting for her to come out.

Dylan stopped short, startled to find him there.

'I knocked,' he said, a strangely considerate thing, coming from her kidnapper. 'You didn't answer, so I wanted to make sure you were all right.'

'Seems like I should be asking you the same thing.' She cautiously walked farther into the main area of the suite. Although there was no reason she should be concerned about the man who was holding her against her will, she was still rattled by what she'd heard in the other room a few hours ago. 'What happened to you last night? You sounded like you were in pretty bad shape.'

He didn't offer an explanation, just stared at her from across the dim room. Looking at him now, she had to wonder if she'd imagined the whole thing. Dressed in a dove gray tee-shirt and tailored charcoal pants, his dark hair perfectly swept back from his face, he looked well rested and relaxed. Still his broody man-of-few-words self, but less on edge somehow. In fact, he looked as though he'd slept like a baby for a full night straight, while Dylan herself felt like roadkill after lying awake speculating about him since the predawn hours.

'You might want to tell your friends that they need to fix the timer on the blinds in here,' she said, gesturing to the tall window that should be bathing the room with daylight but was instead blocked by the remote-controlled window shades. 'They opened on their own last night, then closed before sunrise. Functionality's a bit backward, don't you think? Nice view, by the way, even in the dark. What lake is that out back – the Wannsee? It's kind of big to be the Grunewaldsee or the Teufelssee, and based on all the old trees surrounding this place, I'm guessing we have to be somewhere near the Havel River. That's where we are, right?'

No reaction from the other side of the room, except for a slow exhale as Rio watched her with dark, unreadable eyes.

He'd brought her breakfast. Dylan strolled over to the squat table and dainty sofa in the center of the parlor area, where a bone china plate containing an omelette, sausage links, roasted potatoes, and a thick slab of toast waited. There was a glass of orange juice, coffee, and a starched white linen napkin tucked beneath a gleaming set of real silver flatware. She couldn't resist the coffee as she wandered over to have a look at everything he brought her. She dropped two sugar cubes into the cup, then poured in enough whole cream to turn the coffee a light shade of tan, sweet and milky, just the way she liked it.

'You know, apart from the incarceration portion of my stay, I have to admit that you folks certainly know how to treat your hostages.'

'You're not a hostage, Dylan.'

'No, a prisoner is more like it. Or does *your kind*, as you put it, prefer a less obvious term – detainee, maybe?'

'You are none of those things.'

'Well, great!' she replied with mock excitement. 'Then when can I go home?'

She didn't really expect him to answer. He leaned back in the chair and crossed his long legs, one ankle propped on the opposite knee. He was thoughtful today, like he wasn't quite sure what to do with her. And she didn't miss the fact that as she took a seat on the sofa and began nibbling at the buttered toast, his gaze lingered hotly on her body.

Not to mention her throat.

She flashed back to what he'd said to her several hours ago: *I can smell you, Dylan, and I want to taste you. I want you . . .*

She definitely had not imagined that. The words had been playing in her mind, practically over and over, since he'd growled them at her through the door. And as he watched her so closely now, with a broody interest that was all male, Dylan could hardly breathe.

She dropped her gaze to her plate, suddenly very self-conscious.

'You're staring at me,' she murmured, the silent scrutiny driving her crazy.

'I'm merely wondering how it is that an intelligent woman like you would choose the line of work you're in. It doesn't seem to fit you.'

'It fits well enough,' Dylan said.

'No,' he said. 'It doesn't fit at all. I've read some of the articles on your computer – including a few of the older ones. Articles that weren't written for that rag that employs you.'

She took a sip of her coffee, uncomfortable with his praise. 'Those files are private. I really don't appreciate you excavating my hard drive like you own it.'

'You wrote a lot about a murder case in upstate New York. The pieces I read on your computer were a few years old, but they were good, Dylan. You are a very smart, compelling writer. Better than you may think.'

'Jesus,' Dylan muttered under her breath. 'I said those files are private.'

'Yeah, you did. But now I'm curious. Why did that particular case matter so much to you?'

Dylan shook her head and leaned back from her breakfast. 'It was my first assignment fresh out of college. A little boy went missing in a small town up north. The police had no suspects and no leads, but there was speculation that the father might have been involved. I was hungry to make a quick name for myself, so I started digging into the guy's history. He was a recovering alcoholic who never held a steady job, one of those class-act deadbeat dads.'

'But was he a killer?' Rio asked soberly.

'I thought so, even though all the evidence was circumstantial. But in my gut, I was sure of his guilt. I didn't like him, and I knew if I looked hard enough I'd find something that pointed to his guilt. After a few false leads, I ran across a girl who'd babysat for the kids. When I questioned her for my story, she told me she'd seen bruises on the boy. She said the guy beat his kid, that she'd even witnessed it personally.' Dylan sighed. 'I ran with all of it. I was so eager to get the story out there that I didn't fully check my source.'

'What happened?'

'Turns out the babysitter had slept with the guy and had some personal axe to grind. He was no Father of the Year, but he never laid a hand on his son, and he sure as hell didn't kill him. After I was fired from the newspaper, the case blew apart when DNA evidence linked the boy's death to a man who lived next door to him. The father was innocent, and I took an extended leave from journalism.'

Rio's dark brows arched. 'And from there you ended up writing about Elvis sightings and alien abductions.'

Dylan shrugged. 'Yeah, well, it was a slippery slope.'

He was staring again, watching her with that same thoughtful silence as before. She couldn't think when he was looking at her like that. It made her feel exposed somehow, vulnerable. She didn't like the feeling one bit.

'We'll be leaving tonight, as I mentioned yesterday,' he said, breaking the awkward silence. 'You'll have an early dinner, if you like, then, at dusk, I'll come back to prepare you for travel.'

That didn't sound good. 'Prepare me . . . how?'

'You can't be allowed to identify this location, or the one we're traveling to. So tonight before we leave, I will have to place you in a light trance.'

'A trance. As in, hypnotize me?' She had to laugh. 'Get real. Anyway, that kind of stuff never works on me. I'm immune to the power of suggestion, just ask my mother or my boss.'

'This is different. And it will work on you. It already has.'

'What're you talking about, it already has?'

He gave a vague shrug of his shoulder. 'How much do you recall of the trip from Prague to here?'

Dylan frowned. There wasn't much, actually. She remembered Rio pushing her into the back of the truck, then darkness as the vehicle started rolling. She remembered being very frightened, demanding to know where he was taking her and what he intended to do with her. Then . . . nothing.

'I tried to stay awake, but I was so tired,' she murmured, trying to recall even another minute of what had to have been several hours of travel and coming up blank. 'I fell asleep on the way here. When I woke up I was in this room . . .'

The small curve of his lips seemed a bit too self-satisfied. 'And you'll sleep again this time until I want you awake. It has to be this way, Dylan. I'm sorry.'

She wanted to make some crack about how ludicrous this whole situation was sounding – from the vampire bullshit he'd tried to feed her yesterday, to this nonsense about trances and traveling to secret locations – but suddenly it didn't seem very funny to her. It seemed impossibly serious.

It suddenly seemed all too real.

She looked at him sitting there, this man who was unlike any other man she'd ever known, and something whispered in her subconscious that this was no joke. Everything he'd told her was true, no matter how unbelievable it might sound.

Dylan's gaze fell from his stoic, unreadable face to the powerful arms that were crossed over his thick chest. The tattoos that snaked around his biceps and forearms were different from the last time she'd seen them. Lighter now, just a few shades deeper than his olive skin tone.

Yesterday the ink in them had been red and gold – she was sure of it.

'What happened to your arms?' she blurted. 'Tattoos don't just change colors . . .'

'No,' he said, glancing down at the now-subtle markings. 'Tattoos don't change colors. But *dermaglyphs* do.'

'*Dermaglyphs?*'

'Naturally occurring skin markings within the Breed. They pass down from father to son and serve as an indicator of an individual's emotional and physical states.' Rio pushed up the short sleeves of his tee-shirt, baring more of the intricate pattern on his skin. Beautiful, swirling arcs and geometric, tribal designs tracked all the way up onto his shoulders and disappeared under his shirt. '*Dermaglyphs* functioned as protective camouflage for the forebears of the race. The Ancients' bodies were covered from head to foot. Each generation of Breed offspring is born with fewer, less elaborate *glyphs* as the original bloodlines dilute with *Homo sapiens* genes.'

Dylan's head was spinning with so many questions, she didn't know which one to ask first. 'I'm supposed to believe that not only are you one of the undead, but that the undead can reproduce?'

He scoffed mildly. 'We're not undead. The Breed is a very long-lived, hybrid species that began thousands of years ago on this planet. Genetically, we are part human, part otherworlder.'

'Otherworlder,' Dylan repeated, more calmly than she could believe. 'You mean . . . alien? To be clear here, you're talking about *vampire* aliens. Am I getting that right? Is that what you're saying?'

Rio nodded. 'Eight such creatures crashed on Earth a long time ago. They raped and slaughtered countless humans. Eventually, some of those rapes were done on human females who could sustain the alien seed and carry it to term. Those women were the first known Breedmates. From their wombs, the first generation of my kind – the Breed – took root.'

Everything she was hearing bordered on the knife's edge of pure, delusional insanity, but there was no mistaking the sincerity of Rio's tone. He believed what he was saying, one hundred percent. And because he was so gravely serious, Dylan found it hard to dismiss him.

To say nothing of the fact that she could personally vouch that the marks on his skin, whatever they were and wherever they had truly come from, had done something that defied all logic. 'Your *dermaglyphs* are just a little darker than your skin color today.'

'Yes.'

'But yesterday they were a mix of red and gold because—'

'Because I needed to feed,' he said evenly. 'I needed blood very badly, and it had to be taken directly from an open human vein.'

Oh, Jesus. He really was serious.

Dylan's stomach lurched.

'So, you . . . fed last night? You're telling me that you went out last night and you drank someone's blood.'

He gave only the slightest incline of his head. There was remorse in his eyes, some kind of private torment that made him seem both lethal and vulnerable at the same time. He was sitting there, seemingly intent on convincing her that he was a monster, but she'd never seen a more haunted expression in all her life.

'You don't have fangs,' she lamely pointed out, her mind still rejecting what she was hearing from him. 'Don't all vampires have fangs?'

'We have them, but they're not normally prominent. Our upper canines lengthen with the urge to feed, or in response to heightened emotion. The process is physiological, much like the reaction of our *dermaglyphs*.'

As he spoke, Dylan carefully watched his mouth. His teeth were straight and white and strong behind his full, sensual lips. It didn't look like a mouth meant for savagery, but for seduction. And that probably made it all the more dangerous. Rio's beautifully formed mouth was one that any woman would welcome on her own, never suspecting it could turn deadly.

'Because of our alien genes, our skin and eyes are hypersensitive to sunlight,' he added, as calmly as he might discuss the weather. 'Prolonged ultraviolet exposure is deadly to all of the Breed. That's why the windows are shaded during the day.'

'Oh,' Dylan murmured, feeling her head bob like that made perfect sense.

Of course they had to block out UV light. Any idiot knew that vampires incinerated like tissue paper under a magnifying glass if you left them out in the sun.

Now that she was thinking about it, she'd not once seen Rio out in daylight. In the mountain cave, he was protected from the sun. When he'd tracked her from Jičín to Prague, it had been late evening, total darkness. Last night, he'd gone out to hunt prey but obviously had made sure he was back before dawn.

Get a grip, Alexander.

This man was not a vampire – not really. There had to be some better explanation for what was going on here. Just because Rio sounded calm and reasonable didn't mean he wasn't completely deranged and delusional. A total nutjob. He had to be.

What about the other people in this high-rent estate? Just more vampire fantasists like him, who believed they descended from a solar-allergic alien race?

And here she was, the unwitting participant, abducted and held captive against her will by a wealthy, blood-drinking cult who believed she was somehow linked to them by virtue of a simple birthmark. Hell, it sounded like a story that was tailor-made for a tabloid front page.

But if anything Rio had said was true . . . ?

Good Lord, if there was anything real about what she'd just heard, then she was sitting on a news story that would literally change the world. One that would alter reality for every human being on the planet. A chill ran up her spine when she considered how important this could be.

'I have a million questions,' she murmured, venturing a glance across the room at Rio.

He nodded as he got up from the chair. 'That's understandable. I've given you a lot to absorb, and you'll be hearing even more before it's time for you to decide.'

'Time for me to decide?' she asked, watching as he strode over to the door to leave. 'Wait a second. What am I going to have to decide?'

'Whether you become a permanent part of the Breed, or go back to your old life with no knowledge of us at all.'

She didn't eat the breakfast Rio brought her, and the dinner he delivered later that day sat untouched too. She had no appetite for food, only a gnawing hunger for answers.

But he told her to save her questions, and when he came back in to inform her that it was time for the two of them to leave, Dylan felt a sudden rush of trepidation.

A gate was being thrown open before her, but it was dark on the other side. If she looked into that darkness, would it consume her?

Would there be any turning back?

'I don't know if I'm ready,' she said, held in the mesmerizing snare of Rio's eyes as he came toward her in the room. 'I'm . . . I'm afraid of where we're going. I'm afraid of what I'm going to see there.'

Dylan looked up into the handsome, tragic face of her captor and waited for some words of encouragement – anything to give her hope that she would come out of this all right in the end.

He didn't offer any such thing, but when he reached out and placed his palm to her brow, his touch was gentle, incredibly warm. God, it felt so good.

'Sleep,' he said.

The firm command filtered through her mind like the soft rasp of velvet over bare skin. He wrapped his other arm around the back of her, just as her knees began to sway. His hold on her was strong, comforting. She could melt into that strength, she thought, as her eyes drifted closed.

'Sleep now, Dylan,' he whispered against her ear. 'Sleep.' And she did.

CHAPTER THIRTEEN

One of the Order's black SUVs was waiting inside a private hangar as the small jet out of Berlin taxied in from a corporate runway at Boston's Logan Airport.

Rio and Dylan were the only passengers aboard the sleek Gulfstream twin engine. The jet and its human pilots were on round-the-clock retainer for the Order, although as far as the two flyboys knew, they pocketed their sizable cash salaries on behalf of a very private, very wealthy corporation that demanded – and received – complete loyalty and discretion.

They were paid extremely well to not so much as lift an eyebrow when Rio had carried a dead-to-the-world, psychically tranced woman into the aircraft in Berlin, nor when he took her off the jet in the same condition some nine hours later in Boston. With Dylan resting soundly in his arms, her backpack and messenger bag slung over his shoulder, Rio headed down the brief flight of steps to the concrete below.

As he crossed the short distance to the Range Rover idling in the hangar, Dante got out of the driver's side, jacking one elbow up on the open door. He was dressed in night patrol gear – long-sleeved tee-shirt, fatigues, and combat boots – all of it as black as his thick, shoulder-length hair. A black semi-auto pistol was holstered under his left arm, another gun strapped to his thigh, but it was the two curved titanium blades sheathed at his hips that Dante never left home without.

One of the Order's newer members was with Dante too,

riding shotgun. Ex–Darkhaven Enforcement Agent Sterling Chase, also garbed in combat gear and loaded for bear, gave Rio a nod of greeting from inside the vehicle. Chase looked as hard-ass as any warrior, his razor-cut golden hair covered in a black skullcap, steel blue eyes hard and steady in his lean face, the shrewd gaze a little emptier than Rio recalled it from a few months ago. Now there was hardly any trace of the uptight, holier-than-thou bureaucrat who'd showed up last summer asking the Order for help and then laying down his own rules of how he expected the warriors to work with him. Dante had not-so-affectionately dubbed the Darkhaven Agent 'Harvard,' a nickname that stuck even after Chase left his old civilian life and joined up with the Order.

'Jay-zus,' Dante said, cracking a broad smile as Rio approached with Dylan lying slack in his arms. 'Talk about going off grid, man. Five months is a helluva vacay.' The warrior chuckled as he opened the SUV's back door and helped Rio get Dylan and her gear situated inside. When they were settled, Dante shut them in, then hopped back behind the wheel. He pivoted around to face Rio. 'At least you came home with a nice souvenir, eh?'

Rio grunted, flicking a glance at Dylan sleeping on the back-seat beside him. 'She's a reporter. And a Breedmate.'

'So I heard. We all did. Gideon told us all about your run-in with Lois Lane back there in Prague,' Dante said. 'No worries, man. We're gonna clamp a hard lid on her story and her pictures before any of that shit goes public. As for her, calls have already been made to find her a place in the Darkhavens if that's her choice after all this is over. It's as good as handled.'

Rio didn't doubt a word Dante said, but he couldn't help wondering which way Dylan was going to go in the end. If she chose the Darkhavens, it would only be a matter of time before a savvy Breed male convinced her that she needed him and ought to be his mate. God knew she'd have no shortage of candidates. With her unusual beauty, she would be the flame they all converged on, and the thought of her being pursued by a bunch of sophisticated, smooth-talking, mostly useless civilians set Rio's teeth on edge.

Though why he should give a damn what she did or with whom, he didn't know.

He had no claim on her, other than the immediate goal of thwarting the disaster that her presence was stirring up. Or rather, the disaster he'd invited by wallowing in his own misery instead of blowing that damn cave like he'd been entrusted to do. Being back in Boston only made him wish he was back on that mountainside, pressing the detonator and watching as a ton of rock sealed him in for good.

'What were you doing over there all this time?' Chase asked, a casually phrased question that didn't quite mask the male's suspicion. 'You told Nikolai that you were going to secure the cave and take off on your own for Spain. The way he told it, you'd up and quit the Order. That was five months ago and no word out of you until now, when you show up bringing bad news and trouble. What the fuck gives?'

'Chill it, man,' Dante advised, throwing a dark look across the front seat. To Rio he said, 'Feel free to ignore Harvard. He's had a hard-on all night because he didn't get to play with his Beretta.'

'No, really,' Chase said, not about to give it up. 'I'm curious is all. What exactly happened over there with you since February when we left you on that mountainside with a duffel full of C-4? Why'd you wait this long to do the damn job? Why the change of plans?'

'There was no change of plans,' Rio replied, meeting the measuring gaze of the warrior in the passenger seat. He couldn't be offended by the challenging tone. Chase had every right to question him – they all had the right – and there wasn't much Rio could say in his defense. He'd let his weakness own him these past several months, and now he had to set that to rights. 'I had a mission to carry out, and I failed in it. Simple as that.'

'Well, we're not exactly batting a thousand on this end either,' Dante put in. 'Since we found that hibernation chamber outside Prague, we've been running leads on the possible existence of an Ancient and they've all come up empty. Chase has been doing some covert internal digging with the Darkhavens and the Enforcement Agency, but those sources aren't turning up anything useful either.'

In the passenger seat, Chase gave an affirmative nod. 'It doesn't seem possible, but if the Ancient is out there, the son of a bitch is deep underground and laying very low.'

'What about the Breed family from Germany that was linked to the Ancient back in the Middle Ages?' Rio asked.

'The Odolfs,' Dante said, shaking his head. 'No survivors that we've found. The few who didn't go Rogue and end up dead from Bloodlust over the years turned up missing or dead of other causes. The entire Odolf line is no more.'

'Shit,' Rio murmured.

Dante nodded. 'That's about all we've got. Just a whole lot of silence and dead ends. We're not about to give up, but right now we're looking for a fucking needle in a haystack.'

Rio frowned, considering the difficulties in hiding the existence of an otherworldly creature like the one the Order hunted now. It would be damn hard not to notice a nearly seven-foot-tall, hairless, *dermaglyph*-covered vampire with an insatiable thirst for blood. Even among the most savage dregs of Breed society, the Ancient would stand out.

The only reason the Ancient had gone undetected for as long as it had was because of the hibernation chamber that housed it on the remote mountain in the Czech countryside. Someone had freed the Ancient from its hidden crypt, but the

Order had no way of knowing when, or how, or even if the bloodthirsty creature had survived its awakening.

With any luck, the savage son of a bitch was long dead.

The other alternative was a scenario no one, Breed or human, would want to imagine.

Dante cleared his throat in the long stretch of silence, his tone going serious. 'Listen, Rio. Whatever your deal was these past months you've been AWOL, it's good to have you back in Boston. We're all glad you're back.'

Rio nodded stiffly as he met the warrior's eyes. No sense telling Dante or anyone else that his return was only temporary. The last thing the Order needed was a liability like him in the ranks. No doubt they'd already discussed that subject when Gideon alerted them about Rio's return.

Dante met his gaze in the rearview. 'You ready to roll, amigo?'

'Yeah,' Rio said. 'I'm more than ready.'

The metallic clack of a lock being freed echoed like a gunshot against the tunnel of rough-hewn granite walls. The door was old, the oiled wood as dark as pitch and as aged as the stone that had been hollowed out of the earth to create the long tunnel and the locked chamber secreted at its end.

But here was where the primitiveness of the place ended.

Beyond the stone and wood and crude iron locks was a laboratory equipped with the finest state-of-the-art technology. It had evolved over the years, employing the best science and robotics that money could buy. The staff of humans operating the facility had been collected from some of the most advanced biological institutions in the nation. They were Minions now, their minds enslaved, loyalty unquestioningly ensured.

All for one purpose.

A single individual, unlike any that existed in all the world.

That individual waited at the end of the tunneled corridor, behind the electronic quadruple-bolted steel door. Inside was a cell constructed specifically to hold a man who was no man at all, but a vampiric, alien creature from a planet far different from the one he inhabited now.

He was an Ancient – the last remaining forebear of the hybrid race known as the Breed. Many thousands of years old, he was more powerful than an army of humans, even kept as he was currently, in a managed state of near starvation. The hunger weakened him, as intended, but it also pissed him off, and rage was always a factor when it came to controlling a powerful creature like the one lifting its hairless, *glyph*-riddled head within the cell.

Bars of highly concentrated ultraviolet light caged the cell in two-inch increments, more effective than the strongest steel. The Ancient would not test them; he'd already done that years ago and nearly lost his right arm from the resulting solar burns. He was masked to keep him calm, and to protect his eyes from the intensity of his UV prison. He was naked because there was no need for modesty here, and because it was crucial that his keeper be able to monitor even the most subtle changes in the *dermaglyphs* that covered every inch of his alien skin.

As for the robotic restraints on the creature's neck, limbs, and torso, they were in place as preparation for the day's assorted fluid and tissue extractions.

'Hello, Grandfather,' drawled the one who held the Ancient prisoner for the past fifty-odd years. He himself was very old by human standards – easily four hundred if he was a day. Not that he kept track anymore, and not that it mattered in the least. As one of the Breed, he appeared in the prime of his youth. With the Ancient kept secretly, and successfully, under his control all this time, he felt like a god.

'Yesterday's test results, Master.'

One of the humans who served him handed him a file of

reports. They didn't call him by name; no one did. There were none around who knew who he truly was.

He'd been born the son of Dragos, his sire a first generation Breed male fathered by the very creature contained within the UV prison cell built in this underground lair. Birthed in secret and sent away to be raised by strangers, it had taken him many long years to finally understand his purpose.

Longer still to get his hands on the prize that would lift him to greatness.

'Did you have a pleasant rest?' he idly asked his prisoner, as he closed the file of test results and readings.

The creature didn't answer, just peeled its lips back and breathed in slowly, air hissing through the large, elongated fangs.

He'd stopped speaking about a decade ago, whether from madness, anger, or defeat, his keeper didn't know. Nor did he particularly care. There was no love between them. The Ancient, despite being close kin, was primarily a means to an end.

'We'll begin now,' the keeper told his prisoner.

He entered a code into the computer that would command the robotics in the cell to commence with the extractions. The tests were painful, plentiful, and prolonged . . . but all necessary. Body fluids were collected, tissue samples harvested. So far, the experiments had yielded only minor successes. But there was promise, and that was enough.

By the time the last specimen was retrieved and catalogued, the Ancient slumped with exhaustion in the cell. Its huge body quivered and spasmed as its advanced physiology worked to heal the damage inflicted by the procedure.

'Just one more process left to complete,' the keeper said.

It was this last one that was most crucial – and most primal – for the vampire recuperating behind the UV light bars of his cell.

Locked within another, more rudimentary prison, was a heavily sedated human female, recently captured off the streets. She too was naked, her dyed black goth-styled hair cut away entirely to better expose her neck. Her eyes were unfocused, pupils dilated from the drugs injected into her system a short while ago.

She didn't scream or struggle as she was led out of her confinement by two Minions and into the main holding area of the laboratory. Her small breasts jiggled with each shuffling step she took, and her head lolled back on her shoulders, revealing the little teardrop-and-crescent-moon birthmark she bore underneath her chin. Her bare feet moved listlessly as she was placed into stirrups on an automated seat that would carry her past the UV barrier and directly into the center of the Ancient's cell.

She hardly flinched as the chair tipped back, positioning her for what was to come. Inside the cell, the restraints on the huge male loosened slightly, freeing him to move in on her like the predator he was.

'You will feed now,' the keeper told him. 'And then you will breed on her.'

⊰ CHAPTER FOURTEEN ⊱

It felt goddamn strange to be in the compound again. But as strange as it was, Rio found it even more surreal to be entering his private apartments within the Order's subterranean headquarters just outside Boston proper.

Dante and Chase had gone off to the tech lab as soon as they arrived, leaving Rio to contend with Dylan on his own. He supposed the warriors were also giving him a chance to reacquaint himself privately with his old life – the one Eva had stolen from him a year ago with her betrayal. He hadn't been in his quarters at the compound for a long time, but the place looked exactly as he remembered it. Exactly as he'd left it, following the warehouse explosion that had sent him into the compound's infirmary for several months of hard recuperation.

The apartments he'd once shared with Eva were like a time capsule. Everything was frozen in its place from that hellish night, when he and his brethren had gone topside to take out a lair of Rogue vampires only to walk headlong into a deadly ambush.

An ambush orchestrated by the female who'd been his Breedmate.

And it was here in the compound, after Eva's deception had been uncovered and Rio denounced her, that she put a blade to her own throat.

She killed herself over his bed in the infirmary, but it was here in their living quarters where Rio felt her presence the most. Eva's personal touches were everywhere, from the flamboyant artwork he'd reluctantly agreed to let her hang on the walls, to the large mirrors positioned near the walk-in closet and across the room from the foot of the huge bed.

Rio carried Dylan past the elegant sitting room and through the curtained French doors that led to the bedroom suite. He caught his reflection in the glass as he brought her over to the four-poster bed and carefully placed her on the dark plum bedding.

He cringed at the swarthy, ruined face of the stranger peering back at him. Even dressed in the fine clothes Reichen had given him, he still looked like a monster – all the more so when he saw the limp beauty asleep in his arms and totally at his mercy.

He *was* a monster, and he couldn't lay the blame for that solely at Eva's feet. He'd been born a beast and a killer; now he just happened to look the part as well.

Dylan stirred a bit as he settled her on the mattress and tucked one of the plump pillows under her head.

'Wake now,' he said, brushing his palm lightly over her brow. 'You have rested long enough, Dylan. You may wake up now.'

He didn't need to stroke her cheek in order to lift the trance. He didn't need to let his fingertips linger on the velvety skin with its charming spray of diminutive, peachy freckles. He didn't need to play his touch along the delicate line of her jaw . . . but he couldn't resist taking his time.

Her eyelids fluttered open. The dark brown fringe of lashes lifted, and Rio was caught in the golden-green light of her gaze. Belatedly, he let his hand fall away from her face, but he could see that she knew he'd taken the liberty. She didn't flinch from him, just drew in a soft breath through her parted lips.

'I'm scared,' she whispered, her voice small and thready from the long sleep he'd put her in. She wasn't aware of the trance or the travel. To her human mind, she was still in Reichen's Darkhaven, her consciousness put on pause in the moments before she and Rio left for Boston. 'I'm afraid of where you're taking me . . .'

'You're already here,' Rio told her. 'We just arrived.'

A look of panic bled into her eyes. 'Where—'

'I've brought you to the Order's compound. You're in my quarters, and you're safe here.'

She glanced around her, quickly taking in her surroundings. 'You live here?'

'I used to.' He stood up and backed away from the bed. 'Make yourself comfortable. If you need anything at all, just ask. I'll see that you get it.'

'How about a ride to my place in New York?' she said, her systems clearly coming back online now. 'Or a GPS map of where you're currently holding me, and I'll find my own way home?'

Rio crossed his arms over his chest. 'This is your home for now, Dylan. Because you are a Breedmate, you will be treated with all the respect due you. You'll have food and comfort, whatever you need. You won't be locked inside these apartments, but I assure you there is nowhere for you to run even if you tried. The compound is completely secure. My brethren and I will not harm you, but if you attempt to leave these quarters, we'll know before you take the first step into the corridor. If you try to escape, I will find you, Dylan.'

She was quiet for a long second, watching him speak, measuring his words. 'And then what will you do to me, hold me down and take a bite out of my throat?'

Cristo.

Rio felt all the blood drain from his head at the very thought. He knew she expected the act to be one of violence, but to him the image of pressing Dylan down beneath him as he pierced her tender skin with his fangs was one of total sensuality.

Arousal spiraled through him in a hot coil, all of it pooling in his groin.

He could still feel the silky warmth of her skin in his fingertips, and now another part of him craved to know her. He turned away, angered at his body's swift, urgent reaction to her.

'When I was in Jičín, I heard about a man who was attacked by a demon. An old farmer witnessed it, said this demon came down off a nearby mountain to feed. To drink human blood.'

Rio stood there, staring at the door in front of him while Dylan spoke. He knew the night she referred to, remembered it clearly because it was the last time he'd allowed himself to feed. He'd gone more than two weeks without nourishment when he prowled onto a humble farm outside the forest at the base of the mountains.

He'd been starving and it had made him careless. An old man came upon him – saw the attack, saw Rio holding the human throat in his teeth. It was a reckless slip, and the interruption was likely the only thing that saved Rio's prey from an out of control feeding that might have meant his death. He stopped hunting that very night, afraid of what he might become.

'It was just an exaggeration, right?' Dylan's voice got a little quieter during his answering silence. 'You didn't really do that. Did you, Rio?'

'Make yourself comfortable,' he growled. As he started to leave, he grabbed her messenger bag that contained her laptop computer and digital camera. 'I have things I need to do.'

He didn't wait for her to protest or say anything more, just knew he had to get the hell out of there. A few brisk strides carried him to the open French doors and the living room beyond.

'Rosario . . . ?'

He stopped walking at the sound of her voice behind him. Scowling, he pivoted his head to look back at her. She had lifted up on the bed at some point, now bracing herself on her elbows.

God, she looked deliciously disheveled like that, beautifully drowsy. It didn't take much to imagine this was how Dylan might look after a night of rousing sex. The fact that she was lying against the plum-colored silk of his bed only made the image all the more erotic.

'What?' His voice was a thick scrape of sound in his throat.

'Your name,' she said, like he should know what she meant. She tilted her head as she studied him from across the room. 'You told me that Rio is only part of your name, so I just wondered what it's short for. Is it Rosario?'

'No.'

'Then, what is it?' When he didn't answer right away, her light brown brows knit together in impatience. 'After everything else you've told me these past couple of days, what can it hurt to tell me the name you were born with?'

He scoffed inwardly, recalling all the things he'd been called since his birth. None of them were kind. 'Why is it important to you to know?'

She shook her head, gave a mild lift of her slender shoulder. 'It's not important. I guess I'm just curious to know more about you. Who you really are.'

'You know enough,' he said. A ripe curse slipped off his tongue. 'Trust me, Dylan Alexander. You don't want to know anything more about me than you already do.'

He was wrong about that, Dylan thought, watching Rio stalk away from her and out of the spacious suite. He closed the door behind him, leaving her alone in the softly lit apartment.

She pivoted off the side of the big bed. Her legs were

wobbly, like she hadn't used them for several hours. Like she'd been out cold for the better part of the night. If what he'd said was true – that they'd left Berlin and arrived in the States – then she figured she was missing about nine hours of conscious memory.

Could that really be possible?

Had he truly put her into some kind of trance this whole time?

She'd been stunned to feel his fingers caressing her face as she woke up. His touch had felt so soothing, so protective and warm. But it had been fleeting too, gone as soon as he realized she'd become aware of it.

She didn't want to feel any warmth from Rio, nor toward him, but she could hardly deny that there was something electric in the way he looked at her. There was something unmistakably seductive in the way he touched her. She wanted to know more about him – needed to know more. After all, as his captive it would be in her best interest to learn everything she could about the man who held her. As a journalist hoping to break a big story, it was her duty to gather even the smallest fact and chase it down to its bare truth.

But it was her interest as a woman that bothered Dylan the most.

It was that very personal desire to know more about the kind of man Rio was that sent her gaze roaming around the bedroom. The decor was lush and sultry, an explosion of jewel-tone colors, from the plum silk bedding to the gold-hued paint on the walls. A collection of abstract paintings, so bright they hurt Dylan's eyes, crowded one entire wall of the bedroom suite. Another wall sported a giant, ornately framed mirror . . . strategically placed to reflect the big four-poster bed and whatever might be going on atop it.

'Subtle,' Dylan murmured, rolling her eyes as she wandered over to a double set of doors on another side of the room.

She drew them open and felt her jaw go slack as she looked in on a walk-in closet that had more square footage than her studio apartment in Brooklyn. 'My God.'

She went inside, vaguely aware of even more mirrors in here – and why wouldn't you want to admire yourself from every angle when you had half of Neiman Marcus to choose from?

She was tempted to nose around in what had to be many thousands of dollars worth of designer clothes and shoes, but a bleak thought registered at once: only about a quarter of the closet contained men's clothing. The rest belonged to a woman – a petite woman, with obviously very expensive taste.

These might be Rio's quarters, but he sure as hell didn't live here alone.

Oh, shit. Was he married?

Dylan backed out of the walk-in and closed the doors, wishing she hadn't looked in the first place. She drifted into the living area of the apartment, seeing a woman's touch everywhere now. Nothing remotely close to her own style, but then what did she know about quality interior design? Her best piece of furniture was a Crate and Barrel sleeper sofa she got secondhand.

Dylan let her hand trail over the back of a carved walnut, claw-footed chair as she took in the garishly elegant furnishings of the place. She wandered over to a gold velvet sofa, and paused as her gaze caught on a small assortment of framed photographs on the table behind it.

The first thing she saw was a picture of Rio. He was seated in the open passenger side of a vintage cherry red Thunderbird convertible that had been parked on a moonlit stretch of beach. Dressed in an open black silk button-down and black trousers, he lounged in a lazy sprawl, as much in the car as out of it. His thighs were parted in a casual vee, his bare toes dug into the fine white sand. His dark topaz gaze gleamed with private wisdom, and his smoky smile made him seem equal parts danger and decadent fun.

Good Lord, he was handsome.

To be fair, he was about a hundred miles ahead of hand-some.

The photo didn't seem very old. There were no scars riddling the left side of his face, so the injury he sustained must have been fairly recent. Whatever happened had robbed him of his classic, impossibly good looks, but it was the anger he carried inside him that seemed the bigger tragedy. Dylan looked at the picture of Rio in happier times and she had to wonder how he'd fallen as far as he apparently had in the time since.

She glanced to another picture, this one an antique. It was a sepia-toned studio image of a dark-haired woman with a Gibson Girl updo and a high-necked, frothy lace Victorian dress. Dylan bent down to get a better look, wondering if the exotic beauty with the coy smile might be Rio's grandmother. The dark eyes stared directly into the camera lens, a look of pure seduction. She was gorgeous and sensual, despite the prim fashion of her time.

And her face . . . it seemed strangely familiar.

'Oh, my God.'

Disbelief, as well as an overriding sense of wonder, swamped Dylan as her gaze traveled to another photograph on the sofa table. This one was full-color, obviously taken within the past decade or less . . . and it featured the same woman from the antique picture. This later one was a nighttime shot of a woman standing on a stone bridge in the middle of a city park, laughing as her long black hair blew playfully around her head. She seemed so happy, but Dylan saw a sadness in her dark eyes – pained secrets hiding in the deep brown gaze that was fixed so tightly on whoever it was that took the photo.

And she recognized that face for certain, she realized now,

though not merely from the impossible time range of photographs displayed on Rio's sofa table.

This was the same face she'd seen on the mountain in Jičín . . . the face of a dead woman.

The beautiful ghost who led Dylan to the cave where she found Rio was his wife.

⇥ CHAPTER FIFTEEN ⇤

It was almost as if he'd never been gone.

Rio stood in the compound's tech lab surrounded by Lucan, Gideon, and Tegan, who'd each greeted him with a hand offered in genuine friendship and trust.

Tegan's grasp lingered the longest, and Rio knew that the stony warrior with the tawny hair and gem-green eyes was able to read his guilt and uncertainty through the link of their clasped hands. That was Tegan's gift, to divine true emotion with a touch.

He gave a nearly imperceptible shake of his head. 'Shit happens, man. And God knows we all have our own personal demons yanking our chains. So, no one's here to judge you. Got it?'

Rio nodded as Tegan let go of his hand. As he passed off Dylan's messenger bag to Gideon, he cast a glance toward the back of the lab, where Dante and Chase were cleaning their weapons for the night. Dante gave him a tip of his chin, but Chase's steely look said his jury was still out when it came to Rio. Smart man. Rio figured the ex–Darkhaven Agent's reaction was probably the same one he'd have if the tables were turned and Chase was the one flying in deadstick and in need of a rescue.

'How much does the woman know about us?' Lucan asked.

At nine hundred years old and first generation Breed, the Order's founder and formidable leader could command control of an entire room with just a quirk of his black brows. Rio considered him a friend – all of the warriors were as near as kin to one another – and he hated like hell that he might have disappointed him.

'I only gave her the basics,' Rio replied. 'I don't think she fully believes it yet.'

Lucan grunted, nodding thoughtfully. 'It's a hell of a lot to deal with. Does she understand the purpose behind that crypt in the rock?'

'Not really. She heard me call it a hibernation chamber when Gideon and I were talking, but she doesn't know anything more than that. I sure as hell don't plan to clue her in. Bad enough she saw the damn thing for herself.' Rio exhaled a harsh breath. 'She's smart, Lucan. I don't think it will take her long to start putting the pieces into place.'

'Then we'd better act fast. The fewer potential details we have to clean up later, the better,' Lucan said. He glanced at Gideon, who had Dylan's laptop open on the computer console beside him. 'How hard do you think it will be to hack in and lose those pictures she's sent out via e-mail?'

'Deleting the source files on her camera and computer is easy. Half a minute's work.'

'What about getting rid of the recipients' image and text files?'

Gideon scrunched up his face as if he were calculating the square root of Bill Gates's net worth. 'About ten minutes for delivery of your basic hard-drive wrecking ball to all of the computers on her distribution list. Thirteen, if you're looking for something with a little more finesse.'

'I don't give a rat's ass about finesse,' Lucan said. 'Just do whatever you need to trash the pictures and kill any text references to what she found on that mountain.'

'I'm on it,' Gideon replied, already working his magic on both devices.

'We can destroy the electronic files, but we still need to deal with the people she's been in contact with about the cave,' Rio pointed out. 'Aside from her employer, there's the three women she was traveling with, and her mother.'

'I'm going to leave that to you,' Lucan said. 'I don't care how you go about it – use her to deny the story, discredit her, or go out and find the folks she's talked to and scrub the memory of every last one of them. Your choice, Rio. Just handle it, like I know you will.'

He nodded. 'I give you my word, Lucan. I will fix this.'

The Gen One vampire's expression was as grave as it was certain. 'I don't doubt you. Never have, never will.'

Lucan's confidence was unexpected, and a gift Rio didn't plan to squander, no matter how wrecked he knew himself to be. For so many years, the Order and the warriors serving within it were his chief purpose in life – even above his love for Eva, which had seeded a quiet, but festering resentment in her. Rio was honor-bound to every last one of these men like his own blood kin, pledged to fight alongside them, even die for them. He looked around him, humbled by the grim, courageous faces of the five Breed males whom he knew without question would lay down their lives for him as well.

Rio cleared his throat, feeling awkward for the nearly unanimous welcome from his brethren. Across the lab, the glass doors whisked open as Nikolai, Brock, and Kade strode in from the corridor outside. The three of them were talking animatedly, giving off an air of easy camaraderie as they swept into the lab.

'Hey,' Niko said, a greeting tossed out to no one in particular. His ice-blue gaze lit on Rio for half a second before he looked to Lucan and began relaying the details of the trio's night patrol. 'Smoked a Rogue down by the river about an hour ago. Bastard was sleeping off a kill inside a Dumpster when we found him.'

'Think it was one of Marek's hounds?' Lucan asked, referring to the army of Rogue vampires his own brother had been amassing until the Order stepped in. Marek was dead at the hands of the Order, but the remnants of his army were still vermin in need of extermination.

Nikolai gave a shake of his head. 'This suckhead wasn't a fighter, just an addict scratching his permanent itch for blood. I figure he was only a few nights out of the Darkhaven based on how easy he went down.' The Russian-born vampire looked past Rio to crack a crooked grin at Dante and Chase. 'Any action over on the South Side?'

'Not a damn thing,' Chase muttered. 'Too busy running errands out at the airport.'

Nikolai grunted, acknowledging the comment with a glance in Rio's direction. 'Long fucking time, man. Good to see you in one piece.'

Rio knew the male too well to think the reply was friendly. Of all the warriors in the Order, it was Nikolai that Rio expected to be first in line to defend him – whether or not Rio deserved it. Niko was the brother Rio never had, both of them born in the past century, both having joined the Order in Boston around the same time.

Odd that Niko had been absent for Rio's arrival at the compound, although knowing the vampire and his love for combat, he probably was pissed off that his patrol was cut short with still a couple of hours to go until dawn.

Before Rio could say anything to his old friend, Nikolai's attention swung back to Lucan. 'The Rogue we found tonight was young, but the kill he left behind looked like the work of more than one vampire. I'd like to head back tomorrow night and sniff around, see if we turn up anything more.'

Lucan nodded. 'Sounds good.'

With that out of the way, Niko turned to Kade and Brock. 'Got enough time before sunrise to do a little hunting of our own. Anyone else feeling thirsty all of a sudden?'

Kade's wolflike eyes glittered like quicksilver. 'There's an after-hours place in the North End that's probably just getting interesting. Plenty of sweet young things just ripe for the plucking.'

'Count me in,' Chase drawled, coming out of his chair next to Dante to join the three other unmated males as they started heading for the lab's exit.

For a moment, Rio watched them go. But as Nikolai stepped out to the corridor behind the rest of the pack, Rio hissed a curse and shot after him.

'Niko, wait.'

The warrior kept walking like he couldn't hear him.

'Hold up, man. Goddamn it, Nikolai. What the fuck is wrong with you?'

As Chase, Brock, and Kade paused to look back, Niko waved them on ahead. They continued moving, rounding a corner in the corridor and disappearing from view. After a long few seconds, finally, Nikolai pivoted around.

The face staring back at Rio in the stark white tunnel was hard and unreadable. 'Yeah. Here I am. What do you want?'

Rio didn't know how to answer that. Hostility rolled off his old friend like a winter chill. 'Have I done something to piss you off?'

Nikolai's sharp bark of laughter scraped against the polished marble walls. 'Fuck you, man.'

He wheeled around and began stalking away.

Rio caught up to him in a blink. He was about to grab the warrior's shoulder and force him to stop, but Niko moved faster. He spun back and plowed into Rio broadside with his forearm against Rio's sternum, driving his spine into the hard wall on the other side of the corridor.

'You want to die, you son of a bitch?' Niko's eyes were narrowed, amber firing into the blue as a result of his anger.

'You want to fucking kill yourself, that's your business. Don't ever use me to help you do it. We clear?'

Rio's muscles were tensed and ready for a fight, his combat instincts rising even though he was facing a long-trusted ally. But as Nikolai spoke, Rio's swiftly igniting battle rage ebbed a crucial fraction. Suddenly Niko's fury toward him made sense. Because Nikolai knew that Rio had stayed behind on that Bohemian mountain intending to end his life. If he hadn't known it those five months ago, he sure as hell knew it now.

'You lied to me,' Niko seethed. 'You looked me right in the eye and you lied to me, man. You were never going back to Spain. What were you going to do with that supply of C-4 I gave you? Strap it on and detonate the shit for some private jihadist fun, or maybe you just planned on sealing yourself inside that godforsaken tomb for the rest of eternity? What was it going to be, amigo? Which way did you plan on checking out?'

Rio didn't answer. There was no need. Of all the warriors in the Order, Nikolai knew him best. He saw him for the weak coward that he truly was. He alone knew how close Rio had been to ending the whole damn thing – even before his arrival on that Czech mountain.

It had been Niko who refused to let Rio wallow in self-loathing, making it his personal mission to pull Rio out of his dark tailspin last summer. Niko who took Rio topside with him in the weeks that followed, hunting for him when Rio had been too weak to look after himself. Nikolai, the brother Rio had never had.

'Yeah,' Niko scoffed. 'Like I said. Fuck you.'

He dropped his arm away from Rio's chest and backed off with a growled curse. Rio watched him go, Niko's boots chewing up the polished marble as he stormed off to meet the other warriors already on their way topside.

'Shit,' Rio hissed, raking his hand through his hair.

This clash with Nikolai was just more evidence that he shouldn't have come back to Boston – even if it meant leaving the problem of Dylan Alexander to someone else to handle. He didn't fit in here anymore. He was an outsider now, a weak link in an otherwise solid steel chain of courageous Breed warriors.

Even now he could feel his temples pounding from the rush of adrenaline that had kicked in a few minutes ago, when it looked like Niko wanted to tear him apart. His vision started to swim as he stood there. If he didn't get moving and find somewhere private to host the oncoming mental meltdown, he knew it would likely be only minutes before he woke up ass-planted on the marble right there in the corridor. And frankly, having Lucan and the others come out of the tech lab to stare over him like he was week-old roadkill was not something he wanted to experience.

Rio commanded his legs to start moving, and with no small degree of difficulty, he managed to find his way back to his quarters. He stumbled inside and closed the door behind him, sagging against it as a fresh wave of nausea swept over him.

'Are you okay?'

The female voice came from somewhere distant in the apartment. At first it didn't register as familiar; his brain was struggling to perform basic motor movements, and the bright, crystalline voice didn't seem to belong in this place full of old, musty memories.

He shoved away from the door and dragged himself through the living room toward his bedroom, his skull feeling like it was going to shatter.

Hot water. Darkness. Quiet. He needed all three right away.

He pulled off his shirt and let it fall onto Eva's ridiculous gold velvet settee. He really ought to burn all of her shit. Too bad he couldn't toss the deceptive bitch into the pyre along with it.

Rio clung to his fury for Eva's betrayal, a feeble grounding, but the only thing he had at the moment. He reached the open French doors to the bedroom and heard a small gasp from inside.

'Oh, my God. Rio, are you all right?'

Dylan.

Her name bled through the fog of his mind like a balm. He looked up to find his unwilling guest sitting on the edge of the bed, something flat and rectangular resting on her lap. She set the object aside on the nightstand and rushed over to him in the instant before his knees gave out.

'Shower,' he managed to croak.

'You can hardly stand up.' She helped him over to the bed, where he gratefully collapsed. 'You look like you need a doctor. Is there anyone here who can help you?'

'No,' he rasped. 'Shower . . .'

He was too far gone to use his Breed ability to mentally turn the water on, but he didn't need to try. Dylan was already running to the adjacent bathroom. He heard the sharp hiss of the shower coming on, then Dylan's soft footsteps on the carpet as she came back out to where he was slumped pathetically on his side toward the foot of the bed.

Vaguely he registered the slowing of her stride the closer she got to him. He hardly heard the quick, indrawn breath above him. But there was no mistaking the shaky exhale as she blew out a quiet, pitying oath.

'Jesus Christ.' Too much silence followed her whispered curse. Then, 'Rio . . . My God. What kind of hell have you been through?'

Using every last ounce of strength he had, Rio peeled his eyes open. Big mistake. The horror he saw in Dylan's gaze was undeniable. She was looking at the exposed left side of his body . . . at the chest and torso that had been shredded by shrapnel and nearly flayed off his bones by the flames of the explosion he'd barely survived.

'Did she . . .' Dylan's soft voice drifted off. 'Did your wife have something to do with what happened to you, Rio?'

His pulse froze. The blood that had been beating like a drum in his ears turned to ice as he stared up blearily into Dylan's questioning, concerned face.

'Did she do this to you, Rio?'

He followed Dylan's outstretched hand as she reached toward the item she'd set down on the nightstand. It was a framed photograph. He didn't need to see the picture under the glass to know that it was a snapshot of Eva, from an evening walk they'd taken along the Charles River. Eva, smiling. Eva, telling him how much she loved him, while behind his back she conspired with the Order's enemy to fulfill her own selfish goals.

Rio snarled when he thought of his own stupidity. His own blindness.

'It doesn't concern you,' he muttered, still adrift in the darkness that was rising up on him from within his broken mind. 'You don't know anything about her.'

'She was the one who led me to you. I saw her on the mountain in Jičín.'

An irrational suspicion sharpened his anger to something deadly. 'What do you mean, you saw her? You knew Eva?'

Dylan swallowed, gave a small shrug of her shoulder. She held the picture frame out toward him. 'I saw her . . . her spirit was there. She was there on the mountain with you.'

'Bullshit,' he growled. 'Don't talk to me about that female. She's dead, and that's where she belongs.'

'She asked me to help you, Rio. She sought me out. She wanted me to save you—'

'I said that's bullshit!' he roared.

Fury brought his body up off the mattress like a viper lashing out to strike. He knocked the frame out of Dylan's hands, and his rage hurled it across the room in blinding speed. It crashed into the large mirror on the wall opposite the bed, splintering on impact and sending shards of polished glass exploding out like a hail of tiny razor blades.

He heard Dylan cry out, but it wasn't until he smelled the juniper-sweet scent of her blood that he realized what he'd done.

She held her hand up to her cheek, and when her fingers came away, they were stained scarlet from a small, bleeding gash just below her left eye.

It was the sight of that wound that snapped Rio out of his downward spiral. Like a bucket of cold water thrown over his head, seeing Dylan injured jolted him instantly sober.

'Ah, *Cristo*,' he hissed. 'I'm sorry . . . I'm sorry.'

He moved to touch her, to assess how badly he'd hurt her – and she backed away from him with wide, terrified eyes.

'Dylan . . . I didn't mean to—'

'Stay away from me.'

He reached out, meaning only to reassure her that he meant no harm.

'No.' She flinched, shaking her head wildly. 'Oh, my God. Don't you touch me.'

Madre de Dios.

She was gaping at him in utter horror now. She was trembling, eyes fixed on him in fear and confusion.

When his tongue brushed across the pointed tips of his extended fangs, Rio understood the source of her terror. He stood before her, the vampire he'd told her he was but which her human mind refused to comprehend.

Now, it did.

She was seeing the truth of it for herself, in the physical changes that had come over him and transformed him from scarred madman to a creature out of a nightmare. There was no hiding the fangs that stretched even larger as his hunger for her swelled. No way to mask the elliptical sharpening of his pupils as the amber glow of blood-thirst swamped his vision.

He looked at the small cut, the rivulet of blood trailing down from it so red against the creamy skin of Dylan's cheek, and he could hardly form a coherent thought.

'I tried to tell you, Dylan. This is what I am.'

≼ CHAPTER SIXTEEN ≽

*V**ampire.*'
Dylan heard the word slip past her lips, despite the fact that she could hardly believe what she was seeing.

In a matter of moments, Rio had transformed before her eyes. She stared in shock at the changes she'd just witnessed. His irises glowed like embers, no longer the smoky topaz color they normally were, but an incredible shade of amber that nearly swallowed up his impossibly thinned pupils. The bones of his face seemed starker now, lean, blade-sharp cheekbones and a squared jaw that seemed carved of stone.

And behind the lush cut of his mouth, Rio sported a pair of fangs like something straight out of the movies.

'You . . .' Her voice trailed off as those hypnotic amber eyes drank her in. She sat down weakly on the edge of the bed. 'My God. You really are . . .'

'I am Breed,' he said simply. 'Just as I told you.'

Seated in front of him, her vision filled with the broad musculature of his bare chest. The complicated pattern of skin markings on his forearms tracked up over his shoulders and down along his pectorals. The entire array of markings – *dermaglyphs,* he'd called them the first time she noticed them – were livid with color now, the darkest they'd been yet. Deep reds, purples, and black saturated the beautiful flourishes and arcing lines.

'I can't stop the change,' he murmured, as if he felt obligated to explain himself. 'The transformation is automatic for every Breed male when he senses fresh spilled blood.'

His gaze shifted slightly down from her eyes, to where her cheek burned from the bite of the glass that struck her. She felt the warm track of blood sliding toward her chin like a tear. Rio watched that droplet fall with an intensity that made Dylan tremble. He licked his lips and swallowed, but clamped his teeth together as rigidly as a vise.

'Stay here,' he said, scowling hard, his voice dark and commanding.

Instinct told Dylan she might be smarter to run, but she refused to be afraid. Strange as it seemed, she felt she'd come to know this man over the past handful of days they'd been thrust together. Rio was no saint, that was for sure. He had abducted her, imprisoned her, and she still wasn't certain what he meant to do with her, but she didn't think he was a danger to her.

What she'd just witnessed here wasn't exactly cause for celebration, but in her heart, she didn't fear what he was.

Well, not completely, anyway.

The water was still running in the shower. She heard it turn off, then Rio came out holding a damp white washcloth. He offered it to her at arm's length. 'Press this to the wound. It will stanch the bleeding.'

Dylan took the cloth and held it to her cheek. She didn't miss Rio's long exhale as she covered the gash, like he was relieved he didn't have to look at it anymore. The fiery color of his eyes slowly began to dim, his slender pupils resuming their round shape. But his *dermaglyphs* were still flushed with color, and his fangs still looked deadly sharp.

'You really are . . . aren't you?' she murmured. 'You're a vampire. Holy shit, I can't believe it's true. I mean, how *can* it be true, Rio?'

He sat down next to her on the bed, no less than two feet of space between them. 'I already explained it to you.'

'Blood-drinking extraterrestrials and human women with alien-friendly DNA,' she said, recalling the outlandish story about a vampiric hybrid race she'd tried to dismiss as science fiction. 'It's all fact?'

'The truth is a bit more complicated than your understanding of it, but yes. Everything I told you is fact.'

Incredible.

Absolutely mind-blowingly incredible.

A mercenary part of her nearly shouted with excitement over the potential fame and fortune there would be in breaking such an enormous news story. But it was another part of her – the part that reminded her of the little birthmark on the back of her neck and its apparent connection to this strange new world – that made her feel instantly protective, as though Rio and the world he lived in was a delicious secret that belonged exclusively to her.

'I'm sorry I upset you,' she told him quietly. 'I shouldn't have been nosing around in your things when you weren't here.'

His head came up sharply, dark brows crushed together. The curse he muttered was ripe and vivid. 'You don't have to apologize to me, Dylan. I'm the one at fault. I should never have come in here the way I was. No one should be near me when I'm like that.'

'You seem a little better now.'

He nodded, head slumped down toward his chest. 'The rage subsides . . . eventually. If I don't black out first, it does eventually pass.'

It didn't take much to see him as he had been when he stumbled into his quarters a short while ago. He'd been almost mindless, his limbs hardly working as he struggled with each difficult step. He'd been barely coherent, a shuddering bulk of muscle and bone and unfocused fury.

'What brings it on, Rio?'

He shrugged. 'Little things. Nothing at all. I can never know.'

'Is that kind of rage just part of being what you are? Do all of the Breed have to go through that kind of torment?'

'No.' He scoffed under his breath. 'No, this problem is mine alone. My head's not screwed on right anymore. It hasn't been right since last summer.'

'Was it an accident?' she asked gently. 'Is that what happened to you?'

'It was a mistake,' he said, a brittle edge to his voice. 'I trusted someone I shouldn't have.'

Dylan looked at the terrible damage his body had weathered. His face and neck bore serious scars, but his left shoulder and half of his muscled torso looked like it had been through hell and back. Her heart clenched tightly in her chest when she thought about the kind of pain he must have endured, both in the event that injured him and in what had to have been many long months of recovery.

He sat there so rigidly, so solitary and unreachable even though he was less than an arm's length away from her on the edge of the big bed. He seemed so alone to her. Alone and adrift.

'I'm sorry, Rio,' she said, and before she could stop herself, she put her hand over the top of his where it rested on his thigh.

He flinched as though she'd put hot coals on his skin.

But he didn't move away.

He stared down at her fingers, which rested lightly across his, pale white over buttery olive. When he looked over at her, it was with a stark wildness in his eyes. She wondered how long it had been since he'd been touched with any kind of tenderness.

How long had it been since he'd allowed himself to be touched?

Dylan smoothed her fingers over the top of his hand, studying the incredible size and strength of him. His skin was so warm, so much coiled power in him even when he seemed determined to hold himself perfectly still.

'I'm sorry for everything you've been through, Rio. I mean that.'

His jaw was clamped so hard it made a tendon twitch in his face. Dylan set the cold compress down on the bed next to her, hardly aware that she was moving because her senses were so fixed on Rio and the electricity that seemed to be pooling where their hands connected.

She heard a low rumble gathering from within him, something between a growl and a moan. His gaze drifted down to her mouth, and for a second — one fast, fleeting heartbeat — she wondered if he was going to kiss her.

She knew she should draw back. Move her hand away from his. Anything but sit there unable to breathe as she waited and wondered — *wished so desperately* — that he would lean in and brush his lips against hers.

She couldn't stop herself from reaching out to him now. She moved her free hand up toward his face, and felt a sudden blast of cold air coming at her, pushing at her like a physical wall.

'I don't want your pity,' Rio snarled in a voice she didn't recognize as his own. The rolling Spanish accent was there as always, but the syllables were harsh, the timbre not quite human, reminding her of just how little she understood about him or his kind. He pulled his hand out from under hers and stood up from the bed. 'That cut of yours is still bleeding. You need attention I can't give you.'

'I'm sure it's fine,' Dylan replied, feeling like an idiot for putting herself out there like that with him. She grabbed the damp washcloth and dabbed at her cheek. 'It's no big deal. I'm fine.'

There was no sense talking since it was obvious he wasn't listening to her anyway. She watched him walk past the broken glass of the shattered mirror, into the living room outside. He picked up the cordless telephone and dialed a short sequence of numbers.

'Dante? Hey. No, nothing wrong. But I, ah . . . is Tess there? I need to ask a favor of her.'

Rio paced like a caged animal in the short minutes it took for his rescue to arrive. He stayed out of the bedroom, confining himself to a small space of real estate near the main entry of his quarters. As far away from Dylan as he could get without actually bolting out of the damn apartment and waiting outside.

Madre de Dios.

He'd nearly kissed her.

Still wanted to, and the admission – even to himself – was like a sucker punch to the gut. Kissing Dylan Alexander was a guaranteed way to turn a bad situation into something catastrophic. Because Rio knew without a shred of doubt that if he kissed the fiery beauty, it wouldn't stop there.

Just thinking about feeling the press of her lips on his made his blood quicken in his veins. His *glyphs* pulsed with the colors of his desire – churning in shades of dark wine and gold. And there was no denying the other evidence of that desire. His cock was as hard as granite, and had been since the instant she so unexpectedly laid her hand atop his.

Holy hell.

He didn't dare look back into the bedroom for fear that he wouldn't be able to keep his feet from doing an about-face march through the closed French doors and right into Dylan's arms.

Like she would actually have him, he thought viciously.

That pat of his hand had been a sweet gesture, the kind

of 'there, there' comfort a mother might offer a pouting child.
Or worse than that, it might have been the pained sympathy
of a charitable angel consoling one of God's most unfortu-
nate blunders.

Maldecido.

Manos del diablo.

Monstruo.

Yes, he was all those things. And now Dylan had seen how
ugly he truly was. To her credit she hadn't recoiled at all the
twisted flesh or his fangs, but then she was made of stronger
stuff than that.

But to think she might welcome his touch? That she might
get close enough to his ruined face to let him kiss her?

Not fucking likely. And he thanked God for that, because
it saved him from seeing her disgust. It saved him from doing
something really stupid, like forgetting for even one second
that she was in the compound – in his private quarters – only
until he corrected the mistake he'd made in letting her get
close to that cave. The sooner he could do that and get her
gone, the better.

A staccato rap sounded on the door.

Rio pulled it open with a growl of self-directed frustration.

'You sounded like shit, so I thought I'd come along with
Tess and take a look at you for myself.' Dante's mouth quirked
into that cocky grin of his as he stood at the threshold with
his gorgeous Breedmate close at his side. 'You gonna let us
in, man?'

'Yeah.' Rio backed off to give the couple space to enter.

Dante's mate looked prettier than ever. Her long honey-
brown waves were pulled back in a loose ponytail, and her
wise aquamarine eyes were soft, even when looking Rio full
in the face.

'It's so good to see you,' she said, and without hesitation
she strode over to him and went up on her toes to give him

a quick embrace and a kiss on his cheek. 'Dante and I both have been so worried about you these past months, Rio.'

'No need,' he replied, but he couldn't deny that the concern warmed him.

Tess and Dante had only been together since late autumn of last year; she'd come into the Order's compound with an extraordinary gift for healing and restoring life with her tender hands. Tess's touch held amazing power, but not even she had been able to fix all that was wrong with Rio. He was too far gone by the time Tess arrived. His scars were permanent, both inside and out, though not for lack of trying on Tess's part.

Dante put his arm around his Breedmate in a move that was both protective and reverent, and it was then that Rio noticed the gentle swell of her belly underneath the pale rose tee-shirt and khaki pants she wore. She caught his downward glance and smiled as beatific as the Madonna herself.

'I'm just out of my first trimester,' she said, turning all of that glowing love on Dante now. 'Someone's making it his new mission in life to spoil me rotten.'

Dante chuckled. 'I aim to please.'

'Congratulations,' Rio murmured, genuinely happy for the pair.

It wasn't common for warriors and their mates to raise a family within the Order. Practically unheard of, in fact. Breed males who looked to devote their lives to combat typically weren't the home-and-hearth types. But then Dante never had been one to color within the lines.

'Where is Dylan?' Tess asked.

Rio gestured toward the closed French doors across the room. 'I made an ass of myself in there with her. I had a meltdown and I . . . ah, damn, I shattered a mirror. Some of the flying glass cut her cheek.'

'You're still experiencing the blackouts?' Tess asked, frowning. 'The headaches too?'

He shrugged, not wanting to discuss his own numerous problems. 'I'm okay. Just . . . do what you can to take care of her, all right?'

'I will.' Tess took a small black medical bag from Dante's hands. At Rio's questioning look, she said, 'Since I've been expecting, my healing abilities have dimmed. I understand it's normal for pregnancy to draw a Breedmate's energy inward. It should come back once the baby is born. Until then, I'll have to rely on good old-fashioned medicine.'

Rio cast a look over his shoulder at the bedroom. He couldn't see Dylan, but he figured she was in there needing to see someone kind and gentle. Someone who could patch her up and talk to her like a normal person. Reassure her that she was safe, among people she could trust. Especially after the spectacular display of raging psychotic-turned-lecherous freak he'd put on for her in there.

'It's okay,' Tess said. 'I'll take care of her.'

Dante cuffed Rio in the biceps. 'Come on. There's still an hour or so before dawn. You look like you could use some fresh air, my man.'

⫷ CHAPTER SEVENTEEN ⫸

Dylan was crouched on the floor near the foot of the bed, picking up broken glass, when the French doors opened softly into the bedroom.

'Dylan?'

It was a female voice, the one she'd heard talking quietly with Rio and another man in the other room a minute ago. Dylan looked up and felt the instant warmth of a caring bright teal gaze light on her.

The beautiful young woman smiled. 'Hi. I'm Tess.'

'Hi.' Dylan set a glass shard off to the side and bent to retrieve another.

'Rio asked me to come in and see if you were all right.' Tess carried a small black leather bag as she came into the room. 'Are you okay?'

Dylan nodded. 'It's just a scratch.'

'Rio feels really awful about this. He's been having . . . problems for some time now. Ever since the warehouse explosion last summer. He's lucky to be alive.'

Oh, God. So that explained the burns and shrapnel scars. An explosion did all of that damage? He really had been through hell and back.

Tess went on. 'Because of his brain trauma from the blast, he blacks out from time to time. On top of that, he also has severe headaches, mood swings . . . well, I think you saw for yourself, it's no picnic. He didn't mean for you to get hurt, I promise you that.'

'I'm fine,' Dylan said, not about to worry over the scratch on her cheek. 'I tried to tell him it was no big deal. The cut's not bleeding anymore.'

'That's a relief,' Tess said as she set the medical satchel down on the bureau. 'I'm glad to see it's not as bad as Rio feared. The way he described it to me on the phone, I thought we were looking at half a dozen stitches at least. A little anti-septic and a bandage ought to do the trick.' She walked over to where Dylan had been collecting pieces of the shattered mirror. 'Here – let me help you with this.'

As she approached, Dylan noticed that Tess's palm rested lightly on the little swell of her stomach. She was pregnant. Not that far along from the looks of it, but she beamed with an inner radiance that left no doubt whatsoever.

And the hand that cradled the early stages of a growing baby bump had a small birthmark on it. Dylan couldn't help staring at the scarlet teardrop-and-crescent-moon shape on Tess's right hand – the very same mark Dylan herself had been born with on the nape of her neck.

'You live here?' Dylan asked. 'With . . . them?'

Tess nodded. 'I live with Dante. He's a warrior of the Order, like Rio and the others who live here at the compound.'

Dylan gestured to the tiny birthmark between Tess's thumb and forefinger. 'You're his . . . Breedmate?' she asked, recalling the term Rio had used after he'd seen Dylan's identical birth-mark. 'You're married to one of them?'

'Dante and I were mated last year,' Tess said. 'We're blood-bonded, which connects us in a way that's even deeper than marriage. I know Rio's told you a bit about the Breed – how they live, where they come from. After what happened in here with him, I'm sure you have no doubt about what they are.'

Dylan nodded, still incredulous that any of this could actually be true. 'Vampires.'

Tess smiled gently. 'That's what I thought too, at first. It's not that simple to define them. The Breed is a complicated race, living in a complicated world full of enemies. Things can be very dangerous for them, and for those of us who love them. For the few males who've pledged themselves to the Order, every night is a risk to their lives.'

'Was it an accident?' Dylan blurted out. 'The explosion that injured Rio . . . was it some kind of terrible accident?'

Something pained moved across the other woman's expression. She stared at Dylan for a long moment, as if she wasn't quite sure how much to say. But then she gave a slight shake of her head. 'No. It wasn't an accident. Someone close to Rio betrayed him. The explosion happened during a raid on an old warehouse in the city. Rio and the rest of the Order were ambushed.'

Dylan glanced down and she realized she was staring at the broken picture frame that Rio had hurtled across the room in his fit of rage. She carefully picked it up, flipped it over in her palms. Sweeping away the spiderweb of broken glass over the color snapshot, she stared down at the exotic dark eyes and the smile that didn't quite reach them.

'Eva,' Tess confirmed. 'She was Rio's Breedmate.'

'But she betrayed him?'

'She did,' Tess said after a long pause. 'Eva made a deal with one of the Order's enemies – a powerful vampire who was also the brother of the Order's leader, Lucan. For information that would help this vampire kill Lucan, something Eva wanted as much as Lucan's brother, she was assured of two things. That Rio would live, and that he would be wounded badly enough that he would never be able to fight again.'

'Jesus,' Dylan gasped. 'So she got what she wanted?'

'Not exactly. The Order was ambushed, based on information Eva delivered, but the vampire she bargained with had no intention of upholding his part of their deal. He sent in a bomb. The explosion might have killed them all, but ironically, Rio took the biggest hit. And then he had to learn afterward that it was Eva who made it happen.'

Dylan couldn't speak. She tried to absorb the weight of what it must have been like for him – not only the physical pain of his injuries, but also the emotional hurt of a deception like the one dealt to him.

'I saw her.' Dylan glanced over at Tess and saw her frown deepen, confusion evident in her questioning gaze. Dylan hadn't known this woman for more than a few minutes, and she wasn't used to sharing herself with anyone, especially not the secret that made her so different from other people. But something in Tess's caring eyes let her know that she was safe. She felt an instant affinity that made her trust she was with a friend. 'The dead come to me from time to time – well, women do, anyway. Women who are no longer living. Eva came to me a few days ago when I was hiking with friends on a mountain outside Prague.'

'She . . . came to you,' Tess said cautiously. 'How do you mean?'

'I saw her spirit, I guess you'd say. She led me to a hidden cave. I didn't know it, but Rio was inside. She – Eva – led me there and asked me to save him.'

'My God.' Tess slowly shook her head. 'Does he know this?'

Dylan glanced meaningfully at the destruction lying at her feet. 'Yeah, he knows. When I told him, that's when he really lost it.'

Tess's look was apologetic. 'He has a lot of anger where Eva's concerned.'

'Understandably,' Dylan replied. 'Is he okay, Tess? I mean, considering what he's gone through, is Rio going to be . . . okay?'

'I hope so. We all hope so.' Tess cocked her head slightly, studying her somehow. 'You're not afraid of him.'

No, she wasn't. She was curious about him absolutely, and uncertain of his intentions where she was concerned, but she wasn't afraid of him. Crazy as it was, even after seeing him as he'd been a short while ago in this very room, Dylan wasn't afraid. In fact, just thinking about Rio did a lot of things to her, none of them scary. 'Do you think I should be afraid of him?'

'No,' Tess said without hesitation. 'What I mean is, this can't be easy on you. God knows I didn't take it very well when I first heard all of this talk of blood and fangs and war.'

Dylan shrugged. 'I write for a quasi-tabloid newpaper. Believe me, I've heard a lot of bizarre things. I don't shock easily.'

Tess smiled, but she didn't hold Dylan's gaze for long. The words she didn't say were clear as a bell in those quickly averted eyes: This wasn't just a bizarre tabloid story. This was real.

'What was in that cave, Tess? It was apparently some kind of crypt – a hibernation chamber, I heard Rio call it. But what the hell was in there? Did something get loose up there on the mountainside?'

Tess lifted her eyes, but only gave a small shake of her head. 'I don't think you really want to know.'

'Yes, I do,' Dylan insisted. 'Whatever it was, it's obviously important enough that Rio felt he had to kidnap me and lock me up to keep me quiet about what I saw.'

Tess's silence put a knot of dread in Dylan's gut. The Breedmate knew what was in that cave, and the knowledge of it clearly terrified her.

'Tess, something was sleeping in that hidden tomb – from the look of it, I'd say it had been holed up there for a very long time. What kind of creature was it . . . or *is* it?'

Tess stood up and dropped some broken glass into a waste-basket beside the bureau. 'Let me take a look at your cut. We should clean it up and get a bandage on it so you don't scar.'

Confined within the UV light cell, the Ancient threw his head back and let out a hellish roar. Blood dripped off the huge fangs and onto the broad, naked chest that was livid with the pulsing color of the vampire's *glyphs*.

'Lock down those damn restraints,' barked his keeper, speaking to his Minions through a small microphone in the observation room outside the cell. 'And for crissake, clean up that mess in there.'

The robotic shackles snaked out sharply and caught the Ancient's thick arms and legs. With a programmic command, they seized up tight, yanking him nearly off his feet. He struggled against the bonds, but he wasn't going anywhere. Thrashing futilely, he peeled back his lips and bellowed again. The wordless howl was one of unmistakable fury as his immense body was dominated by industrial-grade titanium and steel.

He was still erect from the breeding that had gone so violently wrong, still lusting for blood and for the body of the lifeless fe-male that was being hastily – and posthumously – evacuated from the cage.

The Breedmate had been savaged. Hard nails and fangs left their mark all over her, and before the Ancient could be pulled off her, the female was dead. She wasn't the first, not even close. Over the nearly five decades since the Ancient had been awakened from his hibernation and brought under his keeper's control, feeding him – and breeding him – had proven to be a very costly, frustrating endeavor.

For all the technology and money at his disposal, there was no science in existence that could replace the kind of base rutting that had taken place in the prisoner's cell a short while ago. Flesh on flesh coupling was the only viable means of conception when it came to the Ancient, and the rest of the Breed as well. But sex was only part of the process. It took ejaculation, along with a simultaneous exchange of blood at that precise moment, for vampire life to take root in a Breedmate female's body.

Normally, bonded couples looking to conceive reveled in the deliberate, sensual act of creating life. Not so in this place. Down here, with the savage, alien creature rendered insane from starvation, pain, and confinement, conception was a life-and-death gamble. Casualties like the one today were part of the equation. Deaths were to be expected.

But there had been successes, and that made all the risk worthwhile. For every Breedmate killed in this process, two others made it out alive . . . with the seeds of a powerful new generation planted deep in their wombs.

The Ancient's keeper smiled privately despite the day's loss.

That powerful new generation was already growing, coming of age in secret.

And its allegiance belonged entirely to him.

⊰ CHAPTER EIGHTEEN ⊱

Rio killed the last couple of hours before dawn topside in the estate's back courtyard with Dante, then headed below to the compound for some alone time in the chapel. The quiet little sanctuary where the Order carried out their most important and personal ceremonies had always been a haven for him. Not now. All he saw in the candlelit space were reminders of Eva's deception.

Because of her, over a year ago they'd had to anoint and shroud one of the Order's most noble members in funeral white and place him on the altar at the front of the rows of pews. Conlan's death in a subway tunnel last summer had been unintentional – the misfortune of being in the wrong place at the wrong time – but his blood was on Eva's hands.

Rio could still see her standing in the chapel at his side, clinging to him and weeping, yet all the while hiding her deceit. Waiting until the next chance she got to collude with the Order's enemies as part of some misguided attempt to see Rio pulled from the Order – even by seeing him maimed – so he could finally belong to her alone.

The irony of it was, he never would have left the Order.

He didn't want to now, and wouldn't, if he felt the least bit useful to the warriors who'd been like kin to him for nearly a century. If he hadn't been robbed of his sanity and his self-control by the blast that might have – should have – killed him.

'Shit,' he muttered, pivoting around to get the hell out of the chapel.

He didn't need to linger there any longer with his old ghosts or the misery they brought him. All it took to revive Eva in his mind was a glance in a mirror or a reflection in a window. He tried damn hard not to do that, not only because of the shock of seeing what stared back at him, but also because he wanted Eva severed from his life completely. Just hearing her name was enough to send him into a fit of uncontrollable rage.

As Dylan could unfortunately attest.

He wondered if she was okay. Tess would have taken excellent care of her, even if her healing touch was absent now that she was pregnant.

But still, Rio wondered. He hated himself for the way he'd reacted. Dylan was probably feeling likewise. If she wasn't too busy pitying him for the mental train wreck he'd proven himself to be.

Feeling as alone and detached as a ghost himself, Rio wandered away from the compound's chapel and down the labyrinth of corridors until he reached the empty infirmary. He took a quick shower in the medical recovery room that had been his home during the months following the explosion, letting the hot water wash away the aches in his muscles and the rising pound in his temples.

And as he cut the spray and toweled off, his thoughts returned to Dylan. It wasn't doing her any good at all to be kept here against her will. And getting her gone meant he had to get that story of hers derailed ASAP.

It was morning now, which may mean lights out for the Breed, but not for the humans living topside. They'd be going about their usual weekday habits, which meant one more day for Dylan's boss at the paper to think about running her story. One more day for the women Dylan had been traveling with to talk about the cave she'd found and speculate on what it might have contained. One more day for Rio's fuckup to put the Order and all of the vampire nation in jeopardy of discovery by humankind.

He threw on a pair of loose navy warm-ups and a tank that were still folded in the closet with a few other things left-over from his extended stay in the infirmary wing. When he stepped into the corridor and navigated his way back to his quarters, it was with new purpose. His head was clearer now, and he was good and ready to get Dylan working on the kibosh to that cave story before another minute passed.

Except when he opened the door to his private apartments, the place was dark. Only a small table lamp glowed in the corner of the living room, like a night light left on for him in case he came back. He glared at the welcome little glow as he slipped inside and quietly shut the door.

Dylan was sleeping. He could see her in his bed in the other room, curled up on top of the duvet. No doubt she was exhausted. The past three days had to have taken a toll on her. Hell, they'd taken a toll on him too.

He walked into the dark bedroom and promptly forgot all about his original purpose in coming into the apartment as he got an eyeful of Dylan's long, bare legs. She was wearing a babydoll tee-shirt and pastel plaid boxers, stuff evidently taken out of her travel bag, which lay open next to the bed.

The cotton combo was nothing overtly sexy as far as sleep-wear went – certainly nothing close to the expensive scraps of lace and satin that Eva used to parade around in for him. But damn if Dylan didn't look good in next to nothing . . . and look good sleeping in his bed.

Cristo, far too good.

Rio pulled a silk throw from a chair in the corner of the room and carried it over to the bed to cover her up. He wasn't doing it merely to be courteous. As one of the Breed, his vision was even sharper in the dark. All of his senses were more acute, and at the moment, they were conspiring to kill him with input about the half-naked female lying so vulnerably within his reach.

He tried not to notice that her breasts were bare beneath the little cap-sleeved shirt, her nipples pressing deliciously against the thin cotton. The temptation to stare at her smooth white skin – especially the exposed wedge of her abdomen where the tee-shirt was twisted and riding up so nicely above her navel – was more than he could handle.

But as he neared the edge of the bed with the blanket, she stirred slightly, shifting her legs and rolling a little farther onto her back. Rio stood there, unmoving, praying she didn't wake up and find him looming over her like a phantom.

Looking at her put a hot ache in his chest. He had no claim on Dylan, but a surge of possession ran through his blood like several thousand volts of live electricity. She wasn't his – wouldn't be his, no matter what path she chose in the end. Whether she wanted a future living among the Breed in a Darkhaven or one lived topside without any recollection of Rio and his kind, she wasn't going to belong to him. She deserved better, that's for sure.

Another man – be he Breed or human – would be much better suited to care for a woman like Dylan. It would be another man's privilege to explore her soft curves and silky skin. Another man's pleasure to taste the delicate pulse that beat in the sweet hollow at the base of her throat. Only another Breed male should have the honor of piercing Dylan's veins with a tender, wholly reverent bite.

It would be the solemn vow of another – never him – to protect her from all harm and to sustain her faithfully and forever with the blood and strength of his immortal body.

Not his right at all, Rio thought grimly as he placed the

blanket over her as lightly as he could. Not one damn bit of her was his to desire.

But yet he did.

God, did he ever.

He burned with want, even knowing he shouldn't. Rio told himself it was purely accidental that his hands brushed along her curves as he dragged the silk coverlet higher. He didn't mean to let his fingers trail through her soft hair, the flame-red waves dampened slightly from a recent washing. He couldn't resist smoothing his thumb along the fine slope of her cheek and over the velvety skin below her ear.

And there was no biting back his whispered curse as his gaze lit on the small bandage that covered the cut he'd given her.

Shit. This was all he truly had to offer her – pain and apologies. And the only reason she was letting him get this close to her now was because she didn't know he was there.

Wasn't awake to see the beast standing over her in the dark, stealing touches and contemplating what it would be like to do far more. Wanting her so badly that his fangs were biting into his tongue, and his lust-changed eyes were throwing off some seriously intense amber light. Those Breed high beams were bathing her in a burnished glow, illuminating every dip and swell and delectable curve.

He drew his hand away from her and she stirred, probably from the heat of his transformed gaze. A quick downward sweep of his lids cut the twin spotlights, plunging the room into total darkness again.

Rio backed away from her without making a sound.

Then he crept out of the bedroom before he could prove himself any more of the thief he feared he could easily become when it came to this female.

At first Dylan thought it was the touch that woke her, but the tender fingers caressing her cheek had been a soothing warmth that made sleep feel more luxurious. It was the abrupt absence of that warmth that pulled her out of what had been a very pleasant dream.

She opened her eyes, seeing nothing but darkness in the bedroom.

Rio's bedroom.

Rio's bed.

She sat up at the realization, feeling awkward as hell that she'd fallen asleep here after taking a shower earlier that night. Or was it day? She didn't know, and couldn't tell, since there were no windows to be found in all two-thousand-plus square feet of Rio's apartment.

The place was dark and still, but Dylan didn't think she was alone.

'Hello?'

A whole lot of quiet was all she heard in response.

She peered out toward the living room and noticed that the lamp she'd left on was off now. And someone definitely had been in here at some point, because whoever it was had covered her with a light blanket that used to be draped over one of the bedroom chairs.

It was Rio. She knew it absolutely.

It had been him beside the bed not a moment ago. His touch that had felt so good against her skin, and so cold when it was gone.

Dylan pivoted around and put her bare feet on the floor. She padded to the closed French doors, opening them softly as she strained to see anything in the lightless living room on the other side.

'Rio . . . are you asleep?'

She didn't ask if he was there; she knew he was. She could feel his presence in the way her heart was racing, blood speeding through her veins. Dylan walked across the carpeted floor to where she remembered seeing a squat ginger jar lamp on a little writing desk. She felt her way there, reaching out carefully for the cold porcelain base of the lamp.

'Leave it off.'

Dylan swiveled her head toward the sound of Rio's voice. He was to her right, near the center of the room. Now that her eyes were adjusting to the lack of light, she could see him in the large, dark form seated on the velvet sofa, his body and long limbs devouring the petite lines of the furniture.

'You can have your bed. I didn't mean to fall asleep there.'

She walked deeper into the room . . . and heard a low growl rumble from his direction.

Oh, God. She froze where she was standing, just a few steps away from the sofa. Was he in the throes of another meltdown like earlier? Or had he not fully recovered from that one yet?

Dylan cleared her throat. Braved another step toward him. 'Are you . . . um, do you . . . need anything? Because if there's something I can do—'

'God*damn* it!' The sound of his voice was more desperate than angry. He pulled one of his faster-than-you-can-blink maneuvers, shooting up off the sofa and moving back against the far wall. As far as he could get from her. 'Dylan, please. Just go back to bed. You need to stay away from me.'

That was probably really good advice. Staying away from a vampire with a traumatic brain injury and a nuclear-grade level of uncontrollable rage was probably about the smartest thing she could do. Yet Dylan's feet kept moving, like all her common sense and survival instincts had packed up and gone on a sudden vacation.

'I'm not afraid of you, Rio. I don't think you're going to hurt me.'

He didn't say anything to confirm or deny it. Dylan could hear him breathing – if the sharp, shallow panting qualified as such. She felt like she was walking up on a wounded wild animal, unsure if reaching out to him was going to win her a bit of uneasy trust or a vicious taste of fang and claw.

'You were in the bedroom with me a few minutes ago . . . weren't you?' She inched steadily forward, undaunted by the weight of his silence or the darkness that concealed him in shadow. 'You touched me. I felt your hand on my face. I . . . I liked it, Rio. I didn't want you to stop.'

He hissed a nasty, violent curse. She felt rather than saw his head come up sharply. There was a pause, and then he must have opened his eyes because the darkness was suddenly pierced by two glowing embers aimed straight at her.

'Your eyes . . .' she murmured, caught like a moth in a flame.

She'd seen Rio's eyes transform from topaz to amber when he'd stumbled into his quarters a few hours ago, but this . . . this was different. There was a smoldering quality to them now, something other than anger or pain. More intense, if that was possible.

Dylan couldn't move, just stood there in the heated path of Rio's gaze, feeling it rake her body from head to toe. Her heart flipped and stuttered as that amber gaze burned over her, into her.

Now he was moving, striding toward her with slow, predatory grace.

'Why did you come up on that mountain?' he asked her, his voice harsh, accusing.

Dylan swallowed, watching him approach her in the dark. She started to say that it was Eva who sent her there, but that was only partly true. The ghost that was Eva had showed her the way, but Dylan returned to the cave because of Rio.

As much as anything – including the job she thought she might be saving with her story of a demon in the Bohemian hills – it was Rio who compelled her to stay in the cave and try to reach out to him when good sense would have told her to flee. It was he who compelled her now, desire for him keeping her feet rooted to the floor when fear should have been sending her running as fast as she could in the opposite direction.

He was right in front of her now, still masked by darkness except for the eerie, seductive glow of his vampire eyes.

'Goddamn it, Dylan. Why did you come up there?' His hands were firm as he took hold of her upper arms. He gave her a little shake, but he was the one who trembled. 'Why? Why did you have to be the one?'

She knew the kiss was coming, even in the dark, but the initial press of his mouth on hers went through Dylan like an uncontained flame. It seared her, hot desire shooting into her core. She melted, losing herself in the brush of Rio's lips – and, oh, Christ – his fangs. She felt the pointed tips of them as he pushed her mouth open with his tongue, forcing her to take what he had to give her now.

Dylan wasn't about to fight it. She'd never known anything as erotic as the graze of Rio's fangs as he kissed her. There was so much lethal power in him; she could feel it, coiled and dangerous, but on the very knife's edge of breaking loose. Rio held her tightly, kissed her harshly, and Dylan had never been so turned on in all her life.

He pushed her down onto the sofa behind her, his strong hands braced at her back to ease the fall. He went with her, the weight of his hard body bearing her down beneath him. She could feel the thick ridge of his sex. It felt enormous and stiff as stone where it wedged between their bodies. Dylan ran her hands up his back, slipping them under the cotton tank he wore so she could feel the flex of his strong muscles as he moved atop her.

'I want to see you,' she gasped in between his hungry kisses. 'I need to see you, Rio . . .'

She didn't wait for his permission.

Casting her hand about, she found the lamp beside the sofa and clicked it on. Soft yellow light bathed the room in illumination. Rio was poised above her, straddling her hips with his knees as he stared down at her in what looked to be pure misery.

His eyes were glowing fiery amber. His features were drawn taut, his jaw held locked but not quite able to mask the astonishing length or sharpness of his fangs. The *dermaglyphs* on his shoulders and arms were churning with color – beautiful, deep saturations in a range of burgundy, indigo, and gold.

And his scars . . . well, she saw them too. Couldn't really ignore them, and she didn't try to.

Dylan came up onto one elbow and reached up to him with her other hand. He flinched, turning his face to the left like he meant to hide his ruined cheek. But Dylan wasn't about to let him hide. Not now. Not from her. She reached out again, tenderly placing her palm against the hard line of his jaw.

'Don't,' he said thickly.

'It's okay.' She gently turned him to face her full-on. With the utmost care, she lightly caressed the scarred skin. She followed the damage to his body, smoothing her fingers down the side of his neck, to his shoulder and biceps, over the skin that had once been as smooth and flawless as the rest of him. 'Does it hurt for me to touch you like this?'

He said something, but it came out strangled, unintelligible.

Dylan sat up fully, lifting herself until her face was level with his. She held his gaze, making sure those thin, catlike pupils stayed rooted on her eyes as she softly stroked his cheek, his jaw, his wonderfully sensual mouth.

'Don't look at me, Dylan,' he croaked, the very thing he'd said before, she realized now. 'Fuck . . . how can you look at me so closely – how can you put your hands on me – and not be revolted?'

Dylan's heart squeezed up like a fist in her breast. 'I'm looking at you, Rio. I see you. I'm touching you. *You,*' she said with emphasis.

'These scars—'

'Are incidental,' she finished for him. She smiled as she glanced down at his mouth and at the perfectly white, perfectly incredible pair of fangs that had sprouted from his gums. 'Your scars are the most ordinary thing about you, if you want to know the truth.'

His lip curled back as if he were going to push her away with more talk of his perceived defects, but Dylan didn't give him the chance. She held his face in her hands and leaned in close, giving him a deep, unhurried, passionate kiss.

She moaned as his hands wove into her hair and he kissed her back.

Dylan wanted him so fiercely, she could hardly stand it. God, the whole thing made no sense – this craving she had for a man she hardly knew and for so many reasons should be terrified of, not kissing like there was no tomorrow.

But she didn't want to stop kissing Rio. She put her arms around his shoulders and drew him down with her, back onto the sofa. His hair was silky against her palm, his mouth hot and questing on hers. His hand was strong but gentle as he slipped beneath the hem of her tee-shirt and smoothed his palm up her stomach and then over her bare breasts. Dylan writhed as he caressed her, his fingers teasing her nipples into hard, aching buds while his tongue played along the seam of her mouth.

'Oh, God,' she gasped, burning for him already.

He wedged himself deeper between her thighs, spreading her wide with his knees and grinding his stiff erection against her through their clothes. She nearly came from the delicious friction of their bodies. Good Christ, she was going to climax for sure if he kept up that fluid rhythm that left no doubt as to what kind of lover he would be once they had their clothes off.

Dylan lifted her feet and locked her ankles around his hips, letting him know that she was willing to go wherever he wanted to take this. She wasn't used to throwing herself at a man's feet – could hardly remember the last time she'd had sex at all, let alone good sex – but she could think of nothing she wanted more than to be making love with Rio. Right here. Right now.

He sucked her lower lip between his teeth as he rolled his hips against hers. She reveled in the graze of his fangs, in the hard, driving thrust of his body and the flex of his muscles under her palms. He slid his hand between her legs, his fingers cleaving her wet, hot flesh, and Dylan could not hold back the cry that curled up from her throat.

'Yes,' she hissed sharply as an orgasm rolled up on her out of nowhere. 'Oh, God . . . Rio . . .'

She was spiraling inside, lost in pleasure, and clutching Rio as her core pulsed with her release. She heard his wild sounding growl, registered dimly that he had broken their kiss to let his lips wander down along the column of her throat. She wrapped her arms around him as he nuzzled her neck, his tongue playing hotly against her tender skin.

The rough stroke of his teeth in that spot startled her.

She tensed, even though she didn't want to be afraid of what might come next. But she couldn't call back the automatic reaction, and Rio drew away from her as if she'd screamed at the top of her lungs.

'I'm sorry,' she whispered, reaching for him but he was already gone, moving off her and taking himself more than an arm's length from the sofa. Dylan sat up, feeling oddly bereft. 'I'm sorry, Rio. I just wasn't sure . . .'

'Don't apologize,' he muttered sullenly. '*Madre de Dios*, do not apologize to me, please. This was my fault, Dylan.'

'No,' she said, desperate that he stay with her. 'I want this, Rio.'

'You shouldn't,' he said. 'And I would not have been able to stop.'

He raked his hand through his dark hair, staring at her with those blazing amber eyes. 'This would have been a terrible mistake for both of us,' he said after a long moment. 'Ah, fuck. It already is a terrible mistake.'

Before she could say anything, Rio simply turned around and left. As the apartment door closed behind him, Dylan pulled her tee-shirt back down and adjusted her skewed boxers. In the quiet he left her with, she pulled her knees up to her chest and wrapped her arms around her shins, then reached over and clicked off the lamp.

⇥ CHAPTER NINETEEN ⇤

Rio lifted a 9mm pistol and aimed it toward a target at the end of the compound's firing range. The gun felt foreign as hell in his hand despite that it was his own weapon, one he'd carried on him for years and had been lethally proficient with . . . before.

Before the warehouse explosion.

Before the injuries that had taken him out of combat and dropped him into a sickbed, broken in mind and body.

Before his blindness to Eva's duplicity had made him question everything he was and ever could be again.

A sheen of sweat broke out on Rio's lip as he held his target in his sights. His trigger finger was shaky, and it took all his concentration to focus in on the small head-and-shoulders silhouette printed on the paper target some twenty yards down the range.

But that was exactly the point of his coming here.

After what had happened with Dylan a few minutes ago, Rio needed a distraction in a major way. Something that would command all of his focus, cool him out. Hopefully dull the edge of the carnal hunger that gnawed at him even now. He wanted Dylan with a need that was still pounding through his veins in a deep, primal beat.

He could still feel her body moving beneath his, so soft and welcoming. So passionately responsive. So accepting of him, even though he was fit only to play Beast to her Beauty.

It was a fantasy he'd let himself indulge in as he'd kissed Dylan, as he pressed her down beneath him and wondered if the intense attraction he felt for her might actually be mutual. No one was that good an actor. Eva had claimed to love him once. The depth of her betrayal had been a shock, but in the back of his mind, he'd known she wasn't happy with him the way he was, in the life he'd chosen as a warrior.

She hadn't wanted him to join in the first place. She'd never understood his need to do some good, his need to be useful. More than once, she'd asked him why she wasn't enough for him. Why loving her, making her happy, couldn't be enough. He had wanted both, but even she had been able to see that he wanted the Order more.

Rio could still recall one night, strolling in a city park with Eva, taking pictures of her on a little bridge over the river. She'd told him that night how she wanted him to leave the Order and give her a baby. Demands he couldn't – or, rather, wouldn't – comply with.

Give it time, he'd told her. The warriors had been putting out fires with a small surge in Rogue activity in the region, so he'd told her to be patient. Once things settled down, maybe they could think about a family.

Looking back, he wasn't sure he'd meant it. Eva hadn't believed him; he'd seen that in her eyes, even then. Hell, maybe it had been at that very moment she'd decided to take matters into her own hands.

He had let Eva down and he knew it. But she had paid him back in spades. Her betrayal had rattled him on a soul-deep level. It had made him question everything, including why the hell he should be taking up precious space in this world.

When Dylan kissed him – when she looked at him full in the face and her eyes reflected back only honesty – Rio could believe, at least for a moment, that he wasn't just a pitiful waste of air and space. When he'd looked into Dylan's eyes and felt her hand cradling his scars, he could believe life might actually be worth living after all.

And he was a selfish bastard for thinking that he had anything to offer a woman like her. He'd already destroyed one woman's life, and nearly his own; he wasn't about to take a second chance with Dylan's life.

Rio narrowed his gaze on the target down the way and forced an iron steadiness into his hold on the gun. He pulled the trigger, felt the familiar kick of his weapon as the Beretta discharged and a bullet went blasting into the smallest center ring of the target's bull's-eye.

'Good to see you haven't lost a bit of your aim. Still dead-on like always.'

Rio set the weapon down on the shelf in front of him. When he turned around it was to find Nikolai standing behind him, his broad back leaned up against the wall. Rio had known he wasn't alone here; he'd heard Niko and the three other unmated warriors talking on the far end of the facility as they cleaned their weapons and rehashed their late-night prowl of the human after-hours club.

'How was the hunting topside?'

Niko shrugged. 'A lot of the usual.'

'Hot babes without enough sense to run when they see you coming?' Rio asked, a tentative stab at breaking the ice that was present between them since his arrival at the compound.

To his relief, Niko chuckled. 'Nothing wrong with loose and easy when it comes to women, my man. Maybe next time you should hang with us. I can hook you up with something sweet and nasty.' Twin dimples notched his lean cheeks. 'You know, if you're not planning to off yourself or anything in the meantime. You dumb bastard.'

It was said without venom, only the solemn knowledge of a friend concerned about one of his own.

'I'll let you know,' Rio said, and he could tell by Nikolai's narrowed look that the warrior understood he wasn't talking about the prospect of getting a little action topside.

Niko's voice dropped to a confidential tone. 'You can't let her win, you know? 'Cause that's what giving up is. Yeah, she screwed you over, and I'm not saying you need to forgive and forget because frankly I don't think I could if I were you. But you're still here. So fuck *her*,' Niko said harshly. 'Fuck Eva. And fuck the bomb that went off in that warehouse. Because you, my friend, are still here.'

Rio scoffed, but it was a weak sound in his tight throat. He tried to clear the obstruction, feeling awkward as hell for caring that someone cared about him. 'Damn, amigo. Just how much Oprah have you been watching since I've been gone? Because coming from you, that was really touching.'

Niko chortled. 'On second thought, forget all that shit I just said. Fuck you too.'

Rio laughed, the first real laugh to come out of his mouth . . . Jesus, in about a full year's time.

'Hey, Niko.' Kade came strolling up from the other end of the facility, the Alaskan's black spiky hair and sharp silver eyes giving him a wild, wolflike look. 'I'm turning in. Tonight if we run into that other Rogue out of the Darkhavens, don't forget you promised he was mine.'

'If I don't get to the suckhead first,' Brock put in, coming up behind the other warrior and smiling as he artfully placed the edge of a huge dagger under Kade's chin.

Brock's rich chuckle boomed out of him good-naturedly enough, but it was plain to see that the warrior the Order had recruited from Detroit would be as grim and thorough as the Reaper himself in combat. He let Kade go, and the two of them continued to argue over dibs on the Rogue as they headed out of the weapons room to their own separate corners of the compound.

Chase was the last to come around from the back of the facility. His black tee-shirt had a long rip down the front, like someone had tried to get a piece of him. Judging by the sated color of the vampire's *glyphs* and the chilled-out look in his normally hard-ass eyes, it appeared he'd taken his fill of everything the club girls were offering topside tonight.

He gave Rio a slight incline of his head in greeting, then spoke to Nikolai. 'If you hear anything more out of Seattle, let me know. I'm curious why a killing of this nature hasn't been acknowledged by the Agency yet.'

'Yeah,' Niko said. 'I'd like to know that myself.'

Rio frowned. 'Who turned up dead in Seattle?'

'One of the longest-standing members of the Darkhaven out there,' Niko said. 'The guy was Gen One, in fact.'

The hairs at the back of Rio's neck did a sudden ten-hut at that bit of news. 'How was he killed?'

Nikolai's look was grave. 'Bullet to the brain, point-blank range.'

'Where?'

'Typically the brain is located in the head region,' Chase drawled, his thick arms crossed over his chest.

Rio slid a narrowed glare on the male. 'Thanks for the anatomy lesson, Harvard. I mean where was this Gen One at when he was killed?'

Niko met Rio's sober look. 'Shot in the backseat of his chauffeured limousine. My contact said the poor bastard was returning from the opera or the ballet or some damn thing, and while he was waiting at a traffic light, someone popped him in the head and vanished before the driver even realized what had happened. Why?'

Rio shrugged. 'Maybe nothing, but when I was in Berlin, Andreas Reichen told me about a Gen One killing that happened recently over there. Only this Darkhaven elder ate it at a blood club.'

'Those private sports clubs have been outlawed for decades,' Chase said.

'Right,' Rio agreed, all sarcasm, since the ex–Darkhaven Agent seemed intent on being a prick. 'So now they print the invitations in invisible ink and you need a secret decoder ring to get past the door.'

'Same MO on the Berlin Gen One?' Niko asked.

'No, not a gunshot wound. According to Reichen's sources, this sports lover ended up losing his head.'

Niko whistled low under his breath. 'That's two of the top three methods for killing a first generation Breed vampire. Option Three being UV exposure, and let's face it, the least effective way unless you have a leisurely ten to fifteen minutes to devote to your work.'

'The two killings could be unrelated,' Rio said, not sure his instincts could be trusted on this anyway. But damn if warning bells weren't clamoring in his head like a cathedral belfry on Easter Sunday.

'Something's off,' Chase said, finally getting with the program. 'I don't like the feel of this either. Two dead Gen Ones in a matter of, what, a week's time? And both of them smelling like executions?'

'We don't know that's what they were,' Niko cautioned. 'Come on, think of the odds here. If you live for a thousand years or so, you're bound to piss someone off. Someone who might want to shoot you in the back of your limo, or guillotine you at a blood club.'

'And the Darkhavens don't want word of either slaying going public?' Rio added.

Chase's tawny brows came together tightly. 'Berlin's on hush mode, too?'

'Yeah. Reichen said they were keeping it quiet to avoid a scandal. Doesn't look good to anyone if a pillar of your community gets toppled in a sports club full of blooded, dead humans.'

'No, it doesn't,' Chase agreed. 'But two dead Gen Ones is a pretty serious hit to the entire vampire nation. There can't be more than twenty first generation individuals still alive among the entire population – Lucan and Tegan included. Once they're gone, they're gone.'

Nikolai nodded. 'That's true. And it's not like we can make any more.'

A chilling thought sank into Rio's gut. 'Not unless we had a live Ancient, a Breedmate, and about twenty years' lead time.'

Both warriors looked at him with grave expressions.

Niko raked a hand through his blond hair. 'Ah, fuck. You don't think—'

'I pray to God I'm wrong,' Rio said. 'But we'd better wake Lucan.'

❧ CHAPTER TWENTY ❧

Being alone after Rio left had made Dylan restless as hell. Her mind was spinning, emotions churning. And she couldn't help thinking about her life back in New York. She had to let her mother know that she was all right at the very least.

Flipping on a lamp, Dylan padded into the bedroom and retrieved her cell phone from its hiding place. She'd practically forgotten about it since she arrived there, having taken it out of her pants pocket and stuffed it under the mattress of Rio's bed the first chance she'd gotten to ditch the thing for safekeeping.

She powered it up, trying to muffle the musical chime as the phone came alive. It was a miracle there was any juice left in the battery at all, but she figured the single bar of remaining power was better than nothing.

Voice mail waiting, the illuminated display informed her.

She had service again.

Oh, thank God.

The number for call-back on the first voice mail was a New York exchange – one of Coleman Hogg's office lines. She retrieved the message and wasn't a bit surprised to hear him sputter and curse about her rudeness in standing up his freelance photographer in Prague.

Dylan skipped the rest of his diatribe and went to the next message. It was her mom, received two days ago, just calling to check in and say she loved her and hoped she was having fun. She sounded tired, that feathery quality to her voice making Dylan's heart go tight in her chest.

There was another message from her boss. This time he was even more angry. He was docking her pay for the cameraman's fee, and he was considering the e-mail he'd received from her about taking extra time abroad to be her resignation. Effective immediately, Dylan was unemployed.

'Great,' she muttered under her breath as she skipped to the next call.

She couldn't really get worked up over the loss of the job itself, but the lack of a paycheck was going to hurt real quick. Unless she found something better, something bigger. Something monumental. Something with real teeth . . . or fangs, as it were.

'No,' she told herself sharply before the idea could fully form in her mind.

No way could she take this story public now. Not when she still had more questions than answers – when she had become a part of the story herself, bizarre as it was to think that.

And then there was Rio.

If she needed one reason to protect what she'd learned about another species existing alongside humankind, he was it. She didn't want to betray him, or put his kind at risk of any sort. She was past that, now that she was coming to know him. Now that she was coming to care for him, as dangerous as that might prove to be.

What happened between them a short while ago rattled her big-time. The kiss had been amazing. The feel of Rio's body pressed so intimately against hers had been the hottest thing she'd ever known. And the feel of his teeth – his fangs – grazing the fragile skin of her neck had been both terrifying and erotic. Would he really have bitten her? And if he had, what would it have done to her?

Based on how fast he bolted out of the room, she didn't expect she would ever have those answers. And really, she shouldn't feel so empty at the thought.

What she needed to do was get herself out of this place – wherever she was – and get back to her own life. Back to being there for her mom, who was probably going crazy with worry now that Dylan had been out of touch for three full days.

The next three incoming calls had been from the runaway shelter, all received yesterday and last night. There were no messages, but the close timing of them seemed to indicate some urgency.

Dylan hit the speed-dial button for her mom's house and waited as the phone rang unanswered on the other end. No answer on her mom's cell phone either. With her heart in her throat, Dylan brought up the number for the shelter. Janet picked up her mom's extension.

'Good morning. Sharon Alexander's office.'

'Janet, hi. It's Dylan.'

'Oh . . . hi, honey. How are you doing?' The question sounded oddly careful, as if Janet already knew – or thought she knew – that Dylan was probably not having a good day. 'Are you at the hospital?'

'The what – no.' Dylan's stomach sank. 'What's going on? Is it Mom? What's wrong?'

'Oh, Lord,' Janet breathed softly. 'You mean, you don't know? I thought Nancy was going to call you . . . Where are you, Dylan – are you back home yet?'

'No,' she said, hardly aware she was talking for the cold ache opening up her chest. 'No, I'm, ah . . . I'm still out of town. Where's my mom, Janet? Is she okay? What's happened to her?'

'She'd been feeling a little run-down after the river cruise the other night, but yesterday afternoon she collapsed here at the shelter. Dylan, honey, she's not doing well right now. We took her to the hospital and they admitted her.'

'Oh, God.' Dylan's whole body felt numbed out, frozen in place. 'Is it a relapse?'

'They think so, yes.' Janet's voice was the quietest it had ever been. 'I'm so sorry, honey.'

Lucan hadn't been happy to be roused out of bed with Gabrielle in the middle of the day, but as soon as he heard the reason for the interruption, the Order's leader was all business, instantly snapped to attention. He'd thrown on a pair of dark jeans and an unbuttoned silk oxford, and came out to the corridor where Rio, Nikolai, and Chase waited.

'We're going to need Gideon to run some record checks,' Lucan said, flipping out his cell phone and speed-dialing the warrior's quarters. He murmured a greeting and an abrupt apology for the intrusion, then gave Gideon the same news Rio and the others had just shared with him. As the four of them headed down the hallway toward the tech lab, Gideon's personal command center, Lucan finished up the short conversation and snapped the cell phone shut. 'He's on the way. I sure hope like hell you're wrong about this, Rio.'

'So do I,' he said, no more eager than anyone else to consider the possibility.

It didn't take Gideon more than a couple of minutes to join the impromptu meeting. He came into the lab in gray sweats and a white muscle shirt, sneakers unlaced like he'd just shoved his feet into them and ran. He dropped ass into the wheeled swivel chair at his computer command center and started launching programs from several of the machines.

'Okay, we're sending feelers out to every reporting agency

and Darkhaven resident bank, including the International Identification Database,' he said, watching the monitors as data slowly began to scroll up on the screens. 'Huh. That's odd. You said one of the two dead Gen Ones was out of Seattle?'

Nikolai nodded.

'Well, not according to this. Seattle came back with zip – no recent deaths reported. No record of a Gen One in their population at all, although that alone isn't completely unheard of. The IID's only been around for a few decades, so it's by no means thorough. We have a few of the Breed's eldest members catalogued, but the majority of the twenty or so Gen Ones still breathing tend to be a bit protective of their privacy. Rumor has it that more than a couple of them are bona fide recluses who haven't been near a Darkhaven for a century or more. I guess they feel they've earned some autonomy after about a thousand or more years of living. Ain't that right, Lucan?'

Lucan, himself aged around nine hundred and not in the IID register, only grunted in response, his gray eyes narrowed on the computer monitors. 'What about Europe? Anything coming back on the Gen One that Reichen mentioned?'

Gideon banged out a lightning-fast sequence on his keyboard, burrowing into yet another secured software system like it was child's play. 'Shit. Nope, nothing showing up there either. I gotta tell you, this level of silence is eerie as hell.'

Rio had to agree. 'So, if no one's reporting Gen One deaths, there could actually be more than just the two we know of so far.'

'That's something we need to find out,' Lucan said. 'How many Gen Ones are registered in the IID across all Breed locations, Gideon?'

The warrior ran a quick search. 'I've got seven between

the States and Europe. I'm sending the report of names and Darkhaven affiliations to the printer now.'

When the single-page listing came off the laser, Gideon swiveled around and handed it to Lucan. He looked it over. 'Most of these names are familiar to me. I know of a couple more that aren't listed. Tegan can probably come up with a couple more too.' He put the list of data down on the meeting table so that Rio and the others could have a look. 'Any Gen One names you see missing from that list?'

Rio and Chase shook their heads.

'Sergei Yakut,' Niko murmured. 'I saw him once in Siberia when I was a kid. He was the first Gen One I ever knew – hell, the only one, until I came to Boston and met Lucan and Tegan. Yakut's name is not on this list.'

'You think you could find him if you had to?' Lucan asked. 'Assuming he's not already some long years dead, that is.'

Nikolai chuckled. 'Sergei Yakut is one mean son of a bitch. Too mean for death. I'm willing to bet he's still alive, and yeah, I think I could probably locate him if he is.'

'Good,' Lucan said, his expression dark. 'I want to get a handle on this fast. Just in case we are looking at a potential serial situation, we need to get names and locations of every Gen One in the population.'

'I'm sure the Enforcement Agency knows of a few more than what we have here,' Chase added. 'I've still got one or two friends left over there. Maybe someone knows something or can point me to someone who does.'

Lucan nodded. 'Yeah. Check it out, then. But I know I don't need to tell you to keep your cards close when you're dealing with them. You may have a few friends in the Agency, but the Order sure as shit doesn't. And no offense to you, Harvard, but I trust those useless Darkhaven ass-kissers about as far as I can drop-kick them.'

Lucan turned a serious look on Rio. 'As for the other potential you brought up – that the Ancient may be revived and being used to breed a new line of first generation vampires?' He shook his head and exhaled a low curse. 'Nightmare scenario, my friend. But it could very well be a solid one.'

'If it is,' Rio said, 'then we'd better hope we get a lead on it soon. And that we're not a couple of decades behind the bastard.'

It wasn't until after he'd said it that Rio realized he was using the word 'we' when talking about the warriors and their goals. He was including himself in his thinking about the Order. More than that, he was actually starting to feel a part of the whole again – a functioning, valid member – as he stood there with Lucan and the others, making plans, talking strategy.

It felt good, in fact.

Maybe there still could be a place for him here after all. He was a mess and he'd made some mistakes, but maybe he could get back to what he was before.

He was still reaching out for that hope as a little beep started up on one of Gideon's monitoring stations for the compound. The warrior wheeled over to the computer, frowning.

'What is it?' Lucan asked.

'I'm picking up an active cell phone signal here in the compound – not one of ours,' he replied, then looked over at Rio. 'It's outbound, originating from your quarters.'

Dylan.

'Holy fuck,' Rio ground out, anger spiking – at himself and at her. 'She said she didn't have one on her.'

Goddamn it. Dylan had lied to him.

And if he'd had his eye on the ball like he should, he would have body-searched her from head to toe before he so much as thought about taking the female at her word.

A reporter with a cell phone in her possession. For all he

knew she could be sitting in his apartments phoning in everything she'd seen and heard to CNN – exposing the Breed to
the humans and doing it right under his fucking nose.

'There was nothing in her bags to indicate she had a cell
with her,' Rio muttered, a feeble excuse and he knew it. 'Damn
it, I should have checked her over.'

Gideon typed something on one of his many control panels.
'I can throw up some interference, shut down the signal.'

'Do it,' Lucan said. Then, to Rio: 'We've got some loose
ends that need to be snipped, my man. Including the one
down the hall in your quarters.'

'Yeah,' Rio said, knowing Lucan was right. Dylan had a
decision to make, and time was getting crucial now that the
Order had other things to contend with.

Lucan put a hand on Rio's shoulder. 'I think it's time I
should meet Dylan Alexander personally.'

'Janet – hello? I didn't get Mom's room number. Hello . . .
Janet? Are you still there?'

Dylan pulled her cell phone away from her ear. *Signal failed.*
'Shit.'

She held the device out in front of her and started pacing
the room, looking for a spot where she might get a stronger
signal. But . . . nothing. The damn thing was dead, just
cut out on her even though the battery hadn't quite choked
yet.

She could hardly think straight for the panicked drum of
her pulse.

Her mom was in the hospital.

Relapse . . . Oh, God.

She narrowly resisted the urge to pitch the dead cell phone
into the nearest wall. 'Damn piece of shit!'

Frantic now, she headed out to the living room to try the
call again –

And nearly jumped out of her skin when the apartment door flew inward like it had been blown open by a storm force gale in the corridor. Rio stood there.

And good Lord, he was pissed off.

'Give it to me.'

His flashing amber eyes and emerging fangs put a knot of fear in her stomach, but she was pissed off too, and torn in pieces over her mother's turn for the worse. She needed to see her. Needed to get the hell out of this unreality she'd been kidnapped into and get back to the things that really mattered to her.

Jesus Christ, she thought, on the verge of losing it. *Her mom was sick again, and alone in some city hospital room. She had to get there.*

Rio strode into the room. 'The phone, Dylan. Give it to me. Now.'

It was then that she noticed he wasn't alone. Standing behind him in the corridor was a tank of a man – easily six-and-a-half feet tall, with a mane of black hair and an air of menace that belied his calm exterior. He hung back as Rio stalked inside and approached Dylan.

'Did you do something to my phone?' she demanded hotly, more than a little terrified of Rio and this new threat but too worried about her mom to care what might happen to her in the next minute. 'What did you do, make it stop working? Tell me! What the hell did you do!'

'You lied to me, Dylan.'

'And you fucking abducted me!' She hated the tears that suddenly ran down her cheeks. Almost as much as she hated her captivity and cancer and the cold ache in her chest that had opened up during her call to the shelter.

Rio put his hand out as he walked up to her. The man in the corridor prowled into the apartment now too. No question about it, he was a vampire – a Breed warrior, like Rio. His gray eyes seemed to penetrate her like blades, and in the same way an animal sensed a predator on the wind, Dylan sensed that where Rio was dangerous, this other man was exponentially more powerful. Older despite his youthful appearance. And more deadly.

'Who were you calling?' Rio demanded.

She wasn't about to tell him. She clutched the slim cell phone in her fist, but at that very instant she felt an energy force pulling at her fingers, prying them open. She couldn't keep them closed no matter how hard she tried. Dylan gasped as her cell phone flew out of her hand and onto the palm of the vampire now standing beside Rio.

'There's a couple of messages here from the newspaper,' he announced darkly. 'And several outgoing calls to other New York numbers. Residence of one Sharon Alexander, a cell number for the same, and a connected call to a blocked number in Manhattan. That's the one we shut down.'

Rio swore vividly. 'Did you tell anyone about us just now? Or about what you've seen?'

'No!' she insisted. 'I haven't said anything, I swear. I'm no threat to you—'

'There is the matter of the pictures you distributed, and the story you sent to your employer,' the dark one reminded her, the way you might remind the condemned of why they were heading for the gas chamber.

'You don't have to worry about any of that,' she said, ignoring Rio's harsh scoff as she spoke. 'That message from the newspaper? That was my boss, letting me know I was fired. Well, technically it was an involuntary resignation, on account of the fact I no-showed an appointment in Prague because I was busy being abducted.'

'You lost your job?' Rio asked, slanting her a scowl.

Dylan shrugged. 'It doesn't matter. But I doubt at this point my boss is going to use any of the pictures or the story I sent him.'

'That's no longer a concern.' The grim one stared at her like he was measuring her reaction. 'By now the virus program we sent him should have wiped out every hard drive in his office. He'll be putting out that fire for the rest of the week.'

She really didn't want to feel the least bit happy about that, but Coleman Hogg up to his quivering jowls in hard drive crashes was one tiny bright spot in an otherwise unbearable situation.

'The same virus went out to everyone you distributed those photos to,' he informed her. 'That takes care of any hard evidence leaks, but we still have to deal with the fact that several people are walking around with knowledge we can't afford to let them keep. Knowledge they could, willingly or unwittingly, pass on to others. So we need to remove that risk.'

Something icy settled in Dylan's gut. 'What do you mean . . . remove the risk?'

'You have a choice to make, Miss Alexander. Tonight you will either be relocated into one of the area's Darkhaven sanctuaries under the protection of the Breed, or you will be returned to your residence in New York.'

'I have to go home,' she said, no decision at all. She looked at Rio and found him staring at her, his face unreadable. 'I have to get back to New York right away. Do you mean I'm going to be free to go?'

That hard gray gaze turned to Rio now, without giving her an answer. 'Tonight you leave for Miss Alexander's home in New York. I want you to handle things with her; Niko and Kade can scrub the other folks she's been in contact with.'

'No!' Dylan blurted. The ice in her stomach suddenly turned into a glacial sort of fear. 'Oh, my God – no, you can't . . . Rio, tell him—'

'End of discussion,' the dark one said, directing his attention at Rio, not her. 'You'll leave at dusk.'

Rio nodded solemnly, accepting the orders like it didn't faze him at all. Like he'd done this sort of thing a hundred times before.

'As of tonight, Rio, no more loose ends.' The flinty eyes slid pointedly to Dylan, then back to Rio. 'Not one.'

As his terrifying friend departed, Dylan turned shakily to Rio. 'What did he mean, remove the risk? No more loose ends?'

Rio glowered over at her darkly. There was accusation in that piercing topaz gaze, a scathing coldness and very little of the wounded, tender man she'd been kissing in this very room just a short time ago. She felt cold under the blast of that hard glare, like she was looking into the face of a stranger.

'I'm not going to let you or your friends hurt anyone,' she told him, wishing her voice didn't falter as she said it. 'I'm not going to let you kill them!'

'No one's going to die, Dylan.' His tone was flat, so detached it was hardly reassuring. 'We're going to take their memory of what they saw in your photographs, and of anything you might have told them about the Breed or the cave. We're not going to hurt anyone, but we need to scrub their minds of any recollection of those things.'

'But how? I don't understand—'

'You don't have to understand,' he said softly.

'Because I'm not going to remember either. Is that what you mean?'

He looked at her for a long moment in silence. She searched his face for some hint of emotion beyond the stony resolve he projected. All she saw was a man fully prepared for the task he'd been given, a warrior committed to his mission. And none of the tenderness she'd seen in him before, or the need she thought he'd felt for her, was going to stand in his way. She was a captive at his mercy. An inconvenient problem he intended to eliminate.

Rio's brows came together slightly as he gave a vague shake of his head. 'Tonight you go home, Dylan.'

She should be happy to hear it – relieved, at least – but Dylan felt oddly bereft as she watched him leave the room and close the door behind him.

CHAPTER TWENTY-ONE

He came back for her after a couple of hours and told her it was time to go. Dylan wasn't surprised that her next conscious memory was waking up in the backseat of a dark SUV as Rio brought it to a stop at the curb outside her Brooklyn apartment building. As she sat up drowsily, Rio met her gaze in the rearview mirror.

Dylan scowled at him. 'You knocked me out again.'

'For the last time,' he said, his voice low, apologetic.

He killed the engine and opened the driver side door. He was alone up front, no sign of the two others who were supposed to be riding along. The ones who'd been ordered to take care of the other 'loose ends' while Rio personally took care of her.

God, the thought of her mom coming in contact with the kind of dangerous individuals that Rio was apparently associated with made her shake with anxiety. Her mother was dealing with enough as it was; Dylan didn't want her anywhere near this dark new reality.

Dylan wondered how fast Rio would catch her if she tried to bolt out of the SUV. If she could get a large enough lead, she might be able to make a run for the subway station into Midtown where the hospital was. But who was she kidding? Rio had tracked her from Jičín to Prague. Finding her in Manhattan might prove a challenge for him . . . for all of about thirty seconds.

But damn it, she needed to see her mom. She needed to be with her, at her bedside, and see her face so she could know for certain that she was okay.

Please Lord, let her be okay.

'I thought you were going to have company for this trip,' Dylan said, hoping by some miracle there had been a change of plans and Rio's friends had stayed behind. 'What happened to the other guys who were supposed to come with you?'

'I dropped them off in the city. They didn't need to be here with us. They'll report back to me when they're finished.'

'When they're finished terrorizing a bunch of innocent people, you mean? How do you know your vampire buddies won't decide to take a little blood donation along with the memories they're going to steal?'

'They have a specific mission, and they'll adhere to it.'

She looked into the smoky topaz eyes staring back at her in the mirror. 'Just like you, right?'

'Just like me.' He got out of the vehicle and came to the back to grab her backpack and messenger bag from the seat beside her. 'Come on, Dylan. We don't have a lot of time to wrap this up.'

When she didn't move, he reached in and startled her with a gentle stroke of her cheek. 'Come on. Let's get inside now. Everything's going to be all right.'

She climbed out of the leather seat and walked up the concrete steps with him to her building's front door. Rio handed her the keys from out of her bag. Dylan turned the entryway lock and stepped inside the stale-smelling, robin's egg blue vestibule, feeling like she hadn't been home in ten years.

'My apartment's on the second floor,' she murmured, but then Rio probably already knew that. He followed close behind her as the two of them climbed the stairs up to her hole-in-the-wall place at the back of the common hallway.

She unlocked the door and Rio walked in ahead of her, keeping her in back of him as though he were accustomed to entering dangerous places and doing it at the front of the line. He was a warrior, all right. If his cautious demeanor and immense size didn't confirm it, the big gun he was concealing in the back waistband of his black cargo pants would have done so in spades. She watched as he checked out the place, pausing next to a computer workstation that sat on a small writing desk in the corner.

'Am I going to find anything on this machine that shouldn't be there?' he asked as he turned it on and the monitor lit him up in a pale blue light.

'That computer is old. I hardly ever use it.'

'You won't mind if I check,' he said, not really a question when he was already bringing up files and having a look at what they contained. He wouldn't find anything but some of her earliest articles and old correspondence.

'Do you have a lot of enemies?' Dylan asked, trailing over to him.

'We have enough.'

'I'm not one of them, you know.' She flipped on a light, more for her benefit than his, since he obviously didn't mind the dark. 'I'm not going to tell anyone about what you've told me, or what I've seen these past several days. None of it, I swear to you. And not because you're going to take those memories away from me either. I would keep your secrets safe, Rio. I just want you to know that.'

'It's not that simple,' he said, facing her now. 'It wouldn't be safe. Not for you, or for us. Our world protects its own, but there are dangers and we can't be everywhere. Letting someone outside the vampire nation carry information about us could be catastrophic. Occasionally it is done, even though it's ill-advised. A human here or there has been trusted with the truth, but it's rare in the extreme. Personally I've never seen it work out well in the end. Someone always gets hurt.'

'I can take care of myself.'

He chuckled, but there was little humor in it. 'I have no doubt. But this is different, Dylan. You're not just a human. You're a Breedmate, and that will always mean you're different. You can bond with a male of my kind through blood and you can live forever. Well, something close to forever.'

'You mean like Tess and her mate?'

Rio nodded. 'Like them, yes. But to be a part of the Breed's world, you would have to cut your ties to the human one. You'd have to leave them behind.'

'I can't do that,' she said, her brain automatically shutting down the idea of leaving her mom. 'My family is here.'

'The Breed is your family too. They would care for you as family, Dylan. You could make a very nice life for yourself in the Darkhavens.'

She couldn't help but notice that he was talking about all of this from a comfortable distance, keeping himself totally out of the equation. Part of her wondered if it would be so easy to turn him down if he were asking her personally to join his world.

But he wasn't doing that at all. And Dylan's choice, easy or not, would have been the same regardless of what he was offering her.

She shook her head. 'My life is here, with my mom. She's always been there for me, and I can't leave her. I wouldn't. Not now. Not ever.'

And she needed to find a way to get to her soon, she thought, weathering Rio's steady, measuring gaze. She didn't want to wait until he decided to start scrubbing her memory now that she'd opted out of the vampire lottery.

'I . . . um . . . I've got to use the bathroom,' she murmured. 'I hope you don't think you're going to stand guard over me while I go?'

Rio's eyes narrowed slightly, but he gave a slow shake of his head. 'Go on. But don't take long.'

Dylan couldn't believe he was actually letting her walk into the adjacent bathroom and shut herself inside. For all his cautious recon of her apartment, he must have missed the fact that there was a small window next to the toilet.

A window that opened onto a fire escape, which led down to the street below.

Dylan turned on the faucet and ran a hard stream of cold water into the sink while she considered the insanity of what she was about to attempt. She had two-hundred-plus pounds of combat-trained, seriously armed vampire waiting for her on the other side of the door. She'd already witnessed his lightning-fast reflexes, so the odds of outrunning him were pretty much zilch. All she could hope for was a sneak escape, and that would mean getting the decrepit window open without making too much noise, then climbing down the rickety fire escape without having it crumble beneath her. If she managed to clear those sizable obstacles, all she'd have to do is start running till she hit the subway station.

Yeah, piece of cake.

She knew it was nuts, even as she hurried to the window and slid the sash lock free. The window needed a good jab to loosen the several coats of old paint that had all but sealed it shut. Dylan coughed a couple of times, loud enough to mask the noise as she knocked the window frame with the heel of her palm.

She waited a second, listening for movement in the other room. When she didn't hear any, she lifted the window and got a faceful of humid city night air.

Oh, Christ. Was she really going to do this?

She had to.

Nothing else mattered but seeing her mom.

Dylan put herself halfway out the window to make sure

the way down was clear. It was. She could do this. She had to try. With a couple of good deep breaths to gird herself, Dylan tapped the flusher and then climbed out the window as the toilet whooshed into action behind her.

Her descent down the fire escape was rushed and clumsy, but in a few seconds her feet touched down on the pavement. As soon as she hit the ground, she gunned it for the subway.

Over the rush of water running in the bathroom sink, Rio had indeed heard the nearly silent slide of the window being pushed open behind that closed door. The flushing toilet didn't quite mask the metallic clank of the fire escape as Dylan carefully climbed out onto it.

She was attempting escape, just as he expected she would.

He'd seen the wheels turning in her head as he talked with her, a look of rising desperation coming into her eyes every moment she was forced to stay in the apartment with him. He'd known, even before she made the excuse of needing to use the bathroom, that she was going to try to get away from him at her first opportunity.

Rio could have stopped her. He could stop her now, as she clambered down the rickety steel ladder to the street below her apartment. But he was more curious about where she planned to run. And to whom.

He'd believed her when she said she had no intention of exposing the Breed to human news outlets. If it turned out she was lying to him, he didn't know what he would do. He didn't want to think he could be so wrong about her – told himself none of that would matter at all if he just wiped her mind clean of the knowledge.

But he'd hesitated to scrub her on the spot after she said she wouldn't leave her human world for that of the Breed. He hesitated because he realized, selfishly, that he wasn't quite ready to erase himself from her thoughts.

And now she was running off into the night, away from him.

With a headful of memories and knowledge that he damn well couldn't allow her to keep.

Rio got up from Dylan's computer desk and walked into the small bathroom. It was empty, as he knew it would be, the window yawning open onto the dark summer night outside.

He climbed out, boots hitting the fire escape for a split second before he leaped from the structure and landed on the asphalt below. Tipping his head back, he dragged the air into his lungs until he caught Dylan's scent.

Then he went after her.

⧫ CHAPTER TWENTY-TWO ⧫

Dylan stood outside the windowed door of her mother's room on the hospital's tenth floor, trying to rally her courage to go inside. The cancer ward was so quiet up here at night, only the hushed chatter from the nurses on duty at their station and the occasional shuffle of a patient's slippered feet as they made a brief circuit around the wing, fingers clasped around the wheeled IV pole that rolled along beside them. Her mom had been one of those tenacious, but weary-eyed patients not so long ago.

Dylan hated to think there was more of that pain and struggle ahead of her mother now. The biopsy the doctors had ordered wouldn't be in for a couple of days, according to the nurse at the desk. They were hopeful that in the likelihood it did come back positive, they might have caught the relapse early enough to begin a new, more aggressive round of chemotherapy. Dylan was praying for a miracle, despite the heaviness in her chest as she steeled herself for bad news.

She hit the hand sanitizer dispenser mounted next to the door, squirted a blob of isopropyl gel into her palms and rubbed it in. As she pulled a pair of latex gloves from the box on the counter and put them on, everything she'd been through in the past several days – even the past few hours – fell away, forgotten. Her own problems just evaporated as she pushed open the door, because nothing mattered right now except the woman curled up on the bed, tethered to monitoring wires and intravenous lines.

God, her mother looked so tiny and frail lying there. She'd always been petite, smaller than Dylan by a good four inches, her hair a richer shade of red, even with the handful of grays that had crept in since the first battle with cancer. Now Sharon's hair was kept short, a spiky, spunky cut that made her look at least a decade younger than her true age of sixty-four. Dylan felt a pang of irrational, but jabbing anger for the fact that a renewed round of chemo was going to ravage that glorious crown of thick copper hair.

She walked softly toward the bed, trying not to make any noise. But Sharon wasn't sleeping. She rolled over as Dylan came close, her green eyes bright and warm.

'Oh . . . Dylan . . . hi, baby.' Her voice was feathery, the only real physical giveaway in her that she was ill. She reached out and took Dylan's gloved hand in a tight hold. 'How was the trip, sweetheart? When did you get back?'

Shit. That's right – she'd supposedly extended her stay in Europe. It seemed like a year had passed in the few days she'd been with Rio.

'Um, I just came home a little while ago,' Dylan answered, a partial lie.

She took a seat on the edge of the thin hospital room mattress, her hand still caught in her mother's clutching grasp.

'I got a little concerned when you changed your plans so abruptly. Your e-mail that you were staying a bit longer by yourself was so short and cryptic. Why didn't you call me?'

'I'm sorry,' Dylan said. The lie she had to keep hurt even worse knowing that she'd made her mom worry. 'I would have called you if I could have. Oh, Mom . . . I'm sorry you don't feel well.'

'I feel all right. Better, now that you're here.' Sharon's gaze was steady, level with a calm resolve. 'But I'm dying, baby. You do understand that, don't you?'

'Don't say that.' Dylan squeezed her mom's hand, then brought the cool fingers up to her lips and kissed them. 'You'll get through this, just like you did before. You're going to be fine.'

The silence – the tender indulgence – was a palpable force in the room. Her mother wasn't going to push the subject, but it was there, like a ghost lurking in the corner.

'Well, let's talk about you instead. I want to hear all about what you've been doing, where you've been . . . tell me about everything you've seen while you were gone.'

Dylan glanced down, unable to hold her mother's eyes if she couldn't tell her the truth. And she couldn't tell her the truth. Most of it would be unbelievable anyway, especially the part where Dylan confessed that she feared she was developing feelings for a dangerous, secretive man. A vampire for crissake. It sounded crazy just to think the words.

'Tell me more about that demon's lair story you're working on, baby. Those pictures you sent me were really something. When is your story going to run?'

'There is no story, Mom.' Dylan shook her head. She was sorry she ever mentioned it to her mother – or to anyone, for that matter. 'Turns out that cave was just a cave,' she said, hoping to convince her. 'Nothing strange about it.'

Sharon looked skeptical. 'Really? But that tomb you found – and the incredible markings on the walls. What was all of that doing in there? It must have meant something.'

'Just a tomb. Probably a very old, tribal burial chamber of some kind.'

'And the picture you took of that man—'

'A vagrant, that's all,' Dylan lied, hating every syllable that passed her lips. 'The pictures made everything seem more important than it was. But there is no story, not even one

suitable for a rag like Coleman Hogg's paper. In fact, he let
me go.'

'What? He didn't!'

Dylan shrugged. 'Yeah, he did. And it's fine, really. I'll find
something else.'

'Well, that's his loss. You were too good for that place,
anyway. If it's any consolation, I thought you did a great job
on that story. Mr Fasso thought so too. In fact, he mentioned
he had contacts with some big news outlets in the city. He
could probably find you something if I asked him to look into
it.'

Oh, shit. A job interview was the last thing she needed to
worry about. Not when the rest of what she'd just heard had
put a knot of dread in her throat. 'Mom – you didn't tell him
about that story, did you?'

'You're darn right I did. I showed off your pictures too.
I'm sorry, but I can't help bragging about you. You're my little
star.'

'Who did you . . . Ah, God, Mom, please tell me you didn't
talk about it with a lot of people . . . did you?'

Sharon patted her hand. 'Don't be so shy. You're very
talented, Dylan, and you should be working on bigger, more
hard-hitting stories. Mr Fasso agrees with me. Gordon and I
talked all about you on the river cruise a couple of nights
ago.'

Dylan's stomach was clenched over the thought of more
people being privy to what she'd seen in that cave, but she
couldn't help noticing the little glint of joy in her mother's
eyes when she mentioned the man who founded the runaway
shelter. 'So, you're on a first-name basis with Mr Fasso now,
are you?'

Sharon giggled, a sound so youthful and impish that Dylan
forgot for a moment that she was sitting beside her mom in
a hospital room in the cancer ward. 'He's very handsome,

Dylan. And utterly charming. I'd always thought him to be so aloof, almost chilly, but he's actually a very intriguing man.'

Dylan smiled. 'You like him.'

'I do,' her mother confessed. 'Just my luck I should find a real gentleman – who knows, maybe my true prince? – when it's too late for me to fall in love.'

Dylan shook her head, hating to hear that kind of talk from her. 'It's never too late, Mom. You're still young. You have a lot of living left to do.'

Shadows crossed her mother's eyes as she looked up at Dylan from her recline on the bed. 'You've always made me so very proud. You know that, don't you, baby?'

Dylan nodded, throat constricted. 'Yeah, I know. I could always count on you, Mom. You were the only one in my life that I could count on. Still are. Two musketeers, right?'

Sharon smiled at the mention of their long-running reference to themselves, but there were tears glistening in her eyes. 'I want you to be all right, Dylan. With this, I mean. With my leaving you soon . . . with the fact that I'm going to die.'

'Mom—'

'Hear me out, please. I worry about you, sweetheart. I don't want you to be alone.'

Dylan wiped at a hot tear that ran down the side of her face. 'You shouldn't be thinking about me now. Just focus on you, on getting better. You need to think positively. The biopsy might not—'

'Dylan. Stop, and listen to me.' Her mother sat up, a stubborn look that Dylan recognized very well coming over her pretty but fatigued features. 'The cancer is back, worse than before. I know it. I feel it. And I've come to terms with it. I need to know that you will be able to come to terms with this too.'

Dylan looked down at their clasped hands, hers masked in

yellow latex, her mother's nearly translucent, the bones and tendons stark beneath the cool, too-pale skin.

'How long have you been looking after me, baby? And I don't mean just since I've been sick. From the time you were a little girl, you were always worrying about me and trying your best to take care of me.'

Dylan shook her head. 'We look out for each other. That's how it's always been—'

Gentle fingers came up under her chin, lifting her gaze. 'You're my child. I've lived for you, and for your brothers too, but you were always my constant. You shouldn't have had to live for me, Dylan. You shouldn't have had to be the adult in this relationship. You should have someone to take care of you.'

'I can take care of myself,' she murmured, not very convincingly when the tears were streaming down her cheeks now.

'Yes, you can. And you have. But you deserve something more out of life. I don't want you to be afraid to live, or to love, Dylan. Can you promise me that?'

Before Dylan could say anything, the door swung open and one of the attending nurses came in with a couple new bags of fluids. 'How we doing, Sharon? How's your pain right now?'

'I could use a little something,' she said, her eyes sliding to Dylan as if she'd been hiding her discomfort until now.

Which, of course, she had been. Everything was much worse than Dylan wanted to accept. She got up from the bed and let the nurse do her thing. After she was gone, Dylan came back over to her mother's side. It was so hard not to break down, to be the strong one as she looked down into the soft green eyes and saw that the spark in them – the fight that needed to be there – was gone.

'Come here and give me a hug, baby.'

Dylan leaned down and wrapped her arms around the

delicate shoulders, unable to dismiss the fragility of her mother's entire being. 'I love you, Mom.'

'And I love you.' Sharon sighed as she settled back against the pillow. 'I'm tired, sweetheart. I need to rest now.'

'Okay,' Dylan answered, her voice thick. 'I'll just stay here with you while you sleep.'

'No, you won't.' Her mother shook her head. 'I won't have you sitting here worrying about me. I'm not going to leave you tonight, or the next day, or even next week – I promise. But you need to go home now, Dylan. I want that for you.'

Home, Dylan thought, as her mother drifted off to a drug-induced sleep. The word felt oddly empty to her when she pictured her apartment and the few possessions she had there. That wasn't home to her. If she had to go somewhere now, somewhere she felt safe and protected, that pitiful hole in the wall wasn't it. Never really had been.

Dylan rose from the bed and turned to leave the room. As she wiped at her teary eyes, her gaze lit on a shadowed face and broad shoulders silhouetted by the hallway lights outside. *Rio.*

He'd found her, followed her there.

Where her every instinct should have been to run away from him, Dylan went to him instead. She pulled open the door and met him outside her mother's room, incapable of speaking as she wrapped her arms around his solid warmth and wept softly into his chest.

⇥ CHAPTER TWENTY-THREE ⇤

He hadn't expected her to run to him when she saw him standing there.

Now that Dylan was in his arms, her body trembling as she cried, Rio found himself at a complete loss. He'd worked up a healthy amount of anger and suspicion in the time it took him to track her across the city. His head was ringing from all the noise, and from the endless, overcrowded presence of humans everywhere he looked. His temples were screaming from the bright lights, all of his senses battering him from within.

But none of that mattered in the long moments he stood there, holding Dylan, feeling her shake with bone-deep fear and anguish. She was hurting, and Rio felt an overwhelming need to protect her. He didn't want to see her in pain like this.

Madre de Dios, but he hated seeing her this way.

He caressed her delicate back, pressed his mouth to the top of her head where it nestled beneath his chin, murmuring quiet words of reassurance. Feeble gestures, but all he could think to do for her.

'I'm so afraid I'm going to lose her,' she whispered. 'Oh, God, Rio . . . I'm terrified.'

He didn't have to guess at who Dylan was talking about. The patient sleeping in the adjacent room had the same creamy coloring, the same fiery-hued hair as the younger version Rio was holding in his embrace.

Dylan tilted her tear-streaked face up at him. 'Will you take me out of here, please?'

'I'll take you anywhere you want to go.' Rio smoothed his thumbs over her cheeks, erasing the wet tracks. 'Do you want to go home?'

Her sad little laugh sounded so broken, lost, somehow. 'Can we just . . . walk for a little while?'

'Yeah. Sure.' He nodded, tucking her under his arm. 'Let's get out of here.'

They walked in silence, down to the elevator and then out of the hospital to the warm night outside. He didn't know where to take her, so he just walked with her. A few blocks up from the hospital was a footbridge that led to the East River promenade. They crossed it, and as they strolled along the water's edge, Rio felt people staring at him as they passed on the walkway.

There were furtive glances at his scars, and more than one wondering look that seemed to question what he was doing with a beauty like Dylan. A damn good question, and one he didn't have a sensible answer for at the moment. He'd brought her into the city on a mission – one that sure as hell didn't allow for detours like this.

Dylan slowed at last, pausing at the iron rail to look over the water. 'My mom got really sick last fall. She thought it was bronchitis. It wasn't. The verdict was lung cancer, even though she never smoked a day in her life.' Dylan went quiet for a long moment. 'She's dying. That's what she just told me tonight.'

'I'm sorry,' Rio said, drawing up next to her.

He wanted to touch her, but he wasn't sure she needed his consolation – wasn't sure she'd accept it. Instead he settled for touching a strand of her loose red hair, easier to pretend he was catching the errant tendril from blowing into her face on the light summer breeze.

'I wasn't supposed to be on that trip to Europe. It was going to be her big adventure with her friends, but she wasn't well enough to go so I took her place. I wasn't supposed to be there. I never would have set foot in that damn cave. I never would have met you.'

'Now you wish you could undo it.' He didn't ask the question, merely stated what had to be simple fact.

'I do wish I could undo it, for her. I wish she could have had her adventure. I wish she wasn't sick.' Dylan turned her head and looked at him. 'But I don't wish I could undo meeting you.'

Rio was stunned silent by her admission. He brought his hand up to the soft line of her jaw, looking down into a face so fair and beautiful it stole his breath. And the way she was gazing up at him – as if he were a man worthy of her, a man she could love . . .

She exhaled a quiet, unsteady breath. 'I would take it all back in a second, Rio. But not this. Not you.'

Ah, Cristo.

Before he could tell himself it was a bad idea, Rio bent his head down and kissed her. It was a gentle meeting of their mouths, a tender brush of lips that shouldn't have made him burn like it did. He reveled in the sweet taste of her, in the way she felt so right in his arms.

He shouldn't want this so badly. He shouldn't feel this need, this tender affection that was kindling inside him every time he thought about Dylan.

He shouldn't be pulling her closer to him, splaying his fingers into the warm silk of her hair as he brought her deeper into his embrace, lost in her kiss.

It took him a long time to break it. But even after he lifted his head, he couldn't stop caressing her face. He couldn't let go of her.

A group of teenagers shuffled past them on the promenade, rowdy human boys in clothes several sizes too big for them, talking loudly and shoving at one another as they went. Rio kept his eyes on the youths, suspicion spiking as he watched the gang pause near the railing and take turns spitting over the edge. They didn't seem overtly dangerous, but they did appear to be the types perpetually ready for trouble.

'Demetrio?'

Rio glanced down at Dylan, confused. 'Hmm?'

'Am I getting close? Your real name, I mean . . . is it Demetrio?'

He smiled, and couldn't resist kissing the freckled tip of her nose. 'No, that's not it.'

'Okay. Well, then, is it . . . Arrio?' she guessed, beaming up at him in the moonlight as she stepped slightly out of his arms. 'Oliverio? Denny Terrio?'

'Eleuterio,' he said.

Her eyes widened. 'Ay-lay-oo-what?'

'My full name is Eleuterio de la Noche Atanacio.'

'Wow. I guess that does make 'Dylan' seem a bit mundane, huh?'

Rio chuckled. 'Nothing about you is mundane, I assure you.'

Her smile was surprisingly shy. 'So, what does it mean – a gorgeous name like that?'

'A loose translation would be 'he who is free and of the night everlasting.' '

Dylan sighed. 'That's beautiful, Rio. My God, your mother must have adored you to give you an amazing name like that.'

'It wasn't my mother's doing. She was killed when I was very young. The name came later, from a Breed family living in a Darkhaven in my homeland. They found me, and took me in as one of their own.'

'What happened to your mother? I mean, you don't have to tell me if you don't – I know, I ask too many questions,' she said, shrugging apologetically.

'No, I don't mind telling you,' he said, finding it remarkable that he really meant that.

As a rule, he hated talking about his past. No one in the Order knew the details surrounding his awful beginnings, not even Nikolai, whom he considered his closest friend. There'd been no need to talk about it with Eva, since they'd met in the Spanish Darkhaven where Rio was raised and she knew his ignoble history.

Eva had politely chosen to ignore the ugly facts surrounding his birth and the years he'd spent as a foundling, killing because he had to, because he didn't know any better. The young savage he'd been before he was brought into the Darkhaven and shown how to live like something better than the animal he'd had to become in order to survive on his own.

Rio didn't want to see Dylan look upon him in fear or disgust, but a bigger part of him wanted to give her the truth. If she could look at his outward scars and not despise him, maybe she would be strong enough to see the ones that ruined him on the inside too.

'My mother lived on the outskirts of a very small, rural village in Spain. She was just a girl – perhaps sixteen – when she was raped by a vampire who'd gone Rogue.' Rio kept his voice low to avoid being overheard, but the nearest humans – the group of adolescent thugs still amusing themselves several yards down the promenade – were paying no attention anyway. 'The Rogue fed on her as he violated her, but my mother fought back. She bit him, apparently. Enough of his blood entered her mouth, and, subsequently, her body. Since she was a Breedmate, the combination of blood and seed resulted in a pregnancy.'

'You,' Dylan whispered. 'Oh, God, Rio. How terrible for her to go through that. But at least she had you in the end.'

'It was a wonder she didn't rout me out of her womb,' he said, looking out at the black, glistening river and remembering his mother's anguish over the abomination she'd given birth to. 'My mother was a simple country girl. She wasn't educated, not in the traditional sense, or in life matters. She lived alone in a cottage in the forest, cast out by her kin years before I came along.'

'What for?'

'*Manos del diablo,*' Rio replied. 'They feared her devil's hands. You remember how I told you that all females born with the Breedmate mark also have special gifts . . . psychic abilities of some sort?'

Dylan nodded. 'Yes.'

'Well, my mother's gift was dark. With a touch and a focused thought, she could deliver death.' Rio scoffed under his breath and held up his own lethal hands. '*Manos del diablo.*'

Dylan was quiet for a moment, studying him in silence. 'You have that ability as well?'

'A Breedmate mother passes down many traits to her sons: hair, skin, and eye color . . . as well as her psychic gifts. I think if my mother had known exactly what was growing in her belly, she would have killed me long before I was born. She did try at least once, after the fact.'

Dylan's brow creased, and she gently placed her hand over his where it rested on the iron grate. 'What happened?'

'It's one of my first vivid memories,' Rio confessed. 'You see, Breed offspring are born with small, sharp fangs. Right out of the womb, they need blood to survive. And darkness. My mother must have figured all of this out on her own, and tolerated it, because somehow I made it out of infancy. To me, it was perfectly natural to avoid the sun and to take my mother's wrist for nourishment. I think I must have been about four years old when I first noticed that she cried every time she had to feed me. She despised me – despised what I was – yet I was all she had.'

Dylan stroked the back of his hand. 'I can't even imagine how it must have been for you. For both of you.'

Rio shrugged. 'I knew no other way to live. But my mother did. On this particular day, with our cottage shutters bolted tight to ward off daylight, my mother offered me her wrist. When I took it, I felt her other hand come up around the back of my head. She held it there, and the pain jolted me like a bolt of lightning arrowing into my skull. I cried out and opened my eyes. She was weeping, great, terrible sobs as she fed me and held my head in her hand.'

'Jesus Christ,' Dylan whispered, her shock evident. 'She meant to kill you with her touch?'

Rio recalled his own marrow-deep shock when he made that same realization for himself – a child watching in terror as the person he trusted above all others tried to end his life. 'She couldn't go through with it,' he murmured flatly. 'Whatever her reasons, she drew her hand away and ran out of the cottage. I didn't see her again for two days. By the time she came back, I was starving and terrified. I thought she'd abandoned me for good.'

'She was afraid too,' Dylan pointed out, and Rio was glad not to hear any trace of pity for him in her voice. Her fingers were warm and reassuring as she took his hand in her grasp. The hand he'd just told her could wield death with a touch. 'The both of you must have felt so isolated and alone.'

'Yes,' he said. 'I suppose we did. It all ended about a year later. Some of the village men saw my mother and took an interest in her, apparently. They showed up one day at the cottage while we were sleeping. There were three of them. They kicked in the door and went after her. They must have heard the rumors about her because the first thing they did was bind her hands so she couldn't touch them.'

Dylan's breath caught in her throat. 'Oh, Rio . . .'

'They dragged her outside. I ran after them, trying to help her, but the sunlight was intense. It blinded me for a few seconds that felt like an eternity while my mother was screaming, begging them not to harm her or her son.'

Rio could still picture the trees – everything so green and lush, the sky so blue overhead . . . an explosion of colors he'd only seen in darker, muted shades when he was out in the safety of night. And he could still see the men, three large human men, taking turns on a defenseless female while her son watched, frozen by terror and the limitations of his five-year-old body.

'They beat her, calling her ugly things: *Maldecido. Manos del diablo. La puta de infierno.* Something snapped in me when I saw her blood run red on the ground. I leaped on one of the men. I was so furious I wanted him to die in agony . . . and he did. Once I understood what I'd done, I went after the next man. I bit him in the throat and fed on him as my touch slowly killed him.'

Dylan was staring at him now, saying nothing. Standing there, so very still.

'The last one looked up and saw what I'd done. He called me the same things he called my mother, then added two more names I'd never heard before: *Comedor de la sangre. Monstruo.* Blood-eater. Monster.' Rio exhaled a brittle laugh. 'Until that moment, I didn't know what I was. But as I killed the last of my mother's attackers and watched as she lay dying in the sunlit grass, some knowledge buried deep within me seemed to come awake and rise up. I finally understood that I was different, and what that meant.'

'You were just a child,' Dylan said softly. 'How did you survive after that?'

'For a while I went hungry. I tried feeding from animals, but their blood was like poison. I hunted my first human about a week after the attack. I was out of my mind with hunger, and I had no experience with finding my own food. I killed several innocent people those first few weeks I was on my own. I would have gone Rogue eventually, but then something miraculous happened. I was tracking prey in the woods when a huge shadow came out of the trees. It was a man, I thought, but he moved so fast and so stealthily I could hardly keep focus on him. He was hunting too. He went after the peasant I'd set my sights on, and with a grace I was sorely lacking, he brought the human down and began to feed from the wound he'd opened in the man's throat. He was a blood-eater, like me.'

'What did you do, Rio?'

'I watched in fascination,' he said, remembering it as clearly as if it had just happened a few minutes ago. 'When it was over, the human got up and walked away as if nothing out of the ordinary had occurred. I was astonished, and when I drew in my breath, that's when the blood-eater saw me hiding nearby. He called me out and after hearing that I was alone, he brought me with him to his home. It was a Darkhaven. I met many others like me, and learned that I was part of a race called the Breed. As my mother had not seen fit to give me a name, my new family in the Darkhaven gave me the one I have now.'

'Eleuterio de la Noche Atanacio,' Dylan said, the words sounding far too sweet as she spoke them. Her hand, as she placed it tenderly on the scarred side of his face felt far too comforting. 'My God, Rio . . . it's a miracle you're standing here with me at all.'

She moved closer to him now, looking up into his eyes. Rio could hardly breathe as she rose onto her toes and tilted his chin down to meet her kiss. Their lips came together for the second time that night . . . and with a need that neither one of them seemed willing or able to conceal.

He could have kissed her forever.

But it was at that precise moment that the quiet promenade erupted in a sudden cacophony of gunfire.

CHAPTER TWENTY-FOUR

Panic flooded Rio's veins like acid.

The gunfire came again, another rapid report that split the night. The sharp staccato pops were coming from somewhere close; in his head they were cannon fire, the sound of them — the shock of a sudden attack — ripping through his senses, filling his mind with a thick fog that swallowed the here and now.

Dylan, he thought fiercely.

Had to keep her safe.

He was only barely conscious of his actions as he grabbed her by the shoulders and threw her down onto the grass beneath him. Her cry of alarm was muted, more felt than heard as he covered her body with his, willing to sacrifice himself for her.

Protecting her was all that mattered.

But as they hit the hard earth together, Rio felt his mind splintering off. Past and present began to blend, mesh . . . morph into a hazy confusion of thought and fracturing logic.

Suddenly he was in the warehouse again — Lucan, Nikolai, and the other warriors moving in on a raid of a Rogue lair in Boston. He was glancing up into the rafters of the abandoned building, noting the movement of enemies in the shadows.

Seeing the silver glint of an electronic device in the suckhead's hands.

Hearing Niko shout a warning that a bomb was set to blow . . .

Ah, fuck.

Rio roared as remembered pain blasted into his head, into every inch of his body. He felt like he was on fire, flesh burning, filling his nostrils with the stench of seared skin and hair.

Cool hands came up to his face, but he was too far gone to make sense of what was real and what was a nightmare from his recent past.

'Rio?'

He heard the soft voice, felt those soothing hands moving over his face.

And, from somewhere not far away the hoots and chortles of several human youths. The laughter was accompanied by the slap of sneakers on pavement, all of it growing distant now.

'Rio. Are you all right?'

He knew that voice. It filtered through the swelling madness that was engulfing him, a lifeline thrown to him in the dark of his mind. He reached for it, feeling her voice ground him where nothing else ever had.

'Dylan,' he managed to rasp out between the panting of his breath. 'Don't want you to get hurt . . .'

'I'm fine. It was only firecrackers.' She smoothed her fingers over the cold clamminess of his forehead. 'Those boys set them off by the railing over there. It's okay now.'

Like hell it was.

He felt one of his blackouts coming on, and coming on fast. He rolled away from Dylan with a groan. 'Shit . . . my head hurts . . . can't think straight.'

She must have leaned over him, because he felt her breath skate across his cheek as she blew out a low curse. 'Your eyes, Rio. Shit. They're changing . . . they're glowing amber.'

He knew they must be. His fangs were biting into his tongue, his skin tightening up all over his body as rage and pain transformed him. He was at his most deadly like this, when his mind was not his own. When his devil's hands were at their most unpredictable, and most powerful.

'We have to get you someplace less public,' Dylan said. She slipped her hands underneath his shoulders. 'Hold on to me. I'm going to help you stand up.'

'No.'

'What do you mean, no?'

'Leave me,' he rasped.

Dylan scoffed. 'Like hell I will. You can't lie out here like this in the middle of Manhattan and expect not to be noticed. Now, come on. Get. Up.'

'I can't . . . don't want to touch you. I don't want to hurt you, Dylan.'

'Then don't,' she said, and put her weight into the task of hoisting him up onto his feet.

Rio had no choice but to put his hands on her shoulders to steady himself as the fog in his mind grew thicker, swallowing up his vision. He fought to keep the blackout at bay, knowing Dylan would be safest only if he remained lucid.

'Lean on me, damn it,' she ordered him. 'I'm going to help you.'

Dylan wedged herself under Rio's arm and took his wrist in her hand, bearing as much of his weight as she could while she tried to find somewhere private for him to deal with the aftershocks of the attack that had come over him. She led him off the riverside walkway and up a one-way side street where there was less traffic, and far less people around to get close enough to see his transformation.

'Still good?' she asked him, hurrying toward an old brick church with plenty of shadows behind it. 'Can you make it a bit farther?'

He gave a nod and grunted, but each step was more sluggish than the last. 'Blacking . . . out . . .'

'Yeah, I kind of figured that,' she said. 'It's okay, Rio. Just hang in with me for another minute, okay?'

No answer this time, but she could feel him working to stay upright and moving. Struggling to stay lucid long enough for her to help him.

'You're doing great,' she told him. 'Almost there.'

She pulled him into the dark behind the building, guiding him to an alcove near a rusted, padlocked door. Using the brick wall as back support for Rio, Dylan carefully eased him down into a sitting position on the ground. She threw a glance in both directions, relieved to see that they were fairly concealed from the side street and any passersby. They were safe there for now.

'Tell me what to do, Rio. What do you need to get through this?'

He didn't answer. Maybe he was incapable. Dylan smoothed his dark hair away from his face and searched his eyes for any sign that he was still cognizant. The thin vertical pupils were always a shock, but no more so than the blast of amber that surrounded them. Rio's eyes burned like hot coals set into his skull. Anyone driving or walking past the small church would have to be blind to miss the otherworldly glow.

Dylan glanced at the old door and its decrepit lock. She'd seen Rio turn on lamps and water spigots with his mind, so pulling off a B&E on the church should have been no big thing. Except he clearly was in no condition to attempt it. His head slumped down onto his chest and with a pained groan, he started listing to the side.

'Shit,' Dylan hissed.

She left him only long enough to search the lightless lot for something heavy. She came back with a piece of broken cinder block that had been keeping the lid of a Dumpster closed.

The brick was rough in her hands, and made an echoing crack and a bright spark as she slammed it against the padlock on the church door. It took two more hard strikes before the lock dropped away with a thump.

'Rio,' she whispered fiercely as she lifted his thick shoulders back up. 'Rio, can you hear me? We have to get you inside. Can you stand up?'

She raised his chin and stared into open eyes that were unseeing now, vacant pits of fire.

'Goddamn it,' she muttered, then winced at the poor choice of expletives, considering she was about to bring an unconscious creature of the night into a heavenly sanctuary for protection.

Dylan eased the church door open and listened for any signs of occupation. It was all quiet, not a single light on inside the small antechamber or in the main area of the nave beyond.

'Okay, here we go,' she said under her breath as she went around to Rio's head and grabbed his arms to pull him over the threshold.

He was heavy as hell, two-hundred-plus pounds of solid muscle and bone, none of it cooperating with her. Dylan tugged and dragged him into the darkness, then closed the door behind them.

It didn't take long to find a couple of candles and a box of matches in the cabinets. Dylan lit the pair of white tapers then ducked back outside to grab the cinder block as a makeshift holder. She stuffed the candles into the cylindrical holes of the cement brick, then went to check on Rio.

'Hey,' she said softly, leaning over his sprawled, unresponsive body where he lay on the floor. His eyes were closed now, but restless behind his lids. A muscle in his jaw twitched, his limbs unmoving yet tense with a coiled energy Dylan could feel as she got near him.

She stroked his face with a feather-light touch, running the backs of her fingers over the flawless cheek that made him so jaw-droppingly gorgeous, and the other side that completely broke her heart. Who could have predicted these past several days, and all the things she would experience? What could possibly have prepared her for meeting this complicated, incredible man?

Would she ever truly be able to forget him, even if he erased himself from her memory like he intended to do?

She doubted it. Even if her mind were forced to forget him, she didn't think her heart ever would.

Dylan bent down and pressed her lips to his slack mouth.

Rio's eyes snapped open. His hands shot around her throat so fast, she didn't have a chance to draw breath enough to cry out.

⇥ CHAPTER TWENTY-FIVE ⇤

He didn't know what yanked him harder out of the dead fog of his mind: the feel of soft lips on his mouth, or the realization a split second later that he was holding a slender throat in his hands. Squeezing tight, fury flowing from the confusion of his blackout into the tips of his fingers where they pressed with deadly intent on a delicate female larynx.

He couldn't let go.

His eyes were open, but he couldn't focus on the face before him. He heard a choked gasp, a moan vibrating against his locked thumbs.

None of it broke him out of the thick darkness.

It wasn't until he felt soft hands come up to his face – his scars – that he felt the first glimmer of clarity.

Dylan.

Cristo . . . he was hurting her.

With a roar, Rio threw himself off her, releasing her the instant he realized what he was doing. He scrambled into the shadows of the unfamiliar surroundings, horrified at what he'd done.

Holy hell . . . what he might have done, if he'd held on any longer.

He heard her suck in a few rapid breaths of air behind him. He waited to hear her footsteps take off at a panicked run. He wouldn't have blamed her. He wouldn't have gone after her either. Not even for the purpose of scrubbing her mind in protection of the Breed and the secret let loose from that Bohemian cave.

If she ran now, she would have her freedom from him completely.

'Go, Dylan. Get far away from me . . . please.'

He heard a rustle of movement as she got up. He closed his eyes, ready to let her go.

Praying she would.

Instead she drew nearer to him. Rio flinched as her hand landed gently on his head and then drifted slowly down his hair.

'Go,' he rasped. 'Before I lose my fucking mind again and do something even worse. For fuck's sake, I might have killed you just now.'

He hissed as she knelt down beside him on the floor. With the slightest coaxing, she brought his head around to face her. 'I'm okay, as you can see. You scared me a little, but that's all. God, Rio . . . how often does this happen to you?'

He scowled and shook his head, not interested in having this conversation right now.

'How do you get through it?' she asked. 'I'd like to help you—'

'You can't.'

He couldn't force his gaze away from her throat as he said it, hard as he tried to avoid looking at the graceful column of Dylan's neck. He hadn't bruised her – a small miracle – but he could still feel the velvety skin against his palms, the heat of her still tingling in his fingertips.

And there, near the hollow at the base of her throat, beat a strong, tempting pulse.

'You need blood, don't you,' she said, too smart to miss the weakness that he couldn't conceal. 'Would it be better for you if you fed?'

'Not from you.'

'Why not, if you need it?'

He cursed, head still pounding from the lingering effects of his meltdown. 'Your blood in my body will create a lasting, unbreakable bond. I would always feel you – be drawn to you – for as long as you are alive.'

'Oh,' she said softly. 'And we definitely wouldn't want that. Not when you prefer to feel isolated and alone.'

Rio scoffed. 'You don't know how I feel.'

'When did you start hating yourself?' she asked, unfazed by the fire he was throwing off with his narrow glare. 'Was it after Eva betrayed you, or much earlier than that? Back in that forest cottage in Spain?'

He snarled, turning away from her before she stoked his anger any higher. He was volatile in his current state, a deadly predator teetering on the very edge of sanity.

Just another good reason why he should put the beast down. Before he hurt someone again. Before he let himself think that the future might hold anything of worth for him.

And damn well before he considered Dylan's reckless offer any longer than he had already.

'My mother's been fighting for her life for nearly a year. You can't wait to throw yours away.'

'What do you think you'd be doing if you let me drink from you now?' he shot back, his voice rough, combative. A bit desperate, even. 'I'm the last thing you need, Dylan. If you reach into the trap to pull me out, I can't promise I won't take your arm off in the process.'

'You're not going to hurt me.'

Rio grunted, a coarse, animalistic sound. 'How do you know I won't?'

'Because I'm going to trust you not to.'

He made the very grave mistake of turning back to look at her. With her eyes on his now, Dylan pulled her hair over to one shoulder and moved closer, until her neck was poised near his mouth. Rio stared at the exposed column of pale skin, his gaze rooting on the rapid tick of her pulse beneath the tender flesh.

He growled a violent curse.

Then he curled his lips off his fangs and sank them into her neck.

Oh . . . God.

Dylan's entire body seized up in the instant Rio's bite penetrated her skin. There was a sudden, piercing shock of white-hot pain, then . . . *bliss.*

Warmth filled her as Rio's lips fastened to the wound he'd made and his tongue coaxed her blood to begin flowing into his mouth. He drew from her with a needy intensity, his fangs grazing her skin, his tongue creating a demanding, delicious friction with each hard, wet pull at her vein.

'Rio,' she whispered, her breath leaking out of her in a long, shuddering sigh.

He made a low noise in the back of his throat, a rumbling growl that vibrated through her skin and bones as he eased her down beneath him to the floor. His strong arms cushioned her, the heat of his body warming her as he covered her.

Dylan melted into him, losing herself in the dizzying pleasure of Rio's darkly erotic kiss. She was burning up inside. She writhed beneath him, desire swamping her as he held her close to him and drank more of her blood.

He was on fire too.

Dylan could feel the rigid line of his cock pressing against her hip as he lay atop her. His thigh was wedged between her legs, spreading her open. She wanted to be naked with him. She wanted to feel him driving into her as he suckled at her neck. She moaned with the need that was rising up in her, making her grind against his thigh.

'Rio . . . I want . . . Oh, God, I need to have you inside me.'

He groaned thickly, his pelvis kicking as he pushed the stiff ridge of his erection harder against her. But at her throat, his suckling grew less needy now, slowing to a calmer tempo. Tender, where Dylan wanted to feel more fire. She felt his tongue sweep over the bite, creating a tingly sensation that traveled through her like electricity. He lifted his head and Dylan moaned at the loss of his mouth on her skin.

'I don't want you to stop,' she told him, reaching for him. 'Don't stop.'

He gazed down at her and said something low under his breath in Spanish. It sounded furious and profane.

Dylan stared up into his scorching amber eyes. 'Now you hate me too, right?'

'No,' he snarled, fangs gleaming in the dim light of the candles.

He pulled one arm out from under her and touched her face. His fingers were shaking, but so very gentle. He smoothed her hair off her brow, then let his hand travel slowly down her cheek, her chin, and along the line of her sternum. Dylan sucked in a sigh as he caressed her breasts. He unbuttoned her shirt in mere moments, then snapped the front closure of her bra.

'You're so soft,' he murmured as his palm covered her bare flesh.

He moved down and kissed her nipple, sucking the pearled tip of her breast into the heat of his mouth. Dylan arched up with the sudden arrow of pleasure that shot through her, her desire spiraling tight as a spring.

Rio came back up to kiss her mouth as he worked the button and zipper of her jeans loose and slipped his hand inside her panties. The coppery tang of her blood on his tongue shouldn't have made her so hot, but knowing he'd fed from her – that he'd taken strength and comfort from her body in such a primal, intimate way – was the strongest aphrodisiac she'd ever known.

And what he was doing to her with his fingers now almost had her coming in his hand.

She cried out, on the verge of losing it. 'Rio, please . . .'

He stripped out of his shirt and pants, then pulled her jeans off. Her panties went slower, as Rio kissed every inch of skin between her thigh and ankle as he eased the scrap of satin down from her legs and cast it aside.

He sat back on his folded knees, gloriously naked. 'Come to me, Dylan.'

She wanted to explore the muscled beauty of his body, but her need for him was more immediate. He took her hands and brought her up onto his lap. His sex thrust up between them, a thick spear of hard flesh. Its broad head glistened with moisture, so temptingly ripe Dylan couldn't resist bending over it and sucking him deep into her mouth.

'*Cristo,*' he hissed, his cock leaping against her tongue.

He tunneled his fingers into her hair as she teased him with a few slow slides up and down the rigid length of him. When she lifted her head, Rio's eyes burned into her. His fangs seemed immense now, his face drawn taut. He caressed her as she climbed up onto him and straddled his thighs.

He kissed her breasts, her shoulder, her throat, her mouth.

'What have you done to me,' he rasped, throwing his head back as she took hold of his sex and guided it into the slick cleft of her body. 'Ah, fuck . . . *Dylan.*'

She seated herself onto him and slowly sank down to the hilt.

Oh, it felt good.

Rio filled her with a heat she'd never known before. At first, Dylan could only hold herself there, unmoving, reveling in the pure heaven of their joined bodies. Rio wrapped his arms around her as she began a slow, shuddering rhythm. He met her stroke for stroke, his erection kicking, surging deeper with each downward thrust of her hips.

It didn't take long for Dylan's climax to build. She'd been more than halfway there before they started, every nerve ending alive with sensation and looking for release. She rode him harder, clutching his shoulders as the first wave of her orgasm flooded over her. She cried out with the pleasure of it, quaking inside, splintering into a million shimmering pieces.

Rio's possessive growl as she came made her smile. He hooked his arms under hers and leaned down, guiding her back onto the floor, their bodies still intimately joined. He drove into her, a hard push of his cock. His tempo was urgent, fierce, full of barely restrained power.

Dylan held on as he rocked against her, reveling in the feel of his muscles bunching and flexing under her palms. Overhead, the candles threw erotic shadows on the ceiling, the flames flaring brighter as Rio buried himself deep inside her and shouted with the force of his release.

As Dylan stroked his strong back, she felt like weeping for the depth of pleasure she'd just experienced with him . . . and for the voice in her head that warned she would be a fool to fall in love with him.

A fact she had to admit, had already come to pass.

⇥ CHAPTER TWENTY-SIX ⇤

If he'd been worried about making more mistakes, particularly where Dylan was concerned, Rio had to admit he'd just crossed one gaping point of no return.

Taking her vein like he had was bad enough; Breed males with even the smallest scrap of honor would never feed from a Breedmate simply for their own gain. That quenching taste of Dylan's blood had pulled him through what would have been hours of anguish, and a blackout that would have left him vulnerable to discovery by humans, other vampires . . . shit. Vulnerable on more levels than he cared to examine.

But whether he'd needed it or not, it had been wrong to take Dylan's blood. Even though she'd given it to him freely, she hardly understood what she was doing – binding herself to him, and for what? Charity. Maybe even pity.

It burned him to think he'd been too weak to turn her away. He'd wanted what she was offering – all of it. And it was a little too late to call his actions back. What he'd done here was irrevocable. He knew it, and maybe instinctively she did too, since she'd become so quiet as she rested in his arms.

Rio was linked to her now, by a bond that could not be undone. With her blood swimming through his body, into his cells, Dylan was a part of him. Until death took one of them, Rio would sense her presence, her emotional state – the very essence of her – no matter how distant their separate futures might take them.

As he stroked the impossibly soft curve of her bare shoulder as she lay in his arms, he had to wonder if the blood bond was somewhat incidental to the profound attraction he was feeling for this woman. He'd felt a connection building with her from the very beginning, ever since she wandered into that cave and he heard her voice in the dark.

Making love with Dylan tonight had been perhaps as big a mistake as drinking from her: now that he'd tasted her passion, he only wanted more. He was selfish and greedy, and he'd already proven to himself that he couldn't count on honor to keep his wants at bay.

He focused instead on her – shallow breaths, careful silence . . . a heaviness within her that had nothing to do with the myriad mistakes that had transpired between them.

She was mourning privately.

'How bad off is she . . . your mother?'

Dylan swallowed, her hair sifting over his chest as she gave a vague shake of her head. 'It's not good. She keeps getting weaker.' Dylan's voice trailed off. 'I don't know how much longer she can fight it. To tell you the truth, I don't know how much longer she will try.'

'I'm sorry,' Rio said, caressing her back and knowing that he could only offer feeble words.

He didn't want Dylan to hurt, and he knew that she was weathering a deep pain. It didn't take a blood bond to tell him that. And he was ten kinds of bastard for doing what he did with her here tonight.

'We can't stay here,' he said, not meaning it to come out like a snarl. 'We need to get moving.'

He shifted beneath her uncomfortably, groaning when he only succeeded in making their position even more awkward. He muttered a curse in Spanish.

'Are you okay?' Dylan asked. She lifted her head and looked up at him, frowning with concern. 'Is the pain coming back now? How do you feel?'

Frustration rose up in his throat on a scoff, but he bit it back. Instead reached out to stroke her cheek. 'Have you always tried to take care of everyone around you before yourself?'

Her frown deepened. 'I don't need taking care of. I haven't needed that in a very long time.'

'How long, Dylan?'

'Ever.'

As she said it, her chin went up a bit, and Rio found it easy to picture Dylan as a freckle-faced little girl stubbornly refusing any and all help, regardless of how badly she might need it. As a woman, she was much the same. Defiant, proud. So afraid to be hurt.

He knew that kind of fear personally as well. He'd walked a similar path from the time he was a child. It was a lonely one; he'd almost not survived it himself. But Dylan was stronger than him in so many ways. He was only now coming to realize just how strong she really was.

And how alone as well.

He recalled that she had passingly mentioned having brothers – a pair of them, both named for rock stars – but he'd never heard her speak of her father. In fact, the only family she seemed to have in her life at all was the woman currently residing in the cancer wing of the hospital down the street. The family she was likely going to lose before long.

'Has it been just the two of you for a while now?' he asked.

She nodded. 'My dad left when I was twelve – abandoned us, actually. They divorced soon afterward, and Mom never remarried. Not for lack of interest.' Dylan laughed, but it was a sad kind of humor. 'My mom has always been a bit of a free spirit, always falling in love with a new man and swearing to me that she's finally found The One. I think she's in love with the state of being in love. Right now, she's crushing on the man who owns the runaway center where she works. God, for her to have so much love left to give even when the cancer is taking so much away from her . . .'

Rio smoothed his fingers down Dylan's arm as she fought the sudden hitch in her voice. 'What about your father? Have you been in touch with him about what's going on?'

She scoffed sharply. 'He wouldn't care, even if I knew where he was and he was sober enough to listen to me. His family was only of value to him when we were bailing him out of trouble or helping him score more booze and drugs.'

'Sounds like a real bastard,' Rio said, anger for Dylan's hurt spiking in his belly. 'Too bad he's gone. I wish I could meet the son of a bitch.'

'You want to hear why he left?'

He petted her hair, watching the candlelight play over the burnished waves. 'Only if you want to tell me.'

'It was my 'gift' as you called it. My weird ability to see the dead.' Dylan idly traced one of his *glyphs* as she spoke, remembering what had to be unpleasant times. 'When I was little, elementary school age and before, my parents never paid much attention to the fact that I occasionally would talk to invisible people. It's not that unusual for kids to have imaginary friends, so I guess they ignored it. Plus, with all the arguing and problems in our house, it wasn't like they heard a lot of what I was saying anyway. Well, not until a few years later, that is. In one of his rare sober moments, my father ran across my diary. I'd been writing about seeing these dead women from time to time, and hearing them speak to me. I was trying to understand why it was happening to me – what it meant, you know? – but he saw it as an opportunity to cash in on me.'

'Jesus.' Rio was despising the man more and more. 'Cash in on you how?'

'He could never hold a job for long, and he was always looking for ways to make a fast buck. He thought if he charged people to come and speak with me – people who'd lost loved ones and were hoping to connect with them somehow – he could just sit back and count the cash as it poured in.' She shook her head slowly. 'I tried to tell him that's not how my visions worked. I couldn't bring them up on command. I never knew when I'd see them, and even when they appeared, it wasn't like I could carry on a conversation with them. The dead women I see speak to me, tell me things they want me to hear, or want me to act on, but that's it. There's no chatting about who's hanging out with them on the Other Side, or any of the other parlor game type of stuff you see on TV. But my father wouldn't listen. He demanded I figure out how to use my skill . . . and so, for a while, I tried to fake it. It didn't last long. One of the families he tried to swindle pressed charges, and my father split. That was the last we ever saw or heard from him.'

Good riddance, Rio thought savagely, but he could understand how that kind of abandonment must have hurt the child Dylan was.

'What about your brothers?' he asked. 'Weren't they old enough to step in and do something about your father?'

'By that time, both of them were gone.' Dylan's voice sounded very quiet, more pained than at any time when she'd been reliving her father's betrayal. 'I was only seven when Morrison died in a car accident. He'd just gotten his license that week, just turned sixteen. My father took him out to celebrate. He got Morrie drunk, and evidently my father was in even worse shape, so he gave the keys to Morrie to drive them home. He missed a turn and ran the car into a telephone pole. My father walked away with a concussion and a broken collarbone, but Morrie . . . he never came out of his coma. He died three days later.'

Rio couldn't contain the growl that boiled up from his throat. The urge to kill, to avenge and protect this woman in his arms was savage, a seething fire in his veins. 'I really need to find this so-called man and give him a taste of true pain,' he muttered. 'Tell me your other brother beat your father to within an inch of his useless life.'

'No,' Dylan said. 'Lennon was older than Morrie by a year and a half, but where Morrie was loud and outgoing, Len was quiet and reserved. I remember the look on his face when Mom came home and told us Morrie had died and our father would be spending a couple days in jail once he got out of the hospital. Len just . . . dissolved. I saw something in him die that day too. He walked out of the house and straight into a military recruiter's office. He couldn't wait to get away . . . from us, from all of it. He never looked back. Some friends of his said he'd been shipped out to Beirut, but I don't know for sure. He never wrote or called. He just . . . disappeared. I just hope he's happy, wherever his life took him. He deserves that.'

'You deserve it too, Dylan. Jesus, you and your mother both deserve more than what life has given you so far.'

She lifted her head and pivoted to face him, her eyes glistening and moist. Rio cupped her beautiful face and brought her to him, kissing her with only the lightest brush of his lips across hers. She wrapped her arms around him, and as he held her there, he wondered if maybe there was a way that he could give Dylan some hope . . . some piece of happiness for her and the mother she loved so dearly.

He thought of Tess – Dante's Breedmate – and the incredible skill she had to heal with her touch. Tess had helped Rio mend from some of his injuries, and more than once he'd witnessed firsthand how she could take away battle wounds and knit broken bones back together again.

She'd said the ability had diminished now that she was

pregnant, but what if there was a chance . . . even a slim one?

As his mind started chugging away on the possibilities, his cell phone went off. He grabbed it from out of the pocket of his discarded jacket and flipped it open.

'Shit. It's Niko.' He hit the talk button. 'Yeah.'

'Where the fuck are you, man?'

He glanced at Dylan, looking so delectably naked in the soft glow of the candles. 'I'm in the city – Midtown. I'm with Dylan.'

'Midtown with Dylan,' Niko repeated, a sardonic edge to his voice. 'I guess that explains why the Rover's sitting at the curb and there's no one here at her place. You two decide to take in a show or something? What the hell's going on with you and that female, amigo?'

Rio didn't feel like explaining at the moment. 'Everything's cool here. Did you and Kade run into any problems?'

'Nope. Located all four individuals and did a gentle little soft-shoe on their memories from the cave.' He chuckled. 'Okay, maybe we weren't so gentle on that asshole she works for at the paper. Guy was a first-class dick. The only one left to do is the female's mother. Tried her home address and the shelter where she works, but no luck either place. You got any idea where she is?'

'Ah . . . yeah,' Rio said. 'Don't worry about it, though. It's under control. I'm going to handle that situation myself.'

There was a beat of silence on the other end. 'Okay. While you're, ah, handling the situation, you want Kade and I to run the Rover out and pick you up? Time's gonna be getting tight soon if we want to make it back to Boston before the sun comes up.'

'Yeah, I need pickup,' Rio said. He rattled off the cross-streets of the hospital complex. 'See you in twenty.'

'Hey, amigo?'

'Yeah?'

'Are we picking you up solo, or should we expect company for the ride back?'

Rio glanced at Dylan, watching as she began putting her clothes back on. He didn't want to say good-bye to her, but bringing her back to the compound with him didn't seem like the kindest thing for him to do either. He'd already dragged her far enough into his problems tonight, first by drinking from her, then by seducing her. If he brought her back with him now, what might he be tempted to do for an encore?

But yet there was a part of him that wanted to hold her close, despite the knowledge that she could – and should – do better than him. He had so little to offer Dylan, yet that didn't keep him from wishing he could give her the world.

'Just call me when you get here,' he told Niko. 'I'll be waiting for you.'

⊰ CHAPTER TWENTY-SEVEN ⊱

Dylan finished getting dressed while Rio made his plans with Nikolai on the phone. He was going back to Boston tonight. From the sound of it, he'd be taking off as soon as the other warriors came to get him. Twenty minutes, he'd said. Not long at all.

And no mention whatsoever of where that left the two of them now.

Dylan tried not to let that sting, but it did. She wanted some indication that what happened between them tonight had meant something to him too. But he was silent behind her in the little back room of the church as he snapped his cell phone closed and started putting his clothes on.

'Are Nancy and the others all right?'

'Yes,' he said from somewhere behind her. 'They're all fine. Niko and Kade didn't harm them, and the process of erasing their memories is painless.'

'That's good.' She leaned over the two half-melted candles and blew them out. In the darkness, she found the courage to ask him the question that had been hanging between them all night. 'So, what now, Rio? When are you going to scrub my memory?'

She didn't hear him move, but she felt the stir in the air as he drew up to her back and his strong, warm hands came to rest softly on her shoulders. 'I don't want to do that, Dylan. For your sake – maybe for my own too – I should erase myself from your memory, but I don't want that. I don't think I could.'

Dylan shut her eyes, holding the tender words close. 'Then . . . where do we go from here?'

Slowly, he turned her around to face him. He kissed her sweetly, then rested his forehead against hers. 'I don't know. I only know that I'm not ready to say good-bye to you right now.'

'Your friends are going to be here soon.'

'Yes.'

'Don't go with them.'

He tilted his chin down and pressed his lips to the top of her head. 'I have to.'

In her heart, even before he said it, Dylan knew he had to go back. His world was with the Order. And regardless of the birthmark that granted her a special place among the Breed, Dylan had to remain with her mom.

She burrowed her cheek into Rio's chest, listening to the solid beat of his heart. She wasn't sure she could let go of him, now that she had her arms wrapped around him. 'Will you come with me, back to the hospital? I want to check in on her one more time tonight.'

'Of course,' Rio said, disengaging from her and taking her hand in his.

They left their makeshift haven in the empty church and walked hand in hand back to the hospital complex. Visiting hours had ended some time ago, but the guard at the front desk seemed used to making exceptions for family members heading up to the cancer ward. He waved Dylan and Rio through, and they took the elevator up to the tenth floor.

Rio waited outside the room as Dylan put her gloves on and opened the door. Her mother was asleep, so Dylan took a seat in the chair beside the bed and just sat there quietly watching her breathe.

There was so much she wanted to tell her – not the least of which being the fact that she had met an extraordinary man. She wanted to tell her mother that she was falling in love. That she was excited and scared and filled with a desperate kind of hope for all that might await in her future with the man standing right outside the hospital room.

She wanted her mom to know that she was falling head over heels in love with Eleuterio de la Noche Atanacio . . . a man like no other she'd ever known before.

But Dylan couldn't say any of those things. They were secrets she had to keep, for now, certainly. Maybe forever.

She reached out and stroked her mom's hair, carefully pulled the thin blanket up under her delicate chin. How she wished her mother could have known one true, profound love in her lifetime. It seemed so unfair that she'd made so many bad choices, loved too many bad men, when she deserved someone decent and kind.

'Oh, Mommy,' Dylan whispered quietly. 'This is so damn unfair.'

Tears welled up and flooded over. Maybe she'd saved a lifetime of crying in preparation of this moment, but there was no stopping them now. Dylan wiped at her tears but they kept coming, too many for her to sweep away with her latex-covered hands. She got up and went around to grab a tissue from the box on her mother's wheeled bed tray. As she dabbed at her eyes, she noticed a ribboned package sitting on a table at the other side of the small room. She walked over and saw that it was chocolates. The box was unopened, and from the look of it, expensive. Curious, Dylan picked up the tiny white card tucked under the silk grosgrain bow.

It read: *To Sharon. Come back to me soon. Yours, G. F.*

Dylan mulled over the initials and realized it had to be the runaway shelter's owner, Mr Fasso. Gordon, her mother had called him. He must have come to visit her sometime after

Dylan had left. And the message on the card sounded a bit more intimate than your basic boss-to-employee, get-well sentiment. . .

Good Lord, could this actually be something more than one of her mom's many disastrous infatuations?

Dylan didn't know whether to laugh or cry even harder at the idea that her mother might have found someone decent. Granted, she didn't know Gordon Fasso outside his general reputation as a wealthy, charitable, somewhat eccentric, businessman. But as far as her mother's taste in men ran, Dylan figured she could – and had – done a lot worse.

She can't hear me.

Dylan froze at the sudden sound of a female voice in the room.

It wasn't her mother's.

It wasn't an earthly voice at all, she realized in the split second before she processed the static-filled whisper and then turned around to face the spirit of a young woman.

I tried to tell her, but she can't hear me . . . can you . . . hear me?

The ghost's lips didn't move, but Dylan heard her speak as clearly as any other specter her Breedmate gift had allowed her to see. She held the sorrowful gaze of a dead girl who looked to be less than twenty years old.

A distant familiarity sparked as Dylan took in the goth clothing and the pair of black braids that hung over the girl's shoulders. She'd seen her before at the shelter. The girl had been one of her mother's favorites – Toni. The runaway who'd no-showed at the job Dylan's mom had gotten for her. Sharon had been so disappointed when she told Dylan about losing Toni to the streets. Now, here that poor lost child was, reaching out at last, but from the grave and truly too far gone for anyone to help her.

So, why was she trying to communicate with Dylan?

In the past, she might have tried to ignore the apparition,

or deny her ability to see it, but not now. Dylan nodded when the ghost asked again if she was being heard.

Too late for me, said the unmoving lips. *But not for them. They need you.*

'Need me for what?' Dylan asked quietly, knowing her own voice never carried into the afterlife. 'Who needs me?'

There are more of us . . . your sisters.

The young woman tilted her head, exposing the underside of her chin. Riding on the slender line of her ethereal skin was the birthmark Dylan knew well.

'You're a Breedmate,' she gasped.

Holy shit.

Had they *all* been Breedmates? All the ghosts she'd ever seen were exclusively female, always young, seemingly healthy-looking women. Had they all been born with the same teardrop-and-crescent-moon stamp that she had?

Too late for me, the ghost of Toni said.

Her form was beginning to break up, fading in and out like a weak hologram. She was becoming transparent, little more than a detached crackle of electricity in the air. Her voice was less than a whisper now, growing weaker as Toni's image dissolved to nothingness.

But Dylan heard what she said, and it chilled her.

Don't let him kill any more of us . . .

Dylan's face was ashen as she came out of her mother's room.

'What happened? Is she okay?' Rio asked, his heart knotting at the thought of Dylan possibly facing her mother's passing all alone. 'Did anything—'

Dylan shook her head. 'No, my mom's fine. She's asleep. But there was . . . Oh, God, Rio.' She lowered her voice and pulled him to a private corner of the hallway. 'I just saw the ghost of a Breedmate.'

'Where?'

'In the room with my mom. The girl was a runaway from the shelter, one my mom was very close to until she went missing recently. Her name was Toni, and she—' Dylan broke off, wrapping her arms around herself. 'Rio, she just told me she was murdered, and that she's not alone. She said there are more like her. She showed me her Breedmate mark and then she told me not to let any more of 'my sisters' be killed too.'

Holy . . . hell.

Dread coiled in Rio's gut as Dylan relayed the unearthly message of warning. Instantly he thought of Dragos's corrupt son, and the very real possibility that the bastard had unleashed the Ancient from its crypt, just as the Order feared. He could be breeding the creature right now, creating multiple new Gen One vampires on multiple females.

For crissake, Dragos's son could be harvesting Breedmates from the four corners of the world for that very purpose.

'She said 'don't let him kill any more of *us*,' like I was in danger as well.'

Rio's skin went tight with foreboding. 'You're sure this is what you saw – what you heard?'

'Yes.'

'Show me.' He took a step toward the room. 'I need to see this for myself. Is it still in there?'

Dylan shook her head. 'No, she's gone now. The apparitions are like mist . . . they don't stay visible for very long.'

'Did you ask her where the others might be, or who it was that killed her?'

'It doesn't work that way, unfortunately. They can speak, but I don't think they can hear me wherever they are. I've tried, but that never works.' Dylan stared at him for a long moment. 'Rio, I think every one of these visitations I've had – from the very first, when I was just a kid – has been the spirit of a dead Breedmate. I always thought it was odd that

I only saw females, young females, who should have been in prime health. When I saw the birthmark under Toni's chin, it all clicked into place in my mind. Rio, I get it now – I *feel* it. They've all been Breedmates.'

Rio ran a hand over his scalp, letting a sharp oath hiss through his teeth. 'I need to call Boston and fill them in on this.'

Dylan nodded, still staring up into his eyes. When she spoke, her voice was a little shaky. 'Rio, I'm scared.'

He pulled her close, knowing what it cost her to admit that, even to him. 'Don't be. I'll keep you safe. But I can't leave you here tonight, Dylan. I'm taking you back with me to the compound.'

She frowned. 'But my mom—'

'If I can help her too, I will,' he said, putting it all out there for her now. 'But first I need to know that you'll be safe.'

Dylan's eyes pleaded with him, then, at last, she gave a small nod of her head. 'All right, Rio. I'll go back with you.'

⇥ CHAPTER TWENTY-EIGHT ⇤

R io didn't trance Dylan for the ride back to Boston. Despite sidelong looks from Nikolai and Kade in the front of the SUV that suggested he was an idiot to break protocol on that, Rio couldn't treat Dylan with anything but total faith. He knew he was taking one hell of a gamble that she could be trusted with the location of the Order's headquarters, even though he wasn't sure how long – or in what capacity – she'd be staying with him there, but he did trust her.

Hell, more than that, he was pretty damn sure he loved her.

He kept that stunning realization to himself, however, seeing very clearly that Dylan was anxious about leaving her mother alone in New York. Each mile they traveled closer to Boston, he felt her heart beat a bit faster. He didn't need to be bonded to her by blood to feel the tang of indecision rolling off her body in waves as she rested quietly against him in the backseat, her gaze fixed on the blur of scenery speeding past the tinted windows.

She didn't want to be here.

Rio didn't doubt that she felt some affection toward him. After tonight, he knew she did. And he had to believe that under different circumstances, she wouldn't feel so much like she wanted to bolt from the moving vehicle and race back home to New York.

'Hey,' he murmured next to her ear as Niko swung the Rover into the gated drive of the compound. 'We're going to figure all of this out, okay?'

She gave him a small smile, but her eyes were sad. 'Just hold me, Rio.'

He drew her farther into his embrace and pressed his lips to hers in a tender kiss. 'I won't let anything bad happen. I promise you that.'

He wasn't entirely sure how he could make good on a sizable vow like that, but seeing the look of hope in Dylan's eyes as she gazed up at him, damn if he wouldn't make it his life's mission to see the promise through, whatever it took.

The SUV rolled through and headed for the Order's secured fleet garage. Rio hated to let go of Dylan as the car came to a stop inside the hangar.

'Home, sweet home,' Kade drawled, opening the passenger door and climbing out.

Nikolai shot Rio a look over the front seats. 'We're gonna head down to the lab. Should we tell Lucan and the others you'll be around shortly?'

Rio nodded. 'Yeah, right behind you. Give me ten minutes.'

'You got it.' Niko glanced to Dylan. 'Listen, I'm really sorry about your mother. That's got to be tough. There just are no adequate words, you know?'

'I know,' she murmured. 'But thank you, Nikolai.'

Niko held her gaze for a moment, then he clapped his palm on the seatback. 'Okay. See you below, my man.'

'Tell Lucan I'm going to be bringing Dylan in on the meeting.'

Both she and Niko threw looks of surprise in his direction.

Outside the Rover, Kade exhaled a wry curse and started laughing under his breath like Rio had lost his mind.

'You want to bring a civilian into a meeting with Lucan,' Niko said. 'A civilian he fully expects that you scrubbed tonight, like he told you to do.'

'Dylan saw something tonight,' Rio said. 'I think the Order ought to hear about firsthand.'

Nikolai considered him in silence for a very long time. Then he nodded like he could see that Rio wasn't going to budge on this. Rio could tell that his old friend realized that Dylan was not merely a civilian, or a mission Rio had failed to execute. By the glint of the warrior's wintry blue eyes, Rio could see that Niko understood just how much Dylan had come to mean to him. He understood, and based on the crooked smile that tugged at the corner of his mouth, he approved.

'Shit, amigo. Yeah. I'll tell him what you said.'

As Niko and Kade strode off to the compound's elevator together, Rio and Dylan got out of the Rover and headed in a couple of minutes behind them. Hands linked, they took the elevator down the three-hundred-foot descent to the Order's headquarters.

It felt strange to walk the labyrinth of secured corridors and not feel like he had for the long months following the explosion – like a lost beast left to roam its lair without place or purpose.

Now, he had both, the heart of which could be summed up in one word: Dylan.

'Will you be comfortable talking about what you saw in that hospital room tonight?' he asked her as they traveled the corridors. 'Because if you'd rather not, I can do it for—'

'No, it's fine. I want to help, if you think I can.'

He stopped her in the long stretch of white marble hallway, not far from the glass walls of the tech lab where his brethren would be waiting.

'Dylan, what you did for me tonight – giving me your blood, staying with me when you had every right to leave me there and never look back . . . Everything that happened between us tonight, I want you to know that it meant something to me. I am . . .'

He wanted to say that he was falling in love with her, but he hadn't said those words in so long – hadn't believed he would ever mean them again, let alone mean them as deeply and honestly as he did now. He stumbled over the admission, and the awkward pause made the chasm seem even wider.

'I am . . . grateful to you,' he said, settling on the other emotion that was filling his heart when he looked at her. 'I don't know that I can ever repay you for all that you gave me tonight.'

Some of the light seemed to dim from her eyes as she listened to him. 'Do you think I would ask you to repay me?' She shook her head slowly. '*De nada*. You don't owe me anything, Rio.'

He started to say something more – some other feeble attempt to explain what she had come to mean to him. But Dylan was already walking ahead of him.

'Shit,' he hissed, raking his hand through his hair.

He caught up to her a few paces up the corridor, just in time to hear Lucan's voice boom through the glass of the tech lab.

'What the fuck do you mean, he's bringing her in with him? My man had better have a goddamn good reason for bringing that reporter back into this compound.'

Any irritation Dylan had felt toward Rio for his polite gratitude was dwarfed by the dread that ran cold in her veins when she heard the Order's leader bellow in outrage. She didn't want to think she needed Rio's protection, but the presence of his broad palm coming to rest at the small of her back as they entered the meeting room full of eight grim-faced, combat-garbed vampire warriors was the only thing that kept her knees from quaking beneath her.

Dylan's eyes made a quick scan of the menace she faced: Lucan, the dark-haired one in charge, was obvious. He'd been with Rio earlier today, laying down the curt instructions that she be taken back home to New York and mind-scrubbed like her mom, her boss, and her friends.

Beside Lucan at an impressive command center of more than half a dozen computer workstations and twice as many monitors was a Breed male with spiky blond hair that looked like it had been raked into a state of total anarchy on the top of his head. He glanced at Dylan from over the tops of thin rectangular sunglasses with pale sky blue lenses. Of all of the warriors gathered there, this one seemed the least threatening, even though he was easily more than six feet tall and had a body as lean and fit and muscular as the others.

'This is Dylan Alexander,' Rio announced to the group. 'I'm sure by now you've heard all about what happened in Jičín, with the cave, and the pictures Dylan took of what was inside.'

Lucan crossed his arms over his chest. 'What I'd like to know is why you apparently ignored mission directives and brought her back with you tonight. She may be a Breedmate, but she's a civilian, Rio. A civilian with media contacts, for fuck's sake.'

'Not anymore,' Dylan interjected, speaking for herself before Rio was forced to defend her. 'My media contacts, such as they were, are gone. And even if they weren't, you have my word that I would never willfully divulge any of what I know to the outside world. I wish I'd never taken those pictures or written that story. I am truly sorry for anything I've done to put the Breed at risk of exposure.'

If they believed her, none of them gave any clear indication of that. The rest of the Order stared at her from where
they were seated at a large conference table, like a jury measuring the convicted. Niko and Kade were there, sitting next
to a black warrior with a skull-trim and shoulders that would
dwarf the biggest NFL linebacker. But if that guy looked
menacing, the one across the table from him was even more
intimidating. With shoulder-length tawny hair and shrewd,
jewel-green eyes, the warrior looked like he'd seen – and likely
done – it all . . . and then some.

He watched Dylan with a narrowed, studying gaze, as did
the remaining two males in the room – a cocky-looking warrior
polishing a rather nasty pair of curved blades, and a military-
type with a tight buzz cut, chiseled chin and cheekbones, and
grim, steel blue eyes.

Rio's arm came around her shoulders. It was a light embrace
that made her feel safe, as if she wasn't standing alone before
this dangerous cadre of combat-trained warriors. Rio
supported her, perhaps her sole ally in the room.

He trusted her. Dylan could feel that trust in the warmth
of his body, and in the tender way he looked at her as he
addressed his brethren.

'You all are aware of Dylan's discovery of the hidden cave
on that mountain, but you haven't heard exactly how it was
that she was able to find it.' Rio cleared his throat. 'Eva showed
her the way.'

A rumble of disbelief – even blatant hostility – rolled
through the room. But it was Lucan's voice that rose above
them all.

'Now you're telling us she's somehow connected to that trai-
torous bitch? Just how the hell is that possible when Eva's been
dead for the past year?'

'Dylan saw Eva's ghost that day on the mountain,' Rio
said. 'That is Dylan's special ability, to see and hear the

dead. Eva appeared to her and guided her to me up in that cave.'

Dylan watched the warriors absorb that bit of news. She could see from nearly every hard face in the room that Eva had no friends among them. And no wonder, considering what she'd done to Rio. What she'd done to them all through her betrayal.

'Tonight Dylan saw another dead female,' Rio said. 'She saw another Breedmate, actually. This time the apparition appeared in her mother's hospital room. The dead girl said something I think you're all going to want to hear.'

He turned to Dylan and gave her a nod to continue the explanation herself. She met the grave stares and carefully relayed everything Toni's spirit had told her, line for line, recalling every word in case it might help make sense of the warning from the Other Side.

'Jesus Christ,' said the warrior over at the bank of computer equipment as Dylan finished speaking. He raked his fingers over his scalp, further mussing the cropped blond spikes. 'Rio, remind me again what you said the other day about someone potentially breeding another population of first generation Breed vampires?'

Rio nodded, and the grim look on his face put a chill in Dylan's spine. 'If the Ancient has been awakened successfully from its hibernation, what's to say it's not procreating? Or being made to procreate?'

As Dylan listened to them talk, pieces of a puzzle she'd been mulling over for the past several days – ever since she set foot in that cave – now clicked into place in her mind. The hidden crypt with its open tomb. The strange, otherworldly symbols on the walls. The unshakable sense of evil that permeated the dark cavern, even though its original occupant was gone . . .

The cave had been a holding tank – a hibernation chamber, just like Rio had inadvertently told her.

And the dangerous creature that had been sleeping inside it was now loose somewhere.

Breeding.

Killing.

Oh, God.

From across the long table, Nikolai shot a frown in Rio's direction. 'With the last of those alien savages back in the baby-making business, the question then would be, how long has he been going at it?'

'And on how many Breedmates,' Lucan added soberly. 'If we truly have a scenario here where Breedmates are being captured and held somewhere, and, in at least a few cases, killed, then I hate to even consider where this could be heading. Gideon, you wanna run a check on Darkhaven records, see if there are any missing persons reports on Breedmates over the past decade or so?'

'On it,' he replied, hitting the keyboard and firing off what appeared to be multiple searches on multiple computers.

The warrior at the conference table who looked like something out of *Soldier of Fortune*, spoke up next. 'Well, nothing short of a miracle, but the Enforcement Agency's Regional Director has actually agreed to a meeting tonight. You want me to mention this newsflash from the dead Breedmate to Director Starkn?'

Lucan seemed to ponder the idea, then he gave a vague shake of his head. 'Let's hold off on that for now, Chase. We're not sure precisely what we're looking for yet, and we'll be upsetting the Agency's apple cart bad enough when we tell them we think the population's few remaining Gen Ones are being targeted for assassination.'

Chase nodded in agreement.

As the group began talking amongst themselves, Lucan walked over to speak with Rio and Dylan privately.

'I appreciate the information,' he told her. 'But as valuable

as it may prove to be, this compound is no place for a civilian.'
He glanced at Rio, those silvery eyes studying him closely.
'She was given a choice and she made it. You know we can't
permit her to stay. Not as a civilian.'

'Yeah,' Rio said. 'I know that.'

Lucan waited, obviously tuned in to the fact that something
intimate had passed between Dylan and Rio. He cleared his
throat. 'So, if you've got something to tell me, my man . . .'

Through the lengthy silence that answered, Dylan unconsciously held her breath. She didn't know what she was waiting
for Rio to say: That he was prepared to challenge Lucan's
rule? That he loved her and would fight to keep her at his
side, no matter what the rest of the Order thought of her?

But he didn't say anything like that.

'I need to talk to Dante,' he told Lucan. 'And I need to
talk to Tess. There's something important I need to ask her.'

Lucan considered him through narrowed eyes. 'You know
what I expect, Rio. You let me know if anything changes.'

'Yeah,' Rio replied.

When Lucan turned and strode back to converse with
Gideon, Rio lifted Dylan's chin on the edge of his hand. 'I
promised you that I was going to try to help your mother,' he
reminded her gently. At her nod, he went on. 'I don't know
if it can be done, but before we can talk about you and I,
that question needs to be answered. I know I can't ask you to
stay with me when you're hurting to be near your family. I
wouldn't ask that of you.'

Hope flickered in her chest. 'But do you . . . want to ask
me to stay with you?'

He caressed her cheek, smoothing her hair back behind
her ear. 'God, yes. I want that, Dylan, very much.'

Rio bent his head down and kissed her, right there in front
of the other warriors. It was brief but so, so sweet. When he
drew back, Dylan felt the eyes of the Order on her – on both

of them. But it was Rio's eyes that held her spellbound. They were heated with desire and tender affection, the huge irises flashing with sparks of amber light.

'Let me take you back to my quarters and get you something to eat. I have to talk to Dante and Tess, but I won't be long.'

⊰ CHAPTER TWENTY-NINE ⊱

Rio's quarters were quiet when he returned to them a short while later. He could smell the trace scents of the other Breedmates who'd been there not long ago to bring her food and keep her company, but it was Dylan's juniper and honey essence that drew him through the empty rooms toward the bedroom suite. The shower was running in the adjacent bathroom, and it didn't take much for him to imagine a lot of rolling steam and sudsy hot water licking her beautiful body.

He approached the partially open door and discovered that the reality was even better than his imagination.

Dylan stood beneath the double heads of the huge walk-in shower, her hands braced on the tiles, spine arched in a graceful curve that caught the drenching blasts of the sprays. Her chin was tilted back, eyes closed. Her fiery hair was soaked to a dark copper shot with gold, clinging to her like wet silk as she rinsed the shampoo from its length.

Frothy white suds ran over the round cheeks of her backside . . . *Cristo*, down between them too, into the tight cleft of her ass and onto her long, slender thighs.

Rio licked his lips, his mouth gone suddenly dry. He felt the ache of his emerging fangs, and the answering throb of his cock as hunger rose within him for this female.

His female, answered an impulse that was purely male, purely Breed.

He wanted her. Wanted her wet and warm beneath him, and he didn't think he could wait too long to have her.

He must have made some kind of noise because Dylan's head came down sharply and turned toward him. Her eyes snapped open, then she smiled at him through the glass . . . a slow, seductive smile that made him wish he was naked right now, climbing under the water with her.

But making love in the darkness of a small church alcove was a far different thing than doing it face-to-face, body to body, in the bright yellow light and mirrored expanse of where they were now. In here, he had nowhere to hide. Dylan would see him – all of him, all of the scars she may not have noticed when they were making love in the dark several hours ago.

Shame made him want to douse the dozen recessed lights overhead. He flicked an irritated glance upward, but Dylan's voice distracted him from the thought.

'Rio . . . join me.'

Madre de Dios, but the sound of that husky invitation was almost enough to distract him from all thought completely . . . except for the one that urged him to take his clothes off and do as she was asking him to.

He met her eyes through the glass of the shower door, his own heavy-lidded and sharp with the flood of swamping amber that was surely turning his pupils into thinnest slivers of black.

'I want you in here with me,' Dylan said. She held his stare as she ran her palms up her flat belly and over the buoyant swells of her breasts. 'Come in here with me . . . I want to feel your hands on me. All over me.'

Holy . . . fuck.

Rio's jaw was clamped so tightly his molars should have shattered. It was damn hard to wallow in self-doubt or shame when the only woman he wanted – a woman he wanted more than anything ever before in his entire existence – was looking at him like she intended to devour him whole.

He got rid of his boots and socks, then stripped out of his shirt and pants and boxers. He stood there, naked, fully erect, his *dermaglyphs* pulsing with all the colors of his desire. Hands fisted at his sides, he let Dylan take a good long look at him. It was excruciating – those first few seconds as her darkening eyes lowered and her gaze swept slowly over him.

He knew what she was seeing. Hell, he could see it well enough for himself: his battered torso, the skin of which was glossy and tight in some places, rough in others, where he still carried tiny pieces of shrapnel embedded several layers down into his flesh. And farther down was the thick red scar that ran down the length of his left thigh, the gash that had almost cost him the limb entirely.

Dylan was seeing all of that ugliness now.

He waited for her eyes to lift.

He waited to see pity in her face, dreaded that he might see revulsion.

'Rio,' she murmured thickly.

Her head came up slowly and her eyes met his. Her peridot gaze was the color of a night-dark forest now, her pupils large beneath the heavy fall of her lashes. There was no pity there, nothing but dusky, feminine desire.

Rio wanted to throw his head back and shout his relief, but the sight of Dylan's parted lips, her hungry eyes drinking him in so wantonly, robbed him of his voice.

She opened the glass door of the shower. 'Get in here,' she demanded, her mouth curling into the most incredibly sexy smile. 'Get in here . . . right now.'

He grinned and stepped inside, joining her under the warm spray.

'That's better,' Dylan purred as she wrapped her arms around him and pulled him down into a deep, wet kiss.

She felt so good against him, all that slick, hot skin, all those exquisite curves. Rio held her close, burrowing his fingers into her wet hair, feeling the warm beat of her pulse against his wrist where it rested at the side of her neck.

'I want to taste you,' she said, already breaking away from his mouth to kiss a slow trail down his throat, to the hollow at its base, then along the line of his shoulder. She sank lower still, playing her tongue over the muscled slabs of his chest, teasing his male nipples into tight little buds. 'You taste good, Rio. I could eat you up.'

He groaned as she let her mouth travel down his sternum, nipping at him as she went along. Her kiss got less playful as she moved toward his scarred left side.

Rio sucked in his breath. 'Don't,' he rasped, awkward panic seizing him when he thought of her getting anywhere near those hideous marks. She glanced up at him in question and he wanted to die from shame. 'It's all right. You don't have to . . .'

'Will it hurt you if I touch you there?' she asked gently, her fingers skating so carefully over the ruined skin. 'Does that hurt at all, Rio?'

He managed a weak shake of his head.

It didn't hurt. What little he could feel through the damaged nerve endings and scars felt good.

Cristo en cielo, it felt so very good to be touched by her.

'Does this hurt?' she asked, pressing the lightest, most caring kiss to the ugliest part of him. 'How does that feel, Rio?'

'Good,' he rasped, his throat going thick, and not just from the sheer pleasure of Dylan's mouth on his body. Her tender gift just now – that sweet, accepting kiss – touched a place in him so deep and forgotten he thought it had been long dead. 'Dylan . . . you are . . . Jesus, but you are the most incredible woman I have ever known. I truly mean that.'

She smiled up at him, beaming now. 'Well, brace yourself, because I'm only getting started.'

Going down on her knees on the tiles before him, Dylan

kissed his pelvis and thighs, lapping at the thin rivulets of water that sluiced down from over his shoulders. Each brush of her mouth near his cock made his erection ratchet tighter, harder. When she reached up and took him in her small wet hands, he thought he was going to lose it.

'How does this feel?' she asked as she stroked him from balls to head and back again, the wicked look in her eyes telling him she knew precisely how it must feel.

Good thing, because he was incapable of talk so long as she was lavishing such slow, rhythmic attention on him.

And as if that weren't glorious enough, Dylan's tongue joined the party too. She slid along the length of his shaft, then wrapped her lips around the head of his cock and sucked him deep into her mouth.

Rio let out a hoarse moan, and it was all he could do to hold his balance as she swallowed even more of him. He shuddered as she tongued the underside of his penis, her mouth moving up and down on him, tightening the pressure that was already building at the base of his spine. A fierce orgasm was roaring up on him like a freight train.

Ah, fuck, if he didn't stop her soon he was going to –

With an animal snarl, he lifted Dylan off his throbbing sex. 'My turn now,' he said, his voice deep and otherworldly.

She gasped as he pushed her back against the tiles and kissed her with the same slow torment she'd dealt to him. He played his mouth along her throat and down between her breasts, where the fluttering drum of her heartbeat danced against his tongue. He kissed her perfect rosy nipples, using only the slightest tips of his fangs to graze her as he moved lower, to the dip of her navel and then the pleasing curve of her hip.

'You taste very good too,' he told her thickly, giving her a glimpse of his fully extended fangs. Her eyes widened, but not in fear. He heard her sharp intake of breath as he bent his head and sucked gently at the sweet little vee of red curls between her thighs. 'Mmm,' he moaned against her creamy flesh. 'You taste very, very good.'

She cried out at the first press of his mouth on her sex, then melted into a slow, sultry moan as his tongue cleaved into the tender folds of her core. He was merciless, wanting to hear her scream from the pleasure he was giving her. He burrowed deeper between her soft thighs, reveling in the sharp twist of his hair as she grabbed his head and held him to her, trembling as he stoked her toward release.

'Oh, my God,' she whispered tightly, her breath panting. 'Oh, Rio . . . yes . . .'

She said his name again, not just the nickname everyone knew him by, but his true name. The one that sounded so right on her lips. She screamed his name as her orgasm overtook her, and it was the most beautiful thing he'd ever known.

Rio wanted to hold her, but his need was too great now. His cock was ready to explode, and he wanted to be inside her -- needed to be - the same way he needed breath and blood to survive.

He stood up and smoothed the wet hair from her face. 'Turn around,' he rasped. 'Put your hands against the tiles and arch your back, like you were when I first came in here.'

With a pleasured smile, she obliged him, planting her palms wide and putting that beautiful backside right in front of him. Rio caressed her flawless skin, letting his fingers trail into the cleft between the round cheeks, and into the slick mouth of her sex. She drew in her breath as he spread her open and played the tip of his cock against the swollen, dark pink folds.

'This is what I wanted to do to you when I saw you in here, Dylan.'

'Yes,' she whispered, trembling as he stroked her so intimately.

He pushed inside and felt the hot walls of her womb grip

his hard flesh. He withdrew, shuddering all the way from the sheer bliss of it. Holy hell, but he wasn't going to last long like this. Nor did he care if he did. He needed to lose himself inside Dylan's warmth, surrender all he had to her, because he knew in his heart that their time together was fleeting.

She would be going back to her world before long, while he remained in his.

Rio wrapped his arms around Dylan's body, holding her as close as he could bring her as his climax started to break over him. He shouted with the sudden blast of his release.

And even after it was over, his arms remained tightly wrapped around the woman he knew he couldn't keep.

⇥ CHAPTER THIRTY ⇤

Dylan wasn't sure how many hours had passed since Rio took her to his bed. They had toweled each other off then made love again, more slowly the second time, as if to memorize every nuance of the moment and hold it close.

As much as she didn't want to think it, Dylan knew she couldn't stay here with Rio much longer. She had a life in progress back in New York, and not being near her mother at a time when she needed Dylan the most was tearing her up inside.

But God, it felt good to lie in Rio's arms like this.

With her cheek resting against his bare chest, Dylan stroked his soft skin, idly tracing the elegant flourish of one of his *dermaglyphs*. The markings were just a shade darker than his olive skin tone now, but as she touched them, color began to infuse the intricate patterns, making them blush with a color she was learning indicated waking arousal.

Still another indication of his interest was starting to rouse as well, nudging hard against her belly.

'Keep that up, and you may never get out of this bed,' he drawled, his deep voice vibrating against her cheek.

'I'm not sure I want to get out of this bed any time soon,' she replied. When she glanced up at him, Rio's eyes were closed, his sensual, wickedly talented mouth curved in a satisfied smile. 'I can't remember ever feeling this happy, Rio. It feels like a dream, being with you like this. I know I have to wake up sometime, but I don't want to.'

His lids lifted and Dylan basked in the warmth of his dark topaz gaze. 'What's happening between us has been . . . very unexpected, Dylan. Until you walked into that mountain cave, I thought my life was over. I knew it was, because I was prepared to end it myself. That very night, in fact.'

'Rio,' she whispered, heart twisting at the thought.

'Nikolai left me with a cache of explosives when the Order first discovered the hidden crypt in February. They all returned to Boston, but I stayed behind. I was supposed to seal the cave so no one else could find it. I promised I would, and told Niko I would go home to Spain for a while, once I had carried out my mission.' He exhaled a short sigh. 'I never intended to leave that mountain. All I had to do was set up the C-4 and detonate it from inside . . .'

'You were going to trap yourself in there?' Dylan asked, horrified. 'My God, Rio. That would have been a long, terrible, lonely way to die.'

He shrugged. 'I didn't care. I thought it would have to be better than living like I was.'

'But you were there for several months before I found the cave. You must have found some hope to keep you from going through with your plans.'

His bitter chuckle seemed to scrape in the back of his throat. 'I delayed at first because I didn't have the balls to finish it. Then my headaches and blackouts started up again, so bad I thought I was losing my mind.'

'Your blackouts – you mean, like what happened to you last night by the river?'

'Yes. They can be pretty bad. I wasn't feeding anymore by then, so starvation only added to the fun. At some point, I lost track of all time.'

'Then I came along.'

He smiled. 'Then you came along.' He lifted her hand and kissed her palm, then the pulse point at her wrist. 'You have been so very unexpected, Dylan. You bring me a happiness I've never known either.'

'Never? Not even . . . before, with Eva?' Dylan hated asking him to compare them, yet she really needed to know the answer. When Rio was quiet for a moment, her heart began to sink. 'I'm sorry. You don't have to tell me. I don't mean to make this awkward for you.'

He shook his head, brows pinched together. 'Eva was sultry and flirtatious. She was a very beautiful woman. Every male who saw her wanted her – Breed and human alike. I was astonished that she noticed me. Even more so when she made it clear that she wanted to be my mate. She pursued me like she did anything else she set her sights on, and my ego knew no bounds. Things cooled between us a bit after I joined the Order. Eva resented sharing me with my calling as a warrior.'

Dylan listened, awash in a very unpleasant state of jealousy for what she was hearing, and regret that she had brought this feeling on herself by forcing him to talk about the woman he'd loved before.

'After the disaster of what happened with Eva, I wasn't looking to open myself up to another woman. But you, Dylan . . .' He picked up a strand of her hair, following the golden-red light in it as the silky wave curled around his finger. 'You are pure flame. I touch you and I ignite. I kiss you and I burn to have more. You consume me . . . like no other woman before you, and, I am certain, like no other ever could again.'

She rose up and kissed him, holding his face in her hands. When she drew back, she couldn't keep from blurting out just how much he meant to her. 'I love you, Rio. It scares me to death to say it out loud, but I do. I love you.'

'Ah, *Dios*,' he whispered roughly. 'Dylan . . . I have been falling in love with you since the very beginning. How you could love me, the way I am now, I don't know . . .'

'The way you are now,' Dylan said, slowly shaking her head in wonder, 'the way you look at me, the way you touch me, how could I not love you? You, Rio. Just as you are now.'

She caressed him with all the emotion she felt for him, letting her fingers skate gently down the rugged left side of the handsome face she would never tire of seeing.

She hardly noticed the scars now. Oh, tragically, there was no reversing what he'd been through. The evidence of the hell he'd survived would always be there, on his face and on his body. But when Dylan looked at Rio, she saw his courage, his strength.

She saw his honor, and to her eyes, he was the most beautiful man she'd ever seen.

'I love you, Eleuterio de la Noche Atanacio. With all my heart.'

Something fiercely tender flashed across his features. With a tight sound caught in his throat, he crushed her against him and simply held her there.

'More than anything, I want your happiness,' he murmured beside her ear. 'I know that your family – your mother's well-being – means the world to you. I know that you need to be with her.'

'Yes,' Dylan whispered. She drew out of his embrace and met his gaze. 'I can't leave her now, Rio. I just . . . I can't.'

He nodded. 'I know. I understand that you need to be there for her, Dylan. But there is a selfish part of me that would try to convince you that this is where you belong now. With me, bonded in blood, as my mate.'

Oh, she liked the sound of that. She recalled quite vividly how incredible it had been to have Rio feed from her vein. She wanted that again . . . now, when the love she felt for him was overflowing her heart.

But she couldn't stay.

'I won't ask it of you now, Dylan. But I want you to know that's what I want, to be with you, always. It's what I'm willing to wait for.'

Joy erupted inside her at the tenderness of his words. 'You'll wait . . .'

'For as long as it takes, I will wait for you, Dylan.' He smoothed a strand of hair from her cheek, and hooked it behind her ear. 'You remember I told you I would try to find a way to help your mother once we came back here to the compound?'

'Yes.'

'That's why I needed to speak with Tess. She is Dante's Breedmate.'

Dylan nodded. 'She helped me clean and bandage my cheek the other day.'

'Right. She's a healer. Before her pregnancy, Tess was gifted with the ability to heal open wounds with her touch alone. She's healed internal ailments as well. There's an ugly little terrier running around the compound that's alive only because Tess was able to cure about half a dozen things that were killing it. Including cancer, Dylan. I didn't want to say anything to you about this until I had a chance to talk with Tess and Dante first.'

Dylan wasn't breathing. She stared at Rio in astonishment, not sure she could trust her ears. 'Tess can cure cancer? But only in animals, right? I mean, you're not saying that she could possibly help . . .'

'Her gift doesn't appear to be limited to animals, but there is a complication. Since her pregnancy, her skills are diminished. She's not sure it could work for your mother, but she told me that she'd be willing to try—'

Dylan didn't let him finish. A hope so bright it was a blinding burst to life inside her as she launched herself at Rio and threw her arms around him in a fierce hug. 'Oh, my God! Rio, thank you.'

He peeled her off him with gentle hands. 'It's not a guarantee. It's only the slimmest possibility, and even that is being optimistic. The odds are very good that Tess won't be able to help.'

Dylan nodded, accepting the idea that it was a long shot, yet elated that there might be even a glimmer of a chance to save her mother.

'She would have to be brought here, to the mansion. Dante won't risk letting Tess travel now that she's expecting. And we can't risk letting your mother know where we're located or what was done to her, so if this is what she wants, it will mean scrubbing her memory of the entire thing once it's finished. And that's still no guarantee that her cancer will be cured.'

'But it's a chance,' Dylan said. 'That's more than what she has now. Without that chance, she probably only has a few more months. And if Tess can help her . . .'

Then that miracle would likely buy her mother years, even decades. At sixty-four and in good health, it wouldn't be unreasonable for her mom to live another twenty-five or thirty years.

At what point would Dylan be willing to abandon her for her own slice of happiness back here with Rio?

She looked at him and saw that the question was one he'd already considered too. He was willing to try to help Dylan's mother because he knew Dylan couldn't bear to lose her, even though he also knew it could mean pushing what he wanted that much farther out of his reach.

'Rio . . .'

'I would wait,' he said solemnly. 'Until you're ready, I will wait for you.'

She closed her eyes and felt his love pour over her like a balm. That he would give her such a selfless gift – the gift of hope – made Dylan adore him all the more. She kissed him with all the devotion she felt in her heart, needing to be close to him . . . to feel him inside her in every way possible.

She thought of the bond he'd mentioned – that of blood, something to be shared as his mate. She wanted that. Needed to feel linked to him in that very primal, exclusively Breed way.

'Make me yours,' she murmured against his mouth. 'Right now, Rio . . . I want you to make me yours through blood. I want to be bonded with you. I don't want to wait for that.'

His low, approving growl made her tingle with anticipation. 'It's unbreakable. Once done, it cannot be undone.'

'Even better.'

She nipped his lower lip and was rewarded with an answering graze of his fangs as he rolled over with her and pressed her down beneath him on the bed. Sparks of amber crowded the smoky topaz color of his irises. His pupils were razor sharp, fixed on her in desire. He kissed her, and Dylan let her tongue play at the tips of his long fangs, dying to feel them piercing the fine skin of her neck.

But Rio drew back, bracing himself over her on his fists. He looked so powerful poised above her, so beautifully, nakedly male. 'I shouldn't do this to you,' he said softly, reverently. 'If you take my blood into your body, Dylan, then I will always be a part of you . . . even if you decide to live your life without me. You will always sense me in your veins, whether you will it or not. I should give you more freedom than this.'

Dylan stared up at him without the slightest reservation. 'I want this, Rio. I want you to be a part of me always. My heart will know you forever, whether or not we bond by blood right now.'

He cursed softly, shaking his head. 'You're sure this is what you want? You're sure that you want . . . me?'

'Forever,' she told him. 'I've never been more sure of anything in my life.'

His breath rasped out of him raggedly as he straddled her waist and sat back on his knees. He brought his wrist up to his mouth. With his hot amber stare fixed on her eyes, Rio curled his lips off his fangs and sank the sharp points into his flesh.

Blood began a steady run down his forearm, the punctures pulsing with each hard beat of his heart. Very gently, he raised Dylan's head and shoulders up from the pillow and held his wound out to her.

'Drink from me, love.'

She felt the hot, wet liquid against her lips, smelled the spicy dark scent of his blood as she drew a breath and covered his bite with her mouth.

The first brush of her tongue across his open vein was electric. Power crackled through her entire body at the first tentative swallow she took from him. She felt her limbs tingle, fingers and toes prickling with a strange, enjoyable heat. The warmth spread, into her chest and stomach, then into her very being. She was melting with the intensity of it, desire starting a swift, steady burn in her core.

And God, he tasted so good.

Dylan drew from him, lost in the pulsing heat he fed her from his veins. She glanced up and found him watching her, his look one of raw need and pure masculine pride. His cock stood fully erect, larger than ever.

Dylan reached for him, stroking him as she suckled hard at his wrist. When she spread her thighs and guided him toward her, Rio threw his head back and hissed, the cords of his neck as taut as cables. He dropped his head back down and she was blasted with amber from his passion-swamped eyes.

It took only the barest flex of her hips to seat him at her core. He entered her on a long, hard thrust, stretching his legs out with hers as he covered her with his body.

'You are mine now, Dylan.'

His voice was thick below her ear, not quite his own now, but sexy as hell. He rocked against her as she drank from him, her climax already screaming to a peak.

As she shattered beneath him in that next blinding second, Rio buried his face into her neck and bit down into her vein.

≼ CHAPTER THIRTY-ONE ≽

It was damn hard to watch Dylan get showered and dressed that next morning, knowing that she was leaving.

But Rio didn't try to stop her. She was going somewhere he couldn't follow – into a daylight world that would probably keep her away from him longer than he wanted to admit. Maybe longer than he could actually bear.

The hours they had shared in his bed, forging a bond through mingling blood and promises that this wasn't really good-bye, had to be enough for him. At least for now.

He couldn't keep her from the life that waited her outside, as much as it killed him to walk her to the compound's elevator and ride the long distance up to the Order's fleet garage above.

They paused together as they stepped out of the elevator. Rio held out the keys to one of his cars. Not one of the sports coupes with the barely legal engines, but a nice, safe Volvo sedan. Hell, he would have put her in an armored tank if he had one to give her. He clicked the remote lock entry button and the Volvo five vehicles back responded with a little chirp.

'You call me every hour and let me know you're okay,' he said, putting the keys and her cell phone in her hand. 'The encrypted number I programmed into your phone comes directly to me. I want to hear from you every hour, just so I know everything's good.'

'You want me to risk getting a ticket for operating a motor vehicle while talking on a cell phone?' She smiled and arched a brow at him. 'Maybe you want to plug me with a GPS chip before I go too?'

'The car's already equipped with GPS,' he said, glad she was keeping it light, especially since he was feeling anything but. 'If you wait here for a second, I'm sure Gideon or Niko could come up with something for you as well.'

Dylan's quiet laugh was a bit hollow. She reached up and smoothed her fingers into the hair at his nape. 'It's killing me to leave you too, you know. I miss you already.'

He pulled her into his arms and kissed her. 'I know. We'll figure this out, work it all out somehow. But I wasn't joking about having you call me every hour from the road. I want to know where you are, and that you make it back safely.'

'I'll be fine.' She shook her head and smiled up at him. 'I'll call you when I get to the hospital.'

'Okay,' he said, knowing he was being unreasonable. Concerned over nothing. Just making one weak excuse after another to cover for the deep need he had to hold her close and keep her there. He released her and took a step back, shoving his hands into the pockets of his loose jeans. 'Okay. Call me when you get there.'

Dylan came up on her toes and kissed him again. When she tried to pull away, he couldn't resist wrapping his arms around her one more time.

'Ah, hell,' he swore harshly under his breath. 'Get out of here before I take you back to my quarters and shackle you to the bedpost.'

'That could be interesting.'

'Remind me later,' he said, 'when you come back.'

She nodded. 'I have to go.'

'Yeah.'

'I love you,' she said, and pressed a tender kiss to his cheek. 'I'll call you.'

'I'll be waiting.'

Rio stood there, fists thrust deep into his pockets as he watched her head for the car. She climbed in and started it up, then slowly rolled the car out of its parking space in the hangar. She gave him a little wave, too smart to slide the window down and give him more time to try to talk her out of leaving.

He hit the button on the hangar's automatic door, and had to shield his eyes from the light pink wash of dawn that filtered in through the estate's surrounding thicket of trees. Dylan drove out into the daylight. Rio wanted to wait until the taillights turned the bend in the property's long drive, but the glare of UV rays was too much for him to take, even for his late-generation Breed eyes.

He punched the keypad again and the wide door closed.

When he got off the elevator back down in the compound, Nikolai was coming up the corridor from the weapons range like hell on wheels. Rio could practically see steam pouring out of the vampire's ears, he was so furious.

'What's going on?' he asked, meeting the cold blue eyes.

'I just got fucked,' Niko replied, and evidently not in a good way.

'By who?'

'Starkn,' he hissed. 'Turns out the Director of the region's Enforcement Agency was just blowing a lot of smoke up our asses. When Chase and I met with the guy last night and told him that we suspect these are targeted hits, he assured us he would put the word out to all the known Gen Ones in the population. Well, guess what he didn't do.'

Rio scoffed. 'Put the word out to all the known Gen Ones in the population.'

'Right,' Niko said. 'My Gen One contact, Sergei Yakut, says he hasn't heard shit out of the Agency in Montreal where he's living now, and neither have any of the other first generation individuals he knows. To top it off, this morning we got word out of Denver of another killing. Another Gen One beheading, Rio. This shit is getting critical fast. Something big is going down.'

'You think Starkn could have a hand in it somehow?'

Nikolai's shrewd blue eyes were icy with suspicion. 'Yeah, I do. My gut is telling me the son of a bitch is dirty.'

Rio nodded, glad for the distraction that could take him away from feeling sorry for himself over missing Dylan and put him back into the Order's business. His business, his world.

When Niko headed off for the tech lab, Rio fell in alongside him, just like old times.

It took about five hours to make the drive from Boston into Manhattan, which put Dylan at the hospital around one in the afternoon. She'd called Rio from the car as she waited for the parking attendant, assured him that she was safe and sound, then she headed into the lobby to grab an elevator to the cancer ward.

God, to think this could be one of the last days her mom might spend in this place. One of the last days she'd be sick. Dylan wanted that so badly, she was almost giddy with the thought as she stepped off at the tenth floor and walked through the swinging double doors that led to her mother's wing.

The nurses on duty were dealing with some kind of printer malfunction, so she just walked past the station without stopping to ask for an update or any news on the biopsy. Dylan paused outside her mom's room door, about to hit the hand sanitizer when she saw that a nurse was just coming out. The woman was carrying an armful of half-empty IV bags. When she saw Dylan, she gave a little nod and a rather sad-looking smile.

'What's going on?' Dylan asked as the nurse came out into the hallway.

'We're taking her off her meds and fluids. Shouldn't be more than another half hour or so before she's released.'

'Released?' Dylan frowned, totally confused. 'What happened? Did we get the biopsy results back or something?'

A mild nod. 'We got them in this morning, yes.'

And based on the flat tone, the results weren't good. Still, she had to ask, because she really didn't want to imagine the worst. 'I'm not sure I understand. If you're taking her off fluids and medication, does that mean she's going to be all right?'

The nurse's expression fell a bit. 'You haven't talked with her yet . . .'

Dylan glanced over her shoulder into the room. Her mother was sitting on the edge of her bed facing the window as she put on a sky blue cardigan sweater. She was fully dressed, hair combed and styled. Looking like she was ready to walk out of the hospital any minute.

'Why is my mother being released?'

The nurse cleared her throat. 'I, um . . . I really think you need to talk with her about that, okay?'

As the woman left, Dylan scrubbed her hands with the alcohol gel and went inside.

'Mom?'

She pivoted on the bed and gave her a big, happy smile. 'Oh! Dylan. I didn't expect to see you back so soon, baby. I would have called you later.'

'Good thing I came when I did. I just heard they're letting you go home in a few minutes.'

'Yes,' she replied. 'Yes, it's time. I don't want to stay here anymore.'

Dylan didn't like the resignation in her mother's voice. It was too light, too accepting.

It sounded a lot like relief.

'Your nurse just told me the biopsy came back this morning.'

'Let's not talk about that.' She waved her hand dismissively and walked over to the table where the now opened box of chocolates sat. She picked up the candies and held them out to Dylan. 'Try one of these truffles. They're delicious! Gordon brought them for me last night – in fact, he was here just minutes after you left. I wish you had waited so you could meet him. He wants to meet you, Dylan. He was very interested when I told him that you're going to need a new job—'

'Oh, Mom. You didn't,' Dylan groaned. It was bad enough her mother had bragged to her boss about Dylan's story regarding the mountain cave, but to have her trying to find Dylan a job from her hospital bed was too much.

'Gordon has connections with a lot of important people in the city. He can help you, baby. Wouldn't it be wonderful if he could help you land something with one of the big news companies?'

'Mom,' Dylan said, more forcefully now. 'I don't want to talk about a job, or about Gordon Fasso, or anything else. All I want to talk about is what's going on with you. Obviously, the test results weren't good. So, why are you being released today?'

'Because that's what I want.' She sighed, and walked over to Dylan. 'I don't want to stay here anymore. I don't want any more tests, or tubes, or needles. I'm tired, and I just want to go home.'

'What did the doctors say? Can we talk with them about the biopsy results?'

'There's nothing more they can do, sweetheart. Except prolong the inevitable, and only for a little while.'

Dylan lowered her voice to just above a whisper. 'What if I told you that I know someone who might be able to make you healthy?'

'I don't want any more treatments. I'm done—'

'This wouldn't be anything like that. It's a kind of . . . alternative healing. Something you can't get in a hospital. It's not a guarantee, but there is a chance that you could be cured completely. I think it might be a good chance, Mom. I think it might be the only one . . .'

Her mother smiled gently as she laid her cool fingers against Dylan's cheek. 'I know how hard this is for you, baby. I do. But the choice is mine to make, on my own. I've had a full life. I'm not looking for miracles now.'

'What about me?' Dylan's voice was thick. 'Would you try it . . . for me?'

In the long silence that answered, Dylan tried desperately to hold back the sob that was rising up in her throat. Her heart was cracked in pieces, but she could see that her mother's mind was made up. It had probably been made up long before this moment. 'Okay,' she said finally. 'Okay, then . . . tell me what you want me to do, Mom.'

'Take me home. Let's have lunch together, and some tea, and let's just talk. That's what I'd really like right now, more than anything.'

\dashv\!\!\Xi CHAPTER THIRTY-TWO \Xi\!\!\vdash

R io didn't hear from Dylan again until late that afternoon. When his cell phone went off in his pocket, he was in the lab with Lucan, Gideon, Niko, and Chase, the five of them discussing Gerard Starkn's apparent snow job and how the Order could best take control of things with the Gen One situation. He excused himself from the meeting and took Dylan's call out in the corridor.

'What's wrong?' It wasn't much of a greeting, but he could sense her upset on the other end as soon as the call connected and the feeling went through him like live electricity. 'Are you okay?'

There was a pause, then: 'I'm okay, yeah. I'm going to be okay eventually, I think.'

'How is your mother?'

'Tired,' Dylan said, sounding weary herself. 'Oh, Rio . . . I've been with her all afternoon at her apartment in Queens. She checked herself out of the hospital today, and she's refusing any further treatment. She wants to . . . she doesn't want to live anymore, Rio. She's made up her mind about that.'

He swore softly, feeling Dylan's anguish like it was his own. 'Did you tell her about Tess?'

'I tried to, but she wouldn't hear it. It's killing me, but if this is what she truly wants, then I know I have to let her go.'

'Ah, love. I don't know what to say.'

'It's all right. I don't know what I need to hear right now.'

\dashv\!\!\Xi 281 \Xi\!\!\vdash

Dylan sniffled a little, but she was holding herself together with admirable courage. 'We spent the day talking – something we haven't been able to do for a long time. It was nice. I told her about you, that I met a very special man and that I love him very much. She's looking forward to meeting you sometime.'

Rio smiled, wishing he could be there right now. 'I'm sure that can be arranged.'

'I talked with her doctor as we were leaving the hospital. He says that realistically, without treatment, Mom probably only has weeks left . . . maybe a couple of months. They're going to give her medicine for the pain, but they warned us that the time she has left isn't going to be easy.'

'Shit, Dylan. Do you want me to come out there tonight? It's almost sundown. If you need me there, I could leave right at dusk and be in the city by around eleven.'

'What about the Order? I'm sure you have other things you have to do.'

'That's not what I asked you.' In fact, he was supposed to be on a mission tonight, but fuck it. If Dylan wanted him with her, Lucan would have to assign someone else to the patrol. 'Do you need me there tonight, Dylan?'

She sighed. 'I'd love to see you. You know I'd never turn you down, Rio. Do you really want to come all this way tonight?'

'Just try to stop me,' he said, sensing her brighten on the other end. In the background now, he heard a truck horn blast. 'Are you driving somewhere?'

'Uh-huh. I'm on my way to pick up some of my mom's things at the shelter. We called her friends over there as we were leaving the hospital, just to fill them in on what's going on. Everyone's pretty worried about her, as you can imagine. And I guess some of the shelter clients and their kids made up a special card for her too.'

'She'll like that.'

'Yeah,' Dylan said. 'I'm going to swing by and grab some takeout for dinner back at Mom's place. She wants baby back ribs, sweet potatoes, and cornbread – oh, and some fancy champagne, as she put it, to celebrate my newfound love.'

'Sounds like you have quite an evening planned.'

Dylan was quiet for a moment. 'It's really good to see her smiling, Rio. I want her to enjoy these next few weeks as much as she can.'

He understood, of course. And as Dylan wrapped up the conversation and promised to call him when she was back at her mother's apartment, Rio wondered how he was going to get through the weeks – perhaps a couple of months – away from Dylan. It wasn't a long time, certainly not by Breed standards, but for a male in love with his mate, the duration was going to seem endless.

He needed to be with Dylan through this.

And he knew that she needed him too.

When he flipped the cell phone closed, he found Lucan standing outside the tech lab doors. Rio had told him earlier about Dylan's mother, and about what Dylan meant to him, how deeply he'd fallen in love with her. He'd laid it all out for Lucan – from the fact that he and Dylan were blood-bonded now, to the offer he'd made her concerning Tess's healing abilities.

Rio didn't know how long Lucan had been standing there, but the shrewd gray eyes seemed fully aware that things were not going well on the other end.

'How is Dylan holding up?'

Rio nodded. 'She's strong. She'll get through this.'

'What about you, my man?'

He started to say that he'd be fine too, but Lucan's stare tore through that bullshit before the words even left Rio's lips.

'I told her I'd be there tonight,' he told the Order's leader. 'I have to go to her, Lucan. For my own sanity, if nothing else. If I stay here, I'm not sure what good I'd be, to tell you the truth. She's the only thing that's held me together in a very long time. I'm a wreck for this woman, my friend. She owns me now.'

'Even more than the Order?'

Rio paused, deliberating over what he was being asked. 'I would die for the Order – for you and any one of my brethren. You know that.'

'Yes. I know you would,' Lucan replied. 'Hell, you almost have, more than once.'

'I'd die to serve the Order, but Dylan . . . *Cristo*. This woman, more than anything before, gives me a reason to live. I have to be with her now, Lucan.'

He nodded soberly. 'I'll put one of the other guys on your patrol tonight. You do what you have—'

'Lucan.' Rio met the male's gaze and held it. 'I have to be with Dylan until she's through this ordeal with her mother. It could be weeks, maybe months.'

'So, what are you telling me?'

Rio cursed under his breath. 'I'm telling you that I'm leaving to be with her, for as long as it takes. I'm quitting the Order, Lucan. I head out for New York tonight.'

'Here's a box for those things, honey.' Janet came into Dylan's mom's office carrying an empty copy paper container. 'It's nice and sturdy and it's got a lid too.'

'Thanks,' Dylan said, setting it down on the cluttered desk. 'Mom is kind of a pack rat, isn't she?'

Janet laughed. 'Oh, honey! That woman hasn't thrown away a note or a greeting card or a photograph since I've known her. She saves everything like it was gold, bless her heart.' The older woman glanced around the room, her eyes going moist with tears. 'We sure are going to miss Sharon around here. She had such a way with the girls. Everyone adored her, even

Mr Fasso was charmed by her and he's not easily impressed. Her free spirit drew people to her, I think.'

Dylan smiled at the sentiment, but it was very hard hearing her mother referred to in the past tense already. 'Thanks for the box, Janet.'

'Oh, you're welcome, honey. Would you like some help finishing up in here?'

'No, thanks. I'm almost done.'

She waited as Janet made her exit, then she went back to the task at hand. It was difficult to tell what might be important to her mother and what could be tossed, so finally Dylan just started gathering papers and old photos by the handful and placing them in the box.

She paused to look at a few of the pictures – her mother standing with her arms around the thin shoulders of two young shelter girls with bad 1980s hair, tube tops, and short shorts; another of her mom smiling behind the counter of an ice cream shop, beaming at the 'Employee of the Month' award the young girl next to her was holding up like a prize.

Her mother had befriended nearly every troubled young woman who came through the place, genuinely invested in seeing them succeed and rise above the problems that had made the girls run away from home or feel that they didn't, or couldn't, fit into normal society. Her mother had tried to make a difference. And in a lot of cases, she had.

Dylan wiped at the tears of pride that sprang into her eyes. She looked for a tissue among the clutter and couldn't find any. Just what she didn't need, to be sitting in her mother's office crying like a baby in front of the evening shift staff.

'Shit.' She remembered seeing a stack of loose paper towels in one of the drawers of the back credenza. Pivoting her mother's chair around, she scooted across the worn carpet and began a quick search of the cabinet.

Ah. Success.

Dabbing at her wet eyes and face, she spun back around and nearly fell out of her seat.

There, standing before her on the other side of her mother's desk, was a ghostly apparition. The young woman was joined by another, both of them wavering in and out of visibility. Then another girl appeared, and still another. And then, finally, there was Toni again, the girl Dylan had seen in her mother's hospital room the other night.

'Oh, my God.' She gaped at them, only half-conscious of the shelter employees going about their business outside, completely unaware of the ghostly gathering. 'Are you all here because of my mom?'

The group of them stared at her in eerie silence, their forms rippling like candle flames caught in a stuttering breeze.

Help them, one of the unmoving mouths told her. *They need you to help them.*

Damn it, she did not have time for this now. She wasn't in the right frame of mind to deal with any of this right now.

But something prickled within her, something that told her she had to listen.

She had to do something.

He won't stop hurting them, said another ghostly voice. *He won't stop the killing.*

Dylan grabbed a scrap of paper and a pen and started writing down what she was hearing. Maybe Rio and the Order could help make sense of it, if she couldn't.

They're underground.

In darkness.

Screaming.

Dying.

Dylan heard the pain and fear in the mingled whispers as the dead Breedmates tried to communicate with her. She felt a kinship to each one of them, and to the ones they said were still alive but in terrible danger.

'Tell me who,' she said quietly, hoping she couldn't be heard outside the door. 'I can't help you if you don't give me something more than this. Please, hear me. Tell me who's hurting the others like us.'

Dragos.

She didn't know which one of them said it, or even if – or how – she might have been heard through the barrier that separated the living from the dead. But the word branded into her mind in an instant.

It was a name.

Dragos.

'Where is he?' Dylan asked, trying for more. 'Can you tell me anything else?'

But the group of them were already fading. One by one, they dissipated . . . vanished into nothingness.

'I almost forgot to give you these, honey.' Janet's singsong voice in the doorway startled a gasp out of Dylan. 'Oh, I'm sorry! I didn't mean to scare you.'

'It's okay.' Dylan shook her head, still dazed by the other encounter. 'What do you have?'

'A couple of pictures I took from the river cruise Mr Fasso hosted earlier this week. I think your mom would like to have them.' Janet came in and put a couple of color prints on the desk. 'Doesn't she look nice in that blue dress? Those girls at the table with her are a few of the ones she was mentoring. Oh – and there's Mr Fasso way in the back of the room. You can hardly make him out, but that's the side of his face. Isn't he handsome?'

He was, actually. And younger than she imagined him. He had to be about twenty years younger than her mother – in his late forties at most, and probably not even that old.

'Will you take these to your mom for me, honey?'

'Sure.' Dylan smiled, hoping she didn't look as rattled as she felt.

It wasn't until Janet had toddled off again that Dylan took a good look at the pictures. A really good look.

'Jesus Christ.'

One of the girls seated at the table with her mom on that river cruise a few short days ago was among the group of dead Breedmates she'd just seen in the office.

She grabbed a stack of older photographs from the box she'd packed them into and sifted through the images. Her heart sank. There was another young woman's face that she'd just seen in spectral form a minute ago.

'Oh, God.'

Dylan felt sick to her stomach as she bolted out of the office for the ladies room. She dialed the number Rio gave her and barely gave him a chance to say hello before she blurted out everything that had just happened.

'One of them said the name Dragos,' she told him in a frantic whisper. 'Does that mean anything to you?'

Rio's sudden silence made the ice in her stomach grow even colder. 'Yeah. Son of a bitch. I know the name.'

'Who is he, Rio?'

'Dragos is the one who created the hibernation chamber in that cave. His son freed the creature that had been sleeping there. He's evil, Dylan. About the worst kind you'd ever want to know.'

≼ CHAPTER THIRTY-THREE ≽

Sharon Alexander was making another pot of tea when a knock sounded on her twelfth-floor apartment door.

'It's open, baby,' she called from the kitchen. 'What'd you do, forget your key?'

'I never had one.'

Sharon jolted at the unexpected boom of a deep male voice. She recognized the dark baritone, but hearing it in her apartment – unannounced, and after dark – was something of a shock.

'Oh. Hello, Gordon.' She tugged self-consciously at her cardigan, wishing she'd put on something less lived-in, more appealing to a sophisticated man like Gordon Fasso. 'I'm . . . well, my goodness . . . this is such an unexpected surprise.'

He sent his cool gaze around the small, embarrassingly cluttered apartment. 'Did I come at a bad time?'

'No, of course not.' She smiled but he didn't return it. 'I was just making some tea. Would you like some?'

'No. I can't stomach the stuff, actually.' Now he did smile, but the slow spreading grin didn't make her feel any more comfortable. 'I stopped by the hospital, but the nurse there told me you were released. I understand your daughter brought you home.'

'Yes,' Sharon replied, watching as he took a leisurely stroll around her living room. She smoothed her hair, hoping it wasn't a complete disaster. 'I really enjoyed the chocolates you gave me. You didn't have to bring me anything, you know.'

'Where is she?'

'Hmm?'

'Your daughter,' he said tightly. 'Where is Dylan?'

For a second, maternal instinct told Sharon to lie and say that Dylan wasn't around and wouldn't be coming back any time soon. But that was ridiculous, wasn't it?

She had no reason to fear Mr Fasso. *Gordon*, she reminded herself, trying to see the charming gentleman he'd shown himself to be recently.

'I can smell her, Sharon.'

The statement was so odd, it took her aback completely. 'You can . . . what?'

'I know she's been here.' He pinned her with an icy glare. 'Where is she, and when is she coming back? These aren't difficult questions.'

A bone-deep chill settled in her as she looked at this man she truly knew so little about. A word skated through her mind as he moved toward her . . . *evil*.

'I told you I wanted to meet the girl,' he said, and as he spoke, something very strange was happening to his eyes. The icy color of them was changing, turning fiery with amber light. 'I'm tired of waiting, Sharon. I need to see the bitch, and I need to see her now.'

Sharon started mouthing a prayer. She backed up as he approached her, but she had few places to go. The walls would hem her in, and the slider in the living room opened onto a short balcony that overlooked a twelve-story drop to the street below. A warm breeze filtered in through the slider screen, and carrying with it the din of the rushing traffic out on busy Queens Boulevard.

'W-what do you want with Dylan?'

He smiled, and Sharon nearly fainted at the sight of his grotesquely long teeth.

No, she thought in near incomprehension. Not teeth at all. Fangs.

'I need your daughter, Sharon. She's an unusual woman, who can help give birth to the future. My future.'

'Oh, my God . . . you're crazy, aren't you? You're sick.' Sharon inched farther away from him, panic hammering in her chest. 'What the hell are you, really?'

He chuckled, low and menacing. 'I'm your Master, Sharon. You just don't know it yet. Now I'm going to bleed you, and you're going to tell me everything I want to know. You're going to help me find Dylan. I'm going to turn you into my slave, and you're going to deliver your daughter right into my hands. And then I'm going to make her my whore.'

He bared those huge, dripping fangs and hissed like a viper about to strike.

Sharon didn't know what possessed her, beyond the consuming terror of what this man – this terrible creature – could do to Dylan. She didn't doubt for a second that he could do precisely what he threatened. And it was that certainty that carried her feet toward the screen door.

Gordon Fasso laughed as she fumbled with the flimsy plastic sliding lock. She threw the screen open.

'What do you think you're going to do, Sharon?'

She backed out onto the balcony but he followed, the broad shoulders of his suitcoat filling the open space of the slider. Sharon felt the rail of the balcony press hard at her spine. Far, far below, horns blasted and engines screamed with the speeding rush of traffic.

'I won't let you use me to get to her,' she told him, her breath rasping through her lips.

She didn't look over the edge. She kept her eyes trained on the glowing embers of the monster's gaze in front of her. And took some small measure of satisfaction when he roared and made a hasty grab for her . . . too late.

Sharon toppled backward over the railing, onto the dark pavement below.

Traffic on the street outside her mother's apartment building was backed up for two blocks. Up ahead in the dark, emergency lights flashed, and police were directing vehicles to an alternate access onto Queens Boulevard. Dylan tried to peer around the minivan in front of her, to what looked like a pretty active crime scene. Yellow tape cordoned off the street below her mom's building.

Dylan tapped the steering wheel, sliding a glance over at the takeout that was getting cold. She was later than she intended. The episode at the runaway shelter had put her back about an hour, and all the phone calls to her mother's apartment had gone to voice mail. She was probably resting, probably wondering what the hell had happened to their little dinner celebration.

She tried the apartment again and got the message service again. 'Shit.'

A couple of kids swaggered by on the sidewalk, coming from the direction of all the activity. Dylan slid the window down.

'Hey. What's going on up there? Are they going to start letting cars through?'

One of the boys shook his head. 'Some old lady took a header off her balcony. Cops are up there trying to clean up the mess.'

Dread settled in Dylan's stomach like a stone. 'Do you know what building?'

'Nah. One of the high-rises on 108th Street.'

Oh, fuck. Oh, holy Christ . . .

Dylan jumped out of the car without even killing the engine. She had her cell phone in hand, dialing her mother as she headed at a dead run up the sidewalk toward all the commotion near the intersection a couple blocks away. As she got closer, cutting into the gathered crowd, her feet slowed of their own accord.

She knew.

She just . . . knew.

Her mother was dead.

But then her cell phone went off like a bank alarm. She stared down at the display and saw her mother's cell number on the lighted screen.

'Mom!' she cried as she picked up the call.

There was silence on the other end.

'Mom? Mom, is that you?'

A heavy hand landed on her shoulder. She whipped her head around and found herself staring into the cruel eyes of a man she'd seen only recently in a photograph from her mother's office.

Gordon Fasso held her mother's pink cell phone in his other hand. He smiled, baring the tips of his fangs. When he spoke, Dylan heard his deep voice vibrate in her ears and in her palm, as his words carried through the speaker of her mother's phone into her own.

'Hello, Dylan. So good to finally meet you.'

⊰ CHAPTER THIRTY-FOUR ⊱

S omewhere in Connecticut, a couple of hours into the drive
from Boston to New York, Rio's chest felt like it had been
yanked open by ice-cold hands. He was on speakerphone with
the compound, trying to find out if Gideon had been able to
uncover any intel about the dead Breedmates Dylan reported
seeing at the runaway shelter. The Order had the pictures
she'd sent from her cell phone, and Gideon was searching for
further missing persons information from the Darkhavens and
human populations.

Rio heard the other warrior talking to him now, but the
words weren't penetrating his skull.

'Ah, fuck,' he groaned, rubbing at the tight blast of cold
that seemed to have moved into the region of his heart.

'What's going on?' Gideon asked. 'Rio? You still with me?'

'Yeah. But . . . something's wrong.'

Dylan.

Something was very wrong with Dylan. He could sense her
fear, and a sorrow so profound it nearly blinded him.

Not a good thing when he was speeding along I-84 at
roughly ninety miles an hour.

'I've got a bad feeling, Gideon. I have to get ahold of Dylan
right now.'

'Sure. Be right here when you're done.'

Rio clicked off the call and dialed Dylan. It rang into voice
mail. Repeatedly.

That bad feeling was getting worse by the second. She was

in real danger – he knew it by the sudden frantic drum of his pulse, his blood bond with her telling him that something terrible was happening to her.

Right now, while she was easily three hours away from him.

'Goddamn it,' he growled, stomping on the gas.

He speed-dialed Gideon again.

'Any luck reaching her?'

'No.' A deeper chill went through him. 'She's in trouble, Gid. She's in pain somewhere. Goddamn it! I should never have let her out of my sight!'

'Okay,' Gideon, the calm one, said. 'I'm going to run a track on the Volvo's GPS, and I'll run one on her cell phone too. We'll locate her, Rio.'

He heard the keyboard clacking on the other end of the line, but the dread in his gut told him that neither device was going to bring him any closer to Dylan. And sure enough, Gideon came back a second later with bad news.

'The car's sitting on Jewel Avenue in Queens, and the cell phone tracks to a location one block away from that. There's no movement coming out of either one.'

As Rio cursed, he heard Nikolai's voice in the background, barely audible over the speaker. Something about Director Starkn and one of the photographs Dylan took.

'What did he just say?' Rio demanded. 'Get Niko on the line. I want to know what he just said.'

Gideon's voice was hesitant . . . and the vivid oath he swore an instant later did nothing to reassure Rio either.

'Damn it, what did he say?'

'Niko just asked me what Starkn was doing in the background of one of Dylan's pictures . . .'

'Which one?' Rio asked.

'The one from that charity cruise her mother was on. The one Dylan ID'd as being the runaway shelter's founder, Gordon Fasso.'

'That can't be,' Rio said, even while a voice inside of him was telling him the exact opposite. 'Put Niko on.'

'Hey, man,' Nikolai said a second later. 'I'm telling you. I saw Starkn with my own eyes. I'd know him anywhere. And the dude standing in the background of this picture is Enforcement Agency Regional Director Gerard fucking Starkn.'

The name sank into his brain like acid as Rio weaved around a sluggish semi-trailer and floored the gas pedal through an empty stretch of pavement.

Gerard Starkn.

What the hell kind of name was that?

Gordon Fasso.

Another odd spelling.

And then there was Dragos, and his treacherous son. Couldn't forget that bastard. He was mixed up in this somehow too, Rio was certain of it.

Could Gordon Fasso and Gerard Starkn be in collusion with Dragos's son?

Oh, Holy Mother . . .

Gordon Fasso. Son of Dragos.

The letters began to jumble and resequence in Rio's mind. And then he saw it, as clear as the blare of red taillights that stretched up ahead of him for about a mile solid.

'Niko,' he said woodenly. 'Gordon Fasso *is* the son of Dragos. Gordon Fasso's not a name. It's a fucking anagram. Son of Dragos.'

'Ah, Christ,' Nikolai replied. 'And if you mix up the letters of Gerard Starkn . . . you get another anagram: dark stranger.'

'That's who's got Dylan.' Rio rolled up on the parking lot of traffic and slammed his hand down on the dashboard. 'Dragos's son has Dylan, Niko.'

She was alive, that much he was sure of, and it was enough to keep him from losing his mind.

But his enemy had her, and Rio had no way of telling where he might have taken her.

And even without the bottleneck that was blocking all south-bound lanes of the highway, he was still some long hours away from the New York state line.

He could be losing her forever . . . right now.

Dylan came awake in the dark backseat of a fast moving vehicle. Her head was thick, her senses dazed. She knew this foggy feeling; she'd been tranced at some point, and was now, somehow, breaking out of it. Through the heavy psychic cloak that had been dropped over her mind, Dylan felt another force reaching out to her.

Rio.

She could feel him in her veins. She could sense him in the power of their blood connection and in her heart as well. It was Rio reaching past Fasso's trance to give her strength, urging her to hang on. To stay alive.

Oh, God.

Rio.

Find me.

The low hum of the road beneath the vehicle's spinning wheels vibrated in her ears. She tried to see where they were heading, but through the bare slit of her lids, all she saw was darkness outside the tinted windows. Treetops rushing by, black against the night sky.

Her face ached from the blow Gordon Fasso had dealt her when she'd fought against her capture. She'd tried to scream, to escape, but he and the bulky guard who accompanied him had proven too strong for her.

Fasso alone would have been far too powerful for her to fight off.

But then, he would be, since he wasn't a man at all, but a vampire.

She had the very real sense that he was not even Gordon Fasso, if that man ever existed.

The monster who had her now was also the one who killed her mother. She didn't have to see her mother's broken body to know that it was Gordon Fasso who murdered her, either by pushing her off that twelfth-floor balcony, or by scaring her so totally that she leapt to her own death to escape him.

Maybe she'd done it for Dylan, a thought that made the loss even harder for Dylan to bear.

But she could grieve for her mother another time, and she would. Right now she had to stay alert and try to find a way out of this horrific situation.

Because if her captor succeeded in bringing her to wherever he intended, Dylan knew that there would be no escaping.

All that awaited her at the end of this path was pain and death.

At some point well into Connecticut, Rio realized that no matter how fast he drove, he stood no chance of finding Dylan. Not in New York, certainly. He was still a couple of hours away, and there was no telling where she was – or even if she was in New York anymore at all.

He was losing her.

Close enough that he could feel her reaching out to him, yet too far to grab hold of her.

'Goddamn it!'

Fear permeated every cell in his body, combined with a sorrow so profound it shredded him from the inside. He was raw, bleeding . . . racked with futile rage.

His vision swam with the rising pound of his temples. His skull screamed as the blackout started crowding his senses.

'No,' he growled, stomping on the accelerator.

He rubbed at his eyes, commanding them to stay focused.

He could not let his weakness overtake him now. He could not fail Dylan – not like this.

'No, goddamn it. I have to reach her. Ah, *Cristo,*' he choked, a broken sob catching in his throat. 'I cannot lose her.'

Go to the reservoir.

Rio heard the static-filled whisper but at first it didn't register. *Croton Reservoir.*

He whipped his head around to the passenger seat and caught a glimpse of dark eyes and sable hair. The image was nearly transparent, and the one face he knew better than to trust.

Eva.

He snarled and cut away from the ghostly hallucination. Until now, he'd only seen Eva in the darkness of his dreams. Her false apologies and tearful insistence that she wanted to help him had just been illusions, tricks of his cracked mind. Maybe this was too.

Dylan's life on the line. He'd be damned before he let his own madness steer him off course now.

Rio, hear me. Let me help you.

Eva's voice crackled like a weak radio signal, but her tone was unmistakably emphatic. He felt a chill on his wrist and looked down to see her spectral hand lighting there. He wanted to shake off her touch like the poison it was, refuse to let Eva betray him again. But when he glanced over at the other side of the car, the ghost of his dead enemy was weeping, her pale cheeks glistening with tears.

You haven't lost her yet, said the unmoving lips that had lied so easily to him in the past. *There is still time. Croton Reservoir . . .*

He stared as her form began to wobble and fade out. Could he believe her? Could anything Eva said be trusted, even in this form? He'd hated her for everything she'd taken from him, so how could he think for one second that he could take her at her word now?

Forgive me, she whispered.

And with one last flicker of visibility . . . she vanished.

'Fuck,' Rio hissed.

He looked out at the endless road ahead of him. He had precious few options here. One wrong move and Dylan was as good as dead. He had to be sure. He had to make the right choice or he would never be able to live with himself if he failed her now.

With a murmured prayer, Rio hit the speed dial on his cell phone. 'Gideon. I need to know where the Croton Reservoir is. Right now.'

There was an answering clatter of fingers flying over a keyboard. 'It's in New York . . . Westchester County, off Route 129. The reservoir is part of an old dam.'

Rio glanced up at the Connecticut highway sign half a mile away from him. 'How far is it from Waterbury?'

'Ah . . . looks like maybe an hour if you take I-84 west.' Gideon paused. 'What's going on? You got a hunch about the dam?'

'Something like that,' Rio replied.

He murmured his thanks to Gideon for the info, then killed the call, hit the gas, and veered into the exit lane.

CHAPTER THIRTY-FIVE

Rio drove like a bat out of hell.

He put all his mental energy into reaching out for Dylan, trying to let her know that he was coming for her. That he *would* find her, or die trying.

He sped along Route 129, hoping he was getting close. He could feel it in his blood that he wasn't far from Dylan now. Their bond was calling to him, urging him on with a certainty that it wouldn't be long before he found her.

And then –

As a dark sedan came flying up the road from the opposite direction, Rio's veins lit up like firecrackers.

Madre de Dios.

Dylan was in that car.

With a hard crank of the wheel, he threw his vehicle into a sideways skid, blocking the road and ready to fight to the death for Dylan. The oncoming sedan's brakes squealed, tires smoking on the pavement. It lurched to a stop, then the driver – a human, by the look of the big man at the wheel – made a sharp right and gunned it up a dark, tree-lined service road.

With a curse, Rio threw his car into gear and went after them.

Up ahead, the sedan crashed through a temporary barricade in the road, then made a hard stop. Two people climbed out of the backseat – Dylan and the vampire who held her.

The bastard had a gun jammed under her chin as he hauled her up the quiet road into the dark.

Rio braked to a stop and leapt out of the driver's seat, his own gun pulled from its holster and leveled at her captor's head. But he couldn't shoot. The chance of hitting Dylan was too great. More than he was willing to risk.

Not that he had much time to consider it.

The huge guard who'd been at the wheel of the sedan came around the car and started firing at Rio. A bullet ripped into his shoulder, searing hot pain. He kept shooting at Rio, trying to drive him back with a relentless hail of gunfire.

Rio dodged the attack and vaulted across the distance using all the Breed power at his command. He fell upon the human – a Minion, he realized as he stared down into the dead eyes. Rio grabbed him by the throat and then put his other hand on the bastard's forehead. He sent all his fury into his fingertips, draining the life out of the Minion with that brief, simple touch.

He left the corpse in the middle of the road and took off on foot to find Dylan.

Dylan stumbled alongside her captor, the hard cold press of a gun's muzzle jammed under her chin. She could hardly see where he was taking her, but somewhere, not very distant, rushing water roared like thunder.

And then gunfire.

'No!' she screamed, hearing the sharp blasts behind her in the dark. She felt a jab of pain and knew that Rio had been hit. But he was still breathing. Thank God, he was still alive. Still reaching out to her through the heat that coursed through her blood.

A cruel yank of her head brought Dylan back around. The vampire who held her forced her to run with him, up the narrow pavement and closer to the source of the falling water.

Before she knew it, they were heading onto a tall bridge. On one side, a reservoir spread out for what looked like miles, the dark water sparkling in the moonlight. And on the other side, a sheer drop from what looked like about two hundred feet.

The spillway below was white with the rush of water cascading over the graduated incline and the huge rocks that spread down into the churning river at its base. Dylan stared over the tall metal rail of the bridge, seeing a certain death in all that furious water.

'Dragos.'

Rio's voice cut through the darkness on the entrance of the bridge.

'Let her go.'

Dylan's captor jerked her to a halt on the bridge. He swung her around, the gun still biting into her jaw. His chuckle vibrated against her, low and malicious.

'Let her go? I don't think so. Come and get her.' Rio took a step toward them and that cold nose of the gun at Dylan's throat stuck even deeper. 'Put down your weapon, warrior. She will die right here.'

Rio glared, amber flashing in his eyes. 'I said let her go, damn it.'

'Put the gun down,' her assailant said. 'Do it now. Or would you prefer to see me tear out her throat?'

Rio's gaze went to Dylan's. His jaw was tight, his tension visible even in the darkness. With a hissed oath, he slowly put his weapon on the ground and stood back up. 'Okay,' he said carefully. 'Now let's finish this, you and I. Leave her out of it, Dragos. Or should I call you Gerard Starkn? Gordon Fasso, maybe?'

The vampire chuckled, clearly amused. 'My little ruse has come to an end, has it? No matter. You're about fifty years too late. I've been busy. What my father started by hiding the Ancient, I am finishing. While the Order has been chasing its ass, taking out Rogues like they were actually making a difference in the world, I've been sowing the seeds of the future. A great many seeds. Today you call me Dragos; soon the world will call me Master.'

Rio inched forward and Dylan's captor turned the gun from its aim on her to Rio instead. Dylan felt the flex of the vampire's muscles as he prepared to squeeze the trigger and she took the only chance she had. With a sharp jut of her hand, she knocked his arm and the bullet shot off into the trees.

She didn't see the blow coming.

Her captor drew his other arm back and let his fist fly, connecting with the side of her head. She went careening, crashing hard onto the pavement.

'No!' Rio shouted.

With a speed and agility that still shocked her, he leapt into the air. Dragos returned the challenge, and with an otherworldly roar, the two powerful Breed males smashed into each other and locked into a fierce hand-to-hand combat.

Rio latched on to Dragos's maniacal spawn in pure rage, the two of them thrashing in midair, each fighting for the chance to kill the other. With a bellow, the vampire spun Rio around and drove him into the metal rail of the bridge. Rio roared, flipping Dragos off him and sending the bastard into the opposite side of the narrow road atop the bridge.

He didn't know how long the battle raged. Neither was willing to stop until the other was dead. Both vampires were fully transformed now, their fangs huge, the night lit up by the blare of two sets of amber eyes.

Somehow Dragos got loose and jumped up onto the railing. Rio followed him, finally driving the bastard down on one knee. Dragos wobbled, nearly losing his balance over the roar of the spillway below. Then he lunged, barreling headfirst into Rio's midsection.

Rio felt his feet slip on the rail. He pitched sharply, then fell.

'Rio!' Dylan screamed from above on the bridge. 'Oh, my God! No!'

Not even a half-second later, Dragos made the same error. But like Rio, he also managed to grab hold of the metal superstructure before the plunge took him down onto the rocks and rushing water.

The fight continued below the bridge, both of them clutching the beams with one hand while they punched and struck each other from their suspension above the wicked drop. Rio's shoulder was burning from the bullet he took earlier. The pain was bringing on a blackout, but he shook it off, focusing all his rage – all his pain, and the fear he'd felt at the thought of losing Dylan – on the task of ending the Dragos line here and now.

And he could feel Dylan giving him strength as well.

She was in his mind and in his blood, in his very heart and soul, lending him her own tenacious determination. He absorbed all of it, using what his bond to Dylan gave him, as he went for another hard strike at Dragos. They continued pounding each other, roaring with the fury of battle.

Until a gunshot ripped out over their heads.

They both looked up and there was Dylan, one of the pistols gripped in her hands. She brought the muzzle down and aimed it at Dragos.

'This is for my mother, you son of a bitch.'

She fired, but Dragos was Breed, and he was faster than she anticipated. He swung away at the last second, getting a better grip farther down the rail. She followed, keeping him trained in her sights. When she went to fire again, one of his hands shot up through the slats and locked on to her ankle.

She fell backward, hitting the bridge hard. Rio heard the breath whoosh out of her lungs, then watched in horror as she was suddenly dragged toward the railing by Dragos's strong grasp on her leg.

In an instant, Rio flung himself up over the rail and onto the road above. He grabbed Dylan's arm in one hand, the dropped pistol in his other.

'Let her go,' he commanded Dragos and brought the gun level with the vampire's head. It was hard to kill one of the Breed, but a bullet to the brain was generally sufficient.

'You think this is over, warrior?' Dragos taunted, fangs flashing. 'This is only the beginning.'

With that he let go of Dylan and dropped, fast as a stone, into the roiling water below. The spillway ate him up, and the river beneath it was pitch dark, impossible to see.

Dragos was gone.

Rio turned to Dylan and gathered her into his arms. He held her close, so relieved that he was able to feel her warmth against him. He kissed her and smoothed away the blood and grit from her face.

'It's over,' he whispered, kissing her again. He stared down at the black water below the bridge, but saw no sign of Dragos in the speeding current. 'You're safe with me, Dylan. It's all over now.'

She nodded and wrapped her arms around him. 'Take me home, Rio.'

⋈ CHAPTER THIRTY-SIX ⋈

Nearly a week had passed since Rio brought Dylan back with him to the Order's compound in Boston . . . back to the home he hoped to make for them with her forever at his side.

He was still healing from the gunshot wound in his shoulder. Tess had tried to speed the mending of his skin after the bullet had been extracted, but as she'd feared, the power of her healing touch was hampered almost entirely by the baby growing in her womb. She wasn't able to help Rio, nor would she have been able to help Dylan's mother.

The funeral for Sharon Alexander had taken place two days ago in Queens. Rio had gone back to New York with Dylan the night before the service – as had the rest of the Order and their Breedmates, in a show of support for the newly mated pair. It pained Rio that he couldn't be at Dylan's side as her mother was laid to rest that sunny summer afternoon, but he was glad for the company that Tess, Gabrielle, Savannah, and Elise were able to provide for her in his place.

Dylan had been brought into the fold like she'd always belonged there. The other Breedmates adored her, and as for the warriors, even Lucan had been impressed with Dylan's willingness to roll up her sleeves and offer her help to the Order. She'd spent the better part of the day in the tech lab with Gideon, poring through IID records and missing persons reports out of the Darkhavens in an effort to identify Breedmates who'd come to her from the afterlife.

Now, as evening approached and the Order was soon to head out on patrols, all of the compound's residents were gathered around the large dining room table in Rio's quarters. As the women shared a meal, the warriors covered Order business and planned the night's missions. Nikolai was soon to be heading out to meet with the Gen One he knew, in the hopes of getting his help to track down the source of the recent slayings.

As for Gerard Starkn, the Order hadn't been surprised to find his New York residence vacant when they'd raided it a few nights ago. The bastard had cleared out entirely, leaving no clues about the double life he'd been leading as Gordon Fasso, AKA the son of Dragos, and zero trace of where he might have fled after his clash with Rio at the Croton dam. A search of the area near the dam had yielded nothing, but Rio and the others weren't about to give up.

There was much yet to be done in the Order's quest to stop the evil Dragos was sowing, but Rio could think of none better to have on his side than the group seated with him now. He glanced around at the faces of his brethren and their mates – his family – and felt a surge of pride, and of deep, humbling gratitude, that he was a part of them once more. For always.

But it was when he turned to look at Dylan that his heart squeezed as if it were caught in a warm fist.

It was she who'd brought him back from the brink. She'd pulled him out of an abyss he never thought he'd escape. Her nourishing blood gave him strength, but it was the boundless gift of her love that truly made him whole.

Rio reached over and took Dylan's hand in his. She smiled as he lifted her fingers to his mouth and kissed them, his eyes locked onto hers. He loved her so deeply, could hardly stand to be away from her now that she was with him. Knowing that she awaited him in his bed every night upon his return from patrol was both a torment and a balm.

'Be careful,' she whispered to him, as he and the other warriors prepared to suit up for their missions.

Rio nodded, then pulled her into his arms and kissed her soundly.

'Jesus,' Nikolai said around a wry chuckle as everyone else began to disperse. 'Get a room, you two.'

'You're standing in it,' Rio shot back, still holding on to Dylan. 'How long before we go topside?'

Niko shrugged. 'About twenty minutes, I'd guess.'

'Long enough,' Rio said, turning a hungry look on his woman.

She laughed and even blushed a little, but there was a definite spark of interest in her eyes. As Nikolai made a hasty exit and closed the door behind him, Rio took Dylan by the hand.

'Just twenty minutes,' he said, soberly shaking his head. 'I'm not sure where to begin.'

Dylan arched a brow at him as she started inching toward the bedroom. 'Oh, I think you'll figure it out.'

Dylan was amazed at just how thoroughly Rio used those twenty minutes.

And when he returned from patrol much later that night, he'd set out to amaze her even more. He'd made love to her for hours, then wrapped her in his strong arms as she drifted off to sleep. She wasn't sure exactly when Rio had left their bed, but it was his absence that woke her about an hour before dawn. She drew on his thick terry robe and padded out of the apartment, following the buzzing in her veins that would lead her to her blood-bonded mate.

He wasn't in the compound or the mansion that sat above it on ground level. He was outside, in the garden courtyard behind the estate. Dressed in just a pair of black warm-ups,

Rio was seated on the wide marble steps that spread out to the manicured lawn, watching a small bonfire a few yards out on the grass. Next to him was a box of framed photographs and a couple of the bright abstract paintings taken from the walls of his quarters.

Dylan looked out at the fire and saw the distorted shapes of more of his belongings slowly being consumed by the flames.

'Hey,' he said, obviously sensing her as she approached him from behind. He didn't look back at her, just stretched his arm out to the side, waiting for her to take his hand. 'I'm sorry if I woke you.'

'It's okay.' Dylan wrapped her fingers around his. 'I don't mind being up. I missed your warmth.'

As she spoke, he pulled her into a tender hold next to him. He circled her thighs with his arm and simply held her there, his gaze still fixed on the fire. Dylan glanced down into the box beside him, seeing the pictures of Eva and a few of the two of them together in happier times. Eva's artwork was in the container, as were some of her clothes.

'I woke up a while ago and realized I needed to clear out a few things that no longer belong in my life,' he said.

His voice was calm, not angry or bitter. Just . . . resolved.

Rio seemed to be in a state of true peace; her sense of it registered all the way into her veins as he embraced her in silence, watching the fire dance on the lawn.

'For the past year, I've hated her,' he said. 'With every breath in my body, I prayed she was burning in hell for what she did to me. I think my hatred for Eva was the only thing that kept me alive. For a long time, it was the only thing I could feel.'

'I know,' Dylan said softly. She tunneled her fingers into his thick hair, caressing his head as he rested his cheek against her hip. 'But it was Eva who led me to you on that mountain. She cared about you, Rio. I think in her own misguided way, she loved you very much. In life, she made some terrible mistakes trying to keep you all to herself. She did some terrible things, but I think she wishes she could correct them in death.'

Rio slowly stood up, still keeping a hold on her as he rose to his feet beside her. 'I can't hate her anymore, because she brought me to you. And not just that day up there in the cave. Eva was in my car the night Dragos took you.'

Dylan frowned. 'You saw her?'

'I was still hours outside of New York, knowing that if Dragos had you, I'd never be able to reach you in time. *Cristo*, the fear that went through me at the very thought—' He broke off and pulled her closer to him. 'I was on the highway, driving as fast as I could, praying like hell for some kind of miracle. Anything to give me hope that I wasn't going to lose you. That's when I heard her voice beside me. I looked over and there she was – Eva, in the car with me. She told me where Dragos had taken you. She gave me the location of the dam, told me to trust her. I didn't know if I could – not ever again – but I also knew that it could be my only hope of finding you. Without her, I would have lost you. She could have told me I'd find you in the middle of a raging inferno and I would have gone in after you. She could have betrayed me again, led me into another ambush, and I would have gone, just for the hope of finding you alive.'

'But she didn't,' Dylan said. 'She told you the truth.'

'Yes. Thank God.'

'Oh, Rio.' Dylan rested her cheek against his chest, hearing the heavy pound of his heart as if it were her own. She felt his love pour into her as warm as sunshine, a love she sent back to him tenfold. 'I love you so much.'

'I love you too,' he said, then tipped her chin up and kissed her, long and slow and sweet. 'I'm going to love you forever, Dylan. If you'll have me, there's nothing I want more than to spend every day – and night – of my life loving you.'

'Of course I'll have you,' she told him, reaching up to smooth her fingertips over his cheek. She smiled slowly and with seductive promise. 'I'll have you every day and night of my life . . . and in every way imaginable.'

Rio growled deep in his throat, a spark of amber lighting in his gaze. 'I like the sound of that.'

'I hoped you would.' She smiled up into his face, a face she would never tire of seeing, especially when he was looking at her with so much tender devotion in his eyes it left her breathless.

She glanced down at the box of Eva's personal effects, then out at the bonfire. 'You know you don't have to do this. Not for me.'

Rio shook his head. 'I'm doing it for both of us. Maybe I'm doing it for her too. It's time to let go of everything that happened before. I'm ready to do that now . . . because of you. Because of the future I see with you. I'm done looking back.'

Dylan nodded gently. 'Okay.'

Rio picked up the box and looked to her to accompany him to the fire. They walked together, silent as they neared the undulating flames.

With a soft push, Rio sent the box of pictures, art, and clothing into the middle of the bonfire. It roared to life for a brief moment, shooting a spray of sparks and smoke high into the dusky periwinkle sky.

In a thoughtful silence, Dylan and Rio watched the fire burn for a while, until the flames grew less hungry, their fuel spent. When it was just smoke and embers, Rio turned to Dylan and brought her into his arms. He held her close, whispering a quiet prayer of gratitude next to her ear.

And in the rising smoke from the dying bonfire behind him, Dylan watched over his broad shoulder as an ethereal, feminine shape took form between the flurry of floating ash.

Eva.

She smiled a bit sadly as she watched the two of them

embrace. But then she gave a slow nod to Dylan and gradually faded away.

Dylan closed her eyes as she wrapped her arms around Rio and buried her face in the solid warmth of his chest. After a little while, her cheek rumbled with the vibration of his voice.

'About that 'having me every way imaginable' promise of yours,' he said, clearing his throat. 'You want to explain some of what you had in mind?'

Dylan looked up at him and smiled, her heart overflowing with love. 'Why don't I show you instead?'

He chuckled, the tips of his fangs already starting to emerge. 'I thought you'd never ask.'

Read on for a preview of the first chapter of the next book in the heart-stopping *Midnight Breed* series.

VEIL
⚜ OF ⚜
MIDNIGHT

⫸ CHAPTER ONE ⫷

On stage in the cavernous jazz club below Montreal's street level, a crimson-lipped singer drawled into the microphone about the cruelty of love. Although her sultry voice was pleasant enough, the lyrics about blood and pain and pleasure clearly heartfelt, Nikolai wasn't listening. He wondered if she knew – if any of the dozens of humans packed into the intimate club knew – that they were sharing breathing space with vampires.

The two young females sucking down pink martinis in the dark corner banquette sure as hell didn't know it.

They were sandwiched between four such individuals, a group of slick, leather-clad males who were chatting them up – without much success – and trying to act like their blood-thirsty eyes hadn't been permanently fixed on the women's jugulars for the past fifteen minutes straight. Even though it was clear that the vampires were negotiating hard to get the humans out of the club with them, they weren't making much progress with their prospective blood Hosts.

Nikolai scoffed under his breath.

Amateurs.

He paid for the beer he'd left untouched on the bar and headed at an easy stroll toward the corner table. As he approached, he watched the two human females scoot out of the booth on unsteady legs. Giggling, they stumbled for the restrooms together, disappearing down a dim, crowded hallway off the main room.

Nikolai sat down at the table in a negligent sprawl.

'Evening, ladies.'

The four vampires stared at him in silence, instantly recognizing their own kind. Niko lifted one of the tall, lipstick-stained martini glasses to his nose and sniffed at the dregs of the fruity concoction. He winced, pushing the offending drink aside.

'Humans,' he drawled in a low voice. 'How can they stomach that shit?'

A wary silence fell over the table as Nikolai's glance traveled among the obviously young, obviously civilian Breed males. The largest of the four cleared his throat as he looked at Niko, his instincts no doubt picking up on the fact that Niko wasn't local, and he was a far cry from civilized.

The youth adopted something he probably thought was a hardass look and jerked his soul-patched chin toward the restroom corridor. 'We saw them first,' he murmured. 'The women. We saw them first.' He cleared his throat again, like he was waiting for his trio of wingmen to back him up. None did. 'We got here first, man. When the females come back to the table, they're gonna be leaving with us.'

Nikolai chuckled at the young male's shaky attempt to stake his territory. 'You really think there'd be any contest if I was here to poach your game? Relax. I'm not interested in that. I'm looking for information.'

He'd been through a similar song-and-dance twice already tonight at other clubs, seeking out the places where members of the Breed tended to gather and hunt for blood, looking for someone who could point him toward a vampire elder named Sergei Yakut.

It wasn't easy finding someone who didn't want to be found, especially a secretive, nomadic individual like Yakut. He was in Montreal, that much Nikolai was sure of. He'd spoken to the reclusive vampire by phone as recently as a couple of weeks earlier, when he'd tracked Yakut down to inform him of a threat that séemed aimed at the Breed's most powerful, rarest members – the twenty or so individuals still in existence who were born of the first generation.

Someone was targeting Gen Ones for extinction. Several had been slain within the past month, and for Niko and his brothers in arms back in Boston – a small cadre of highly trained, highly lethal warriors known as the Order – the business of rooting out and shutting down the elusive Gen One assassins was mission critical. For that, the Order had decided to contact all of the known Gen Ones remaining in the Breed population and enlist their cooperation.

Sergei Yakut had been less than enthusiastic to get involved. He feared no one, and he had his own personal clan to protect him. He'd declined the Order's invitation to come to Boston and talk, so Nikolai had been dispatched to Montreal to persuade him. Once Yakut was made aware of the scope of the current threat – the stunning truth of what the Order and all of the Breed were now up against – Nikolai was certain the Gen One would be willing to come on board.

First he had to find the cagey son of a bitch.

So far his inquiries around the city had turned up nothing. Patience wasn't exactly his strong suit, but he had all night, and he'd keep searching. Sooner or later, someone might give him the answer he was looking for. And if he kept coming up dry, maybe if he asked enough questions, Sergei Yakut would come looking for him instead.

'I need to find someone,' Nikolai told the four Breed youths. 'A vampire out of Russia. Siberia, to be exact.'

'That where you're from?' asked the soul-patched mouthpiece of the group. He'd evidently picked up on the slight tinge of an accent that Nikolai hadn't lost in the long years he'd been living in the States with the Order.

Niko let his glacial blue eyes speak to his own origins. 'Do you know this individual?'

'No, man. I don't know him.'

Two other heads shook in immediate denial, but the last of the four youths, the sullen one who was slouched low in the booth, shot an anxious look up at Nikolai from across the table.

Niko caught that telling gaze and held it. 'What about you? Any idea who I'm talking about?'

At first, he didn't think the vampire was going to answer. Hooded eyes held his in silence, then, finally, the kid lifted one shoulder in a shrug and exhaled a curse.

'Sergei Yakut,' he murmured.

The name was hardly audible, but Nikolai heard it. And from the periphery of his vision, he noticed that an ebony-haired woman seated at the bar nearby heard it too. He could tell she had from the sudden rigidity of her spine beneath her long-sleeved black top and from the way her head snapped briefly to the side as though pulled there by the power of that name alone.

'You know him?' Nikolai asked the Breed male, while keeping the brunette at the bar well within his sights.

'I know *of* him, that's all. He doesn't live in the Darkhavens,' said the youth, referring to the secured communities that housed most of the Breed civilian populations throughout North America and Europe. 'Dude's one nasty mofo from what I've heard.'

Yeah, he was, Nikolai acknowledged inwardly. 'Any idea where I might find him?'

'No.'

'You sure about that?' Niko asked, watching as the woman at the bar slid off her stool and prepared to leave. She still had more than half a cocktail in her glass, but at the mere mention of Yakut's name, she seemed suddenly in a big hurry to get out of the place.

The Breed youth shook his head. 'I don't know where to find the dude. Don't know why anyone would willingly look for him either, unless you got some kind of death wish.'

Nikolai glanced over his shoulder as the tall brunette started edging her way through the crowd gathered near the bar. On impulse, she turned to look at him then, her jade-green gaze piercing beneath the fringe of dark lashes and the glossy swing of her sleek, chin-length bob. There was a note of fear in her eyes as she stared back at him, a naked fear she didn't even attempt to hide.

'I'll be damned,' Niko muttered.

She knew something about Sergei Yakut.

Something more than just a passing knowledge, he was guessing. That startled, panicked look as she turned and broke for an escape said it all.

Nikolai took off after her. He weaved through the thicket of humans filling the club, his eyes trained on the silky black hair of his quarry. The female was quick, as fleet and agile as a gazelle, her dark clothes and hair letting her practically disappear into her surroundings.

But Niko was Breed, and there was no human in existence who could outrun one of his kind. She ducked out the club door and made a fast right onto the street outside. Nikolai followed. She must have sensed him hard on her heels because she pivoted her head around to gauge his pursuit and those pale green eyes locked on to him like lasers.

She ran faster now, turning the corner at the end of the block. Not two seconds later, Niko was there too. He grinned as he caught sight of her a few yards ahead of him. The alley she'd entered between two tall brick buildings was narrow and dark – a dead end sealed off by a dented metal Dumpster and a chain-link fence that climbed some ten feet up from the ground.

The woman spun around on the spiked heels of her black boots, panting hard, eyes trained on him, watching his every move.

Nikolai took a few steps into the lightless alley, then paused, his hands held benevolently out to his sides. 'It's okay,' he told her. 'No need to run. I just want to talk to you.'

She stared in silence.

'I want to ask you about Sergei Yakut.'

She swallowed visibly, her smooth white throat flexing.

'You know him, don't you.'

The edge of her mouth quirked only a fraction, but enough to tell him that he was correct – she was familiar with the reclusive Gen One. Whether she could lead Niko to him was another matter. Right now, she was his best, possibly his only, hope.

'Tell me where he is. I need to find him.'

At her sides, her hands balled into fists. Her feet were braced slightly apart as if she were prepared to bolt. Niko saw her glance subtly toward a battered door to her left.

She lunged for it.

Niko hissed a curse and flew after her with all the speed he possessed. By the time she'd thrown the door open on its groaning hinges, Nikolai was standing in front of her at the threshold, blocking her path into the darkness on the other side. He chuckled at the ease of it.

'I said there's no need to run,' he said, shrugging lightly as she backed a step away from him. He let the door fall closed behind him as he followed her slow retreat into the alley.

Jesus, she was breathtaking. He'd only gotten a glimpse of her in the club, but now, standing just a couple of feet from her, he realized that she was absolutely stunning. Tall and lean, willowy beneath her fitted black clothing, with flawless milk-white skin and luminous almond-shaped eyes. Her heart-shaped face was a mesmerizing combination of strength and softness, her beauty equal parts light and dark. Nikolai knew he was gaping, but damn if he could help it.

'Talk to me,' he said. 'Tell me your name.'

He reached for her, an easy, nonthreatening move of his hand. He sensed the jolt of adrenaline that shot into her bloodstream – he could smell the citrusy tang of it in the air, in fact – but he didn't see the roundhouse kick coming at him until he took the sharp heel of her boot squarely in his chest. *Goddamn.*

He rocked back, more surprised than unfooted.

It was all the break she needed. The woman leapt for the door again, this time managing to disappear into the darkened building before Niko could wheel around and stop her. He gave chase, thundering in behind her.

The place was empty, just a lot of naked concrete beneath his feet, bare bricks and exposed rafters all around him. Some fleeting sense of foreboding prickled at the back of his neck as he raced deeper into the darkness, but the bulk of his attention was focused on the female standing in the center of the vacant space. She stared him down as he approached, every muscle in her slim body seeming tensed for attack.

Nikolai held that sharp stare as he drew up in front of her. 'I'm not going to hurt you.'

'I know.' She smiled, just a slight curve of her lips. 'You won't get that chance.'

Her voice was velvety smooth, but the glint in her eyes took on a cold edge. Without warning, Niko felt a sudden, shattering tightness in his head. A high-frequency sound cranked up in his ears, louder than he could bear. Then louder still. He felt his legs give out beneath him. He dropped to his knees, his vision swimming while his head felt on the verge of exploding.

Distantly, he registered the sound of booted feet coming toward him – several pairs, belonging to sizable males, vampires all of them. Muted voices buzzed above him as he suffered out the sudden, debilitating assault on his mind.

It was a trap.

The bitch had led him there deliberately, knowing he'd follow her.

'Enough, Renata,' said one of the Breed males who'd entered the room. 'You can release him now.'

Some of the pain in Nikolai's head subsided with the command. He glanced up in time to see the beautiful face of his attacker staring down at him where he lay near her feet.

'Strip him of his weapons,' she said to her companions. 'We need to get him out of here before his strength returns.'

Nikolai sputtered a few ripe curses at her, but his voice strangled in his throat, and she was already walking away, the thin spikes of her heels clicking over the field of cold concrete underneath him.

The New York Times bestselling Midnight Breed series

LARA ADRIAN

VEIL
❦ OF ❧
MIDNIGHT

'Adrenaline-fuelled, sizzlingly sexy, darkly intense
. . . addictively readable series.' *Chicago Tribune*

Bound by blood, addicted to danger, they'll enter the darkest
and most erotic place of all . . .

A warrior trained in bullets and blades, Renata cannot be
bested by any man – vampire or mortal. But her most powerful
weapon is her extraordinary psychic ability – a gift both rare
and deadly. Now a stranger threatens her hard-won inde-
pendence – a golden-haired vampire who lures her into a
realm of darkness . . . and pleasure beyond imaging . . .

Robinson
978-1-84901-109-9
£6.99

www.constablerobinson.com

To order *Veil of Midnight*, or any other **Lara Adrian** title, simply contact The Book Service (TBS) by phone, email or by post.

No. of copies	Title	RRP	ISBN	Total
	Kiss of Midnight	£6.99	978-1-84901-106-8	
	Kiss of Crimson	£6.99	978-1-84901-107-5	
	Midnight Awakening	£6.99	978-1-84901-108-2	
	Veil of Midnight	£6.99	978-1-84901-109-9	
	Ashes of Midnight	£6.99	978-1-84901-105-1	
	Shades of Midnight	£6.99	978-1-84901-282-9	
	Grand Total			£

FREEPOST RLUL-SJGC-SGKJ, Cash Sales Direct Mail Dept.,
The Book Service, Colchester Road, Frating, Colchester, CO7 7DW

Tel: +44 (0) 1206 255 800
Fax: +44 (0) 1206 255 930

Email: sales@tbs-ltd.co.uk

UK customers: please allow £1.00 p&p for the first book, plus 50p for the second, and an additional 30p for each book thereafter, up to a maximum charge of £3.00.

Overseas customers (incl. Ireland): please allow £2.00 p&p for the first book, plus £1.00 for the second, plus 50p for each additional book.

NAME (block letters): _____
ADDRESS: _____
_____
_____ POSTCODE: _____

I enclose a cheque/PO (payable to 'TBS Direct') for the amount of £_____
I wish to pay by Switch/Credit Card
Card number: _____
Expiry date:_____ Switch issue number:_____